Praise for Marta Perry and her novels

"While love is a powerful entity in this story,
danger is never too far behind. Top Pick!"
—*RT Book Reviews* on *Season of Secrets*

"Set within the Amish community,
with a strong, sympathetic heroine at the center
of a suspenseful plot, Perry's story hooks you
immediately. Her uncanny ability to seamlessly
blend the mystery element with contemporary
themes makes this one intriguing read."
—*RT Book Reviews* on *Home by Dark*

"Marta Perry illuminates the differences between
the Amish community and the larger society
with an obvious care and respect for ways and
beliefs.... She weaves these differences into the
story with a deft hand, drawing the reader
into a suspenseful, continually moving plot."
—*Fresh Fiction* on *Murder in Plain Sight*

"*A Christmas to Die For*...is an exceptionally written
story in which danger and romance blend nicely."
—*RT Book Reviews*

D0708850

SOUTHGATE VETERANS
MEMORIAL LIBRARY
14680 DIX-TOLEDO ROAD
SOUTHGATE, MI 48195

MARTA PERRY

Hide in Plain Sight

☙

Buried Sins

HARLEQUIN® LOVE INSPIRED® CLASSICS

If you purchased this book without a cover you should be aware that this book is stolen property. It was reported as "unsold and destroyed" to the publisher, and neither the author nor the publisher has received any payment for this "stripped book."

Recycling programs for this product may not exist in your area.

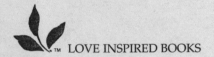 ™ LOVE INSPIRED BOOKS

ISBN-13: 978-0-373-65162-7

HIDE IN PLAIN SIGHT AND BURIED SINS
Copyright © 2013 by Harlequin Books S.A.

The publisher acknowledges the copyright holder of the individual works as follows:

HIDE IN PLAIN SIGHT
Copyright © 2007 by Martha Johnson

BURIED SINS
Copyright © 2007 by Martha Johnson

All rights reserved. Except for use in any review, the reproduction or utilization of this work in whole or in part in any form by any electronic, mechanical or other means, now known or hereafter invented, including xerography, photocopying and recording, or in any information storage or retrieval system, is forbidden without the written permission of the editorial office, Love Inspired Books, 233 Broadway, New York, NY 10279 U.S.A.

This is a work of fiction. Names, characters, places and incidents are either the product of the author's imagination or are used fictitiously, and any resemblance to actual persons, living or dead, business establishments, events or locales is entirely coincidental.

This edition published by arrangement with Love Inspired Books.

® and TM are trademarks of Love Inspired Books, used under license. Trademarks indicated with ® are registered in the United States Patent and Trademark Office, the Canadian Trade Marks Office and in other countries.

www.LoveInspiredBooks.com

Printed in U.S.A.

CONTENTS

Books by Marta Perry

Love Inspired

*Hunter's Bride
*A Mother's Wish
*A Time to Forgive
*Promise Forever
  Always in Her Heart
  The Doctor's Christmas
  True Devotion
†Hero in Her Heart
†Unlikely Hero
†Hero Dad
†Her Only Hero
†Hearts Afire
†Restless Hearts
†A Soldier's Heart
  Mission: Motherhood
**Twice in a Lifetime
**Heart of the Matter
**The Guardian's Honor
**Mistletoe Prayers
  "The Bodine Family Christmas"
  Her Surprise Sister

Love Inspired Suspense

Tangled Memories
Season of Secrets
††Hide in Plain Sight
††A Christmas to Die For
††Buried Sins
Final Justice
Twin Targets

*Caldwell Kin
†The Flanagans
**The Bodine Family
††The Three Sisters Inn

MARTA PERRY

has written everything from Sunday-school curricula to travel articles to magazine stories in more than twenty years of writing, but she feels she's found her writing home in the stories she writes for the Love Inspired Books lines.

Marta lives in rural Pennsylvania, but she and her husband spend part of each year at their second home in South Carolina. When she's not writing, she's probably visiting her children and her six beautiful grandchildren, traveling, gardening or relaxing with a good book.

Marta loves hearing from readers, and she'll write back with a signed bookmark and/or her brochure of Pennsylvania Dutch recipes. Write to her c/o Steeple Hill Books, 233 Broadway, Suite 1001, New York, NY 10279, email her at marta@martaperry.com or visit her on the web at www.martaperry.com.

HIDE IN PLAIN SIGHT

After all those years she had protected her two younger sisters, Rachel and Caroline were independent now. That was only right. Still, some irrational part of her mind seemed to be saying: *You should have been here*.

A black-and-yellow sign announced a crossroad, and she tapped the brakes lightly as she approached a curve. She glanced at the dashboard clock. Nearly midnight.

She looked up, and a cry tore from her throat. A dark shape ahead of her on the road, an orange reflective triangle gleaming on the back of it... Her mind recognizing an Amish buggy, she slammed on the brakes, wrenching the wheel with all her strength. *Please, please, don't let me hit it—*

The car skidded, fishtailing, and she fought for control. Too late—the rear wheels left the road and plunged down into a ditch, tipping crazily, headlight beams spearing toward the heavens. The air bag deployed, slamming into her. For an instant she couldn't breathe, couldn't think.

As her head began to clear she fought the muffling fabric of the air bag, the seat belt harness digging into her flesh. Panic seared along her nerves, and she struggled to contain it. She wasn't a child, she wasn't trapped—

A door slammed. Voices, running feet, and someone yanked at the passenger door.

"Are you hurt? Can you talk?"

"Yes." She managed to get her face free of the entangling folds. "I think I'm all right, but I can't reach the seat belt."

ONE

She had to get to the hospital. Andrea Hampton's fingers tightened on the steering wheel as that call from the Pennsylvania State Police replayed in her mind in an endless loop. Her sister had been struck by a hit-and-run driver while walking along a dark country road—like this one. They didn't know how badly she was injured. Repeated calls to the hospital had netted her only a bland voice saying that Rachel Hampton was undergoing treatment.

Please. Please. She wasn't even sure she believed any longer, but the prayer seemed to come automatically. *Please, if You're there, if You're listening, keep Rachel safe.*

Darkness pressed against the windows, unrelieved except for the reflection of her headlights on the dark macadam and the blur of white pasture fence posts. Amish country, and, once you were off the main routes, there were no lights at night except for the occasional faded yellow of oil lamps from a distant farmhouse.

If she let herself picture Rachel's slight figure, turning, seeing a car barreling toward her... A cold hand closed around her heart.

For everything there is a season, and a time
to every purpose under heaven: a time to be born
and a time to die; a time to plant and a time to
uproot; a time to kill and a time to heal.
—*Ecclesiastes* 3:1–3

This story is dedicated to my gifted editor, Krista Stroever. And, as always, to Brian.

"Hold on. We'll get you out." A murmured consultation—more than one person, then. The scrape of metal on metal, and the door shrieked in protest as it was lifted.

"The buggy." Her voice came out in a hoarse whisper. "I didn't hit it, did I?"

"No," came a curt male voice, and then a flashlight's beam struck her face, making her blink. "You didn't."

Hands fumbled for the seat belt, tugging. The belt tightened across her chest, she couldn't breathe— and then it released and air flowed into her protesting lungs.

"Take a moment before we try to move you." He was just a dark shadow behind the light. In control. "Be sure nothing's broken."

She wanted to shout at him to pull her free, to get her out of the trap her car had become, but he made sense. She wiggled fingers, toes, ran her hands along her body as much as she could.

"Just tender. Please, get me out." She would not let panic show in her voice, even though the sense of confinement in a small, dark space scraped her nerves raw with the claustrophobia she always hoped she'd overcome. "Please."

Hands gripped her arms, and she clung instinctively to the soft cotton of the man's shirt. Muscles bunched under the fabric. He pulled, she wiggled, pushing her body upward, and in a moment she was free, leaning against the tip-tilted car.

"Easy." Strong hands supported her.

"Are you sure she is all right, Calvin Burke?" This

voice sounded young, a little frightened. "Should we take her to the hospital?"

"The hospital." She grasped the words. "I'm all right, but I have to get to the hospital. My sister is there. I have to go there."

She was repeating herself, she thought, her mind still a little fuzzy. She couldn't seem to help it. She focused on the three people who stood around her. An Amish couple, their young faces white and strained in the glow of the flashlight.

And the man, the one with the gruff, impatient voice and the strong, gentle hands. He held the light, so she couldn't see him well—just an impression of height, breadth, the pale cloth of his shirt.

"Your sister." His voice had sharpened. "Would you be Rachel Hampton's sister?"

"Yes." She grabbed his hand. "You know her? Do you know how she is? I keep calling, but they won't tell me anything."

"I know her. Was on my way, in fact, to see if your grandmother needed any help."

"Grams is all right, isn't she?" Her fear edged up a notch.

"Just upset over Rachel." He turned toward the young couple. "I'll take her to the hospital. You two better get along home."

"*Ja,* we will," the boy said. "We pray that your sister will be well." They both nodded and then moved quickly toward the waiting buggy, their clothing melting into the darkness.

Her Good Samaritan gestured toward the pickup

truck that sat behind her car. "Anything you don't want to leave here, we can take now."

She shoved her hand through the disheveled layers of her hair, trying to think. "Overnight bag. My brief-case and computer. They're in the trunk." Concern jagged through her. "If the computer is damaged..." The project she was working on was backed up, of course, but it would still be a hassle if she couldn't work while she was here.

"I don't hear any ominous clanking noises." He pulled the cases from the trunk, whose lid gaped open. "Let's get going."

She bent over the car to retrieve her handbag and cell phone, a wave of dizziness hitting her at the movement. Gritting her teeth, she followed him to the truck.

He yanked open the passenger side door and shoved the bags onto the floor. Obviously she was meant to rest her feet on them. There was no place else to put them if she didn't want them rattling around in the back.

She climbed gingerly into the passenger seat. The dome light gave her a brief look at her rescuer as he slid behind the wheel. Thirtyish, she'd guess, with a shock of sun-streaked brown hair, longer than was fashionable, and a lean face. His shoulders were broad under the faded plaid shirt he wore, and when he gave her an impatient glance, she had the sense that he carried a chip on them.

He slammed the door, the dome light going out, and once again he was little more than an angular shape.

"I take it you know my grandmother." Small surprise, that. Katherine Unger's roots went deep in Lancaster County, back to the German immigrants who'd swarmed to Penn's Woods in the 1700s.

He nodded, and then seemed to feel something more was called for. "Cal Burke. And you're Rachel's older sister, Andrea. I've heard about you." His clipped tone suggested he hadn't been particularly impressed by whatever that was.

Still, she couldn't imagine that her sister had said anything bad about her. She and Rachel had always been close, even if they hadn't seen each other often enough in the past few years, especially since their mother's death. Even if she completely disapproved of this latest scheme Rachel and Grams had hatched.

She glanced at him. As her eyes adjusted to the dim light, she was able to see a little more, noticing his worn jeans, scuffed leather boots and a stubble of beard. She'd thought, in that first hazy glimpse as he pulled her out of the car, that he might be Amish—something about the hair, the pale shirt and dark pants. But obviously he wasn't.

"I should try the hospital again." She flipped the cell phone open.

Please. The unaccustomed prayer formed in her mind again. *Please let Rachel be all right.*

"I doubt they'll tell you any more than they already have." He frowned at the road ahead. "Have you tried your grandmother's number?"

"She never remembers to turn her cell phone on." She punched in the number anyway, only to be sent straight to voice mail. "Grams, if you get this before I see you, call me on my cell." Her throat tightened. "I hope Rachel is all right."

"Ironic," he said as she clicked off. "You have an accident while rushing to your sister's bedside. Ever occur to you that these roads aren't meant for racing?"

She stiffened at the criticism. "I was not racing. And if you were behind me, you must have seen me brake as I approached the curve. If I hadn't…" She stopped, not wanting to imagine that.

His hands moved restlessly on the wheel, as if he wanted to push the rattletrap truck along faster but knew he couldn't. "We're coming up on Route 30. We'll make better time there."

He didn't sound conciliatory, but at least he hadn't pushed his criticism of her driving. Somehow she still wanted to defend herself.

"I'm well aware that I have to watch for buggies on this road. I just didn't expect to see anyone out this late."

And she was distracted with fear for Rachel, but she wouldn't say that to him. It would sound like a plea for sympathy.

"It's spring," he said, as if that was an explanation. "*Rumspringa,* to those kids. That means—"

"I know what *rumspringa* means," she snapped. "The time when Amish teenagers get to experience freedom and figure out what kind of life they want. You don't need to give me the Pennsylvania Dutch tour. I lived in my grandparents' house until I was ten."

"Well, I guess that makes you an expert, then."

No doubt about it, the man was annoying, but she hadn't exactly been all sweetness and light in the past half hour, either. And he was taking her to the hospital.

"Sorry. I didn't mean to snap. I guess I'm a little shaken."

He glanced at her. "Maybe you should have them check you out at the hospital. You had a rough landing."

She shook her head. "I'll probably be black-and-blue tomorrow, but that's it." She touched her neck gingerly. Either the air bag or the seat belt had left what felt like brush burns there. The bruises on her confidence from the fear she'd felt wouldn't show, but they might take longer to go away.

Apparently taking her word for it, he merged onto Route 30. The lights and activity were reassuring, and in a few minutes they pulled up at the emergency entrance to the hospital.

"Thank you." She slid out, reaching for her things. "I really appreciate this."

He spoke when she would have pulled her bag out. "I'm going in, too. May as well leave your things here until you know what you're doing."

She hesitated, and then she shrugged and let go of the case. "Fine. Thank you," she added.

He came around the truck and set off toward the entrance, his long strides making her hurry to keep up. Inside, the bright lights had her blinking. Burke caught her arm and navigated her past the check-in desk and on into the emergency room, not stopping until he reached the nurses' station.

"Evening, Ruth. This is Rachel Hampton's sister. Tell her how Rachel is without the hospital jargon, all right?"

She half expected the woman—middle-aged, gray-haired and looking as if her feet hurt—to call security. Instead she gave him a slightly flirtatious smile.

"Calvin Burke, just because you've been in here three or four times to get stitched up, don't think you own the place." She consulted a clipboard, lips pursing.

Andrea stole a look at him. It wasn't her taste, but she supposed some women went for the rugged, disreputable-looking type.

Ruth Schmidt, according to her name badge—another good old Pennsylvania Dutch name, like Unger—picked up the telephone and had a cryptic, low-voiced conversation with someone. She hung up and gave Andrea a professional smile.

"Your sister has come through surgery fine, and she's been taken to a private room."

"What were her injuries?" She hated digging for information, as if her sister's condition were a matter of national security. "Where is my grandmother? Isn't she here?"

The woman stiffened. "I really don't know anything further about the patient's condition. I understand Mrs. Unger was persuaded to go home, as there was nothing she could do here. I'd suggest you do the same, and—"

"No." She cut the woman off. "I'm not going anywhere until I've seen my sister. And if you don't know anything about her injuries, I'll talk to someone who does."

She prepared for an argument. It didn't matter what they said to her, she wasn't leaving until she'd seen Rachel, if she had to stay here all night.

Maybe the woman recognized that. She pointed to

a bank of elevators. "Third floor. Room 301. But she'll be asleep—"

She didn't wait to hear any more. She made it to the elevator in seconds and pressed the button, the fear that had driven her since she left Philadelphia a sharp blade against her heart. Rachel would be all right. Grams wouldn't have gone home unless she was convinced of that. Still, she had to see for herself.

A quick ride in the elevator, a short walk across the hall, and she was in the room. Rachel lay motionless in the high, white hospital bed. Both legs were in casts, and hospital paraphernalia surrounded her.

Light brown hair spread out over a white pillow, dark lashes forming crescents against her cheek. Rachel looked about sixteen, instead of nearly thirty. Her little sister, whom she loved, fought with, bossed, protected. Her throat choked, and the tears she'd been holding back spilled over.

Cal picked up a five-month-old newsmagazine and slumped into a molded plastic chair. The dragons guarding the third floor wouldn't have let him in, obviously, so he'd just wait until the sister came back down again. Maybe tonight wasn't the time, but he had a few things he'd like to say to Andrea.

He frowned, uninterested, at the magazine, seeing instead the face of the woman who'd just gone upstairs. On the surface, she'd been much like he'd expected from the things her sister and grandmother had said and from the photo on Katherine's mantel.

Glossy, urban, well dressed in a rising young executive way, with silky blond hair falling to her collarbones in one of those sleek, tapered cuts that every television newswoman wore now. Eyes like green glass, sharp enough to cut a man if he weren't careful.

Well, he was a very careful man, and he knew enough not to be impressed by Ms. Andrea Hampton.

Not that her sister or grandmother had ever bad-mouthed her, but the picture had formed clearly enough in his mind from the things they said, and from her absence. Her elderly grandmother and her sister were struggling to get their bed-and-breakfast off the ground, and Ms. Successful Young Executive couldn't be bothered to leave her high-powered life long enough to help them.

Not his business, he supposed, but despite his intent to live in isolation, he'd grown fond of Katherine and her granddaughter in the time he'd been renting the barn on the Unger estate. He'd thought, when his wanderings brought him to Lancaster County, that he just wanted to be alone with his anger and his guilt. But Katherine, with her understated kindness, and Rachel, with her sweet nature, had worked their way into his heart. He felt a responsibility toward them, combined with irritation that the oldest granddaughter wasn't doing more to help.

Still, he'd been unjust to accuse her of careless driving. She'd been going the speed limit, no more, and he had seen the flash of her brake lights just before she'd rounded the curve.

Her taillights had disappeared from view, and then he'd heard the shriek of brakes, the crunch of metal, and his heart had nearly stopped. He'd rounded the

curve, fearing he'd see a buggy smashed into smither-
eens, its passengers tossed onto the road like rag dolls.

Thank the good Lord it hadn't come to that. It had
been the car, half on its side in the ditch, which had
been the casualty.

Come to think of it, somebody might want to have
a talk with young Jonah's father. The boy had said he'd
just pulled out onto the main road from the Mueller
farm. He had to have done that without paying much
attention—the approaching glow of the car's lights
should have been visible if he'd looked. All his attention had probably been on the pretty girl next to him.

He didn't think he'd mention that to Andrea Hampton. She might get the bright idea of suing. But he'd
drop a word in Abram Yoder's ear. Not wanting to get
the boy into trouble—just wanting to keep him alive.

Giving up the magazine as a lost cause, he tossed
it aside and stared into space until he saw the elevator
doors swish open again. Andrea came through, shoulders sagging a bit. She straightened when she saw him.

"You didn't need to wait for me."

He rose, going to her. "Yes, I did. I have your things
in my truck, remember?"

Her face was pale in the fluorescent lights, mouth
drooping, and those green eyes looked pink around
the edges. He touched her arm.

"You want me to get you some coffee?"

She shook her head, and he had the feeling she
didn't focus on his face when she looked at him. His
nerves tightened.

"What is it? Rachel's going to be all right, isn't she?"

"They say so." Her voice was almost a whisper, and

then she shook her head, clearing her throat. "I'm sure they're right, but it was a shock to see her that way. Both of her legs are broken." A shiver went through her, generating a wave of sympathy that startled him. "And she has a concussion. The doctor I spoke with wouldn't even guess how long it would be until she's back to normal."

"I'm sorry to hear that." His voice roughened. Rachel didn't deserve this. No one did. He could only hope they caught the poor excuse for a human being who'd left her lying by the side of the road. If he were still an attorney, he'd take pleasure in prosecuting a case like that.

Andrea walked steadily toward the exit. Outside, she took a deep breath, pulling the tailored jacket close around her as if for warmth, even though the May night didn't have much of a bite to it.

"I'll just get my things and then you can be on your way." She managed a polite smile in his direction.

"How do you plan to get to your grandmother's? I called to have your car towed to the Churchville Garage, but I don't imagine it'll be drivable very soon."

She shoved her hair back in what seemed to be a habitual gesture. It fell silkily into place again. "Thank you. I didn't think about the car. But I'm sure I can get a taxi."

"Not so easy at this hour. I'll drive you." He yanked the door open.

"I don't want to take you out of your way. You've done enough for me already, Mr. Burke." Her tone was cool. Dismissing.

He smiled. "Cal. And you won't be taking me out

of my way. Didn't you know? I'm your grandmother's tenant."

He rather enjoyed the surprised look on her face. Petty of him, but if she kept in better contact with her grandmother, she'd know about him. Still, he suspected that if he were as good a Christian as he hoped to be, he'd cut her a bit more slack.

"I see. Well, fine then." She climbed into the truck, the skirt she wore giving him a glimpse of slim leg.

He wasn't interested in any woman right now, least of all a woman like Andrea Hampton, but that didn't mean he was dead. He could still appreciate beautiful, and that's what Andrea was, with that pale oval face, soft mouth and strong jawline. Come to think of it, she'd gotten the stubborn chin from her grandmother, who was as feisty a seventy-some-year-old as he'd met in a long time.

She didn't speak as he drove out of the hospital lot. He didn't mind. God had been teaching him patience in the past year or so, something he'd never thought of before as a virtue. He suspected she'd find it necessary to break the silence sooner than he would.

Sure enough, they'd barely hit the highway when she stirred. "You said you were my grandmother's tenant. Does that mean you're living in the house?" Her hands moved restlessly. "Or inn, I guess I should say, given Grams's and Rachel's project."

She didn't approve, then. He could hear it in her voice.

"I rent the barn from your grandmother. The newer one, behind the house. I've been there for six months now, and in the area for nearly a year."

Healing. Atoning for his mistakes and trying to get right with God, but that was something he didn't say to anyone.

"The barn?" Her voice rose in question. "What do you want with the barn? Do you mean you live there?"

He shrugged. "I fixed up the tack room for a small apartment. Comfortable enough for one. I run my business in the rest of it."

"What business?" She sounded suspicious.

He was tempted to make something up, but he guessed she'd had enough shocks tonight. "I design and make wood furniture, using Amish techniques. If you pick up any wood shavings on your clothes, that's why."

"I see." The tone reserved judgment. "Grams never mentioned it to me."

"Well, you haven't been around much, have you?"

He caught the flash of anger in her face, even keeping his eyes on the road.

"I speak with my grandmother and my sister every week, and they came to stay with me at Easter, not that it's any of your concern."

They were coming into the village now, and he slowed. There wasn't much traffic in Churchville, or even many lights on, at this hour. The antique shops and quilt stores that catered to tourists were long since closed.

He pulled into the drive of the gracious, Federal-style Unger mansion, its Pennsylvania sandstone glowing a soft gold in the light from the twin lampposts he'd erected for Katherine. He stopped at the door.

He wouldn't be seeing much of Andrea, he'd guess.

She'd scurry back to her busy career as soon as she was convinced her sister would recover, the anxiety she'd felt tonight fading under the frenzied rush of activity that passed for a life.

"Thank you." She snapped off the words as she opened the door, grabbing her bags, obviously still annoyed at his presumption.

"No problem."

She slammed the door, and he pulled away, leaving her standing under the hand-carved sign that now hung next to the entrance to the Unger mansion. The Three Sisters Inn.

TWO

Andrea had barely reached the recessed front door when it was flung open, light spilling out onto the flagstones. In an instant she was in Grams's arms, and the tears she didn't want to shed flowed. They stood half in and half out of the house, and she was ten again, weeping over the mess her parents were making of their lives, holding on to Grams and thinking that here was one rock she could always cling to.

Grams drew her inside, blotting her tears with an unsteady hand, while her own trickled down her cheeks. "I'm so glad you're here, Dree. So glad."

The childhood nickname, given when two-years-younger Rachel couldn't say her name, increased the sensation that she'd stepped into the past. She stood in the center hall that had seemed enormous to her once, with its high ceiling and wide plank floor. Barney, Grams's sheltie, danced around them, welcoming her with little yips.

She bent to pet the dog, knowing Barney wouldn't stop until she did. "I went to the hospital to see Rachel. They told me you'd already gone home. I should have called you...."

Grams shook her head, stopping her. "It's fine. Cal phoned me while you were with Rachel."

"He didn't say." Her tone was dry. Nice of him, but he might have mentioned he'd talked to Grams.

"He told me about the accident." Grams's arm, still strong and wiry despite her age, encircled Andrea's waist. Piercing blue eyes, bone structure that kept her beautiful despite her wrinkles, a pair of dangling aqua earrings that matched the blouse she wore—Grams looked great for any age, let alone nearly seventy-five. "Two accidents in one night is two too many."

That was a typical Grams comment, the tartness of her tone hiding the fear she must have felt.

"Well, fortunately the only damage was to the car." She'd better change the subject, before Grams started to dwell on might-have-beens. She looked through the archway to the right, seeing paint cloths draped over everything in the front parlor. "I see you're in the midst of redecorating."

Grams's blue eyes darkened with worry. "The opening is Memorial Day weekend, and now Rachel is laid up. I don't know..." She stopped and shook her head. "Well, we'll get through it somehow. Right now, let's get you settled, so that both of us can catch a few hours sleep. Tomorrow will be here before you know it."

"Where are you putting me?" She glanced up the graceful open staircase that led from the main hall to the second floor. "Is that all guest rooms now?"

Grams nodded. "The west side of the house is the inn. The east side is still ours." She opened the door on the left of the hall. "Come along in. We have the back stairway and the rooms on this side, so that'll give us our privacy. You'll be surprised at how well this is working out."

She doubted it, but she was too tired to pursue the subject now. Or to think straight, for that matter. And Grams must be exhausted, physically and emotionally. Still, she couldn't help one question.

"What was she doing out there? Rachel, I mean. Why was she walking along Crossings Road alone after dark?"

"She was taking Barney for a run." Grams's voice choked a little. "She's been doing that for me since she got here, especially now that things have been so upset. Usually there's not much traffic."

That made sense. Rachel could cut onto Crossings Road, perpendicular to the main route, without going into the village.

She trailed her grandmother through the large room that had been her grandfather's library, now apparently being converted into an office/living room, and up the small, enclosed stairway. This was the oldest part of the house, built in 1725. The ceilings were lower here, accounting for lots of odd little jogs in how the two parts of the Unger mansion fit together.

Grams held on to the railing, as if she needed some help getting up the stairs, but her back was as straight as ever. The dog, who always slept on the rug beside her bed, padded along.

Her mind flickered back to Grams's comment. "What do you mean, things have been upset? Has something gone wrong with your plans?"

She could have told them, had told them, that they were getting in over their heads with this idea of turning the place into an inn. Neither of them knew anything about running a bed-and-breakfast, and Grams was too old for this kind of stress.

"Just—just the usual things. Nothing for you to worry about."

That sounded evasive. She'd push, but they were both too tired.

Her grandmother opened a door at the top of the stairs. "Here we are. I thought you'd want your old room."

The ceiling sloped, and the rosebud wallpaper hadn't changed in twenty years. Even her old rag doll, left behind when her mother had stormed out of the house with them, still sat in the rocking chair, and her white Bible lay on the bedside table. This had been her room until she was ten, until the cataclysm that split the family and sent them flying off in all directions, like water droplets from a tornado. She tossed her bags onto the white iron bed and felt like crying once more.

"Thanks, Grams." Her voice was choked.

"It's all right." Grams gave her another quick hug. "Let's just have a quick prayer." She clasped Andrea's hands, and Andrea tried not to think about how long it had been since she'd prayed before tonight.

"Hold our Rachel in Your hands, Father." Grams's voice was husky. "We know You love her even more than we do. Please, touch her with Your healing hand. Amen."

"Amen," Andrea whispered. She was sure there were questions she should ask, but her mind didn't seem to be working clearly.

"Night, Grams. Try and sleep."

"Good night, Dree. I'm so glad you're here." Grams left the door ajar, her footsteps muffled on the hall carpet as she went to the room across the hall.

Andrea looked at her things piled on the bed, and it seemed a gargantuan effort to move them. She undressed slowly, settling in.

She took her shirt off and winced at the movement, turning to the wavy old mirror to see what damage she'd done. Bruises on her chest and shoulder were dark and ugly where the seat belt had cut in, and she had brush burns from the air bag. She was lucky that was the worst of it, but she shook a little at the reminder.

After pulling a sleep shirt over her head, she cleaned off the bed and turned back the covers. She'd see about her car in the morning. Call the office, explain that she wouldn't be in for a few days. Her boss wouldn't like that, not with the Waterburn project nearing completion. Well, she couldn't make any decisions until she saw how Rachel was.

Frustration edged along her nerves as she crossed to the window to pull down the shade, not wanting to wake with the sun. This crazy scheme to turn the mansion into a bed-and-breakfast had been Rachel's idea, no doubt. She hadn't really settled to anything since culinary school, always moving from job to job.

Grams should have talked some sense into her, instead of going along with the idea. At this time in her life, Grams deserved a quiet, peaceful retirement. And Rachel should be finding a job that had some security to it.

Andrea didn't like risky gambles. Maybe that was

what made her such a good financial manager. Financial security came first, and then other things could line up behind it. If she'd learned anything from those chaotic years when her mother had dragged them around the country, constantly looking for something to make her happy, it was that.

She stood for a moment, peering out. From this window she looked over the roof of the sunroom, added on to the back of the house overlooking the gardens when Grams had come to the Unger mansion as a bride. There was the pond, a little gleam of light striking the water, and the gazebo. Other shadowy shapes were various outbuildings. Behind them loomed the massive bulk of the old barn that had predated even the house. Off to the right, toward the neighboring farm, was the "new" barn, dating back to the 1920s.

It was dark now, with Cal presumably asleep in the tack room apartment. Well, he was another thing to worry about tomorrow. She lowered the shade with a decisive snap and went to crawl into bed.

Her eyes closed. She was tired, so tired. She'd sleep, and deal with all of it in the morning.

Something creaked overhead—once, then again. She stiffened, imagining a stealthy footstep in the connecting attics that stretched over the wings of the house. She strained to listen, clutching the sheet against her, but the sound wasn't repeated.

Old houses make noises, she reminded herself. Particularly her grandmother's, if her childhood memories were any indicator. She was overreacting. That faint, scratching sound was probably a mouse, safely distant from her. Tired muscles relaxed into the soft bed, and exhaustion swept over her.

She plummeted into sleep, as if she had dived into a deep, deep pool.

Andrea stepped out onto the patio from the breakfast room, Barney nosing out behind her and then running off toward the pond, intent on his own pursuits. A positive call from the hospital had lifted a weight from her shoulders and she felt able to deal with other things. She paused to look around and take a deep breath of country air.

Not such pleasant country air, she quickly discovered. Eli Zook must be spreading manure on his acreage, which met the Unger property on two sides. How were the city tourists Rachel expected to have as guests going to like that? Maybe they'd be pleased at the smell of a genuine Amish farm.

They'd have to admire the view from the breakfast room. The flagstone patio had stood the years well, and now it was brightened by pots overflowing with pansies and ageratum. The wide flower bed dazzled with peonies and daylilies. She had knelt there next to Grams, learning to tell a weed from a flower.

Moving a little stiffly, thanks to her bruises, she stepped over the low patio wall and followed the flagstone path that led back through the farther reaches of the garden, weaving around the pond and past the gazebo with its white Victorian gingerbread. When she glanced back at the house, morning sunlight turned the sandstone to mellow gold, making the whole building glow.

Rounding the small potting shed, she came face-to-face with the new barn. An apt expression, because she'd always thought the barn had more character than a lot of people. Lofty, white, a traditional bank barn with entries on two levels, it had the stone foundation and hip roof that characterized Pennsylvania Dutch barns. More properly Pennsylvania Swiss or German, her grandfather had always said, but the name stuck.

It hadn't seen much use since her grandfather had stopped farming and leased the fields to the Zook family, but the stone foundation showed no sign of deterioration, and the wooden planks looked as if they had a fresh coat of white paint.

A small sign on the upper level door was the only indication that Cal Burke did business here. And how much business could he do, really? The only way into his shop was via the rutted lane that ran along a hedge of overgrown lilacs that bordered the house. She glanced toward the road. Yes, there was a tiny sign there, too, one that could hardly be read from a passing car. The man needed a few lessons in marketing.

She walked up the bank to the door and tapped lightly. Stepping inside, she inhaled the scent of wood shavings and hay. Music poured from a CD player that sat on a wooden bench. Cal apparently liked Mozart to work by. He bent over a pie safe, totally absorbed as he fitted a pierced tin insert to a door.

He obviously hadn't heard her, so she glanced around, wanting to see any changes before she spoke to him. There weren't many. In the center threshing floor he'd installed a workbench and tools, and the rest of the space was taken up with pieces of furniture in various stages of construction. The mows and lofts on either side already held hay and straw, probably stored there by Eli Zook.

She took a step forward, impressed in spite of herself by his work. They were simple oak pieces, for the most part, done in the classic style of Pennsylvania Dutch furniture. There was a three-drawer chest with graceful carving incised on the drawer fronts, a chest stenciled with typical tulips and hearts, a rocking chair with a curved back.

Cal did have a gift for this work, and he was certainly focused. Sun-bleached hair swung forward in his eyes, and he pushed it back with a sweep of one hand, all of his movements smooth and unhurried. He wore faded jeans and a blue plaid shirt, also faded, the sleeves rolled up to the elbows. A shaft of sunlight, beaming down from the open loft door, seemed to put him in a spotlight, picking out gold in his brown hair and glinting off tanned forearms.

She moved slightly just as the music stopped. The sole of her loafer rustled stray wood shavings, and he looked up. The pierced tin clattered to the floor, the sound loud in the sudden stillness.

"I'm sorry. I didn't mean to disturb you."

"It's all right." He straightened, leaning against the pie safe, and watched her approach.

She hadn't noticed his eyes last night. The light had been too dim, for the most part, and she'd been too upset. Now she saw that they were a light, warm brown, flecked with gold like his hair.

He waited until she stopped, a few feet from him, before he spoke again. "Any news from the hospital?"

"We called first thing. Rachel had a good night, and she's awake and asking for us." She couldn't stop the smile that blossomed on the words.

"Thank God." He smiled in return, strong lips curving, lines crinkling around his eyes, his whole face lighting. For an instant she couldn't look away, and something seemed to shimmer between them, as light and insubstantial as the dust motes in the shaft of sunshine.

She turned to look at the furniture, feeling a need to evade his glance for a moment. She wouldn't want him to think he had any effect on her.

"So this is your work." She touched a drop leaf table. "Cherry, isn't it?"

He nodded, moving next to her and stroking the wood as if it were a living thing. "I've been working mostly in oak and pine, but Emma Zook wanted a cherry table, and Eli had some good lengths of cherry that I could use."

"It's beautiful. Emma will be delighted, although if I remember Amish customs correctly, she won't say so."

A faint smile flickered in his eyes. "'For use, not for pretty,' she'll say. Anything else might sound like pride."

"That's Emma, all right." Nostalgia swept through her. Emma Zook had helped Grams in the house for years, and her sturdy figure, always clad in a long dress and apron, was present in Andrea's earliest memories.

As children, they'd played with the Zook youngsters, so used to them that they never saw the Amish clothing or dialect as odd. She'd caught up a bit with Emma over breakfast. As she'd expected, all the children except Levi were married and parents by now. Levi—well, Levi would always be a child, no matter how old he was.

"The Amish have the right idea," Cal said. "No reason why something can't be both useful and beautiful."

She traced the scalloped edge of the drop leaf. "This certainly qualifies."

"Two compliments in as many minutes." He drew back in mock surprise.

"I believe in giving credit where credit is due. You make lovely furniture. I just can't help but wonder why you're doing it in my grandmother's barn."

Where did you come from, and why are you here? That's what she was really asking. How could this man have made such inroads into her family when she hadn't even known about him?

He shrugged. "I came to this area to learn Amish furniture techniques. When I needed a place to set up shop, she had an empty barn. We came to an agreement."

She'd like to ask what that agreement was, but he could answer that it wasn't her business. Which it wasn't, but anything that affected her grandmother and sister mattered to her, whether she'd been back recently or not.

"You're not from around here," she tried.

"No. I'm not."

Most people liked talking about themselves. Cal Burke seemed to be the exception.

"You're a little hard to find. How do you market your work?"

He shrugged again. "There are plenty of machine-made copies out there, but if people are asking around for good, handmade furniture done in the old Amish style, they'll find me or one of the others who do it."

"That's no way to do business." His marketing strategy, if that's what it was, exasperated her so much that she couldn't stop the words. "You have something people want, so make it easy to find you. You could probably double or triple your business if you did a little advertising."

"I don't want to double my business. There are only so many pieces I can make by hand in a month, and they sell okay. What am I going to do with more customers than I can satisfy?"

She blinked, looking at him. As far as she could tell, he was serious. "If you hired a few people to help you—"

"Then it wouldn't be my furniture people were buying."

"But you could make more money—"

He shook his head with an impatient movement that made the hair flop in his eyes again. "I make enough to get by, and I enjoy my work. Your corporate approach wouldn't work for me."

She stiffened. "If you mean I'm practical, I don't consider that an insult. Although I suspect you meant it that way."

"Just recognizing a difference in how we see things, that's all." His voice was mild, but his eyes had turned frosty. "If you came out here to tell me how to run my business, I thank you for your interest."

"No." She bit off the word. The world needed practical people like her. They kept the dreamers afloat.

But she didn't suppose it would do any good to tell him so. "My grandmother wants you to know that we'll be going to the hospital shortly. She asks if you'll keep an eye out for the painters and let them in." Somehow it seemed important that he know the favor was for Grams, not her.

"I'd be glad to."

"I thought she could call you, but she said you never answer your phone."

"Really bugs you, doesn't it?" His expression suggested internal laughter. "I don't like to jump when the phone rings. If anybody wants me, they leave a message."

She bit back another comment about his business methods. Or lack of them. Why should she care if the man frittered away his prospects for want of a few sensible steps?

"I see." She kept her tone perfectly polite. "Thank you for taking care of the painters. My grandmother will appreciate it."

She turned and walked away quickly, suspecting that if she looked back, she'd find an amused smile on his face.

"But I can't. I really can't." Andrea looked from her grandmother to her sister. Both faces were turned toward hers, both expectant, waiting for an answer she couldn't possibly give. "I'm extremely busy at work right now."

"Surely your employer will give you the time off." Grams was serenely confident. "Your family needs you."

Rachel didn't say anything. She just leaned back

against the raised head of the hospital bed, her face almost as white as the pillow.

She'd tell herself they were ganging up on her, but that wasn't true. They were depending on her, just as Rachel and her baby sister Caroline had depended on her during those years when Mom had relocated the family from place to place, nursing her grudge against Grams and Grandfather and depriving her children of the only stable home they'd ever known.

Andrea was the oldest. She was the responsible one. She'd take care of it.

The trouble was, she was responsible to her job, as well, and there couldn't possibly be a worse time for her to take off. Gordon Walker would not understand his right-hand woman requesting a leave to help her family. He hadn't even taken time away from work when his wife was in labor with their twins.

Of course, he and his wife were now divorced, and he saw his daughters once a month if he was lucky.

She tried again. "I'm in the middle of a very important project, and I'm on a deadline. I couldn't take time off now. It wouldn't be fair to the company."

It wasn't fair to her, either. Maybe that thought was unworthy, but she couldn't help it. The promotion her boss had been dangling in front of her for the past year would be hers when this project was completed. Her position with the company, her stable, secure life, would be assured.

"Can't someone else take over for you?" Grams's brow furrowed. "We've already accepted reservations for our opening weekend. All the rooms are booked. We can't turn those people away now."

Grams's sense of hospitality was obviously offended at the thought, even though these would be paying guests. Andrea could see it in her eyes. An Unger didn't let people down.

I'm a Hampton, too. She thought bleakly of her father. They're pretty good at letting people down.

Rachel tried to push herself up on the bed a little, wincing, and Andrea hurried to help her.

"Take it easy. I don't think you should try to do that on your own. Those casts must weigh a ton."

"If they don't, they feel like it." Rachel moved her head restlessly on the pillow.

Looking into Rachel's eyes was like looking in a mirror. Green eyes, cat's eyes. All three Hampton girls had them, even though otherwise they didn't look at all alike.

She was the cool, conservative blonde. That was how people saw her, and she didn't find anything wrong with that. It fit with who she wanted to be.

Rachel, two years younger, was the warm one, with her heart-shaped face and her sunny-brown hair. She had the gift of making friends and collecting strays everywhere she went. Sweet, generous, she was the family peacemaker, always the buffer.

And they'd needed a buffer, she and Caroline. Her youngest sister had been born an exotic orchid in a family of daisies. She certainly looked the part. In her, the green eyes sparkled and shot fire. Her hair, a rich, deep red, had been worn in a mass of curls to below her shoulders the last time Andrea had seen her. Currently, as far as she knew, Caroline was making pottery in Taos. Or maybe it was turquoise jewelry in Santa Fe. Andrea couldn't keep up.

"I could come home in a wheelchair. We could get some extra help and I could supervise." But the tears that shone in Rachel's eyes belied the brave words, and she thumped one hand against the side rail of the bed, making the IV clatter.

"Honey, don't." Andrea caught the restless hand, her heart twisting. "It'll be all right."

But how would it be all right? How could she be true to herself and yet not let them down?

Rachel clung to her, much as she had when Mom had taken them away from Grams and Grandfather so many years ago. "You mean you'll do it?"

"We'll find some way of handling the situation. I promise."

Rachel gave a little sigh, relaxing a bit, though worry still puckered her brows.

"Good," Grams said. "I knew we could count on you."

She'd told her boss she couldn't be back until Monday, though she'd continue working while she was here. She was only a phone call or an e-mail away, after all. By then, she'd somehow convince Grams and Rachel that with Rachel laid up for who knows how long, starting a bed-and-breakfast didn't make sense.

A glance at Rachel's face assured her that now was not the time to mention that. Rachel was far too fragile.

She'd discuss it with Grams later. Giving up the inn was the best thing for everyone, especially Rachel. Once she was healed, she could get another restaurant job in a minute with her skills, and if she needed help to get through until then, Andrea or Grams would certainly provide that.

Right now she had to do something to wipe that strained expression from Rachel's eyes. "Did you hear about my adventure getting here last night? Rescued from a ditch by your handsome tenant. Hope you don't mind my using your car while mine's in the body shop."

"Grams told me Cal brought you to the hospital. He is a hunk, isn't he?" Some of the tension eased out of the pale face. "So, you interested, big sis?"

"I wouldn't want to tread on your territory." She smiled. "We made a deal a long time ago, remember? No boyfriend poaching."

"Sad to say, Cal doesn't see me as anything but little-sister material." She wrinkled her nose. "I have to admit, when I first met him, I thought there might be something, but the chemistry just isn't there."

Andrea didn't bother to analyze why she was relieved. "I understand he's been around for about a year?" She made it a question for both of them.

"Just about," Grams agreed. "He stayed over at the Zimmerman farm for a while, I think, when he first came to the area."

"You never mentioned renting the barn to him when we talked." Grams and Rachel had come into the city for dinner just a month ago, but in all their talk about the inn, they hadn't brought up their resident tenant.

"Didn't we? I thought you knew about him."

The vagueness of it got under her skin. "Where did he come from? What did he do before? What does Uncle Nick think of him?" Her grandfather's business partner had a solid, no-nonsense attitude that Grams lacked.

"I don't know. Does it matter?" Grams frowned a little, as if Andrea had said something impolite. "And it's not James Bendick's business."

Rachel moved slightly. "He's a nice guy. That's all we need to know."

It wasn't all *she* needed to know. Perhaps the truth was that Grams hadn't mentioned him because she'd known exactly the questions Andrea would ask and didn't want to answer them. Grams did things her own way, and she'd never appreciated unsolicited advice.

"I believe I'll get some coffee." Grams stood, picking up her handbag.

"I'll get it for you, Grams," she offered.

Her grandmother shook her head. "You stay here and talk to Rachel. I want to stretch my legs a bit."

Andrea watched her leave, her heart clutching a little. Grams wouldn't admit it, but she was slowing down. Grams had always been so strong, so unchanging, that age had sat lightly upon her. It had seemed she would never let it get the better of her. But that had been an illusion.

A weight settled on Andrea's shoulders. She had to make the right decisions now. Rachel, Grams—she was responsible for both of them.

"Are you okay, Dree?"

She shook off the apprehension before she turned to look at her sister. "Sure. Just worried about you. Did the police talk to you about the accident?"

Rachel nodded. "The township chief was in before

you got here. It doesn't sound as if they have much evidence. He wanted to know if I remembered anything."

"Do you?"

Rachel moved restlessly. "I don't remember anything that happened after about noon yesterday."

THREE

Cal let himself in the side door of the Unger mansion, toolbox in hand. He'd told Katherine that he'd fix the loose post on the main staircase, but that wasn't his only reason for being there.

He'd been mulling it over, praying about it, most of the day. Prayer was still new enough to him that he wondered sometimes whether he ought to be asking for guidance about simple everyday things. Still, it was comforting to feel that Someone cared.

And this wasn't a selfish thing. He wanted a sense of whether he should speak to Andrea about her grandmother. Seemed to him the answer was yes, although that might just be his need to do something.

Two years ago, he'd have found it laughable to think he'd be so concerned about an elderly woman who wasn't even a relative, but he hadn't been much of a human being, either, back then. Now—well, he cared about Katherine Unger.

Katherine was kind, proud and too stubborn to ask for help even when she needed it. She'd be appalled, probably, if she realized how much he'd learned about her concerns just by listening. If she knew he intended to talk to Andrea, she'd be outraged.

But someone had to. Emma Zook could, but she might be too much in awe of Katherine to do it. So he would. He reached the stairs and pulled out a hammer. He'd been watching for an opportunity to speak to Andrea alone since she'd returned from the hospital, but she'd been holed up in the second-floor family quarters. Maybe a little noise would draw her out.

Sure enough, it didn't take more than a few hearty blows with the hammer before Andrea appeared at the top of the stairs, looking annoyed. She marched down to him.

"What are you doing?" She'd exchanged the pants and jacket she'd been wearing this morning for a pair of dark jeans and a green top that matched her eyes. "I'm trying to do some work upstairs."

"Sorry. You brought work with you?"

"Of course. I couldn't just walk out in the middle of the week."

Even when rushing to her sister's side, she hadn't left the job that seemed so important to her. She reminded him of himself, the way he used to be. That probably went a long way toward explaining why she annoyed him so much. He wasn't too fond of that guy.

He rested his elbow on the banister. "Wouldn't your boss give you a break under the circumstances?"

For a moment she hesitated, and he could almost read her thoughts. She had the kind of superior who wouldn't, as a matter of fact, and she didn't want to admit it.

"I didn't ask," she said finally. "I have responsibilities, and I meet them." She frowned. "What are you doing here, anyway?"

"Katherine asked me to take care of this loose place in the banister." He wiggled the carved wood gently, mindful of its delicate reeding. "I had time to get to it this afternoon."

"I didn't realize you work for my grandmother."

"I don't. I'm just being neighborly." He still hadn't figured out the best approach. "Look, I know this is none of my business—"

"But it's not going to stop you," she finished for him. "All right. You won't be content until you have your say, so get it over with." She planted one hand on the railing, standing up a step so that their faces were level.

"You don't beat around the bush, do you?"

"I try not to." A slight frown appeared between her brows. "Does that bother you?"

"On the contrary, it makes it easier." If she wanted it straight from the hip, she'd get it. "Your grandmother and sister have been running themselves ragged, trying to get the inn ready. They needed help even before Rachel was hurt, but now it's worse. With Rachel in the hospital, your grandmother shouldn't be in the house alone. Did she tell you she's spotted a prowler out in the grounds recently?"

She sent him a startled glance, hand tightening on the railing. "No. Did she call the police?"

"By the time they got here, the person was long gone." He shrugged. "They didn't take it too seriously, figuring it was just someone curious about the inn. Still, there have been some minor incidents of vandalism in the area lately and a few break-ins. I've been trying to keep an eye on things. But she shouldn't be staying here at night by herself."

"You're right about that." She sounded faintly bewildered that she was agreeing with him. "As for the rest, I'm not sure how best to help her."

He was surprised that she was taking it so well, but perhaps she'd been giving some thought to the problem. She just hadn't come to the right conclusion yet.

"Move in, take over for Rachel, get the inn up and running," he said promptly. "Your grandmother can't do it by herself."

"My job—"

"—can get along without you for a while."

"You don't know that." If her glare had been a blow, it would have knocked him over. "I'd be risking a lot to stay here now."

"I get it. I had bosses like that once." He had a feeling he'd *been* that kind of a boss.

"Then you should understand. Maybe I can hire someone to help out."

He shook his head. "I'm not saying more workers wouldn't make things go faster, but what's needed is someone to oversee the whole project. Your grandmother isn't up to that anymore."

"You think I don't know that?" She fired up instantly. "She shouldn't be attempting something so ambitious at her age. She ought to just relax and enjoy life."

"How is she supposed to do that? What's she going to live on, air?" He clamped his mouth shut. He'd gone too far, even though his intentions were good.

"What are you implying?" She grabbed his arm to keep him from stepping away. "My grandmother doesn't need to worry about money."

Was she putting on a front?

"Maybe you ought to have a serious conversation with your grandmother."

Her grip tightened. "Tell me what you meant. What do you know, or think you know?"

Fine, then. "I know I offered to lend her the money for the renovations, but she took out a loan on the house instead. I know Emma works for free half the time. I know the signs of financial trouble. If someone doesn't step in, namely you, your grandmother could lose this place that means the world to her."

He yanked his arm free and grabbed the toolbox. "I'll come back later and fix this."

Andrea was actually shaking. She watched Cal's broad back as he retreated down the hall. She should talk to Grams—no, she should find out first from someone she trusted if there was any truth to Cal's allegations. Emma. Emma knew everything that went on here.

But even as she thought it, there was a tap on the front door, followed by a quick, "Anyone here?"

"Uncle Nick." She hurried to the door, to be swept into a hug. Soft whiskers and a scent of peppermint—that was Uncle Nick.

He held her at arm's length. "Well, if you're not a sight for sore eyes, Andrea. You're looking beautiful, as always."

"And you're the biggest flatterer in town, as always. You haven't aged a bit."

She made the expected response automatically, but it was true. Maybe the beard and hair were a little whiter, his figure in the neat blue suit just a bit stouter, but his cheeks were still rosy and firm as apples. He had an aura of permanence and stability that was very welcome.

"Ah, don't tell me that. I know better." He shook his head. "This is a sad business about Rachel."

She linked her arm with his. "She's going to make a complete recovery—the doctors have promised. Come into the library. We have to talk."

He lifted bushy white eyebrows. "Where's your grandmother?"

"Taking a nap, thank goodness. She needs one, after yesterday's upsets."

He nodded, glancing around the room and taking in the computer setup and file cabinets. "It's sad to see this fine old room turned into an office. What your grandfather would have said, I don't know."

There didn't seem to be an answer to that. She gestured him to a chair, sitting down opposite him.

He was surveying her with shrewd, kind blue eyes. "You're worried, aren't you? Tell Uncle Nick about it."

She had to smile. He wasn't really their uncle, nor was his name Nick. Caroline had called him that when she was three because to her eyes, James Bendick, Grandfather's junior partner, looked like St. Nicholas.

"That's what you always said. And you solved our problems with chocolate and peppermints."

"It's a good solution."

"Not for this problem." The worry, dissipated for a moment in the pleasure of seeing him, weighed on her again. "Tell me the truth, Uncle Nick. Is Grams in financial trouble?"

"Who told you that? Not your grandmother." His voice had sharpened.

"No. Cal Burke told me. He seems to think she could lose the house."

"I'd call that an exaggeration." He frowned. "And I'm not sure what business it is of his, in any event."

"Never mind him. Tell me what's going on. I thought Grandfather left her well-off. I've never questioned that."

"Your grandmother never questioned it, either. Sad to say, maybe she should have."

"But the properties, his investments…" She couldn't believe it. "Explain it to me."

Uncle Nick's lips puckered. "I'm not sure I should. Your grandmother—"

"Grams is depending on me." Normally she'd appreciate his discretion, but not now. "I have to know what's wrong in order to help her."

He hesitated, looking distressed. Finally he nodded. "Your grandfather decided, a few years before his death, to sell most of his properties. He didn't want to take care of them."

"I thought he enjoyed that." One of her earliest memories was of riding along with Grandpa when he went out the first day of every month to collect the rents from his tenants. That had been her first taste of business, and she'd wanted to be just like him.

Uncle Nick shrugged. "People change. He wanted

to invest the money himself." His gaze dropped. "He wasn't very good. If only he'd held on to the property until the real estate market went up, your grandmother would be sitting pretty."

"As it is…" She could hardly take it in. Still, she'd certainly known how determined Grandpa was to do as he chose. Something chilled inside her. She, of all people, knew just how stubborn he could be.

"She has this place left, but not enough to maintain it." His voice was brisk, as if he didn't want to dwell on what had been. "I'm not sure how you feel about this idea of theirs to turn the place into an inn."

"I think it's a bad move," she said promptly. "Rachel is a great cook, but she doesn't know anything about running an inn. And Grams doesn't need the stress at her age."

Nick beamed at her as if they were the only two sensible people left on earth. "The practical course is for your grandmother to sell. She could pay off the home equity loan she took for the renovations and have enough to live very comfortably for the rest of her life."

"I wish she agreed."

He nodded. "She has her own stubborn streak, that's for sure. I was worried about her living here alone since your grandfather died, but she'd never listen to me. It was a little better after Rachel moved back, but even so…"

"Cal Burke is out at the barn." With the phone he never answered. What good did that do?

"Burke." He repeated the name. "I suppose he's better than nothing, but what do we know about him?"

Not much. She shared his concern.

"And there have been a rash of thefts. People breaking into isolated farmhouses. You know what this area is like—folks have lived here for generations, never giving a thought that Great-aunt Eva's dough box might be worth a small fortune to a crooked dealer."

She almost wished she hadn't asked, but it was better to face the facts, no matter how unpleasant.

"What are we going to do?" It was good to feel that she had an ally. "Rachel and Grams want me to stay and open the inn. They don't seem to understand that I have a position I can't walk away from."

He patted her hand. "If you make it clear you can't, they'd have to face facts."

"I've tried. Without success."

"You'll have to keep trying." He rose. "Give my best to your grandmother, and tell Rachel that I'll see her later." He gave her a quick hug. "I know you'll do the right thing. You always do."

"Can I carry that for you, Andrea?"

Andrea stopped reluctantly. She'd noticed Cal down the block when she'd left Snyder's General Store to walk back to the house, but she hadn't been eager to talk to him. Just because he was right about her grandmother's finances didn't mean she had to like it.

He caught up with her, and she handed over the shopping bag, taking in the dress shirt and neat gray slacks he wore. She blinked, exaggerating her surprise.

"You didn't know I'd clean up this well, did you?" He smiled, apparently ready to forgive and forget. "Have a hot date?"

"No, just out for supper at the Dutch Inn. It's chicken and dumpling night. What about you?"

She gestured toward the bag he now carried. "Grams needed a few things from the store, and I didn't want to drive to New Holland to the supermarket."

"So you went to Snyder's, where you get a hot serving of gossip with every bag of groceries."

She couldn't stop a smile. "Some things never change."

"Did you get the latest popular opinion on who I am and why I'm here?"

She was surprised that he spoke so easily about it. "Opinion is divided. You're either a famous author hiding from a deranged fan or a bank robber sitting on his loot until it cools off. That one came from Etta Snyder's ten-year-old son. Her teenage daughter considers you a tragic figure recovering from a terrible loss."

She felt a sudden qualm. What if any of them proved true?

But he didn't seem affected. "I'll let you guess which it is." They walked past the Village Soda Shop and Longstreet's Antiques, their steps matching. "Did you get the whole scoop from Bendick? I saw him come in."

She stiffened. Her family troubles weren't his affair. Didn't he understand that?

His eyebrows lifted. "Okay. Right. I'm interfering."

She fought with herself for a moment. Interfering. Aggravating. But he already knew, so who was she kidding by refusing to answer him?

"Uncle Nick confirmed what you said." She bit off

the words, resenting the fact that he'd known what she should have.

"Sorry. I wish I'd been wrong." His voice had just the right degree of sympathy.

Some of her resentment ebbed away. This wasn't his fault. "I can't grasp it. When I was small, I thought my grandfather was the wisest, kindest man in the world."

Her opinion about the kindness had changed when Grandfather let them go without a word, writing them out of his life except for the college funds he'd provided. Surely he could have mended the quarrel with Mom if he'd really cared about them. But even so, she'd never doubted his business acumen.

"You can still have good memories of him." His tone warmed.

She could only nod, her throat choking up. She would like to remember Grandfather as she'd once seen him, without thinking about how he'd let her and her sisters down. Or how he'd apparently failed Grams.

"Why didn't my grandmother tell me? I would have helped."

She could feel his gaze on her face. "Maybe it doesn't matter why. Now that you know, you'll do the right thing."

He sounded like an echo of Uncle Nick, except that they didn't agree about what that right thing was.

"Uncle Nick told me he's been worried about Grams. He said there have been problems with antique thieves. That prowler you mentioned—" She came to a stop, frowning at him.

He stopped, too, leaning an elbow on top of the

stone wall that surrounded the church across the street from Grams's house. "Could be connected, I suppose."

"Nick said they hit isolated farmhouses. Grams's place is right on the edge of the village."

"It's also big, concealed by plenty of trees and out-buildings, and for the most part has had only one elderly woman in residence. There aren't any houses to the east, and in the back, the farms are too far away for troublemakers to be spotted." His frown deepened as he looked across the road toward the house.

She shivered a little at the thought. He was right—the mansion was isolated in spite of the fact that it fronted on the main road. Crossings Road, where Rachel had been injured, snaked along one side, leading toward distant farms and making it easy for someone to approach from the back. "Surely no one would try to break into the house."

"They wouldn't have to. The outbuildings are crammed to the roof with stuff. Furniture, mostly. And that's not including the attics of the house itself. No one knows what's there."

"You mean there's no inventory?"

His lips twisted in a wry smile. "I'm sure you'd have a tidy inventory, with the approximate value listed for every item."

"Of course I would." Her voice was tart. He didn't need to act as if efficiency were a sin. "For insurance purposes, if nothing else."

"That's how your mind works, but not your grand-mother's."

"I suppose not." Her grandmother was an odd mix-ture—clever about people, but naive about business, which had been her husband's prerogative. "You're trying to give me nightmares, aren't you?"

He gave a rueful smile and shoved away from the wall. "Sorry about that." He touched her hand in a brief gesture of sympathy. Warmth shimmered across her skin and was gone. "I figured I shouldn't be the only one."

Andrea was still wrestling with the difficulties when she went up to her room that evening, hoping to concentrate on some work. A half-dozen times she'd nearly confronted Grams about the financial situation, but each time a look at her grandmother stopped her. Grams looked so tired. So old.

She'd never thought of her grandmother as needing someone to take care of her. Now she'd have to, even though she suspected Grams wouldn't take kindly to any suggestion that she couldn't manage her own affairs.

Well, she'd let the topic ride until tomorrow, at least. Maybe by then she'd have come up with some tactful way of approaching the subject and Grams would, she hoped, have had a decent night's sleep.

She opened her laptop. In an instant she was completely engrossed in work.

Finally the numbers began to blur on the screen. She got up, stretching, and walked to the window. Full dark had settled in, and her attention had been so focused on the computer screen that she hadn't even noticed. Maybe she'd been trying to shut out the human problems that she found so much more difficult to deal with than figures.

Her eyes gradually grew accustomed to the darkness. She could make out the pond now, the forsythia bushes along it, and the pale line that was the flagstone path.

She stiffened. There—by the toolshed. That wasn't a bush—it was a person. She froze, watching the faint gleam of a shielded light cross the door of the shed.

He was breaking in. She whirled, racing out of the room and across the hall to burst in on her grandmother, who sat up in bed with a Bible on her lap. Barney jumped up, ears pricking.

"Andrea, what—"

"There's someone prowling around by the toolshed. Call the police and alert Cal. I'm going to turn the outside lights on."

She could hear Grams protesting as she bolted down the stairs, the dog at her heels.

FOUR

Andrea reached the back door and slapped the switch that controlled the outside lights. They sprang up instantly, bathing the area with soft illumination. The yellow glow was probably intentional on Rachel's part. It fit well with the style of the two-and-a-half-century-old building, but at the moment, Andrea would rather have harsh fluorescents that lit up every shadowy corner.

She peered through the glass pane in the door, shivering a little. The dog, pressing against her leg, trembled, too, probably eager to get outside and chase whatever lay in the shadows.

The flowers were mere shapes that moved restlessly in the breeze, as if they sensed something wrong. She strained to see beyond the patio. There was the pale outline of the pond, and beyond it nothing but angular shadows.

She heard a step at the top of the stairs behind her.

"I tried Cal, but there was no answer. Perhaps it's him you saw outside."

If so, she was going to feel like an idiot for overreacting. "Does he usually look around the grounds at night?" He'd mentioned looking for the prowler, and after their conversation, that seemed likely. The tension eased.

"Sometimes. But I called the police anyway. Now, don't start worrying about it." Grams seemed to be reading her mind. "I'd rather be safe than sorry."

But she couldn't help the chagrin she felt. City-dweller, jumping to conclusions at the slightest thing.

Well, if so, Cal was the one who'd spooked her, with his talk of prowlers and thieves. He and Uncle Nick had done the job between them.

A heavy flashlight hung on the hook next to the back door, just where Grandfather had always kept one. Clutching the collar of the excited dog, she opened the door, then reached up and took the flashlight.

"Andrea, don't go out," Grams said. "I'm sure it's fine, but wait for the police. Or Cal. He'll come to the house when he sees all the lights on."

Obviously Grams wasn't worried. A little embarrassing, to have her elderly grandmother reassuring her.

"I'll just step outside and flash the light around. See if I can spot Cal. Or anyone."

The dog surged forward, tail waving, apparently welcoming this change in his usual routine. Did the waving tail indicate he sensed a friend?

She edged down the two steps to the patio, lifting the flashlight to probe the shadows beyond the pond. Even as she did, the wail of sirens pierced the night.

She must have relaxed her grip at the sound, because Barney pulled free and darted off toward the lane, letting out an excited bark. Turning, she caught a glimpse of what might be a dark figure. Her heart jolted. She swung the light toward it, but the beam didn't reach far enough to show her anything suspicious.

The dog barked again, a high, excited yip.

If it had been an intruder, he'd be thoroughly scared away by the dog, the lights and the sirens. The lane led to the road—if he went that way, he might run straight into the arms of the police, although he'd hardly be so foolish.

She swung the light back toward the shed where she'd first glimpsed the figure. Everything was still. Reassured by the wail of the police car as it turned in the drive, she crossed the patio, flashing the light around. Nothing seemed to be disturbed.

Cal had said the outbuildings were stuffed to the rafters with furniture. She focused the flashlight on the toolshed. Nothing moved now. The shed was a dark rectangle, with a darker rectangle for the door.

She frowned, trying to pick out details in the shaft of light. Memory provided her with an image of the door as she'd seen it earlier, and tension trailed along her nerves. There had been a padlock on the door. If it was open, someone had been breaking in.

She glanced toward the house. Grams stood in the lighted doorway, peering out.

"Grams, I'm going to check the toolshed. Please don't come out."

"Be careful." Grams sounded a little shaky.

"I will. But if anyone was here, he's long gone by now." She called the words back over her shoulder, moving toward the shed. If something had been stolen on her second night here, she was going to feel responsible.

A mental list began to take shape. Get better outdoor lighting, whether it enhanced the ambience or not. Ask the police to make a regular swing by the property. New locks on any building that held something of value. If what Cal had said was right, that could be any of the half-dozen or more outbuildings.

Every building should be properly inventoried. If it hadn't been done when her grandfather died, it should be done as soon as possible.

Grams and Rachel hadn't thought of that—their minds didn't work that way, as Cal had pointed out. Hers did. He hadn't intended a compliment, but she considered her organizational skills an asset. If her mother had been a bit more meticulous, maybe they wouldn't have spent so much time evading the bill collectors.

She shook that thought off, because remembering those days gave her a queasy feeling in her stomach and an inclination to check her bank balance, just to be sure she was all right.

Hardly surprising. Other children's bogeymen had been monsters and snakes. Hers had been collection agencies.

"Barney! Come, Barney." Her grandmother's voice fluted over the dark garden.

She glanced back the way she'd come to see the dog's pale coat as he bounded toward Grams. Apparently Barney hadn't been in time to take a piece out of their intruder.

Ahead of her, the entrance to the toolshed yawned

open, sending a faint shiver of fear across her skin. She hadn't been imagining things. Someone had been here.

A few steps took her to the shed door. With a vague thought of fingerprints, she didn't touch it. She'd shine the light inside, that's all. There was no way of knowing if anything was missing, but at least she could see if it looked disturbed. And get an idea of what she had to deal with.

She leaned forward, light piercing the darkness, giving her a jumbled view of wooden pieces—straight chairs, tables, shelves, even an old icebox, jammed on top of each other...

A quick impression of movement, a dark figure. She couldn't react, couldn't even scream as a hand shot out, shoving her into the toolshed.

She barreled into the edge of a table, cracking her head on something above it. Stars showered through the darkness. She stumbled, hitting the floor just as the door banged shut.

For an instant dizziness engulfed her, followed by a wave of sheer, uncontrollable panic. She was shut in, she was alone in the dark—

She bolted to her feet, grabbed at the door, fumbling for a handle, a latch. "Let me out!"

Shout, don't cry, don't let yourself cry or the panic will take over.

"Help! Help me!"

The door jerked open, and she hurtled out. She caught back a sob, her hands closing on the soft fabric of a shirt and solid muscle. She knew him by instinct before she could see him.

"Cal—there was someone here. Did you see him?"

He pulled her clear of the door and slammed it shut. "Are you okay?"

"Yes." They'd had this exchange before, hadn't they? "I'm fine. Did you see him?"

"I saw him." He sounded grim. "Not enough to describe him, unfortunately. You?"

She shook her head. "Just a blur of movement when he pushed me into the shed. I'm sorry."

He grunted, a frustrated sound. "I was following him. If you hadn't sounded the alarm, I might have caught him."

Cal shook his head in response to Katherine's repeated offer of another cup of chamomile tea. "No, thanks, I've had plenty." One cup of the pale brew was surely enough to satisfy the demands of politeness.

"I think that's everything we need." The young township cop sat awkwardly at the kitchen table, looking half-afraid to touch the delicate Haviland cup and saucer that sat in front of him.

"Do you think you'll catch the thief?" Katherine was as much at ease in her kitchen, wearing a fuzzy red bathrobe, as if she sat in the parlor.

"That might be too much to expect, Grams." Andrea spoke before the cop could come up with an answer. "None of us actually saw the man, and he didn't take anything, as far as we know."

While the cop's attitude toward Katherine was one of respect bordering on awe, the glance he turned on Andrea was simply admiration.

Cal understood. Even casual and disheveled, wearing jeans and a loose blue shirt, Andrea was cool and elegant.

And frosty, when she looked at him. Apparently his comment about her interfering with his pursuit of the intruder still rankled.

"I'd best be on my way, ma'am." The cop rose, settling his uniform cap over a thatch of straw-colored hair as he headed for the back door. "We'll do the best we can to keep an eye on the place."

"Thank you, Officer." Katherine was graciousness itself. "We appreciate that."

Once the door closed behind him, Cal shook his head. "That won't be often enough. The township cops have too much territory to cover and too few men. What you need out there is better lighting."

"That's just what I was thinking." Once again Andrea looked faintly surprised to find herself agreeing with him. "I'll call about it in the morning."

"I don't think that's necessary. If we leave on the lights we have, that should suffice." Katherine set a cup and saucer in the sink, the china chattering against itself, betraying her emotion.

"I can install them," he said, knowing she was probably worrying about the cost, "if Andrea gets the fixtures."

Andrea nodded. "Of course." Her gaze crossed his, and he knew they were thinking the same thing. "It'll be my contribution to the renovations."

"I don't want you to spend your money on this." Katherine's eyes darkened with distress. "After all, you didn't think the inn was a good idea."

She probably still didn't, but she managed a smile.

"I have to take part. The sign does say The Three Sisters Inn, after all." She put her arm around her grandmother's waist and urged her toward the stairs. "You go up to bed, Grams. I'll just talk to Cal about the lights, and then I'll see him out."

"Thank you, dear." Katherine patted her cheek, and then came over to touch him lightly on the shoulder. "And you, Cal. I don't know what we'd have done without you tonight."

"No problem," he said easily. "Have a good night's sleep."

She nodded. "Come, Barney." The dog padded obediently after her. "That's my good, brave dog," she crooned, starting up the stairs. "You were so clever to chase the bad man away."

He waited until he heard her door close to shake his head. "I've never been overly impressed with Barney's intelligence, and tonight confirmed that. He ran to me, recognizing a friend, instead of chasing the prowler."

Andrea frowned. "Even if he's not the brightest dog in the world, you'd think he'd go after a stranger."

That thought had occurred to him, too, but he didn't see anything to be gained by pursuing it now. If this was the same person who'd broken into several farmhouses, he could be someone local, even someone who'd been to the house before.

She sat down across from him, apparently willing to forget her annoyance in the need to talk with someone. "Do you think he was planning to steal something tonight, or just checking things out for a future visit?"

"I'm not sure." He balanced the silver teaspoon on his finger. Silver, good china, antiques—there was plenty here to tempt a thief. "He may have wanted to see where the best stuff was. I would expect him to come with a truck of some sort if he planned to haul away any antiques. Pennsylvania German pieces tend to be pretty hefty, to say the least."

"I suppose you're right. He did break the lock, though."

"Meaning he wouldn't have done that unless he planned to take something? I'm not sure you're right. He couldn't know what was there unless he got in to have a look around."

"I guess." She ran her hands through the silky strands of blond hair in a gesture of frustration. "I don't even know what's in the shed. How could they get away without a proper inventory when my grand-father died?" She sounded slightly outraged, as if lack of the right paperwork was a moral failing.

"Maybe that's a good job for you." It would keep her busy, anyway.

"I can't imagine how long that would take. More time than I have, at any rate. But I'll call a locksmith and have decent locks put on all those buildings."

A slight feeling of sympathy surprised him. Andrea was trying to do the right thing for her grandmother, even if she didn't agree with her decisions.

"I can put new locks on. We'll get them when we go for the light fixtures tomorrow."

"We?" Her eyebrows lifted.

"We. Unless you're well-informed as to the best type of light fixtures and locks to use."

Her eyes narrowed, and he could almost see her

trying to pigeonhole him. "I thought you were a carpenter, not a handyman."

"I know a little about a lot of useful things."

"In that case, I'm surprised you didn't offer to do the lights and the locks before," she said tartly. "Since you were so quick to warn me about the danger."

"I did. Numerous times." He rose, carrying his cup and saucer to the sink. "Katherine always turned me down. She held tightly to the illusion that this place was still safe. After tonight, I don't think that's an issue, sadly. She'll let us do it."

"You really don't need to help." Andrea's chair scraped as she shoved it in, the only sound in the room other than the ticktock of the ornate Black Forest mantel clock. "I'm sure my grandmother appreciates your offer, but I can hire someone. I'll pay—"

He swung around, annoyed that she thought this was about money. "I said I'd do it."

"It's my responsibility." That stubborn jaw was very much in evidence. "Why should you be involved?"

"Because I live here, too. Because your grandmother and your sister have both been kind to me."

Because they can accept me as I am, without needing a dossier on my past.

Her hands moved, palms up, in a gesture of surrender. "All right, then. If you feel that way about it, I guess we'd better head out to the hardware store tomorrow."

"Fine." He strode toward the door and pulled it open. "Be sure you lock this behind me."

"You don't need to remind me of that." The ghost of a smile touched her lips as she came to the door and reached for the dead bolt. "I'm a city-dweller, remember? Locking up is second nature to me."

She stood close in the dim light, with the half-opened door between them like a wedge. Her face looked softer in the shadows, more vulnerable.

The way it had looked when she'd catapulted out of the shed practically into his arms. He'd felt her heart racing in the instant she'd pressed against him. She'd been panic-stricken, although she was hardly likely to admit that to him.

"Katherine could use a few street smarts. But I can't see her changing at this time of her life, so we'll have to take care of it for her."

She nodded, but he thought there was still a question in her eyes. About him. She wasn't like Katherine and Rachel in that regard. She didn't accept anyone at face value.

No, if Andrea stuck around for long, she'd be trying to find out more about him. She'd have to know, just so she could fit him into her neat classification system. And if she did, it would only raise more questions in her mind. Why would a rising young attorney in a prestigious firm throw it all over after winning the case of his career? She'd want to know the answer.

She wouldn't. No one here knew but him. His conscience would never let him forget the mistake he'd made in his rush to get ahead, or the child his stupidity had returned to an abusive father. It had cost his career to right that wrong, and he didn't figure he was finished paying yet. But that wasn't Andrea's business.

"Good night." His fingers brushed hers lightly as he grasped the door to pull it shut behind him. "Pleasant dreams."

"So basically it was much ado about nothing." Andrea gave Rachel her most reassuring smile the next morning. "Really. Stop looking so worried."

Of course Rachel couldn't help it, tethered as she was to a wheelchair by the two heavy casts. The chair was parked by the window, but she didn't look as if she'd been enjoying the view of the hospital's helipad.

"I knew we should have taken more security measures, especially after thieves broke into the Bauman farmhouse and vandals knocked over some of the gravestones in the church cemetery." She brushed a soft brown curl behind her ear with a quick gesture, brow crinkled. "But Grams still thinks this place is as safe as it was fifty years ago, and anyway, she said—" She stopped abruptly, guilt plainly written on her face.

"Relax, Rachel. I talked to Uncle Nick. I know about Grams's finances."

Rachel blinked. "He told you?"

"Yes. What I want to know is, why didn't you tell me?" She forced the hurt out of her voice.

Discomfort made her sister move restlessly in the wheelchair. "You know Grams. She's proud. The only reason I found out was because I happened to be visiting when she hit a low point."

"So you came up with the idea of starting the bed-and-breakfast to help her." How disapproving did she sound? Apparently some, because Rachel's gaze slid away from hers.

"It seems like a good use for the house. Nobody needs a huge place like that just to live in."

"Exactly." She sat down in the vinyl padded chair that was all the room offered for a visitor, turning it to face Rachel. "So wouldn't Grams be better off to sell? The place is way too big for her, and I don't think she should have the worry of starting a business at this time of life."

"You don't understand." Rachel straightened, eyes flashing. "Grams loves that place. Unger House has been her home for fifty years. How can you act as if it would be easy for her to give it up?"

That was as much anger as she'd seen from Rachel since Caroline stole her boyfriend in tenth grade. She leaned forward, resting her hand on her sister's.

"I know it wouldn't be easy, but doesn't that point come to everyone? When people get older, they usually have to move into a place that's more manageable. I'm sure Grams understands that."

Rachel's expression was unusually stubborn. "She's not ready for that. Besides, she always assumed there'd be family to take over Unger House one day. Us."

That was like a blow to the stomach. "She—why would she think that? It's been years since we left."

"Not that long, as Grams sees it." Rachel tilted her head, surveying Andrea with an expression that suggested she just didn't get it. "You're the one who had the most time here. I'd think you'd have lots of good memories."

"Good memories?" Something hardened in her. "What I remember is being dragged out of the house with half our belongings, Caro screaming, Grams crying, and Grandfather standing there like a statue. As if he didn't care."

"Oh, honey." Rachel patted her hand as if she was the one who needed comfort. "I know how bad that was, but can't you think about all the good times, instead? We were happy here once."

She jerked her feelings back under control, shoving the images from that day behind a closed door. In her ordinary life, she never let them out. Here, she'd been tripping over them every other minute, it seemed.

"You've always been the peacemaker, Rachel, trying to make everyone else feel good." Lucky Rachel had the gift of being able to separate out the bad stuff and remember only the happy times. She didn't, it seemed.

"There were lots of good things," Rachel insisted. "Remember the time the power went off in the big snowstorm, and Eli and Levi Zook brought the horse and sleigh and took us for a ride over the fields to their place? Having the power go off wasn't a problem for them, since they don't depend on it anyway."

"I remember." She couldn't help a smile. "Caroline tried to teach Eli and Emma's kids how to do the hokey-pokey. I don't think they appreciated it."

"The point is that if Grams wants to stay at Unger House, I'm ready to help her do it. The bed-and-breakfast seemed like the logical answer." She rubbed the wrinkle that formed between her brows. "My getting hurt wasn't part of the plan, but I still think if they'd let me go home, we could work it out. Emma's a good cook, and if I'm there to supervise—"

"Absolutely not." That was one thing she was sure

of in this situation. "I've talked to the doctors. You need rest, healing and therapy, in that order. No coming home until they give the okay."

Rachel looked at her steadily. "If I do that, how is Grams going to get the inn ready to open? She can't do it herself. Just making all the decisions, let alone the work—"

"She won't be doing it by herself." She'd reached the point she'd probably known all along she would. This wasn't her dream, but she couldn't let her family down. "I'll stay and do my best to get the inn off the ground."

She could only hope that she wouldn't have to sacrifice her job in order to do it.

FIVE

Andrea hurried through the center hallway toward the rear of the house, pausing in the small room that had been first a summer kitchen, then later a playroom for her and her sisters. They'd loved the huge fireplace, big enough to roast a whole side of beef. They'd pretended they were Cinderella, sweeping the hearth. Come to think of it, Caroline had always gotten to play Cinderella. She'd been the wicked stepmother.

That was how Rachel had made her feel at her suggestion of selling Unger House—like the wicked stepmother. That stung, with its implication that Rachel cared more, understood more, than she did. She still thought selling was the logical solution, but she was smart enough to know when a plan, logical or not, didn't stand a chance of success.

So she was heading to the hardware store with Cal, putting off the two things she was least eager to do today. Confronting her grandmother about the financial situation, for one. And then telling her boss she needed a leave of absence. Knowing him, she'd be lucky if he didn't simply give her a choice—her family or her job.

Something winced inside her at that. She deserved that promotion. She'd worked hard for it, sacrificing everything else in her drive to succeed. It wasn't fair that she might lose it now.

She pushed through the swinging door to the kitchen. "Emma, do you need anything—"

She stopped, nerves jumping. Emma was not in sight, but a man stood with his back to her—tall, broad, black pants and a black jacket, his hand in a drawer of the hutch that held the everyday china.

"What are you doing?" The edge to her voice was put there by fear, but she wouldn't give in to the feeling. Wouldn't let herself think about the dark figure that had shoved her into the toolshed. It was broad daylight now, and she wasn't afraid.

The man froze, then turned slowly toward her. It was like watching a mountain move. His face became visible, and something jolted inside her. The face was oddly unformed, as if a sculptor had started working on it and then walked away, uninterested in finishing. Blue eyes, rounded cheeks like a child's...

Emma hurried in from the pantry, her white apron fluttering, eyes worried behind wire-rimmed glasses. "What are you doing, Levi? You remember Andrea, don't you?"

"I remember him." Andrea tried to soften her embarrassment with a smile. Of course. She should have recognized him at once. Emma's oldest son was two years older than she was chronologically. Mentally, he was still the child he'd been long ago. "How are you, Levi?"

"Say good day," Emma prompted, but he just shook his head, taking a step back until he bumped the hutch.

"That's all right," Andrea said, trying to smooth over the uncomfortable moment. "Maybe later Levi will want to talk to me."

Levi's round blue eyes filled with tears. With an incoherent sound, he turned and ran from the kitchen, the screen door slamming behind him.

She could kick herself. "I'm so sorry." She turned to Emma. "I didn't mean to upset him that way."

"He will be fine." Emma didn't seem upset. "He just needs time to get used to new people."

"Doesn't he remember me?" Her own childhood memories were flooding back faster and faster, no matter how much she tried to block them out.

Emma shook her head. "He knows you, for sure. He just doesn't understand about how people change. I'll tell him a couple of times about how you're Andrea all grown-up. He'll be fine."

Certainly Emma didn't seem worried about the incident. Her oval face, innocent of makeup, was as serene as always. Whatever grief she'd endured over Levi's condition had long ago been accepted as God's will, the way she'd accept a lightning strike that hit the barn or a bumper crop of tomatoes to take to market as God's will.

Andrea went to press her cheek against Emma's, affection surging within her. Maybe she'd be a better person if she had a little of that kind of acceptance.

"Well, you tell Levi I was happy to see him, anyway." She dismissed that flare of apprehension that had gripped her when she'd seen him at the hutch. "Rachel was just reminding me of the big snowstorm, when we came to your house in the sleigh. Levi helped his father drive the horses, I remember."

"Ach, I will tell him." Emma beamed at the reminiscence, rubbing her hands on the full skirt of her plain, wine-colored dress. "He will remember that, he will."

They'd all played together then—Amish and English—it hadn't mattered to the children. Emma's oldest daughter, Sarah, had been her exact age. She'd longed go to school with Sarah in the simple white schoolhouse down the road, instead of getting on the yellow school bus for the trip to the consolidated elementary.

"How is Sarah? Married, I know from my grandmother."

"Married with six young ones of her own, and training to be a midwife, besides." Emma's pride was manifest, though she'd never admit it.

"Please greet her for me, too." They'd all grown and gone their separate ways. Only Levi had remained, a child still, but in a man's body. "I'm going to the hardware store with Cal to get some new lights and locks. I wondered if you needed anything."

Emma's plump face paled. "Locks? Why? Has something happened?"

She'd assumed Grams would have mentioned it, but possibly they hadn't had a chance to talk before Grams set off for the hospital.

"We had a prowler last night." She didn't want to alarm Emma, but surely it was better that she know. "He tried to get into the old toolshed."

"Did you—did you get a look at this person?" Emma's hands twisted together under her apron.

She shook her head, sorry now that she'd mentioned it. She didn't want to distress Emma. Probably she, like Grams, still thought of this area as perfectly safe.

"He ran away when he heard the dog and the sirens." Maybe it was just as well not to mention her closer encounter with the man. "We're going to put up brighter lighting in the grounds. Hopefully that will keep any troublemakers away."

"Ja." Emma pulled open the door under the sink, peering inside. *"Ja,* maybe it will. I can't think of anything that I need from the store."

Andrea hesitated a moment, studying the tense lines of Emma's shoulders under the dark dress, the averted face. The thought of a prowler had upset her more than expected, but Andrea didn't know what to do to ease her mind.

"Don't worry about it, please, Emma. I'm sure the lights will solve the problem. And if you're concerned about walking back and forth to the farm, I'd be happy to drive you."

"No, no." Emma whisked that offer away with a sweeping gesture. "I am fine. No one will bother me."

There didn't seem to be anything else to say, but Andrea frowned as she walked to the door. They couldn't afford to have Emma upset. Grams needed her more than she ever had.

They both did, if they were really going to open the inn on time, and though she could hardly believe it of herself, it seemed she was committed to this crazy venture.

* * *

From his perch on the stone wall that wound along the patio, Cal watched the black-clad figure vanish from sight around the barn. He and Levi had reached the point that Levi would sometimes speak to him, but today he'd rushed past without a word. Something had upset him, obviously.

Cal latched his hands around his knee. Andrea had said she'd meet him, and he'd guess she was the type to be on time. So he'd come a bit early, not wanting to give her a reason to say he'd kept her waiting.

Sure enough, she hurried out the back door, checking her watch as she did. She looked up, saw him and came toward him at a more deliberate pace.

"Sorry. Have you been waiting?"

"Only for a couple of minutes." He got up leisurely. "I saw Levi come running out."

"I suppose you think I frightened him."

He held both hands up in a gesture of surrender. "Peace. That wasn't aimed at you. I know how shy he is. It's taken months to get him to the point of nodding at me."

A faint flush touched her cheeks. "I guess that did sound pretty defensive, didn't it? I was startled that Levi didn't seem to remember me."

He fell into step beside her as they walked toward the stone garage that had started life as a stable. "I take it you knew him when you were children."

What had she been like as a child? Flax hair in braids, he supposed, probably bossing the others around because she was the oldest.

She nodded, those green eyes seeming fixed on

something far away. "They were our neighbors. Emma's daughter Sarah was my closest friend." She shook her head. "It seems odd now, when I think of it. As if it happened in a different world."

That, he thought, was the most unguarded thing she'd said to him yet. "I suppose it was, in a way. Childhood, I mean."

"The differences didn't seem so great to a child. We drove my grandfather crazy by talking in the low German dialect the Zook children used at home."

"He didn't like that?" He gestured her toward the truck. When she hesitated, he opened the passenger door for her. "We may as well take this. Rachel's compact doesn't have much trunk room."

She nodded, climbing in. When he slid behind the wheel, she went on as if the interruption hadn't happened.

"I'm not really sure why he objected. His family was what the Amish call 'fancy' German, just as they call themselves the 'plain folk.'" She shrugged. "He didn't insist—maybe he knew that would just make us more determined. Or maybe he saw that Emma's family was good for us." Some faint shadow crossed her face at that.

"Sounds as if you and your sisters had a good childhood here," he said lightly. "I was an urban kid, myself. Never saw a real cow until I was twelve."

"Good?" Again that shadow. "Yes, I guess. Until it ended."

He glanced toward her. "Ended sounds rather final."

She blinked, and he could almost see her realizing

that she'd said more to him than she'd intended. She shrugged, seeming to try for a casual movement.

"Everyone outgrows being a kid. Can we get what we need at Clymer's Hardware, or do we have to go farther?"

Obviously the subject was closed. Maybe only the encounter with Levi had opened her that much. Something had happened to put a period to that innocent time, maybe the same thing that had kept her away from here for so long. Whatever it was, she wasn't going to tell him.

So be it. He wouldn't pry, any more than he wanted someone prying into his life. "Clymer's. I know your grandmother likes to use local businesses if she can."

"Fine."

He pulled into the lot next to the frame building with old-fashioned gilt lettering on the glass windows. He loved going into the village hardware store. It was nice to be in a place where people knew your name, as the song said.

Clymer's was as much a center for male gossip as the grocery store was for female gossip, in the way of small towns. Here they'd be talking about who needed new fencing and how the alfalfa was coming along.

Andrea slid out quickly, and he followed her to the door. She stepped inside, pausing as if getting her bearings.

"Lighting fixtures are in the back." He nodded toward the aisle.

Detouring around kegs of nails and the coil of rope that hung handy to be measured off, they headed back to where sample fixtures hung, gleaming palely in the daylight. Ted Clymer looked up from the counter where he was working a crossword puzzle and raised a hand in greeting. Ted seemed to figure if his customers needed any help, they'd ask for it. Otherwise, he left them alone.

Andrea came to a halt in the midst of racks of light fixtures. She turned toward him. "I'm not too proud to admit when I'm out of my depth. What do you think we need?"

Since he'd already decided, he was relieved that they weren't going to argue about it. He chose two brands and set the boxes in front of her. "Either one of these would do the job."

"Which do you recommend?"

He put his hand on the more expensive brand. "This will cost more to begin with, but it's higher rated. Still, the other one will serve."

She shook her head decisively. "I don't want to worry that they'll have to be replaced in a couple of years. How many do you think we need to cover the area?"

"I'd say six would do it." He glanced at the racks. "Ted doesn't have that many out, but he probably has more in the back."

She picked up the box. "I'll ask him to get them while you're picking out the locks." Her smile flickered. "You don't need to ask my opinion. Just get what you think will work best."

So apparently Andrea trusted him in that, at least, and she wasn't grudging the money spent on something her grandmother needed. He watched her walk toward the counter. Even in khaki pants and a fitted denim jacket, she had just enough of an urban flair to let you know she didn't belong here.

Too bad. Because Katherine would like having her around, not because it mattered to him.

It took a few minutes to find locks that satisfied him. Nothing would keep out a really determined thief, but these would discourage anyone who was looking for a lock that could be popped quickly and quietly.

He headed back to the counter, his hands full, but checked when he saw the person who stood next to Andrea, talking away as if they were old friends. Margaret Allen. He'd be willing to bet that no legitimate errand had brought her into the hardware store. It was far more likely that she'd spotted them from across the street and decided to check up on the competition.

He approached and dropped the locks on the counter, their clatter interrupting the conversation. "That's it for us, Ted. Ring us up."

He turned, forcing a smile. "Hello, Margaret. How's business?"

She returned the smile with one that had syrup oozing off it. Margaret looked, he always thought, like a well-fed, self-satisfied cat, and never so much as when she was asserting her position as the owner of the finest inn in the county. Just how far would she go to maintain that status? The question had begun pricking at the back of his mind lately.

"How nice to see you, Cal. I was just telling Andrea how wonderful it is of her to come and help her grandmother at such a sad time. Poor Rachel. I'm afraid all their visions of starting a bed-and-breakfast will be lost. Still, I always say that every cloud has a silver lining, and I'm sure in the end, this disappointment will be for the best. Don't you agree, Andrea?"

Andrea looked a little dazed at the flood of saccharine. "Yes, I mean—"

"We have to go." He handed Andrea the credit card Ted had been patiently holding out. "Lots to do. Nice seeing you, Margaret." He scooped up boxes, handing the bag containing the locks to Andrea, and nudged her toward the door.

She shot him an annoyed look. "I'm glad to have met you, Ms. Allen. I'll tell my sister you asked about her."

They reached the pickup, and he started loading fixtures quickly, not having any desire to hang around for another interrogation from Margaret.

Andrea dropped the bag with the locks into the pickup bed. "You didn't have to be rude to that poor woman. She was just expressing her concern."

"Right." He shook his head. "That was Margaret Allen." He pointed to the Georgian mansion across the street with its twin weeping willows overhanging the wrought iron fence. "That Margaret Allen, owner of The Willows bed-and-breakfast."

"She said she was a friend of my grandmother's." Andrea climbed in, frowning at him as he got behind the wheel. "Maybe she did gush a bit, but I'm sure she meant well."

"A bit?" He lifted an eyebrow. "You looked as if you were drowning in it."

Her lips twitched. "Just because she runs another B and B, that doesn't make her the enemy."

"In her mind, it does. Believe me. She takes pride

in having the only inn in Churchville, and she doesn't like to share the limelight, or the tourist dollars, with anyone." He pulled out onto Main Street for the short drive home.

"Surely there's enough tourist trade to go around."

He shrugged. "Ask Rachel, if you don't believe me. She's the one who's had to deal with her. The other B and B operators in the county have been support- ive, by and large, but Margaret created one problem after another."

"What could she do? Surely you don't think she was our prowler."

That was a thought that hadn't occurred to him, and he filed it for future consideration. "I don't see her wandering around in the dark, no, but she has played dirty. Complaints to the township zoning board, com- plaints to the tourist bureau, complaints to the bed- and-breakfast owners association. All couched in such sickeningly sweet language you'd think she was doing them a favor by putting up roadblocks."

"Maybe she was." It was said so softly he almost missed it.

"Is that what you'll tell your grandmother when you bail and leave them on their own?" The edge in his voice startled him. He hadn't meant to say that.

He felt Andrea's gaze on him and half expected an explosion. He didn't get it.

"Think what you like." Her tone dismissed him, as if he were no more important in the scheme of things than the barn cat. "But as a matter of fact, I'm not leaving. I'm staying until I can be sure that my grand- mother and sister are all right."

It silenced him for a moment. "What about your job?"

Her fingers clenched in her lap. "I don't know. Talking to my boss is a pleasure I haven't had yet."

"I'm sorry. I hope he understands."

"So do I." Her fingers tightened until her knuckles were white.

"It means that much to you?"

"Yes. It does." She clipped off the words, as if he didn't have the right to know why.

She was willing to sacrifice something that was important to her for the sake of someone else. The few people who knew the truth about him might say he'd done the same, but he'd done it as much for himself as for anyone else, because he'd known he couldn't live with himself if he hadn't.

It had brought him unexpected benefits in the long run—helped him to know what he wanted from life, brought him to faith. Still, he couldn't assume that would be the result for Andrea's sacrifice.

"I hope it works out for you, Andrea. Really."

He glanced across the confines of the front seat at her. There was something startled, a little wary, in her eyes. As if she wasn't sure whether she believed him. Or maybe as if it mattered what he thought.

SIX

Andrea sat in the room she still thought of as her grandfather's library that afternoon, frowning over the rather sketchy records Rachel seemed to be keeping on the inn's start-up. Sketchy didn't cover it. Surely Rachel had better records than this. If not, they were in more trouble than she'd imagined.

She flipped through the file folder, her frustration growing. Hadn't Rachel been saving receipts, at least? Grams might know if she had records elsewhere. Maybe, like Grandfather, she preferred to do it all by hand, although he had been far more organized than this.

Grandfather's tall green ledgers had been a fixture of their childhood. Presumably the insurance and real estate business he'd shared with Uncle Nick had long since been computerized, but she'd always associate her grandfather with those meticulously handwritten ledgers. She glanced at the shelf where they'd once stood in a neat row, but it was now occupied by a welter of tourist brochures and bed-and-breakfast books. Rachel must have moved them.

The front door closed, and Barney gave the excited yelp that meant the center of his existence had returned. The scrabble of his nails on the plank floor was followed by the crooning voice Grams reserved for him. Andrea had to smile. She couldn't imagine her dignified grandmother talking baby talk to any other creature but Barney.

"Andrea?" Her grandmother came in, followed by the excited dog. "Good, you're here. I'd like to speak with you."

The determined set to Grams's jaw told her that any questions about Rachel's record-keeping would have to wait. Grams clearly had an agenda of her own.

Andrea swung the leather swivel chair around so that she faced the wingback tapestry chair that was Grams's favorite. The desk chair had been Grandfather's. It was too big for Andrea, and she felt slightly uncomfortable in it, as if she sat in the boss's chair without permission.

"How's Rachel? Did you tell her I'll come to see her this evening?"

Grams sat down, her expression lightening a little. "I thought she seemed a bit stronger today. She didn't look quite so pale. Nick had been in with a lovely arrangement of roses, and Pastor Hartman came just as I was leaving."

"That's good." Good that Rachel seemed better, and good that she was having other company. Perhaps that would keep Grams from feeling guilty if she couldn't be there every minute.

"Yes." Grams fondled the dog's ears for a moment, frowning a little. "I understand from Rachel that you know about my financial situation. That James Bendick told you."

That must really rankle, or Grams would be using the nickname that she'd adopted along with the children. "Please don't blame Uncle Nick, Grams. I'd already guessed some of it, and I made him tell me what was going on."

That didn't seem to have the desired effect. Grams still looked severe. "Nevertheless, he doesn't have the right to discuss my affairs without my permission. I'll have to speak to him about it."

The threat to be spoken to by Grams had been such a part of her childhood that it almost made her smile. *Andrea Katherine, do I have to speak to you?* The words echoed from the past.

Grams was taking this too seriously for smiling, however, and they had to discuss the situation, whether Grams wanted to confide in her or not.

"Uncle Nick probably thought I'd heard it already, from you. Which I should have. Why on earth didn't you tell me about the financial problems? You must know I'd help any way I can."

Grams turned her face away, and for a moment Andrea thought she wasn't going to answer. Then she realized that her grandmother was looking at the portrait of Grandfather that hung over the mantelpiece on the other side of the room.

"I didn't want you to think ill of your grandfather. Or any more than you already do."

The words were spoken so softly that it took a moment for them to register. And when they did, Andrea felt a flush rise on her cheeks. "I don't know what you mean."

Grams looked at her then, her blue eyes chiding. "Yes, you do, Andrea. You've never forgiven him for the quarrel with your mother."

It was like being slapped. She'd never dreamed that Grams guessed her feelings. Obviously she hadn't been as good at hiding them as she'd thought. She took a breath, trying to compose herself. She couldn't let whatever lingering resentment she had affect what she did now.

"It was a long time ago, Grams. What's important is what's going on now."

Her grandmother shook her head slowly, delicate silver earrings echoing the movement. "The past is always important, Andrea. Your grandfather was a good man. He gave me a comfortable life, and I won't hear a word against him just because he made a few wrong business decisions."

It must have been more than a few, some practical part of her mind commented, but she shooed away the thought. She had to help Grams, but she'd hoped to steer clear of Grandfather's mistakes, knowing that would hurt her.

"He loved you very much, Grams."

For the first time since her return, Andrea stared directly at the portrait. Her grandfather's image stared back—blue eyes as piercing as she remembered, the planes of his face still strong even when the painting was done, to commemorate Grandfather's retirement from the state legislature at sixty-five. He looked like a man you could count on.

But he also looked stubborn. In the case of his daughter, the stiff-necked stubbornness had won out over any other consideration, including his grandchildren.

"He loved you, too, dear. I know you find that hard to believe, but he did."

"He let her take us away." The voice of her childhood popped out before she could censor it.

Grams reached out to grasp her hand. "He couldn't stop her. She was your mother." She shook her head. "I know you think he could have mended things with her, but you must be old enough now to see how it was. He was proud, and your mother—well, she was willful. They could never stop the quarrel long enough to admit they loved each other."

Willful, reckless, lavish with both affection and temper—yes, she knew what her mother had been like. How had two such solid citizens as her grandparents have produced Lily Unger Hampton? That had to be one of the mysteries of genetics.

"I'm sorry, Grams." To her horror, she felt tears well in her eyes. "I know it hurt you, too." But her grandmother would never know just how bad it had been for her precious grandchildren, at least not if Andrea could help it.

"He grieved when you were taken away." Grams's voice was soft. "You have to believe that, my dear."

Not as much as we did. You were the grown-ups, you and Grandfather, and our mother and father. Why didn't you take better care of us? She wouldn't say that, but she couldn't help feeling it.

Shaking her head, Grams got up. She dipped her

hand into a Blue Willow Wedgwood bowl that sat on top of the desk, retrieving the small key. She handed it to Andrea.

"It fits the bottom drawer on the right." She nodded to the massive mahogany desk that had been Grandfather's. "I want you to look inside."

Something in her wanted to rebel, but she couldn't ignore the command in her grandmother's eyes. She bent and unlocked the drawer, pulling it open. Inside were long rectangular boxes, three of them—the sort of archival boxes that preserved documents. The top box had a name, written in black ink in Grandpa's precise lettering. *Andrea.*

She lifted that one, setting it on the desk blotter to remove the lid. Her throat tightened. A picture, drawn by a child's hand, showed two figures—a white-haired man in a navy suit, a child with yellow braids. Before she could dwell on it, she flipped through the rest of the contents.

Report cards, more drawings, dating back to the earliest attempts that were no more than ovals on sticks for figures. Always two of them—grandfather and granddaughter. A handmade valentine, with a lopsided heart pasted onto a white doily, signed with a red crayon. *To Grandfather from your helper.*

She remembered making that one, sitting at the kitchen table, asking Emma to aid with the spelling. Emma, always more adept in German than English, had called Grams in to advise.

Tears stung her eyes, and she fought to keep them from falling. Grams meant well. She was trying to prove that Grandfather had loved her. But if he'd loved her enough to save all these things, why hadn't he loved her enough to do whatever it took to stay a part of her life?

A hot tear splashed on the valentine, and she blotted it away. Yes, Grams meant well. But looking at these reminders didn't make the situation better. Seeing them just made it worse.

Cal rounded the shed on his way to the kitchen. His stride checked abruptly.

Andrea sat on the low stone wall where he'd sat earlier, but she didn't seem to be waiting for anyone. Her cell phone was pressed to her ear, and judging by the expression on her face, the conversation wasn't going well.

He detoured to the walk that circled around, taking him toward the door at a safe distance from her. She'd probably come out to the garden to ensure her privacy, and he wouldn't intrude. But he couldn't prevent a certain amount of curiosity. Was it her boss who put that expression on her face?

Or was it a boyfriend, unhappy at her prolonged absence from the city? That thought generated a surprisingly quick denial. No one had mentioned a boyfriend in Andrea's life, but then again, why would they, to him?

He went on into the kitchen, where he consulted Emma about the exact finish on the piece he was making for her, enjoying prolonging the conversation with a smattering of the low German he'd been attempting to learn. It must still be plenty fractured, judging by her laughter.

That had been one of the things that had surprised him about the Amish when he'd come here. He'd expected, from outward appearances, a dour people, living an uncomfortable life as if it were a duty.

Instead he'd found people who laughed readily and who took as much enjoyment in plowing all day in the sun as they did from sitting on the porch on a summer's evening. Work was not something that was separate from play—all things held their own intrinsic satisfaction, because they were done in obedience to God's will.

It was a lesson he'd been trying to learn, but he suspected that even the trying was self-defeating. He couldn't will himself into finding peace and joy in the everyday things of life. That only happened when he forgot the effort and simply lost himself in what he was doing.

When he went out the back door again, Andrea still sat on the wall. Afternoon sunlight, filtering through the leaves of the giant oak that shaded the patio, turned her silky blond hair to gold. The cell phone lay next to her.

"Hi." He nodded toward the phone. "I didn't want to interrupt you."

"An interruption might have improved the conversation." She grimaced. "No, I take that back. It would just have prolonged it."

"Your boss?" That instinctive sympathy came again.

"He did *not* take the news well. Not even when I assured him I'd keep working on the project from here."

"Did you point out that telecommuting is fast becoming the norm in some businesses?"

"He doesn't think telecommuting will do the trick at this point." She shrugged. "I can't really argue with that. He's probably right."

He propped one foot on the wall and leaned an elbow on his knee. "I assume he finally accepted the inevitable."

"Well, he's not firing me outright, so I suppose that's a good sign. But I suspect my promotion has just moved off into the distant future." Her eyes clouded at that. "I'll do everything I can from here, and my assistant will do what she can, but he'll still be inconvenienced."

"A little inconvenience never hurt anyone. Maybe he'll learn to appreciate you more." He'd like to remove the dismay from her face, but that wasn't within his power.

"Somehow I doubt that."

He sat down next to her. No use pretending he didn't care about her troubles. He couldn't help doing so. "This promotion—it means a lot to you."

A fine line formed between her brows. "It means… security."

Whatever he'd expected her to say—recognition, success, the corner office—it hadn't been that. "Security? That sounds like something I'd expect from a fifty-year-old who's thinking about retirement."

She stiffened. "Security is generally considered a good thing, believe it or not. You don't have to be fifty to think about it. In fact, if you wait until you're fifty, you've put it off too long."

"You're young, smart and, I suspect, talented at what you do." He smiled. "And those are good things, too. They'd be appreciated in plenty of places. Your grandmother says—"

"My grandmother doesn't know anything about business. But you do, don't you?" She swung the full impact of those green eyes on him.

"What makes you say that?" He backtracked, wondering where he'd made a mistake. "I'm just a craftsman."

"You do a pretty good imitation of the country hick from time to time, but that's not who you are, is it?"

He shrugged, almost enjoying parrying with her. She'd never hit on the truth, so what difference did it make?

"I told you I grew up in the city. Any little vestiges of urban sophistication should wear away, in time."

"I'm not talking about growing up in the city." She brushed that away with a wave of her hand. "I'm talking about the corporate mind-set. You understand it too well to be a bystander."

He rose, the enjoyment leaving. He didn't like the turn the conversation was taking. "Hey, I was just trying to be sympathetic."

She studied him for a long moment, her brow furrowed with uncertainty. And he suspected she didn't like being uncertain about anything.

"If that's true, I appreciate it," she said finally. "But I still don't believe you're just a simple craftsman."

His tension eased. She wasn't going to make an issue of it, and even if she did—well, he hadn't committed any crime. At least, not any that the law would call him to book for. Whatever guilt he still carried was between him and God.

"And you're not just a simple financial expert, are you? You're also a granddaughter, a sister, and now an innkeeper."

"Don't remind me." She rubbed at the line between her brows, as if she could rub it away. "I know you won't appreciate how this pains me, but my sister's idea of keeping track of start-up costs consists of throwing receipts in a file."

"She uses a file? I thought my cigar box was pretty sophisticated."

That got a smile, and the line vanished. "You're not going to make me believe that, you know."

"Maybe not." He sobered. "But I hope you'll believe that if anything happens that worries you, you can call me. Any time. I promise I'll answer my phone."

She looked startled. "You mean—but surely with the new lights and the locks, no one would try to break in."

"Sounds a little melodramatic with the sun shining, but I'm still not comfortable about the situation." An ambitious thief might want to see what he could get before the inn opened, filling the place with visitors. And an ambitious rival might think one more incident would be enough to scuttle the inn plans for good. "Just—call me."

Her gaze seemed to weigh him, determining whether and how much to trust him. Finally she nodded.

"All right. If I see or hear anything that concerns me, I'll call you. I promise."

She'd made a promise she didn't expect she'd have to keep, Andrea thought as she drove home from the hospital that evening. She appreciated Cal's concern, but surely the measures they'd taken would discourage any prospective thief.

Now all she had to worry about was hanging on to her future at work, ensuring Rachel's healing, and getting the inn off and running. Those concerns had actually begun to seem manageable.

The layer of dark clouds that massed on the horizon didn't dampen her optimistic mood. Rachel had looked almost normal tonight, joking about the casts and finally rid of the headache that had dogged her since the accident. Andrea hadn't realized how worried she was about her sister until the weight had lifted with the assurance that Rachel was her buoyant self again.

They had spent nearly two hours going over all of Rachel's plans for the inn, and in spite of her sister's undoubted lack of financial expertise, they probably had a reasonable chance of success. They had a beautiful, historic building in an unmatched setting, and Grams was a natural hostess. With Emma's housekeeping ability and Rachel's inspired cooking, they should be in good shape.

The cooking was the immediate problem, but surely they could find a way around that until Rachel was well. If Andrea could just get them set up on a sound financial system, the whole thing could work. She might still have doubts about the wisdom of Grams taking on such a project at her age, but at least she was no longer convinced they were headed for disaster.

She pulled up to the garage, giving an approving nod to the lights Cal had installed. It would take a brazen thief to attempt to break in now, even though darkness took over beyond the buildings with only the pale yellow glow from a distant farmhouse to break it.

She parked and walked quickly to the side door that led directly into the family quarters. From upstairs, Barney gave an experimental woof and then quieted, apparently recognizing her step. Grams must have already gone to bed.

Andrea made the rounds of the ground floor, checking the doors that Grams had already no doubt checked. Everything was locked up and secure. She hurried through the library, not looking toward the portrait. Thinking about her grandfather was not conducive to a good night's sleep.

Upstairs, she opened the door to Grams's bedroom. Her grandmother was already asleep, her Bible open on her lap. Barney looked up, tail slapping the floor. Andrea removed the Bible, open to the twenty-third Psalm. Had that comforted Grams enough to send her to sleep? Faint longing moved through her. She wanted…

She wasn't sure what. Faith, like Grams had? Like Cal apparently had? But faith wasn't to be manufactured just because she felt responsibility weighing on her. She turned off the bedside lamp, tiptoed out and shut the door.

A cool breeze wafted into the hall from the open window. She glanced at it, deciding to leave it open, and went on into her bedroom.

The new lights cast reflections on her ceiling. Comforting reflections. They could all sleep well tonight, including Cal. She wouldn't be calling him.

* * *

Andrea jolted awake. Shoving the sheet aside, she reached for the bedside lamp, heart pounding. Then the noise came again, and she subsided, relaxing. Thunder, that was all. The threatening storm had arrived. Even as she thought that, rain slashed against the house.

Jumping out of bed, she hurried to the windows, but no sprinkles dampened the wide sills. The rain wasn't coming in this direction, but it might well be raining in the hall window.

She hurried out into the hallway. The sheer white curtains on the window billowed inward, and she rushed to pull down the sash, bare toes curling into a slight dampness on the floor beneath her feet. She could imagine Grams's reaction if she woke to soaked curtains.

There were no lights on this side of the house. Darkness pressed against the panes, mitigated only by reflections of the dim night-light Grams always left on in the hall. She stood there for a moment, looking into the dark, until it was split by a vivid flash of lightning.

She jerked back, gasping. In the brief instant of light—had that been a figure, standing just by the shelter of the lilac hedge?

She pressed her hand against her chest, feeling the thud of her heart. Imagination, that was all. She was spooking herself, seeing menace where there was nothing... But there had been something that night by the toolshed. Was their prowler making another visit?

Lightning snapped again, closer now, one sharp crack illuminating the grounds below as sharply as a spotlight. Showing her the dark figure of a man.

She drew back, clutching the curtain instinctively in front of her, as if he could see her standing there in the flimsy cotton nightshirt. She slid to the side of the window. Stared out, focusing her eyes on the spot, trying to still the rasp of her breath. If the lightning flashed again, she'd be ready.

A volley of lightning, thunder following it so fast that the storm must be right over the house. It showed her, as if in a series of jagged still pictures, the figure turning, the brim of a hat, tilting up toward the window where she stood, frozen. The face was a pale blur, but the clothing—even in dark outline, the clothing looked Amish.

Impossible. But she had to believe the evidence of her own eyes, didn't she? Even as she watched, the figure moved, raising one arm as if he shook his fist at her.

She stumbled backward, heart thudding, breath catching, and then bolted for the bedroom and her cell phone. The doors were locked, he couldn't get in, call Cal, call the police....

Cal answered on the first ring, sounding as if he fought his way awake. "Yes, what?"

"There's someone, a man, out on the east side of the house."

"Andrea?" His voice sharpened. "Are you sure?"

"The lightning makes it as bright as day. He's there, watching the house. We didn't put lights—"

They hadn't thought they needed to where there were no outbuildings to be broken into. Maybe the intruder's goal wasn't the outbuildings. Maybe it was the house itself.

"I'll be right there. Don't go out, you hear me?"

"I won't. I'll go down to the side door and meet you there." She glanced across the hall. "My grandmother's exhausted. I don't want to wake her again unless I have to."

"Right. Don't call the police until I see what's up. And don't open the door." He clicked off without a goodbye.

It wasn't until she stood there shivering in the dark that she realized that at least one part of her relief at hearing his voice on the phone was the conviction that it couldn't be Cal out there in the dark, playing tricks.

Quickly she pulled sweatpants and a sweatshirt on, stuffing her feet into slippers. She hadn't realized she'd been considering that possibility, even subconsciously. But what, as Uncle Nick had said, did they really know about Cal?

Well, she knew now that he wasn't their prowler. And she knew that comfort had flooded through her at the sound of his voice.

Maybe it was better not to dwell on that. She grabbed a flashlight and went softly down the stairs. Should she have called the police? Maybe, but if she did, Grams would waken, would be subjected to that upset yet again.

Wait, as Cal had said. See what he found.

She huddled against the side door, gripping the flashlight, wishing for even the dubious comfort of Barney at this point. If Cal didn't appear soon, she'd have to do something.

A dripping face appeared outside the glass, and her heart threatened to leap from her chest before she recognized Cal. She unlocked the door, trying to ignore the shaking of her fingers, and pulled him in out of the rain.

She switched on the hall light. Like her, Cal wore sweatpants and sweatshirt, but his were wet through.

"I'm sorry. You're soaked." Well, that wasn't very coherent. "Should I call the police?"

"No use." He shook his head, water spraying from his drenched hair. "He's not there now."

"If he ever was?" She knew her quick anger was just reaction to strain. "I saw him. He was there."

"Relax, I believe you. The lilac bushes were broken, the grass tamped down, as if he'd stood there for some time." His fingers closed over hers. They were wet and cold, but somehow they warmed her. "Tell me what you saw."

"A man. I can't say how tall he was—I was looking down from the upstairs window." She kept her voice low, not wanting to stir up the dog. "I didn't make out the face, but Cal—he was wearing Amish clothing."

He frowned. "Are you sure?"

"I know it doesn't make any sense, but I'm sure. Dark pants and jacket, white shirt, the hat—if it wasn't an Amishman, it was someone doing a good imitation."

"I'd almost rather believe that." His voice was troubled. "The Amish aren't exactly noted for producing prowlers. You never met a more law-abiding bunch."

She shivered. "That's not all. It—he—the figure seemed to be looking up at the window where I was standing. He raised his arm, as if he were shaking his fist at me. And if you tell me I was dreaming—"

"I don't doubt you." Without seeming to know he was doing it, Cal pulled her closer. "But we've got to think this through before we do anything. Can you imagine the repercussions if something like this hit the newspapers?"

"I hadn't thought of that, but I see what you mean." Like it or not, and they didn't, the Amish were newsworthy. A story like that could get out of control in hours. She glanced up the stairs. "I don't want Grams upset, and that would devastate her."

"Well, whoever he was, he's gone now." Cal brushed damp hair back from his brow. "Are you okay if we hold off making a decision until we can talk this over in the morning?"

She was insensibly comforted by the way he said *we*. Whatever came, she wasn't alone in this. "Yes, all right. After all, he didn't really do anything except lurk. The house is locked up securely."

"Good." He squeezed her hand. "I'll take another look around before I go back to the barn. We'll talk in the morning. Meantime, try to get some sleep, or your grandmother will want to know why your eyes are so heavy." He turned to go back out into the rain.

"Wait. Do you want an umbrella?"

"Why?" Cal paused on the threshold, his smile flashing. "I can't get any wetter than I already am. Good night. Lock the door."

"No chance I'll forget that."

He vanished almost at once into the darkness beyond the reach of the light. She locked the door, realizing that she was smiling.

Amazing. If anyone had told her fifteen minutes ago that she'd find anything to smile about tonight, she'd have said they were crazy.

SEVEN

Cal frowned at the mug of coffee in his hand and then set it out of the way on the barn floor. He needed something to get his brain moving after the previous night's alarms, but caffeine wasn't doing the job.

He picked up a sanding block and knelt next to a reproduction of an old-fashioned dry sink, running the fine sandpaper along its grain. This was better than coffee for what ailed him.

What he really needed was to talk with Andrea, but he'd known better than to go to the inn first thing this morning. Katherine would be up and Emma already busy in the kitchen, making it impossible to have a private conversation. He'd have to wait until after their breakfast was over, at least.

He ran his hand along the curved edge of the dry sink's top. Smooth as silk—that was what he wanted. Taking shortcuts at this stage would show up eventually in the finished product, ruining the piece for him.

Even the work didn't chase away his troubled thoughts, unfortunately. He couldn't stop chewing on the implications of what Andrea had seen. Or thought she'd seen.

A few days earlier, he might have been tempted to believe she was making up her tale of a prowler, just to convince her grandmother to sell. Now, he knew her better. Andrea wouldn't do that.

No, he didn't doubt that she'd seen someone, but was it beyond belief that the man, whoever he was, wasn't Amish? She'd seen a figure in dark clothes, but peering out into the storm from an upstairs window, she couldn't have seen all that much. Maybe her imagination had taken the prowler's dark clothing and filled in the rest.

Somehow he didn't relish the idea of bringing that up with her.

"Cal?"

He straightened at the sound of Andrea's voice, dismayed at the flood of pleasure he felt at the sight of her. She stood for a moment in a stripe of sunlight at the barn door.

"Come in. How are you? Nothing else happened, did it?"

She came toward him, the sneakers she wore making little sound on the wide planks of the barn floor. In jeans and a loose denim shirt worn over a white tee, she almost looked as if she belonged here.

"It was quiet enough," she said. "I didn't sleep much, though. I woke at every creak, and believe me, a house that old creaks a lot."

"How about some coffee?" He gestured toward the pot that sat on a rough shelf against the wall. "It won't be as good as Emma's, but at least it's hot."

"None for me, thanks. Grams insisted on giving me

three cups of herbal tea this morning, because I looked tired. I don't have room for coffee."

"She didn't ask any difficult questions, I hope." If she'd told her grandmother about what had happened...

Andrea shook her head. "No. And I didn't mention anything about last night." She ran her hand along the top of the dry sink, much as he had done, a wing of silky hair falling across her cheek as she looked down. "But I can't just ignore what happened."

"I know." He frowned, wondering if it were wise, or even possible, to keep her from voicing her suspicions. "Do you want to go to the police?"

"Depends upon what moment you ask me." Her smile flickered. "I spent my wakeful night going over and over it and changing my mind every thirty seconds or so."

He bent, picked up a couple of sanding blocks, and tossed one to her.

She caught it automatically. "What's this for?"

"Try it." He knelt, running his block along the side of the piece. "It's very soothing."

"Just what I need—to be soothed while intruders trample through Grams's yard and try to break in." But she sat down on the floor in front of the dry sink and began sanding lightly.

"Trample?" He raised an eyebrow.

"You know what I mean." She sanded for a moment longer, frowning. "He was there. He was watching the house."

"I know." He silenced the urge to tell her what he thought she should do. It was her decision, not his.

"You're right. This is soothing. How did you learn to do this? The furniture, I mean, not just sanding."

"My dad's father." His voice softened, as it always did at the thought of his grandfather. Whatever he knew about being a good man, as well as a good carpenter, came from him. "He figured everyone should know how to do something useful, just in case."

"He sounds like a wise man."

She glanced up at him, smiling. For an instant their faces were close—so close he could see the flecks of gold in those green eyes, mirroring the gold of her hair. So close he could feel the movement of her breath across his cheek.

Her eyes widened, and he heard the catch of her breath. He put the sanding block down with a hand that wasn't entirely steady and sat back, away from her. That was—well, unexpected. Not surprising that he found her attractive, but shocking in the strength of that pull toward her. And disturbing that she felt it, too.

Andrea looked down at the sandpaper in her hand. She cleared her throat. "Well, I have to make a decision about calling the police."

So they were going to ignore what had just happened. Maybe that was best.

"If you tell the police the person you saw was Amish—"

"I know. It will cause problems, problems for the community, problems for Grams. I don't want that. But I have to do something. I can't help wondering…" She looked at him again, eyes guarded. "What if it was Levi?"

"Levi." He had to adjust his perspective. "That

didn't occur to me. Do you have some reason for thinking that?"

She shook her head. "Only that I've seen him around the house. At one time, I'd have said I knew him, but not any longer. Does he ever come over here at night?"

"I've never seen him." Everything in him wanted to reject the idea. "Look, you know he's like a child—a gentle child. If it were Levi last night, he certainly didn't intend any harm. From what I've seen, his parents keep close tabs on him, so it's hard to believe he could have been wandering around after dark."

"Somebody was." She moved restlessly. "You mentioned there'd been some vandalism in the area. Could it have something to do with that?"

"I don't know. The incidents have been pretty harmless, as far as I've heard. Mailboxes knocked down. Somebody threw a bucket of purple paint at an Amish house. The police seem to think it's caused by teenagers looking for a little excitement. Nothing here was damaged, but maybe they're branching out into intimidation." He'd rather imagine it was random mischief, not deliberate malice toward the inn.

She nodded, frowning. "What do you think we should do?"

We. The simple pronoun stopped him for a moment. Andrea considered him an ally. She didn't want to make this decision alone, and she didn't want to worry her elderly grandmother, or Rachel, stuck in a wheelchair. So she'd turned to him.

All the resolutions he'd made about living a detached life here were on the line. Panic flickered. He couldn't make himself responsible for them.

But he'd put himself in this position. He'd interfered, and he couldn't back away and say it was none of his concern just because his emotions were getting involved.

"It seems to me that the police are already doing about all they can do, under the circumstances. The fact that you saw a prowler again probably wouldn't change anything."

He was being drawn in. He was starting to think like a lawyer again. He didn't want to, but he couldn't help it.

"I suppose not, but doing nothing doesn't resolve the situation."

"Look, why don't you give it a day or two? Let me talk to some of my Amish friends, sound them out about it. See if there's any animosity toward the inn among the Amish community." Doing so might harm the delicate balance of his relationship with them, but the alternative was worse.

She studied him for a moment, as if weighing his sincerity. "All right." She got to her feet too quickly for him to reach out a helping hand. "If you'll do that, I'll talk to Uncle Nick. He may have some ideas, and I'm sure he'd keep anything I tell him in confidence. He wouldn't want to upset Grams."

Obviously Andrea wasn't one to leave everything in someone else's hands, but maybe she was right. Bendick did seem to have his finger in a lot of pies in the township.

"What about Levi? Do you want me to talk to Emma?"

"No. I'll see if I can bring it up without upsetting

her." She shook her head. "I'm not looking forward to it."

"Better to talk to her than let the suspicion affect your attitude toward him."

"True enough. If I didn't say it before, thank you, Cal. For last night, and for being willing to help. I appreciate it. And Grams would, if she knew."

"Any time."

He meant it, but he had to be careful. Andrea had broken through barriers he'd thought were completely secure, and trying to deny the attraction he felt was pointless.

But that attraction couldn't go anywhere. The life Andrea prized was the kind of life that had nearly destroyed his soul.

The gold lettering on the plate glass window jolted the cool facade Andrea had meant to maintain for this visit. Unger and Bendick, Real Estate and Insurance. She hadn't imagined that Grandfather's name would still be on the business.

It was a name that stood for something in this quiet country village. Uncle Nick probably hadn't been eager to give that up, and she couldn't blame him.

Grams had assured her that Uncle Nick would be in the office on a Saturday morning. Fortunately she hadn't asked why Andrea wanted to see him.

A bell tinkled when she opened the door. Clever of Uncle Nick to retain the old-fashioned flavor, even when he was dealing with visiting urbanites looking for a little piece of country to call their own. Or maybe especially then.

The woman behind the mission oak desk looked up inquiringly, and in an instant Andrea went from being the appreciative observer to being that ten-year-old trailing her grandfather around town. There was Betty Albertson, her grandfather's faithful secretary, peering at her over the half-glasses she wore at her desk.

Those half-glasses had fascinated Andrea. Betty wore them so far down her pointed nose that they seemed in constant danger of sliding right off, like a sled down Miller's Hill.

"Betty, how nice to see you. It's been a long time." Conventional words, giving her the moment she needed to remind herself that she was no longer ten, no longer interested in the stash of chocolate bars in Betty's top right desk drawer.

Sharp gray eyes now matched gray hair, pulled smoothly back into the same sort of French twist Betty had worn when her hair had been a mousy brown. For a moment she thought the secretary didn't recognize her, but then she smiled.

"Andrea Hampton. Land, it has been a while. You look as if life agrees with you."

Did she? With everything she valued turned upside down in the past few days, it hardly seemed likely.

"I see you're still running Unger and Bendick single-handedly."

The joke had always been that Betty knew more about the business than both partners combined. She'd been so fiercely loyal to Grandfather that it occasionally seemed she resented even the distraction of his family.

Betty's smile tightened. "Mr. Bendick offered to

hire more help, but I prefer to handle things on my own."

She'd given offense, even though it hadn't been intended. "I'm sure no one could do it better. My grandfather often said you were worth more than a dozen assistants."

"Did he?" A faint flush warmed Betty's thin cheeks. "That was kind of him. He was always so thoughtful."

Betty had her own memories of Grandfather. "Is Uncle Nick-Mr. Bendick—in? I'd like to see him for a moment."

Betty's gaze flicked toward the closed office door that bore his name, again in faded gold. "This isn't a good time. We get swamped on Saturdays. Why don't I ask him to stop by the house later?"

Andrea glanced around, half amused, half annoyed. "It doesn't look that busy right now. Surely he can spare me a few minutes."

Betty's lips pressed together, nostrils flaring, but then she mustered an unconvincing smile. "He's on the phone. If you want to wait, I'll try to slip you in when he finishes."

Plainly Betty had transferred the devotion she'd once had for Fredrick Unger to his junior partner. "I'll wait." She crossed the faded Oriental carpet to the row of wooden chairs against the far wall and sat.

Betty blinked, perhaps wondering if she'd gone too far. "Well, that's fine. I didn't mean anything, I'm sure."

"I won't take long, I promise."

She couldn't get into an argument with the woman, just because she was hyperprotective of her employer.

If anything, she ought to feel sorry for Betty, leading such a narrow life. She probably didn't get out of Churchville from one year to the next. Andrea vaguely remembered an elderly mother that Betty looked after.

The schoolhouse clock on the wall above the desk ticked audibly. As a child, sitting on this same chair, legs swinging, she'd been mesmerized by the jerky movement of the hands. Photos surrounded the clock, recording events from the early days of Churchville. Grandfather at the ground breaking for the school, at the dedication of the bank, at some long-ago Fourth of July celebration.

The door to the inner office opened. Uncle Nick blinked and then hurried toward her, hands outstretched.

"Andrea, this is a surprise. Betty, why didn't you tell me Andrea was waiting?"

Betty slid the half-glasses down to look over them. "You were on the phone. And now you have an appointment to show the Barker place."

"I certainly have a few minutes to talk with Andrea."

"You know how interested those people are. You don't want to be late."

"Why not? They've kept me waiting at every appointment." He took Andrea's arm, winking at her once his back was turned to Betty. "We have time for a little chat."

He led her into his office and closed the door, then gave her a quick hug. "I'm sorry about that. The woman thinks I can't do a thing unless she reminds me."

"I don't want to mess up a sale."

He shook his head. "Pair of uptight yuppies who think they want a country place but don't like anything that's in their price range." He beamed at her. "I'm glad you stopped in for a visit before you head back to the city."

"As a matter of fact, I'm not going back for a while."

"Now, Andrea, don't tell me you let them talk you into doing something rash. Your job—"

"My job will wait. Right now my family needs me."

His dismayed expression was almost comical. "My dear, I'm sorry. Is your boss all right with your taking time off?"

She shrugged. "He's not happy, but I'm afraid it can't be helped." Her mind flickered to Cal, saying that maybe he'd learn to appreciate her more. "I have to stay, at least until the inn is up and running."

The elderly swivel chair creaked when he sank down in it. His eyes were troubled, and he ran his hand along his jaw.

"I wish we could find some other way of dealing with this."

"I appreciate your concern, Uncle Nick, but it's all right. Really." She took a breath. How to word this without alarming him or sending him running to Grams? "That's actually not what I came to talk to you about."

He blinked. "Is something wrong? Something else, I mean?"

"Not exactly. Well, you know about the prowler. We haven't had any damage, but it made me wonder if there's anyone who might have a grudge against the family."

"Against Katherine?" He sat upright, outrage in his voice. "Your grandmother is universally respected. You know that."

It was said with such vehemence that she couldn't doubt it was true of him. "Has there been anything— someone who thought Grandfather had treated him unfairly, or some dispute about property lines?"

He was already shaking his head. "Nothing at all. I'm sure the prowler was simply an isolated incident. Those security lights you put up should do the trick."

So he knew about the lights already. She'd forgotten how quickly the township grapevine worked.

"What about turning the house into a bed-and-breakfast? Have there been any ill feelings about that?"

"Mostly from Margaret Allen, maybe a few other old-timers who hate change, don't want to see any more tourists brought in." He shook his head. "They're fighting a losing battle on that one. But I'd say they're not the type to prowl around in the dark, especially Margaret."

He had a point. "She's more likely to bury a person under a pile of platitudes."

"That's our Margaret." He chuckled, then sobered again. "But I'm concerned about you. Your grandmother, dear woman that she is, doesn't understand the sacrifice she's asking you to make. Maybe I could hire someone to help out—"

"Thanks, Uncle Nick." She was touched by his kindness. "I appreciate that, but no."

"Really, my dear." He rose, coming back around the desk. "I want to help. It's the least I can do—"

The door opened and Betty marched in, holding

out a briefcase. "Mr. Bendick, you must leave or you'll keep those people waiting." She sounded scandalized at the thought.

"Yes, yes, I'm going." He snatched the case and sent Andrea an apologetic look. "Think about what I said. I'll talk to you later."

She nodded. "I will. Thank you, Uncle Nick."

He hurried out, letting the front door slam behind him.

"He worries about your grandmother," Betty said, her voice almost accusing.

Several annoyed retorts occurred to her, but she suppressed them. "There's no need. I'm there with her, and Cal Burke has been very helpful."

"Well, he would be, wouldn't he?"

Andrea blinked. "What do you mean?"

"It's none of my business, of course." Betty patted the smooth twist of gray hair. "But I'm the one who typed the lease, so I can't help knowing, can I?"

She resisted the impulse to shake the woman. "Knowing what?"

"Why, about his lease on the barn. Mr. Bendick warned your grandmother, but she wouldn't listen."

She took a step toward Betty. "What?" she snapped.

"She's renting that barn to him at a ridiculously low price. Almost nothing. It worried Mr. Bendick something awful. Cal Burke is bound to help out. He doesn't want your grandmother to sell, because then he'd lose the nice deal he talked her into."

The lease clutched in one hand, Andrea charged toward the barn, anger fueling her rush. When she found Cal, he wasn't going to know what hit him. She held on to the anger, knowing at some level that if she let it slip, even more hurtful feelings would surface.

Betrayal. She'd already experienced enough betrayal in her life.

She hurried up the slope and shoved the heavy door aside. Her rush carried her several feet into the barn before she realized she was alone.

She stood for a moment, looking at the scattered pieces of furniture as if Cal might be hiding behind one of them. Nothing split the silence except her own labored breathing.

Instinct sent her outside again, where she looked around, frowning. The inn grounds and the surrounding farmland dozed in the Saturday-afternoon sunshine.

And already the anger was seeping away, leaving space for pain and regret. How could she have been so foolish as to trust the man? She knew better than to let herself be taken in by a plausible stranger, the way Grams undoubtedly had.

Maybe he was in the apartment he'd created for himself in the tack room. She followed the path around the corner of the barn. She'd find him and make him admit that he was taking advantage of her grandmother. If there was an explanation for this…

But there couldn't be. She stifled that notion. There could be no logical reason for Cal to have talked Grams into renting him the barn at what anyone would consider a token amount. No wonder Uncle Nick had been upset.

Upset didn't begin to cover it for her.

She rounded the corner and stopped. She'd been prepared to find the story-and-a-half tack room annex changed, but she hadn't expected this.

The rough-hewn door had been replaced by a paneled one with nine-pane beveled glass. A bow window curved out at the front of the building, with a flagstone path leading to the entry.

Irritation prickled along her skin. He'd probably talked Grams into paying for all this, creating a cozy nest for himself at someone else's expense.

Her feet flew over the stones, and she gave a peremptory rap on the door.

The door swung open before she had a chance to raise her hand for another knock.

Cal stood there, smiling. Welcoming.

"Good, you're here. How did you make out with Bendick?"

For a moment she could only stare at him. They'd become partners. She'd agreed to investigate with him.

Before she'd known he was a cheat.

She stalked inside. The old tack room had certainly been transformed. Wooden built-ins lined the walls on either side of a fieldstone fireplace. The wide plank floors were dotted with colorful Navajo rugs that contrasted with the solid Pennsylvania Dutch furniture. The open space was living room, dining room, and kitchen combined, with an eating bar separating the kitchen section. An open stairway led up to a loft that must be the bedroom.

Cal closed the door. "Do you like it?"

Anger danced along her nerves. "Yes. Did my grandmother pay for this?"

He blinked. Then his face tightened, brown eyes turning cold. "Maybe you should ask your grandmother that."

"I'm asking you." Small wonder Grams hadn't confided in her about this dubious rental. She'd have known how Andrea would react. If Grams planned to run the inn on these lines, she'd be bankrupt in a month.

Cal looked at her steadily. "You'd better tell me what this is about, Andrea. I'm not good at guessing games."

He leaned against the bar between kitchen and living room, elbows propped on it. The pose might have looked casual, if not for the muscle that twitched in his jaw, belying his outward calm.

"This." She thrust the lease at him, appalled to see that her hand was shaking. "How did you talk my grandmother into this? She might be naive about business, but surely she realized how ridiculous the rent is. And for both your home and your business—you really got a great deal, didn't you?"

He made no move to take the paper, but his hands curled into fists. "Did you talk to your grandmother?"

"I'm talking to you. The person who's cheating her." *The person who lied to me and made me let my guard down. The person I thought I could trust.*

Cal thrust himself away from the counter, taking a step toward her. "You don't believe that." He stopped, shaking his head. "My mistake. I guess you do."

"I was the one who made the mistake. I trusted you." She would not let her voice break. "How could you do this to an old woman?"

His face might have been carved from a block of

wood. "That lease is between your grandmother and me. You don't come into it at all."

"My grandmother asked me to help her with her business."

He raised an eyebrow. "As far as I know, Katherine didn't sign a power of attorney, turning her affairs over to you. If she wants to talk to you about my rental, she will. Are you worried that she's squandering away your inheritance?"

Fury boiled over, threatening to scald anyone in its path. "I'm trying to protect my grandmother from people who would take advantage of her."

Like you, Cal. It wouldn't have been hard to get her to trust you. I did, and I'm a much tougher case than Grams. Something twisted and hurt under the anger.

"I see." Nothing changed in his expression, but he seemed suddenly more distant. "I can't help you, Andrea. The details of my lease are between me and Katherine."

"Anyone who knows the rent you're paying would know you're cheating her."

"That's for Katherine to decide. You're not the owner. And even if you were, you can't throw me out." He nodded toward the paper in her hand. "I have a lease, remember?"

She stared at him, baffled and furious. Then she turned and slammed her way out.

EIGHT

"I don't know what you thought you were doing." The glare Grams directed at Andrea left no doubt about what Grams considered her actions. Interfering.

"I'm trying to help you. That's all." Andrea sat up a bit straighter. Being called onto the library carpet made her feel about eight.

"Going to my tenant behind my back is not helpful, Andrea Katherine."

When Grams resorted to using both names, the situation was serious. "I'm sorry, but I'm worried about you. If you'd let me know how bad the financial situation is—"

"You'd have told me I should sell the place." Grams finished the thought for her. Her face tightened, and she suddenly looked her age. "That's why I didn't tell you. I didn't want to argue about it."

That was more or less what Rachel had said, but how could Andrea keep silent when the people she loved best in the world seemed bent on the wrong course?

"Are you so sure selling wouldn't have been for the best?" She kept her tone soft.

Grams shook her head. "You're more like your grandfather than you want to admit. That's what he would have said, too, even though this place has been in his family for close to two hundred years."

Grams was right about one thing. She didn't care to be told she was like her grandfather.

If saving Unger House meant enough to Grams that she'd go against what she believed Grandfather would have wanted, then no argument of Andrea's would sway her.

"I've already agreed that I'll do all I can to help you. But if you want to involve me in the business, I have to understand what's going on. When Betty told me—"

"Betty!" Grams's nostrils flared. "What right does she have to talk about my concerns, I'd like to know."

"I'm sure she was just reflecting Uncle Nick's feelings." She shouldn't have mentioned Betty. Relations had always been strained between Grandfather's wife and his secretary.

"Nick is a good friend." Grams's face softened. "He worries too much, but he means well."

"I mean well, too, even if you think I'm going about it the wrong way."

"I know that." Grams's voice gentled a little. Maybe the storm was over, even if the problem wasn't resolved. "Rachel and I appreciate the fact that you're willing to stay here and help us."

"I want to get you on a good business basis, so that you have a chance to succeed. As far as the rental is concerned…" She couldn't let it go without trying once more to show Grams that Cal was taking advantage of her. "The barn is yours to do as you like with, but

I have to tell you that the rent you're charging is extremely low by current standards."

Grams was already shaking her head. "You don't understand."

"How can I, when you won't tell me about it?"

For a moment the situation hung in the balance. If her grandmother continued to treat her like a child who had to be protected from the facts, this would never work.

Finally Grams nodded. "I suppose you ought to know." She glanced toward the portrait over the fireplace. "When Cal approached me about renting the barn, I couldn't imagine how he'd live there. But he was willing to do all the work on the apartment himself. If you've seen it, you'll have to admit he's done a fine job, and he insisted on paying for everything that went into the renovation."

She'd misjudged him in that respect, at least. To her surprise, Andrea was relieved.

"He's certainly increased the value of the building," she admitted. "But even so, to lock yourself into a contract with that low a rent could be a problem." Cal's turning the lease against her still rankled.

"We agreed that as his business picked up, the rent would increase." Grams flushed, as if she found the discussion of money distasteful. "He insists on paying me more every month, more than he should. I don't want to feel as if I'm accepting charity."

No, Grams wouldn't like that feeling. She had always been the giver, not the recipient.

Andrea took a deep breath. "I'm sorry, Grams. I

shouldn't have gone to Cal without talking to you about it first."

"No. You shouldn't have." Grams gave her the look that suggested Andrea's manners weren't up to what was expected of an Unger. "Now I think we'll both see Cal and apologize."

"Both…"

Words failed her. Grams proposed to lead her by the hand and make sure she apologized properly, the way she had when Andrea had left the farm gate open and the Zook cows had gotten out.

"Grams, I can handle this myself. It's my mistake."

Her grandmother stood, every inch the lady. "It was my error, as well, in not telling you. We'll both go."

Apologizing to Cal alone would have been embarrassing. Doing it with Grams looking on was humiliating. It didn't help to know that she deserved it.

If she kept herself busy enough, maybe she could forget that awkward scene with Cal. At least that's what Andrea had been telling herself since Grams left to spend the evening with Rachel at the hospital. Unfortunately, it didn't seem to be working.

She shoved away from the desk in the library, blinking as she tried to focus her eyes on something other than the computer screen. It was getting dark, and she hadn't bothered to turn on any lights.

She stretched, rubbing at the tension in the back of her neck. She'd started entering data for the inn into the desktop hours ago. As far as she could tell, neither Grams nor Rachel had touched the computer since they'd bought it, supposedly for the business, and that increased her worries over their chances for success. Running a B and B wasn't just about being a good cook or a good host. It was a business. She hadn't been kidding when she'd told Cal about Rachel's idea of a filing system.

And that brought her right back to Cal again. He'd been gracious when she'd apologized. Pleasant, even.

She frowned at Barney, who'd taken up residence on the hearth rug, seeming to transfer his allegiance to her when Grams wasn't around. "I'd be just as happy if he hadn't been so nice about it. You understand, don't you?"

Barney thumped his tail against the rug. The only thing he understood was that someone was talking to him. He rose, stretching very much as she had, and padded over to her. She patted the silky head that pressed against her leg.

"I'm being ridiculous, I suppose."

He didn't comment.

It had been a difficult situation, made worse by Grams accepting part of the responsibility for the mis-understanding. She'd actually admitted that she should have told Andrea the whole story.

That had hit her right in the heart. She didn't want her grandmother to feel any less in charge than she'd always been.

I don't know how to balance all this. The discovery that she was actually taking her problems to God startled her, but it felt right. Maybe Grams's quiet faith was having an impact on her. *Usually I think I can handle anything, but I can't. I need guidance. I have to know*

*what I should do—about Grams, about the inn, even
about Cal. Please guide me. Amen.*

Maybe it wasn't the most perfect of prayers, but
the admission that she couldn't see her way somehow
made her feel a bit better.

And as for Cal having such an inside glimpse of
their family dynamics—well, maybe she'd be lucky
enough not to be alone with him for the next few days.
Or ever.

Barney whined, his head coming up, and he let out
a soft woof.

"What is it, boy? Do you hear Grams coming?" She
peered out the side window, but there was no sign of a
car turning into the drive.

The sheltie whined again, then paced to the door
and nosed at it.

"You want to go out? I guess it has been a while."
She opened the library door and then followed the dog
through to the back hallway.

"Okay, out you go." The lights Cal had installed
showed her the garden, the outbuildings, the barn, and
beyond them, the dark, silent woods and pasture. All
was quiet.

Barney bounded out, the screen door banging behind him. He'd be a few minutes at least, needing to
investigate every shadow before coming back inside.

She leaned against the doorjamb, tiredness sinking in. Tomorrow was Sunday, and that meant church
with Grams in the morning and an afternoon visit to
Rachel. Probably she ought to try and find the rest of
the receipts Rachel thought she had saved, just in case
any of them required an explanation.

In typical Rachel fashion, the receipts had, her sister thought, been tucked away in one of Grandfather's ledgers, which she vaguely remembered putting on the top shelf of the closet which stored kitchen and dining room linens.

Of course. What a logical place to keep receipts they would need to produce come tax time, to say nothing of Grandfather's ledgers. Rachel hadn't inherited any of his organizational genes, that was clear. Obviously Andrea would either have to do the business taxes for them or hire someone locally who'd keep after them all year long.

She opened the closet, frowning at the creaking that came from the hinges. Sometimes it seemed everything in the house had its own sound, all of them together creating a symphony of creaks, cracks, whines and pops. Hopefully none of their guests would be the nervous sort.

The deep closet had shelves against its back wall, accessible only after she'd moved several metal pails, a corn broom and two mops. What the closet didn't have was a light, but the fixture in the hallway sent enough illumination to show her that there appeared to be a book of some sort on the top shelf, stuck between two roasting pans big enough to cook the largest turkey she could imagine. She'd need something to stand on in order to reach the shelf.

She propped the closet door open with one of the mops and retrieved a chair from the kitchen, glancing out the screen as she passed. No sign of Barney yet. She could only hope he hadn't found a rabbit to chase or worse, a skunk. She doubted they had enough to-mato juice in the house to cope with that.

The very fact that she knew the remedy for a dog's encounter with a skunk gave her pause. That certainly wasn't part of her normal urban life. Since she'd been back in this house, all sorts of things were resurfacing from her early years.

Grasping the chair with both hands, she carried it into the closet and climbed onto it. She reached up to find that her fingertips fell inches short of the top shelf. That was what came of having twelve-foot ceilings. How on earth had her sister gotten the book up there to begin with? And why did she think that a logical place to put it?

She could go in search of a stepladder, but maybe if she put her foot on one of the lower shelves, she could boost herself up enough to reach the book.

She wedged her toe between two stacks of table linens that someone, probably Emma, had stored carefully in plastic bags. Bracing her left hand against the wall, she stretched upward, groping with her right. Her fingertips brushed the soft leather cover of the ledger. Memory took her back to Grandfather's desk, sitting on a high stool next to him, watching as he entered figures in a neat row.

This is the proper way to do it, Drea. If I keep the records myself, then I know they're accurate.

She blinked, willing away the childhood memory, and stretched until her hand closed on the edge of the book. Victory in her grasp, she started to pull it down. The palm that was braced against the wall slipped, the chair wobbled, then tipped. In an instant she was falling, tangled helplessly in chair legs and sliding linens, landing with a thud that would probably leave a bruise on her hip.

A board creaked out in the hallway, separate from the clatter of her fall. Before she could look the door slammed shut, leaving her in total darkness.

Her breath caught, and she pressed her lips together. *Don't panic. It's all right. All you have to do is get up and open the door. If you could cope with being trapped in the car and shoved into the toolshed, you can cope with this.*

She untangled herself, willing her heart to stop pounding, and fumbled with sweat-slicked hands for a knob. And realized there was none on the inside of the door.

Be calm. You're all right. Grams will be home soon.

But another voice was drowning out the calm, reasonable adult. It came welling up from someplace deep inside her, erupting with all the violence of a child's terror.

"Let me out!" She pounded on the door, unable to hold back the fear she didn't understand. "Let me out! Someone help me! Help!"

The child inside was crying, hot, helpless tears. *Someone help me. Father, please, help me.*

Cal rounded the corner of the toolshed, his sneakers making little sound on the damp grass. He could see the garage now, illuminated by one of the lights he'd installed, with the door still standing open. Katherine and Andrea must have gone to the hospital to see Rachel.

He frowned absently, coming to a halt and gazing around, probing the shadows, searching for anything that was not as it should be. It would be best if he got back to his own place before they returned. He and Andrea had already butted heads too many times today.

He wasn't sure whether it had been worse to bear her accusations or to listen to her apology. At least when she'd been throwing her fury toward him, he'd had the shield of his righteous anger.

It was only afterward that he began to wonder just how righteous that feeling had been. The hard lessons of the past had driven him to God, but he suspected he still had a lot to learn about living the way God expected.

Andrea had at least been furious with him on behalf of someone else. His feelings had been motivated entirely by something much more personal. He'd thought they'd been on the road to becoming friends. Now it was clear they'd never be that, and disappointment had fueled his anger. Maybe he hadn't expressed it, but he'd felt it, and that was just as bad.

He'd turned to head back to the barn when he saw Barney dash across the garden toward the inn door. Odd. Katherine wouldn't leave the dog outside when the place was empty. How had he gotten out of a locked house?

"Barney!" He took a few steps along the path toward the patio. "What are you doing out here?"

He expected the dog to turn and run to him with his usual exuberant greeting. Instead Barney pawed at the door, ignoring his voice.

The back of his neck prickled. Something wasn't

right here. Apprehension pushed him into a trot that covered the rest of the way to the house in seconds.

Even so, by the time he reached Barney, the dog was howling, pawing at the door frantically. Cal grabbed for the collar even as he realized that the noise he heard was more than just the dog.

Somewhere in the house, someone cried for help.

He yanked open the unlocked door, scrambling into the back hall and stumbling over the eager dog. "Barney—"

He shoved the animal out of his way. Barney skidded, claws scrabbling on the bare floor, and then launched his body at the narrow, paneled door of the hall closet.

Dog and door collided with a thud that echoed the pounding from inside. Cal's pulse thudded so loudly in his ears that it took a second to isolate the voice.

Andrea—but an Andrea who was a far cry from the brisk, efficient woman he knew. She sounded terrified. If someone had hurt her...

"It's okay," he shouted. Anything to dispel that panicky note in her voice. "Andrea, it's okay. I'm here. I'll get you out."

"Hurry." Her voice sounded muffled, as if she'd clamped her hand over her mouth.

He grabbed the small knob that released the catch, turned it, and Andrea tumbled into his arms. She grasped him, her fingers digging into his shoulders, her breath coming in harsh gasps.

He'd sensed her claustrophobia when she'd been closed in the toolshed for seconds. Now—now she was in the grip of a full-blown attack, as terrified as if she'd been faced with death instead of closed-in darkness.

"It's okay." He put his arm around her, feeling the tremors that coursed through her body. "Come with me." He piloted her toward the library, switching on lights as they went, sensing that nothing could be too bright for her at the moment. "You're safe now. Tell me what happened. Did someone hurt you?"

Her hand went up to her mouth as if to hold back sobs. She took one ragged breath and then another, seeming to gain a bit more control with each step they took away from the closet. Barney danced around them, trying to push his way between their legs, making little throaty sounds that sounded sympathetic.

"I'm all right." Andrea probably had to force the words out, and he felt the tension that still gripped her body.

"You're fine," he soothed. He switched on the lamp next to the sofa and eased her to a sitting position. She still gripped his hand tightly, so he sat down next to her.

Barney, balked of his clear intent to take that space, had to be content with putting his head in Andrea's lap.

Cal smoothed his fingers over hers. "Did someone push you? Attack you?" He thought of the dark figure she'd seen out in the rain, and his alarm ratcheted upward. He should search the house, but he couldn't leave her in this state.

"No, nothing like that." She wiped away tears with her fingers. "At least—" She hesitated. "I don't think anyone was there. Probably the door just slammed shut when I lost my balance."

The slight shading of doubt in her voice had all his senses on alert. "Did you see someone? Hear someone?"

"I didn't see anyone."

Andrea straightened, putting up one hand to rub the back of her neck, as if tension had taken up residence there. Her usually precise blond hair tumbled about a face that was paler than usual, and her jeans and white shirt were smudged with dust. None of that was typical of Andrea, but it was somehow endearing.

Focus, he reminded himself. "You didn't see anyone. Did you hear something then?"

She shrugged, attempting a smile that was a mere twitch of her facial muscles. "You know how old houses are. This place makes all sorts of sounds even when it's empty."

"And it makes noises when someone is there. Someone who shouldn't be." His tone was grim. The back door had been standing open. Who knew how many other entrances had been just as accessible?

"I heard a creak that I thought came from the hallway, just before the door swung shut, but that doesn't mean anything. All the floors slant, and the door might swing shut on its own." She sounded as if she were trying to convince herself. "Besides, what could anyone gain by shutting me in a closet?"

Just saying the words put a tremor in her voice. The wave of protectiveness that swept over him startled him with its strength. He had no business feeling that way about Andrea.

He cleared his throat. "Maybe he wanted to keep you from seeing him. Or maybe—" Another, more disquieting thought hit him. "You're claustrophobic, aren't you? How many people know about that?"

"What do you mean?" Her fingers tightened, digging into his hand, and her voice rose. "Are you saying someone would do that deliberately to upset me?"

"Or to scare you off." He put his other hand over hers in a gesture of comfort and then frowned, groping for a rational thought that seemed to be lost in a sense of awareness of her.

"That's—that's ridiculous." But she didn't sound convinced.

"Look, Andrea, I'm beginning to think there's more going on here than we realize. First Rachel's accident, and then this business with the prowler—either the Hampton women are prey to a lot of bad luck all at once, or someone is willing to go to extremes to keep the inn from opening."

"Rachel." Her eyes darkened with fear as she zeroed in on the possibility of a threat to her sister. "But that was an accident. The police haven't found any evidence of anything else."

"I'm not trying to scare you." He raised a hand to brush a strand of silky hair back from her face. His fingers lingered against the smooth skin of her cheek without his mind forming the intent.

"I'm not afraid." She attempted a smile that trembled on her lips. "In spite of the evidence to the contrary. But Grams, and Rachel—"

"I know. I don't like it, either." He wanted to wipe the worry from her face, but he wouldn't lie to her, pretending everything was all right when it so obviously wasn't. "Maybe I'm wrong. Maybe it's all a coincidence. But I don't like you being alone." Vulnerable, he wanted to add, but suspected she wouldn't appreciate it.

"I'm not alone. You're here. I appreciate—" She looked into his eyes and seemed to lose track of the rest of that sentence.

He understood. His rational thought processes had gone on vacation. All he could think was that she was very close, that her skin warmed to his touch, that he wanted to protect her, comfort her…

He closed the inches that separated them and found her lips. For an instant she held back, and then she leaned into the kiss, hands tightening on his arms, eyes closing. He drew her nearer, trying to deny the emotion that flooded through him, wiping out all his barricades in a rush of feeling.

"Andrea." He murmured her name against her lips, not trusting himself to say more. This shouldn't be happening, but it was. He'd probably regret it later, but now all he wanted was to hold her.

He'd told himself they couldn't be friends. Maybe they couldn't, but maybe they could be much more.

NINE

Andrea wrapped her fingers around the coffee mug, absorbing its heat. The warmth generated by Cal's kiss had dissipated when he'd drawn back, looking as confused by what had happened as she was.

Maybe they'd both sensed the need to change the tempo a bit at that point. Cal had gone to search the house, leaving the dog with her. Barney had padded at her heels while she fixed coffee and carried a tray back to the library, apparently mindful of his duty to guard her. The journal, Rachel's receipts tucked inside, lay next to the computer, the innocent cause of her problems.

She stroked the sheltie's head. In spite of Cal's doubts about Barney's intelligence, the dog had seemed to know she was in trouble.

"Good boy," she told him. "If it hadn't been for you…" Well, she didn't want to think about that.

"If it hadn't been for Barney, you'd still have been all right." Cal came into the room as he spoke. "Your grandmother would have come home and found you soon, even if I hadn't heard the dog."

She knew he was trying to make her feel better, but

she didn't want to think about what she'd have been like if she'd been closed in the closet all this time. Cal didn't understand the panic. No one did who hadn't experienced it.

"Did you find anything wrong anywhere?"

"No actual sign of an intruder, but there are far too many ways into a house this size." He frowned, looking as if he'd like to go around putting bars on the windows. "And I'm not saying that closet door couldn't have swung shut on its own, or even from the vibration when you fell, but it still seems pretty stable."

"Is that supposed to make me sleep well tonight?"

She watched as he took a mug, poured coffee and settled on the couch opposite her. She liked the neat economy of his movements.

"I'd put safety over a good night's sleep anytime." He looked toward the windows. "Your grandmother should be back soon, shouldn't she?"

She glanced at the grandfather clock in the corner and nodded. "I don't want her upset about this. It was just an accident. You agree?"

"Let's say I'm about eighty percent convinced of that. You're sure it wasn't a person you heard before you fell?"

He leaned toward her, propping his elbows on his well-worn jeans. As usual, he wore a flannel shirt, this time over a white tee, the sleeves folded back. Also as usual, his brown hair had fallen forward into his eyes.

"It was a creak. That's all. I told you—this house has a language all its own. Surely if someone had been there, I'd have heard him running away."

An image popped into her mind—the large, dark

figure she'd seen outlined by the lightning. Her fingers tightened on the mug. If he'd been in the house, he would have made more noise than a gentle creak.

"Well, maybe. Unless he was smart enough to slip away the minute he heard you fall."

"You searched the house. You didn't find any signs someone had gotten in," she pointed out.

Lines crinkled around his eyes. "Does that mean you trust me?"

"Yes." The word came out so quickly that the sureness of it startled her. Maybe tomorrow she'd be back to being suspicious of him, but at the moment she was just glad he was here.

"Well…good." He seemed a little taken aback by her quick response. "Have you given any more thought to what I asked you? Does anyone else around here, other than family, know about your claustrophobia?"

She shook her head, wanting to reject the possibility. "I don't know. I suppose someone could. The Zook family probably knew." Levi popped into her mind, and she pushed him out again. He wouldn't remember something like that. "It was a lot worse when I was a child. I don't even remember what triggered it the first time, so I must have been pretty young."

"It didn't start when you left here, then."

She blinked, surprised at his linking the two things. "No. Why would you think that?"

The light from the Tiffany lamp on the end table brought out gold flecks in his eyes. "It's just that I've gathered it was a pretty traumatic time for all of you."

"Has my grandmother talked about our leaving?"

She asked the question carefully, not sure she wanted to hear the answer.

"Only in a general way, saying how much it grieved her when you left."

"It wasn't our choice." Her voice was tart with remembered pain. "The adults in our lives didn't give Rachel and Caro and me any say in what happened."

"They don't, do they? My folks split up when I was twelve, and I always had the feeling that what happened to me was an afterthought. Did your parents—"

She nodded, her throat tight. "Our dad left. Not that he'd been around all that much to begin with." She frowned, trying to look at the past as an adult, not as the child she'd been. "He kept losing jobs, and Mom—well, she couldn't cope. That was why we moved in here, I suppose. Our grandparents were the stable element in our lives."

"And then you lost them, too." Setting his mug aside, he reached across the space between them to take her hands, warming her more than the coffee had.

"My mother quarreled with Grandfather." She shook her head. "I'm not sure what it was all about—maybe about Daddy leaving. It all happened around the same time. I just remember a lot of shouting. And then Mom telling us we were going away, hustling us out of the house before we even had time to pack everything."

"Where did you go?"

She shrugged. "Where *didn't* we go is more like it. Mom never seemed able to settle in one place at a time. We moved constantly, usually one step ahead of the bill collectors."

Her hands were trembling. Silly to be so affected after all this time, but he grasped them tightly in his.

"I'm sorry," he said softly. "I shouldn't have brought it up."

"It's all right. We all grew up okay, in spite of it. And there was a trust fund from my grandparents to see us through college."

"Still, it can't have been easy, having your whole world change so quickly. Is your father a part of your life now?"

"No." Maybe it was odd that his absence didn't bother her more, but he'd never exactly been a hands-on father. "We haven't heard anything from him from that day to this."

"And your mother?"

"She died a couple of years ago. Driving under the influence, apparently. In Las Vegas." She pressed her lips together for a moment. "We hadn't seen much of her since we'd all been out on our own."

He moved his fingers over her hand, offering comfort. "Sounds as if your parents let the three of you down pretty badly."

She shook her head, the words seeming to press against her lips, demanding to be released. "It was Grandfather who let me down. Let us down, I mean. We counted on him. He could have stopped her. But he just stood and watched us leave and never said a word."

All the pain of that betrayal, held at bay over the years she'd been away, came sweeping back, threatening to drown her. That was why she so seldom came here, she knew it now. She didn't want to remember, and the memories were everywhere here.

"You really think your grandfather could have prevented what happened? Unless he was able to have her declared an unfit mother…"

She jerked her hands away. "I don't want to talk about it anymore." He didn't understand. Grandfather—he could do anything, couldn't he? Or was that a ten-year-old's view of the world?

Cal recaptured her hands. "I'm sorry," he said again. He brought her fingers to his lips so that she felt his breath with the words. "I wish I could make it better."

"Thank you." She whispered the words, shaken by the longing she felt to let him comfort her, to close the space between them and be in his arms again…

The sound of car wheels on gravel had her sitting up straight. She drew her hands from his, hoping he couldn't guess what her thoughts had been. She didn't know whether she was glad or sorry that Grams was home, ending this.

"Remember, not a word to Grams. About any of this."

He nodded. Then, too quickly for her to anticipate it, he leaned forward and touched her lips with his.

The organ was still playing behind them when Andrea and her grandmother stepped out into the May sunshine after worship. Andrea tucked her hand unobtrusively into Grams's arm as they went down the two shallow steps to the churchyard. She'd seen the sparkle of tears in Grams's eyes more than once during the service.

Actually, the minister's prayers for Rachel's recovery had made her own eyes damp. She'd expected to feel guilty, if anything, at going back to church after letting regular attendance slip out of her life over the past few years. Instead she'd felt welcomed, and not just by the congregation. The awareness of God's presence, growing in her heart since she'd returned, had intensified to the point that her heart seemed to swell. Grams had looked at her with a question in her eyes once or twice, as if she sensed what was happening.

"I see everyone still gathers out here after the service," she said as they reached the walk and moved away from the steps to allow others to come down. She wasn't ready yet to talk about this renewed sense of God in her life.

People clustered into small groups as they cleared the stairs, exchanging greetings, catching up on the news. A long folding table had been set up to one side, bearing pitchers of iced tea and lemonade. Several children had already started a game of tag among the tilted old gravestones. A few late tulips bloomed, bright red against gray markers.

Grams patted her hand. "Some things don't change. Once you and your sisters did that in your Sunday best."

"I remember. We didn't have any silly superstitions about cemeteries after playing here every Sunday."

The small church, built of the same stone as the inn, was almost completely surrounded by its graveyard, with burials dating back to the early 1700s. A low stone wall enclosed both church and churchyard. Even now, one little girl was emulating a tightrope walker on the top of it.

"Let me guess." Cal spoke from behind her, his low

voice sending a pleasurable shiver down her spine. "You used to be the daring young girl walking on the wall."

"Whenever my grandmother wasn't looking." She turned toward him as Grams began talking to the pastor. "I didn't realize you attended church. Here, I mean."

"If you're not House Amish or Mennonite, this is where you worship in Churchville, isn't it?" He glanced toward her grandmother. "Katherine didn't suspect anything last night?" he asked softly.

"She didn't seem to, but it's hard to be sure. When we were kids, we thought she had eyes in the back of her head and an antenna that detected mischief."

"There was probably plenty, with three girls so close in age."

She smiled, shaking her head. "Fights, mostly, over who took what from whom. Caroline, our youngest sister, was such a good actress that she could convince almost anybody of anything. Except Grams, who always seemed to know the truth. I just hope her antenna wasn't working last night."

"She'd probably have said something, if so. She's not one to keep still where people she cares about are concerned."

She nodded, but as her gaze sought her grandmother's erect figure, the smile slipped away. Grams had changed since Grandfather's death, and she hadn't even noticed it. The strength they'd always counted on was still there, but it was muted now. Or maybe Rachel's accident had made her vulnerable.

"I see now how much this place means to her." She

pitched her voice low, under the animated chatter that was going on all around them. "I don't want anything that's going on to affect that."

His hand brushed hers in a mute gesture of support. "You can't always protect people, even though you care about them."

She glanced up at him, ready to argue, but maybe he had a point. She'd protected her little sisters during those years under their mother's erratic care, but eventually they'd been on their own. The situation was reversed now with Grams. She'd always been the strong one, and now she had to be protected, preferably without her realization.

Cal raised an eyebrow, lips quirking slightly. "Not going to disagree?"

"I would, but I see one of your favorite people coming. I'm sure you'll want to talk to her."

"Not Margaret." The hunted look in his eyes amused her. "It'll be tough to keep a Sunday state of mind with Margaret spreading her version of good cheer around."

She couldn't respond, because Margaret was swooping down on them. *Swooping* actually seemed the right word—the floating handkerchief sleeves of her print dress fluttered like a butterfly's wings.

"Cal. And Andrea. How nice to see the two of you together. Again. So lovely when young people find each other." Margaret put one hand on Cal's arm, and Andrea suspected it took all of his manners to keep from pulling away.

"We weren't lost," he said shortly. "We were just talking about the inn."

In a way, she supposed they had been, since that

was what concerned Grams most at the moment. "Cal's been helping us with some of the repairs," she said. To say nothing of rescuing her from dark closets.

"You are such a sweet boy, to help a neighbor who's in distress."

The expression on Cal's face at being called a sweet boy suggested she'd better intervene before he was reduced to rudeness.

"Just about everyone has been very helpful in getting the inn ready to open." Except Margaret, she supposed. "It's coming together very well."

"Is it?" Shrewdness glinted in Margaret's eyes for an instant. "I was under the impression you're nowhere near ready to open for Memorial Day weekend. Sad, to have to cancel those reservations. It doesn't give the impression of a truly professional establishment. I'd be glad to take those guests, but naturally I'm completely full for that weekend."

"I don't know what makes you think that, but we're not canceling any of our reservations." She certainly hoped that was true. "You'll be pleased to know that we expect to open on schedule."

Margaret's eyes narrowed. "That's delightful. Of course, everyone won't be as happy for you as I am. Still, one has to break eggs to make an omelet." She turned away, sleeves fluttering. "Excuse me. I must go and talk to the dear reverend about the strawberry festival."

Andrea managed to hold back words until the woman was out of earshot. "What did she mean?" she muttered. "Who won't be glad to see us open on time?"

Cal cupped her elbow with his hand. "I think your grandmother's ready to leave."

She planted her feet, frowning at him. "Answer the question, please."

A quick jerk of his hand pulled her close to him, and he lowered his head to speak so no one could hear. "A few of the old-timers don't like the idea of another inn opening, increasing the tourist traffic in town."

"Nick mentioned something about that, but he really made light of their attitude." So light, in fact, that she hadn't considered it since.

"Did he?" He was probably wondering why she hadn't said anything to him. "Well, one of those people has your grandmother cornered at the moment, so I think we'd better go to the rescue."

Grams was talking with Herbert Rush, an old friend of Grandfather's. Or rather, it looked as if he was talking at her—and not about something pleasant, to judge by the color of his face and the way his white eyebrows beetled over snapping blue eyes.

Andrea hurried over, sliding her hand through Grams's arm. "Are you about ready to leave, Grams?" She fought to produce a polite smile. "How are you, Mr. Rush?"

The elderly man transferred his glare to her. "How am I? I'm unhappy, that's how I am. The last thing this village needs is another thing to draw tourists. I wouldn't have believed it of your grandmother. Turning a fine old showplace like Unger House into a tourist trap. Someone should do something about that. Your grandfather must be turning over in his grave."

"On the contrary, I'm sure my grandfather is proud

of my grandmother, as he always was." She pinned a smile in place. Grams wouldn't appreciate it if she allowed anger to erupt. She turned toward the gate, grateful for Cal's presence on Grams's other side.

Apparently this place wasn't as idyllic as she'd been thinking, and Grams was getting the full picture of its less appealing side.

He seemed to be making one excuse after another to walk over to the inn these days. Cal rounded the tool-shed, checking the outbuildings automatically. Since sunset was still an hour away, he couldn't even tell himself that he was making his nightly rounds.

He wanted to see Andrea again. That was the truth of it. A moment's sensible thought told him that pursuing a relationship with her was a huge mistake, but that didn't seem to be stopping him from finding a reason to be where he might see her.

Well, that wish was going to be disappointed, because a quick glance told him the garage was empty. She and Katherine hadn't returned from their visit to Rachel.

But someone else was around the place, judging by the late-model compact that sat on the verge of the drive. Frowning, he quickened his steps. Probably nothing, but with all the odd things happening lately, it didn't do to take anything for granted.

His muscles tightened. A woman was on the side porch, shading her eyes as she peered through the glass in the door. He shot forward.

"What are you doing?"

He reached the bottom of the steps as she spun around, her mouth forming a silent O of surprise.

"I—you startled me." She grasped the railing. "I'm looking for Andrea Hampton. I knocked, but no one answered."

"She's out just now." The adrenaline ebbed, leaving him feeling he'd been too aggressive. She was younger than he'd thought at first glance, probably no more than twenty-two or three. Blond hair in a stylish, layered cut, a trim suit that looked too dressy for a Sunday afternoon in Churchville, a pair of big brown eyes that fixed on him as if asking for help. "Can I do anything for you?"

She came down the three steps so that they stood facing one another, looking up at him as if he could solve all her problems. "Is she going to be back soon? Ms. Hampton, I mean." Then, seeming to feel something else was called for, she added, "I'm Julie Michaels, her assistant."

He couldn't help the way his eyebrows lifted. So Andrea's office was following her here. "Cal Burke." He wasn't sure what to do with the woman. Telling her to go away certainly wasn't an option, though the urge to do so was strong. "I'm not sure when—"

The sound of tires on gravel took the decision out of his hands. "Here she is now."

At the sight of them, Andrea pulled to a stop in front of the woman's car. She slid out, frowning a little.

He reached Katherine's door and opened it, his gaze on Andrea as she came around the car. "I spotted her looking in the window. Is she really your assistant?"

"She is." There was a note in her voice he couldn't quite define.

Then she walked quickly toward the young woman. "Julie. I'm surprised to see you here."

Surprised and not particularly welcoming, if he read her correctly. Now what was that about? None of his business, of course, but still… He helped Katherine out and closed the door.

"I stopped by to pick up the report."

Andrea's brows lifted. "I said I'd e-mail it in tomorrow. There was no need for you to come all this way."

"I was in the area anyway," she said. "I just thought it would be helpful. I didn't mean to be in the way." Her tone suggested a puppy that had received a swat instead of a pat.

"That was very thoughtful." Katherine stepped forward, holding out her hand. "I'm Andrea's grandmother, Katherine Unger." The glance she shot Andrea said that she was disappointed in her manners.

He was probably the only one who saw Andrea's lips tighten. "I'll get the file for you." She turned and went quickly into the house, leaving the three of them standing awkwardly.

Julie turned toward the patio, her hurt feelings, if that's what it had been, disappearing in a smile. "What a lovely place. You must be a wonderful gardener, Ms. Unger."

"I have a great deal of help. Come onto the patio where you can see the flowers."

He could go back to his workshop, but some instinct made him trail along behind them. Andrea hadn't expected this visit, and she didn't like it. Why?

"I'm sure Andrea must be a big help to you. It's great that she could take time off when you need her." Julie bent to touch the petals of a yellow rose that had just begun to open.

"Yes, yes, it is." Katherine's smile wavered a bit. "I don't know what I'd do without her at this time, with her sister in the hospital."

"I heard about the accident. I'm so sorry." The woman's words sounded sympathetic, but there was something watchful in those big eyes. "How long do you think you'll need to have Andrea stay?"

That seemed to be his cue. He spoke just as Katherine opened her mouth to respond. "Is that a Japanese beetle on the rosebush?"

Katherine turned away from the woman instantly, bending over to peer anxiously at the small leaves, brushing them with her fingers. "I don't see anything. Are you sure, Cal?"

He guided her a few steps away, keeping her focused on the flowers. "It was over here. I just caught a glimpse."

Knowing Katherine's devotion to her flowers, that should keep her occupied for a few minutes. And off the subject of Andrea's departure. That hadn't been a casual query, and the idea of the woman trying to pump Katherine raised his hackles.

The back door swung open. Andrea strode toward them, a manila folder in her hand. She held it out to Julie.

"Here you are. Please ask Mr. Walker to call me if he has any questions."

"I will." She tucked the folder under her arm. "You

have such a lovely home here, Ms. Unger. Thank you for letting me see your garden." She glanced wistfully toward the house.

He took Katherine's arm before she could issue an invitation to a tour. "Let me give you a hand up the steps. Emma sent one of the grandkids over to mention potato salad and cold ham for a late supper if you came home hungry."

"She spoils me." Katherine took his arm, leaning on it a bit more heavily than usual. "I guess I will go in, now. Goodbye, Ms. Michaels."

He shepherded her into the house and saw her settled in her favorite chair. When he got back outside, the Michaels woman was pulling out of the drive. Andrea sat on the stone wall at the edge of the patio, frowning.

"That wasn't exactly a disinterested call, was it?" He sat down next to her.

She glanced at him, eyebrows lifting. "What do you mean?"

"While you were inside, your assistant tried to pump your grandmother about how long you'd be away from work."

"I should have expected that." Her lips tightened. "Did she succeed?"

"I headed her off. How long has she been trying to look just like you?"

For an instant she stared at him, and then her face relaxed in a slight smile. "You don't miss much. Believe it or not, when I hired her, Julie was just out of college, with brown hair halfway down her back, glasses and a wardrobe that consisted of discount store polyester suits."

"She found a role model in you. I guess that's natural enough."

"At first it was flattering. It took me a while to realize that she didn't just want to emulate my style of clothing. She wants my job. And she sees my absence from the office as her golden opportunity to step right into my shoes."

"Your boss wouldn't be that stupid, would he?"

She shrugged, eyes worried. "The more days I'm gone, the easier it will be for her. If I stay too long, he may just decide he can do without me altogether." Her fingers clenched on her knees. "I can't let that happen. I can't lose everything I've worked for."

Something twisted inside him. She'd go, just like that. It was what he'd thought all along, but knowing he'd been right about her didn't make him feel any better.

"So that's it. Is your job really more important to you than your family?"

She swung toward him, anger sweeping the anxiety from her face. "I don't think you have the right to ask me that."

Matching anger rose. "Why? Because I'm an interfering outsider?"

"No." Green eyes darkened. "Because you expect me to spill my feelings and share my decisions when you're not willing to tell me a single thing about you."

TEN

She shouldn't have said that. Andrea wanted to refute the words, to deny that she cared in the least about his secrets. But it was already too late. Whatever she did or said now, Cal would know that the imbalance in their relationship mattered to her.

She could feel the tension in him through the inches that separated them, could sense the pressure to shoot to his feet and walk away.

But he didn't. He sat, staring down at the edging stones along the patio, where the setting sun cast wavering shadows from the branches above. His profile was stern, the planes of his face looking as if they'd been carved from one of the planks of wood he used.

Doubt assailed her. Whatever it was that made him look that way—did she really want to know? She sensed that if he told her, that truth could change their relationship in incalculable ways.

He moved slightly, not looking at her—just the slightest shrug, as if he tried to ease the tension from his shoulders.

"You told me once I had too much of a corporate mind-set to be just a carpenter. Remember that?"

"Yes." *I don't want to know.* But she did. She did.

"I was a lawyer." He grimaced slightly. "Guess I still am, in a way, but I'll never practice again."

That was her cue to ask why, but she wasn't ready for that. She settled for an easier question. "Where? Not around here."

"Seattle." He leaned back, bracing his hands on the wall. The pose could have looked relaxed, but it didn't. "You wouldn't know the firm, but it's one of the big guns there."

"Prestigious." Her mind grappled to reconcile the informal country carpenter with a big-city lawyer. Difficult, but she'd always known there was something.

"You could say that. When I landed the position, I knew I had it made. Straight to the big leagues—not bad for an ordinary middle-class kid who didn't even know which fork to use." A thread of bitterness ran through the words. He shot her a sideways glance that questioned. "Can you understand how overwhelming that could be?"

"I think so." Cal had been young, ambitious, intelligent, and he'd gotten the break that ensured his future. She of all people knew what that felt like. "But something went wrong."

His hands clenched against the stone, the knuckles whitening. "Not for a long time. I threw everything into the job, and it paid off. I was on the fast track to partnership, and nothing else mattered."

He was circling the thing that caused him pain, getting closer and closer. She sensed it, and wanted, like a coward, to close her ears, but she couldn't.

"The senior partner called me in. Assigned me to

the case of my career. One of our biggest clients was involved in a child custody dispute with his ex-wife. I was just the sort of aggressive bulldog he wanted to represent him. Win, and opportunities would open to me that I couldn't have imagined."

"You accepted." Of course he had. He wouldn't have evaded that challenge, any more than she would.

"Sure. I threw myself into the case, determined to do the best job any attorney could." He looked at her then, his brown eyes very dark. "I trusted the client. You have to believe that."

She nodded, throat tight. She thought she saw where this was going now, and already his tension infected her, so that her hands pressed tight against the stone, too.

He shrugged, mouth twisting. "I did a great job. Lived up to everyone's expectations. Demolished the opposition and won the case." He was silent for a moment, as if he had to steel himself to say the next thing. "Then I found out that my client had been lying. He really was molesting his six-year-old daughter."

She'd been prepared for it, she'd thought, but it still hit her like a blow to the heart. "The little girl—"

Dear Lord, could anything be worse?

"Yes. The child I gave back to her father."

"It wasn't just you," she said quickly. "It was a judge's decision, surely. And the mother must have had legal representation."

"I told myself that. All the arguments—that it wasn't just my responsibility, that I had a duty to represent my client, that our legal system is adversarial and everyone deserves representation. It didn't change anything. The bottom line was still the same."

"What did you do?" He'd have done something. She knew that about him.

"Went to the senior partner. He told me to forget it. I'd done my job, and it was out of my hands."

"You couldn't."

"No. Couldn't ignore it. Couldn't go to the mother without putting the whole firm in jeopardy. So I did the only thing open to me. I went to the client and told him either he relinquished custody to his ex-wife, or I blew the whistle on him. It would have meant disbarment or worse, but I'd do it."

He took a deep breath, and she had the sense he hadn't breathed in a long time. She hadn't, either.

"Did it work?"

He nodded. "Guess I was convincing enough, especially when I resigned from the firm." His voice roughened. "I saw the child back into her mother's care, but God alone knows how much damage was done to her in the meantime."

That was the guilt he carried, then. That was why he lived the way he did.

"Cal, you did everything you could. He was the criminal, not you."

He grimaced. "Nice of you to defend me. I spent months trying to tell myself that, until finally God forced me to face the truth. I'd been so ambitious, so determined to succeed, that I'd let myself get sucked into a life that didn't take into account any of the important things, like faith, honesty, other human beings.

I had to stop making excuses before I could repent and begin again."

That's what he was doing here, then. Starting over. Looking for peace in this quiet place where values still applied.

"You did the right thing." Maybe her opinion didn't matter, but she had to say it. She met his gaze. "You couldn't have done anything else."

Something in his eyes acknowledged her words. He didn't speak. They didn't touch. But they were closer than if they'd been in each other's arms. She seemed to be aware of everything about him—of every cell in his body, of the blood coursing through his veins.

She took a breath, letting the realization crystallize in her mind. She cared about him, far more than she'd known. She admired him more than she could say.

But what he'd just told her had shut out any possibility of a relationship between them, because the life she longed to keep was the very one he'd never go back to.

Emma, going up the attic steps ahead of Andrea, pushed the door open, letting a shaft of sunlight fall on the rough wooden stairs. Rough, but not dusty, Andrea noticed. Obviously Emma's cleaning fanaticism extended even to the attics of the old house.

"All of the quilts are packed away in trunks," Emma said. "It is good that they'll be useful again."

"I just hope they're still in decent shape after being in storage for so long." She emerged into the attic, which stretched out into the shadowy distance, marked by the looming shapes of discarded furniture.

Lots and lots of furniture. Cal had said the place

was packed to the rafters, and he was right. Her un-practiced eye identified a dining room set that surely wasn't genuine Duncan Phyfe, was it?

Emma, weaving her way through odd pieces of furniture, let out an audible sniff. "I put them away proper. They'll just need a bit of airing, that's all."

If Emma had done it, of course it would have been done properly. She was the one who'd suggested the quilts when Andrea and Grams had been debating about drapes and bedcovers for the guest rooms.

"The English will like having Amish-made quilts in the rooms," she'd said matter-of-factly.

She was right. Their guests would come to Lancaster County to see the Amish, who ironically only wanted to be left alone, and they would be thrilled at the idea. So she and Emma were on a hunting expedition in the attic for quilts and anything else that would give the guest rooms a unique touch.

Concentrating on the decorating just might keep her mind from straying back, again and again, to that conversation with Cal the previous day. On second thought, nothing was strong enough to do that.

Cal. He'd wrung her heart with his story, and in the dark silence of the night, she'd found herself filling in all the things he hadn't said.

He'd given up everything—his career, his future, his friends—because it was the right thing to do. Plenty of people would have rationalized away their responsibility in the situation, but not Cal. He'd taken on even more than his share, and now seemed content that it was what God expected of him.

She approached that thought cautiously. Somehow it

had never occurred to her, even when she was attending church regularly, that God might have a claim on one's business life. That God might require sacrifice, on occasion. That was an uncomfortable idea, but once planted, it didn't seem amenable to being dismissed.

Emma knelt in front of a carved wooden dower chest, one of several lined up near the window. Andrea hurried to join her, thinking that her jeans were more appropriate to kneeling on the wide-planked floor than Emma's dress.

Concentrate on the task at hand. The practical one was to choose the quilts for the bedrooms. The unspoken one was to use this opportunity to talk to Emma about Levi, to try and get a sense of whether he might have been the dark figure she'd seen the night of the storm.

Leave the theological considerations for later. And any thought of her feelings for Cal for later still.

Emma lifted the chest lid, exposing bundles wrapped in muslin sheets. She took out the first one, unwrapping it. Andrea grasped the sheet and spread it out so that the quilt wouldn't touch the floor.

"Squares in Bars," Emma said, naming the pattern as she unfolded it. "My mother made many quilts for your grandmother. This was one of hers."

Andrea's breath caught as the colors, rich and saturated, glowed like jewels in the sun streaming in the many-paned attic window. The quilt was bordered in a deep forest-green, with the squares done in the blues, maroons, pinks, purples and mauves of Amish clothing.

"It's beautiful." Drawn to touch, she stroked the colors. "Your mother was an artist."

Emma shook her head. "Just usual work. She was quick with the needle, I remember."

That was the closest thing to pride she'd ever heard from Emma.

"Here is one that belongs in your room." Emma pulled back the sheet on the second quilt. "Do you remember?"

Remember? She couldn't speak as the pattern came into view, myriads of diamonds expanding from the center in vivid and unexpected bursts of color. She touched it gently. How many nights had she fallen asleep trying to count the number of diamonds in the quilt?

"I remember," she said softly, her throat going tight. "Your mother made this one, too, didn't she?"

Emma nodded, her plain face softening a little at Andrea's reaction. "Sunshine and Shadow. It was her favorite pattern."

"Is that what it's called? I don't think I ever knew. I can see why—the alternating bands of dark and light are like the bands of sunlight and shadow made by the rails of a fence."

Emma traced a line of dark patches. "It's the pattern of life. Sometimes sun, sometimes shadow. Like Scripture says, 'To everything there is a season, and a time to every purpose under Heaven.' But always God is with us."

The words squeezed her heart. Would Emma consider Levi one of the dark bands? She never seemed to show disappointment or sorrow with him. Maybe this was the moment to ask, but Andrea couldn't seem to force the words out.

"I should put it in a guest room, though, not keep it for myself." But her hands clung to the quilt. Or maybe to the memory of how safe she'd felt, sleeping under it.

Emma shook her head in a decided way. "Your grandmother ordered it from my mother just for you, when she knew you were coming to live here. It made her so happy to fix that room up for you, and how she smiled when it was all finished."

The image came clear in her mind, even from those few words. A younger Emma, a younger Grams, spreading the quilt on her bed, Grams's face lit with pleasure.

"Those were happy times, when we were here," she said, hoping her voice didn't sound as choked as it felt.

"Yes." Emma seemed to be looking back, too. "It was good, all of you children together, those days when the house was so full. We are in the *daadi haus,* now, Eli and Levi and me, and Samuel and his family have the farmhouse."

Andrea sat back on her heels, her arms filled with the quilt. "Does it grieve you, that Levi won't have a family of his own?"

Emma considered for a moment. "No, not grieve. He is as God chose to make him. I accept that as God's will."

The question she had to ask stuck in her throat, and she pushed it out. "I thought I saw Levi one night from my window. Does he go out after dark by himself?"

"No." The expression on Emma's face couldn't be disguised. Fear. Stark, unreasoning fear filled her face before she bent over the chest, hiding it. "No." Her voice was muffled. "Levi does not go out after nightfall. It would not be right."

Something cold closed around Andrea's heart. The unthinkable had happened. Emma was lying to her.

Cal walked into the hallway of the inn from the kitchen and paused, looking around. He hadn't been in since the painters finished, and he let out a low whistle. Katherine should be pleased. The Three Sisters Inn was a showplace, all right, with the parlors restored to their former grandeur. He might not know much about decorating, but he knew elegant when he saw it.

He put his hand on the newel post, sturdy now since he'd finished the repairs. Emma had said that Andrea needed some help moving things up in the guest rooms. He couldn't very well say no, but he wouldn't mind a little more time elapsing before seeing her again.

He'd told her things he hadn't told anyone else. He'd like to say he didn't know why, but that wouldn't be true. He knew. He cared about her. That was why.

It wouldn't go anywhere, that caring, and she knew that as well as he did. They were too different, and the life she prized was one that he'd never return to.

He started up the stairs. Well, she'd probably be as eager as he was to restore some barriers between them.

He reached the open center hallway on the second floor and glanced around. The doors stood open to the guest rooms—four on this floor, three more upstairs. Andrea was nowhere to be seen, so he went on up the narrower staircase to the third floor.

The rooms here were smaller and didn't seem quite

finished. It looked as if Andrea had been putting most of her efforts into the second floor.

A loud thud sounded somewhere over his head, startling him. He yanked open the door to the attic stairway. "Andrea?" He bolted up the stairs.

"I'm all right." Her voice reassured him as he opened the second door at the top of the stairs.

"Good thing. I thought that was you. What are you trying to do?" He picked his way through pieces of furniture to where she stood.

"I want to take this stand down to the blue bedroom." She tugged at the recalcitrant piece that lay fallen on its side, obviously the thud he'd heard. "It's heavier than it looks."

"It's solid mahogany." He bent to shift it upright, and then took a step back, looking at it. "Nice piece. What's that?" Something had fallen out when the door on the front of the stand swung open.

Andrea picked up several oversize green books. "Grandfather's ledgers." She dusted them off with the tail of her pale blue shirt and flipped one open. "Goodness, this dates back to before I was born."

"Seems like a funny place to store them."

She wrinkled her nose. "Rachel, getting the place ready to turn into an inn. Things that were in her way got stuck into the most unimaginable places. We really should do some serious sorting and organizing. These ledgers should be kept for their part in Unger house history, if nothing else."

She bent over the book. For a moment she was engrossed in her find, and he could watch her as closely as he wanted. With her blond hair pulled back in a ponytail and a streak of dirt on her cheek, she didn't look much like the sleek urban professional.

She glanced up, catching his grin before he could erase it. "What's funny?"

"Just thinking you look a little different, that's all."

"You try rummaging through this attic without getting dirty, in spite of Emma's ferocious cleaning," she said. "You certainly were right about this place. Grams could start selling things off to an antique dealer and fund the inn for the foreseeable future."

"Your grandmother mentioned some interest from one of the local antique dealers, but she's reluctant to part with anything. Or maybe the prospect of sorting seems overwhelming. Are you ready to start an inventory?"

"Don't tempt me." She glanced around as if she'd like to do just that. "You wouldn't believe the stash of handmade quilts Emma and I found up here this morning."

Any potential embarrassment had evaporated in the face of Andrea's calm attitude. She'd found her way back to an easy friendliness, and that was for the best.

"Something you can use, I take it?"

She nodded, but the smile slid from her face. "I had a chance to sound her out about Levi. She insists that he's never out alone at night, so he couldn't be the person I saw."

"Did you believe her?"

She looked at him, distress filling her eyes. "I've known her most of my life. I'd have said she'd never lie. But no, I didn't believe her."

Her voice shook a little on the words, and he knew how much it hurt her.

"I'm sorry. Look, it may not mean anything. If it was Levi, he hasn't come back. Nothing's happened for a couple of days. Whoever he was, our prowler seems to be scared off."

She nodded. "And now that I've mentioned it, I'm sure Emma will make sure that Levi doesn't do any late-night wandering."

"Right." It was worth agreeing to see the concern fade from her eyes. He just hoped they were right and the prowler was a thing of the past.

He seized the stand. "Well, shall we get this downstairs?"

"Yes, thanks. I appreciate the help. Rachel's coming home in a couple of days, and the opening is in less than a week." She tried to take the other side, but he pulled it away from her.

"I've got it. Just do the doors for me."

"Macho," she said, teasing, and went to open the door.

He muscled the stand down the stairs and around the bend at the bottom. Andrea closed the door while he leaned against the wall, trying not to breathe hard.

"Let's leave it here until I have a chance to clean it."

He nodded and started down the next flight of stairs. "Anytime you want heavy moving done, you know who to call."

She followed him. "But—did you want something, before I waylaid you with the stand?"

"Emma sent me upstairs. Guess she thought you could use an extra hand."

"My thanks to both of you." She paused as they approached the landing. "That sounded like the side door." She passed him and hurried on down the stairs.

When they reached the bottom, no one was there. She glanced into the library. "Margaret." She didn't sound especially welcoming. He couldn't say he blamed her.

Margaret scurried across the room, holding out an armload of peonies. "I just brought these in for your sister. I hope you don't mind—I thought they might cheer her long recuperation. Hello, Cal. You're here again, I see."

He nodded. It was probably best to ignore the comment.

"Of course I don't mind." Andrea took the flowers. "But why did you come in the side? Wasn't the front door open?"

"I didn't." Margaret looked surprised. "I came in the front."

He'd have said the sound had been from the side door, too. Odd.

There was a rap at the front door, and James Bendick popped his head in. "Andrea—oh, there you are. And Margaret." He came in, holding a bouquet of pink roses. "I heard Rachel is coming home, so I brought her these, but someone beat me to it. Margaret, those must be straight from your beautiful borders."

Margaret batted her eyes at him. "You're such a flatterer, James."

"This was sweet of you, Uncle Nick." Andrea took the flowers, putting the ledgers down on the drop leaf table in the hallway to do so.

Bendick seemed to be determined to ignore him. Perversely, Cal leaned against the newel post, wondering how long it would take for the man to acknowledge his presence.

"Those look like some of your grandfather's old ledgers." Bendick flipped one open. "Dating back to the Dark Ages, I see."

"Cal and I found them in the attic. I thought Grams might enjoy seeing them."

Having Cal forced on his attention, Bendick nodded. "Burke. Helping out, are you?"

"Just doing the heavy moving." Cal pushed away from the post. "I'll be going, Andrea. Give me a call if you need anything else brought down."

"I will. And thank you, Cal."

If her smile was anything to go by, Andrea must have bought his suggestion that they'd seen the last of their prowler. He just hoped he was right.

He went quickly past the parlors to the side door, reached for it, and then stopped.

The side door was the only one where someone entering wasn't likely to be seen, either from the kitchen or the library. It had been locked when he'd come over. He'd tried it first before entering through the kitchen.

Now the door stood ajar. Someone had come in. Or gone out.

ELEVEN

Andrea sank down in a kitchen chair, grateful for the mug of coffee Emma set in front of her. The morning was only half over, but she'd been working nonstop. It was time to take a break.

Grams sat at the end of the table with her usual cup of tea. "Do you think the bedroom for Rachel is all right? I hate the idea of putting her in the maid's room."

"It's fine," she said quickly, before Grams could get the idea of making a change after all the work they'd already done to prepare a ground floor room for Rachel's homecoming. "She has to be on this floor because of the wheelchair, and that room is perfect. It has its own bath."

"She will be close to the kitchen," Emma added, stirring something in the large yellow mixing bowl. "She will like that, she will."

Obviously Emma was on her side in this. Neither of them wanted to start rearranging furniture at this point.

"Once she's home, we can see if there's anything else we can do to make her more comfortable," Andrea pointed out.

"I suppose you're right." Grams still looked a bit doubtful, probably over the idea of a daughter of the house being relegated to the maid's room. Rachel had certainly lived in worse when she was in culinary school, but Grams wouldn't want to hear that.

"What are you making, Emma?" A change of subject was in order.

"Rachel's favorite cake. Banana walnut." She emptied a cup of walnuts into the mixture. "Black walnuts from our own tree will make it extra good."

She inhaled the scent of bananas and walnuts. "Smells wonderful. I'd best stay away while it's baking, or I might be tempted to get into it before Rach gets home tomorrow."

Rachel home tomorrow, and the grand opening on the weekend. That would go well—it had to. Of course it would be a shame that Rachel couldn't make her special breakfasts, but Emma would serve hearty Amish meals instead and the guests would be delighted.

And once that was over, she could make plans to get back to work. They would need more help after she left, of course, but Emma's daughter-in-law seemed eager for the work, and she'd pay the salary herself, if necessary.

She glanced at Grams, wondering how she'd feel if Andrea inquired more closely into her finances. She'd opened up a little, but Andrea still didn't feel she had a good handle on how secure Grams was.

And then there was the other regret. Cal. Her mind drifted toward the night they'd kissed, and she pulled it firmly back. There was no sense in thinking about what might have been. They both recognized the attraction and the caring, but the differences between them were just too great.

Still, she couldn't ignore that sense of loss.

"I'm just relieved we've had no further problems with prowlers," Grams said. "I'd hate to have our guests upset. Those lights were a fine idea."

Grams didn't know, of course, about the other incidents, and Andrea had no intention of telling her. There were too many possibilities for troublemakers—Levi, sneak thieves, teenagers intent on vandalism, even the holdouts in the community who were opposed to the decision to open the inn. It didn't really matter who it was, as long as it stopped.

"Andrea?" Grams was looking at her questioningly.

"Yes, I'm sure you're right. There's nothing more to worry about."

Grams reached across the table to touch her hand lightly. "Thanks to you. I don't know what we'd have done without you."

Andrea clasped her grandmother's hand, the fragility of fine bones under the skin making her aware again that Grams needed taking care of. "I loved doing it."

"You have so much business sense." Grams's eyes grew misty. "Just like your grandfather."

She wasn't sure she wanted to be compared to her grandfather, but she knew that to Grams it was a high compliment. "Thank you."

"I'm thinking it's time I turned my business affairs over to you. Nick has been very helpful, of course, but he's not family. You'll do it, won't you?"

For a moment she couldn't speak. If she'd needed

anything to assure her that Grams thought of her as a competent adult, this would do it.

"Of course I will." She blinked back surprising moisture in her eyes. "I'd be honored."

"That is good." Emma used a spatula to get the last bit of batter into the pan and then smoothed the surface with a practiced swirl. "'There is a time to every purpose under Heaven.'" She quoted again the words she'd said earlier, and they seemed to resonate. "A time to turn things over to the younger generation. Eli and me, we still have plenty to do, but now it's our son's turn to manage."

"The Amish know how to do it right," Grams said, smiling. "They build the *daadi haus* for the older couple and turn the farm over to the next generation. Everyone has a role to fill."

"Ja." Emma carried the oblong pan over to the old gas range that took up half of one wall. "It is good to know where you belong."

She bent over, cake pan in one hand, and pulled open the oven door with the other.

There was a loud whooshing sound. Before Andrea could move, flames shot out of the oven, right in Emma's face.

Cal sat beside Andrea on the patio wall, waiting. The paramedics were in the kitchen with Emma. So was her husband, Eli. He and Andrea had been relegated to the outside as unnecessary.

Levi stood next to the gray buggy that was pulled up in the driveway. He'd buried his face in the horse's mane, and once in a while his shoulders shook.

"Do you think I should attempt to comfort him?" Andrea said softly.

He shook his head. "I tried, just before you came out. It seemed to make him worse, so I gave up. He'll be all right as soon as he knows his mother is fine."

"Is she?" Andrea's lips trembled, and she pressed them together in a firm line.

He covered her hand with his where it lay on the stone wall between them, and the irrelevant thought passed through his mind that when she was gone, he wouldn't be able to look at this wall in the same way.

"I'm sure she will be." He hoped he sounded positive.

Her fingers moved slightly under his. "You didn't see. It was awful. Thank goodness Grams knew what to do. She had a wet towel on Emma's face before I'd even figured out what happened."

"I don't suppose you ever saw a gas oven blow out. She probably has. It used to be a fairly common accident, years ago. Since most of the Amish cook with gas, it still happens—did while I was staying out at the Zimmerman place, but luckily no one was hurt."

What about this time? He wasn't sure what he thought, not yet. He didn't want to believe someone had tampered with the stove, but it didn't do to take anything for granted.

"Tell me what happened."

Andrea's face tightened. "I don't want to go over it again."

"I don't suppose you do, but we have to figure out what caused this."

Her eyes met his, startled. "You think it wasn't an accident?"

"I don't know what I think, yet. That's why I want to ask you a few questions." He was surprised to hear that lawyer's voice coming out of his mouth.

She took a breath, seeming to compose herself. "Emma was baking a cake. For Rachel's homecoming. I guess she'd been preheating the oven. Yes, I'm sure she had, because I remember seeing her turn it on." She shrugged. "There isn't anything else to tell. She opened the oven door to put the cake in, and the flames came out in her face." She shivered. "I hate to sound stupid, but what made it do that?"

"The pilot light was blown out—it had to be. The gas built up in the oven, and when the door was opened, that was all it took to ignite."

"It could have happened accidentally." She sounded as if she were trying to convince herself.

"I suppose so," he agreed. "When was the last time the oven was used?"

"Last night—no, I take that back, we didn't use it last night. It would have been in the morning yesterday, when Emma baked."

Something tingled at the back of his mind. "Why did you say last night?"

"Well, it's silly, really. Grams and I were laughing about it. Emma insists on leaving something cooked for our supper, and then I put it in the oven to heat. And she always asks, so I don't even dare to heat it in the microwave. Emma doesn't hold with microwaves."

"It might have been safer, this time."

She nodded. "Anyway, neither of us was very hungry last night, so we just had sandwiches. We were joking about who had to confess to Emma." Her voice shook again, and she turned her hand so that her palm was against his, clasping it tightly. "Cal, it had to be an accident. No one would do that deliberately."

"Maybe. But too many odd things have been happening for me to write them all off as coincidence."

The back door opened. The paramedics came out, carrying their gear, and headed for their truck. Then Eli emerged, supporting Emma, who held a wet dressing to her face. Levi gave an inarticulate cry and shambled toward them.

Eli caught him before he could grasp Emma in a bear hug, talking to him softly and urgently in the low German the Amish used among themselves. Levi nodded, touched his mother's sleeve, and then went to unhitch the horse.

Andrea approached, holding her hand out tentatively. "Emma, I'm so sorry. Are you all right?"

"Ja." Eli answered for her. "The glasses protected her eyes, praise God. Her face is painful, but it will heal."

Emma came from behind the dressing for a moment, her skin red and shiny. "You take care of your grandmother, now. And my cake—"

"Don't start worrying about the cake. You can make another one for Rachel when you're completely recovered."

They watched as Eli and Levi handed her up carefully into the buggy. Levi took the reins.

"I'll come by later to see how you are," Andrea called as the buggy creaked slowly away.

She looked as if she wanted to go after them, do something to make this better. He touched her arm.

"Maybe we'd better check on Katherine."

"Yes, of course." She ran her fingers through her hair. "I'm beginning to think I'm not very good in an emergency."

"You'll do." He followed her into the house, wondering. If this had been deliberate—but there wouldn't be any way to prove it. Still, he wanted a look at the stove.

He got his chance almost immediately, when Andrea, seeing how shaken Katherine was, took her grandmother upstairs to lie down. He waited until they'd disappeared up the steps and then opened the oven door.

When Andrea came back a few minutes later, he was still bending over the open door.

"Did you find anything?"

He shrugged. "Only how easy it would be to blow out the pilot. You'd better have someone come from the gas company to check it out, but I don't think he'll find anything wrong."

He closed the door. Andrea sagged against the kitchen counter, as if her bones had gone limp.

"Rachel comes home tomorrow. The first guests arrive on Saturday, and now Emma is out of action. What could anyone have to gain by tampering with the stove?"

He shrugged. "Someone might have thought it would delay the opening."

"Who would care?" She flung her hands out in frustration.

"Margaret cares. She doesn't want the competition.

And there are those who don't want anything to draw more tourists here."

She shook her head at that. "I can't believe anyone would hurt Emma for such a reason."

He hesitated, but she had to know. "It might not have been aimed at Emma."

She blinked. "What do you mean?"

"If anyone knew that you usually heated up supper, the target might have been you."

"But—how would they know? And even if one of us mentioned it, how could they be sure Emma wouldn't take it into her head to bake something?"

He frowned. "That's the thing. Yesterday afternoon, when I came in, I tried the side door, but it was locked. When we came down from the attic, Emma had already gone, but she always uses the back door. I found the side door was not only unlocked, but ajar."

"You mean someone might have come in then and tampered with the stove."

He couldn't tell whether she accepted it or not. "Could have. Could have had a good idea you'd be the next to use it. Could have been a lot of things, but there's no proof."

"No." Her face was pale. "There's not remotely enough to take to the police."

"Maybe I'm being overly suspicious. I hope so. But I don't like it."

"Neither do I." She rubbed her forehead. "It has to be just an accident. There's an innocent explanation for all of this, surely."

"I hope so." He wanted to say he'd protect her, but he didn't know if he could. And he certainly didn't have that right. He reached out to touch her cheek, the caress lingering longer than he intended.

"Take care of yourself, Andrea. Call me if anything, anything at all, strikes you as odd."

"I will."

But she was probably thinking the same thing he was. How did you protect yourself against something as amorphous as this?

"No, thank you, it's wonderful, but I can't eat another bite." Andrea tried to soften the refusal with a smile. Nancy Zook, wife of Eli and Emma's son Samuel, held a cherry pie in one hand and a peach pie in the other. After the huge serving of Schnitz un Knepp— ham hock, dried apples and dumplings—she'd thought she'd never eat again, but Nancy had urged a sliver of pie on her.

"Ah, it's nothing. Soon it will be time to make the strawberry preserves. We will send some over to you." Nancy put the pies down on the table and turned to offer seconds to the rest of the Zook family—Eli, Samuel, their five children and Levi.

Emma was keeping to her bed for the evening, but when Andrea had slipped over to the attached *daadi haus* to see her, she'd been insistent that she'd be back at work soon. Given the painful-looking blisters on her face, Andrea doubted it.

She'd walked over to the Zook farm late in the afternoon to bring get-well wishes and roses from her grandmother. The insistence that she stay to supper had been so strong that she couldn't have refused without insult, especially after they learned that Grams was having supper at the hospital with Rachel.

The room looked much like any farmhouse kitchen, with its wooden cabinets and linoleum floor. A wooden china closet held special dishes. One difference was that the only wall decoration was a large calendar featuring a picture of kittens in a basket. In most Old Order Amish communities, only such a useful picture could be placed on the wall.

She sipped strong coffee, glancing around the long, rectangular table with its covering of checkered oilcloth. The children chattered amongst themselves softly, mindful of having an English guest. With their round blue eyes and blond hair, the girls in braids, the boys bowl-cut, they looked very alike.

Eli and Samuel talked about the next day's work. Levi sat silent, looking down at his pie. His clean-shaven face was unusual for an Amish adult male, but the beard was a sign of marriage. His soft round cheeks were like those of the children.

Had the figure in the rain had a beard? She wasn't sure. She didn't want to think it, but nothing that had been done would be beyond Levi's capabilities.

She glanced at the gas range. He'd know about the pilot light. But he'd never hurt his mother. That was a ridiculous thought.

A small voice at the back of her mind commented that he might have expected it to be her. All of the Zook family would know about the supper arrangements.

She wanted to reject the idea, but she couldn't. Levi seemed so uneasy with her presence at the table. He'd sent her only one startled glance when she first sat down, his blue eyes as wide as those of a frightened deer, and since then he'd kept his gaze fixed firmly on his plate, showing her only the top of his blond head.

A low rumble of thunder had all of them looking toward the windows.

"Ach, a storm is coming yet." Eli pushed his chair back. "We must get the outside chores done quickly."

The children scurried from the table, diving toward the door in their eagerness to be first out.

"I'd better leave if I don't want to get soaked on the way home." Andrea rose and held out her hand to Nancy. "Thank you so much for the wonderful meal."

"It's nothing." Nancy bobbed her head in a formal little gesture. "Would you be wanting Levi to walk you back?"

"No." That came too quickly. "I'm sure he has work to do. I'll be fine, but I'd better run."

She hurried out the back door, waving to the children as she headed for the path that went around the pond and through a small woodlot before coming out behind the barn where Cal had his shop.

Thunder rumbled again, closer now. It had been foolish not to bring a jacket, with afternoon thunderstorms forecast. Still, if she hurried, she could probably beat the rain home.

The breeze picked up, ruffling the surface of the pond and making the tall ferns that bordered it sway and dance. The scent of rain was in the air, and lightning flashed along the horizon. The distant farms, each marked by twin silos, seemed to wait for the rain.

She scurried past the pond with a fleeting memory of sailing homemade boats on it with the Zook children. The path plunged between the trees, and it was suddenly dark. She slowed, watching the path, having no desire to trip on a tree root and go sprawling.

A trailing blackberry bramble caught at her slacks, then tugged the laces of her sneakers, pulling one free of its knot. She bent, quickly retying it. Quiet—it was so quiet here. Even the birds must have taken shelter from the coming storm.

But as she rose, a sound froze her in place. Was that a footstep, somewhere behind her?

She looked back, seeing nothing, but the undergrowth was thick enough to hide a figure unless it was close. Too close.

That thought got her feet moving again. Hurry. Don't think about the possibility of someone behind you. Think about the fact that the last thing Cal told you was to be careful. Is this being careful?

Cal. She yanked out her cell phone. Better to risk feeling foolish than get into trouble. She could still feel those strong hands that pushed her into the toolshed.

Cal answered almost at once.

"It's Andrea. I'm on the path coming back from Zook's farm. Maybe I'm being silly, but I thought I heard someone behind me."

"I'm on my way." The connection clicked off.

She'd stopped long enough to make the call, and now the sound was closer. The bushes rustled as if a body forced its way through them.

Could be a deer. But even as she thought the words she started to run, feet thudding on the path, instinct telling her to flee like a frightened animal.

Around the twists in the path, careful, careful, don't trip. If you fall, he could be on you in a moment.

The sounds behind her were louder now, as if the follower had given up any need for secrecy. She didn't dare look behind her. To lose even a second could allow him to catch up.

Lightning flashed, close now, and the boom of thunder assaulted her ears. She was nearly out of the woods, just a little farther...

She spurted into the open like a cork from a bottle, and as she did the heavens opened. In an instant she was drenched and gasping as if she'd been shoved into a cold shower.

Don't stop, don't stop...

And then she saw Cal running toward her. Relief swept over her. She was safe.

TWELVE

Cal put another small log on the fire he'd started in his fireplace and watched flames shoot up around it. Maybe the fire would warm and comfort Andrea. It was probably better than putting his arms around her, which was his instinctive reaction.

He put the poker back in the rack, glancing toward her. She sat on the sofa, wearing one of his flannel shirts, towel-drying her hair. She looked vulnerable, which made it even harder to keep his distance.

He had to find a way to help her, but he had to do it without wrecking the hard-won peace he'd found since he'd come here. Getting emotionally involved with a woman who couldn't wait to get away from this life would be a mistake. So would reverting to acting and thinking like a lawyer.

"Thanks." Andrea looked up at him, producing a faint smile. "For the fire and the hot chocolate. I've already had enough coffee to keep me up half the night."

He sat down in the armchair, a careful distance from her. "Can you tell me about it now?"

"There's not much to tell." She frowned, absently toweling the damp hair that clung to her neck. "I'd gone over to see how Emma was, and Nancy insisted I stay for supper. When we noticed the storm coming up, they all scattered to do their chores, and I headed down the path. I'd just reached the woods when I thought I heard someone behind me."

"Back up a little. Did you see where Levi was when you left?"

"I'm not sure. Nancy offered to have him walk me back, but I said no." Her gaze met his. "I'm a little ashamed of that. I'm letting suspicion make a difference in how I treat people. That's not right."

"Maybe so, but it's probably unavoidable. So you don't know where he went at that point?"

"I think he headed for the barn with the boys, but I'm not positive, but just because I was at Zook's farm, that doesn't mean Levi was the one who followed me."

"No, but it's more probable than that someone else was hanging around, watching you."

He could see the shiver that went through her at the suggestion, and regretted it. But somehow they had to get to the bottom of this.

"So you never actually saw the person who followed you."

"No. Just heard him. At first I thought it was an animal, but once I started to run—" She wrapped her arms around her, as if comforting herself, and the too-long sleeves of the shirt flopped over her hands. "I'm sure what I heard was a person."

"I didn't see him, either." He frowned. What could anyone hope to gain by such a stunt?

Andrea shoved her hair back from her face. "That doesn't mean he wasn't there." Her voice was tart.

"I didn't mean that. I'm trying not to think like a lawyer, but old habits die hard." He'd thought he had it licked before Andrea came, involving him in her problems.

That wasn't fair. The trouble had already been here, but something about Andrea's arrival seemed to have brought it out.

"It's not that bad to think like an attorney, is it? After all, you are one."

"I'm a carpenter," he said. "Any resemblance to the person I used to be is a mistake."

A slight frown wrinkled her brows. "I can understand your grief and guilt. But do you think that necessarily means you can't be an attorney?"

His turn to frown. "You think I'm wasting my life here. Is that it? Believe me, I've gained far more than I lost in making the change. Peace. A new relationship with God." He paused, his momentary irritation dissolving. "In my old life, I'd have been embarrassed if someone brought up God in conversation. Am I embarrassing you?"

"No." Her face softened. "Maybe it's the impact of this place. I've thought more about faith since I came back than I had in the past year. Feeling—I don't know. Tugged back, I guess."

"I'm glad." He reached across the space between them to take her hand. Her fingers were cold, and he tried to warm them with his. "Even when you go away…"

He stopped. He didn't want her to leave. That was the truth, however irrational it might be. She wouldn't stay. Her life was elsewhere.

"When I leave—"

Her eyes met his, and he saw in them exactly what he felt. Longing. Tenderness. Regret.

Be careful. You're not going to kiss her again. It would be a mistake, getting entangled with someone who is determined to leave.

He rose, moving to the fireplace and leaning on the mantel. Take himself out of range.

"As far as this incident is concerned…" He frowned, trying to concentrate on the problem. "Most likely the person who followed you was Levi, simply because no one else could have known you were there. But if stopping the inn from opening is the object of all this harassment, why would he care?"

"I suppose that must be the motive—at least I can't think of any other reasonable hypothesis." She frowned. "It still seems overly dramatic to think that any of these solid, law-abiding Pennsylvania Dutchmen would resort to trying to scare me away just to eliminate another B and B."

"None of it is very logical." He had to get a handle on some aspect of the situation. He might have a better chance of doing that if his heart didn't perform such peculiar acrobatics whenever he looked at Andrea.

"There's still nothing to take to the police. I can just imagine their reaction to my story of being followed coming back from the Zook farm."

"They wouldn't be impressed, I'm afraid." They'd be polite, of course, but what could they do? It wasn't as if she'd been attacked. That thought sent a coldness settling deep inside him. The incident with the stove was an attack, but he couldn't prove it, or that she had been the target.

Andrea glanced at her watch and then shot to her feet. "Look at the time. I have to get home before Grams. I can't let her see me like this."

"You look pretty good to me." He pushed away from the mantel. "Sort of casually disheveled."

"I look as if I've been dragged through a knothole," she said tartly. She started for the door.

He followed her. "I'll walk you back."

"You don't need—"

"I'll walk you back," he repeated firmly, opening the door. "No more wandering around alone, okay?"

He thought she'd flare up at that, but she just nodded. "I'll take the dog with me everywhere I go. He might not be the brightest of creatures, but at least he'll make noise."

He wanted to offer himself instead of the dog, but that wouldn't be wise, not when just being within six feet of her made him want to kiss her. Like now.

He yanked the door open. The rain had subsided to a faint drizzle. "You're right. We'd better go."

Before he gave in to the powerful need to have her in his arms.

"Just grate the cheese." Laughter filled Rachel's voice as she sat in her wheelchair in the kitchen, the table pushed aside to give her more room. "Go on, use the grater. It won't bite you."

"I'm not so sure." Andrea gingerly lifted the metal grater, wary of its sharp teeth. Still, anything that had Rachel laughing had to be good.

Afternoon sun streamed through the kitchen windows, but she was making a breakfast frittata. At least, she was attempting to. She began grating the cheese into the earthenware bowl Rachel had chosen, trying to keep her fingers out of reach of the grater's teeth.

"You really think I can prepare a breakfast that will satisfy the guests." She frowned. "Make that three breakfasts, if Emma doesn't come back until next week."

"Look at it this way," Rachel said. "You're not so much cooking as being my hands. I'm really cooking. You're following directions."

The cheese stuck on the grater, and she gave it a shove. The bowl tipped, the grater flew up, and cheese sprinkled like snowflakes over the tile floor.

She looked at Rachel. "Your hands just made a mess."

Rachel's lips twitched. Then, as if she couldn't hold it back, she began to laugh.

Andrea glared, but an irrepressible chuckle rose in her throat.

"Go ahead, laugh. I never claimed to be able to cook. That's your department. I eat out or open a frozen dinner, and my cheese comes already grated in a bag."

"I'm sorry." Rachel's green eyes, so like her own, brimmed with laughter. "It's just that you're so competent on the computer and all thumbs in the kitchen."

"It's a good thing there's one area of my life that's under control."

But was it? The computer represented the business world to her, and how could she know what was happening back at the office when she was stuck here? E-mailing her assistant wasn't the same as being there, especially when that assistant had her eyes on Andrea's job.

"I'd be just as out of place in your office," Rachel said. "Here, hand me the bowl. Maybe I can set it in my lap and do the grating."

"No, I'm determined now. I will learn how to do this." She began again, careful to keep the bowl steady. "After all, you'll have to learn how to keep the reservations on the computer after I leave. I'll get to laugh at you then."

"Did you really get all that computerized?" Rachel shook her head. "I kept putting off trying, because it looked so hard."

"It'll be much easier once you get used to it. Much of your traffic will come from the Web site I started, especially when we get some more pictures up. Right now I just have the basics." That was one good thing accomplished, and the computer really would make running the inn easier, if she could get Rachel in the habit of using it.

"I'm astonished. You've done more in two weeks than I did in six months."

She must be getting more sensitive, because she detected immediately the note in Rachel's voice that said she was comparing herself unfavorably with her big sister.

"That's nonsense," she said firmly. "The renovations are all credited to you, and as for the garden..." She glanced out the kitchen window at the borders filled with color. "The guests will love looking at that while they have their breakfast. Always assuming I manage to make anything edible."

"You'll be fine," Rachel said. "You just have to do one main hot dish for each day. We'll serve fresh fruit cups, that special Amish-recipe granola that Grams gets from the farmer's market, and the breads and coffee cakes that Nancy offered to make. It'll be fine."

"Thank goodness for Nancy. She promised us Moravian Sugar Cakes for the first morning. I'll gain a pound just smelling them." She looked down in surprise, realizing she'd actually grated the entire block of cheese without getting any bloody knuckles. "We have to remember to bring flowers in to put on the tables, too."

Rachel nodded, turning the chair so that she could see out the screen door toward the garden. "I wish I'd been able to get the gazebo moved. That was one thing I intended that I didn't get to."

"Move the gazebo?" Andrea glanced out at the white wooden structure with its lacy gingerbread trim. "Why?"

Rachel shook her head. "You really don't have an eye for a garden, do you? It's in quite the wrong place, where it doesn't have a view. It makes the garden look crowded, instead of serving as an accent piece."

"I'll take your word for it." She wiped her hands on a tea towel. "What do I do next?"

Before Rachel could answer, the telephone rang.

Rachel picked it up. "Three Sisters Inn," she said, a note of pride in her voice. But a moment later her face had paled, and she looked at Andrea with panic in her eyes.

"Just a moment, please." She covered the receiver with her hand. "It's Mr. Elliot—has a reservation for the weekend, an anniversary surprise for his wife. He claims he received an e-mail from us, canceling, saying we aren't going to be open yet. You didn't—"

"Of course not." For a moment she stared at her sister, speculations running wildly through her mind. Then she reached for the phone. Redeem the situation first, if she could, and figure out where the blame lay later.

"Mr. Elliot?" It was her businesswoman voice, calm, assured, in control. "I'm terribly sorry about this misunderstanding, but we certainly didn't cancel your reservation."

"You didn't send this e-mail?" He sounded suspicious.

"No, sir, we didn't. My sister has been hospitalized, and perhaps something went out without our knowledge." That made it sound as if they had a vast staff capable of making such an error.

"Seems a sloppy way to run an inn," he muttered, but the anger had gone out of his voice. "So we're still on for the weekend."

"Yes, indeed." She infused her voice with warmth, even as her mind seethed with possibilities. "And we'll provide a very special anniversary cake to surprise your wife. Don't worry about a thing."

When she finally hung up, her hand was shaking.

Rachel stared at her. "They're still coming?"

"Yes. But it's a good thing he was angry enough to want to blow up at us, or we'd never have known."

"The other guests—" Rachel's eyes darkened with concern.

"I'll get the list and call them right away." She hurried into the library, headed for the computer, hearing the wheels of Rachel's chair behind her.

"Maybe we can reach them before they have a chance to make other plans." Rachel sounded as if she were clinging hard to hope.

"Cross your fingers." Andrea paused. "The person who planned this overreached herself. If she'd waited until the last minute, we'd probably have been sitting high and dry with no guests."

"She?"

"She. I can't prove it, but I know perfectly well who did this."

"It had to be Margaret. She was in the library the other day with access to the computer. She even said something to me Sunday about hearing we wouldn't be able to open in time. But what can I do? There's no way to prove it."

Andrea had spotted Cal making his nightly rounds with a flashlight and called him in. Grams and Rachel had gone to bed early, and the house was quiet.

They sat on the sofa in the old summer kitchen that still bore remnants of the playroom it had been when she and her sisters had lived in the house. Games were stacked on the shelves to the right of the fireplace, and if she opened the closet, she'd find a few toys that Grams hadn't wanted to give away.

Cal frowned, staring absently at the cavernous fireplace. "You could bring a civil suit against her, but that would be using a bazooka to rid the house of mosquitoes."

"Not worthwhile, obviously, but I hate letting her get away with it. And the nerve of her—she just walked in the library when we were upstairs, calmly accessed the reservation records on my computer, and sent the e-mails."

He glanced at her. "The computer was on?"

"Don't remind me of how easy I made it for her. I not only had it on, it was open to the reservations. Well, it's password protected now, but it certainly got us off to a bad start."

"Did you lose any of the reservations?"

"Only one. The others consented to rebook after I'd groveled a bit."

That surprised a smile out of him. "I didn't think you knew how to do that."

"That's a lesson I learned early in my career. If there's a problem, don't waste time defending yourself. Just fix it."

"Not a bad philosophy. I'll bet you didn't know running a B and B would have so much in common with your real life."

His words were a reminder that her time here was coming to an end. She fought to ignore the hollow feeling in the pit of her stomach.

"Anyway, I'm absolutely certain Margaret's guilty of monkeying with the computer, but would she prowl around at night or dress up in Amish clothes to stand out in the rain? I don't think so."

"Anyone with such a fund of insincerity can't be trusted, but I'm inclined to agree with you about that.

She'd be afraid of being caught in an embarrassing position."

"I'd like to catch her at something." She shook her head. "That sounds vengeful, doesn't it? Grams would be ashamed of me. It's just that we've all worked so hard—"

"I know." He squeezed her hand. "Are you ready for guests to arrive on Saturday?"

"I think we're in good shape, but I'm certainly glad Grams didn't tell them they could arrive Friday night. Rachel's been walking me through cooking the breakfast meals. We actually ate my artichoke and sausage frittata for supper, and it wasn't half-bad. And Nancy Zook is providing all the baked goods we need."

He nodded. "I heard from Eli that she's agreed to help out some, at least until Rachel's on her feet again."

"I expect I'll be coming back on weekends, at least through the busy season."

Did that sound as if she were asking for something—some hint of where they stood? She hated having things unresolved.

"I'm glad we'll still get to see you." His tone was as neutral and friendly as if he spoke to Eli Zook.

Maybe that answered the question in her mind. Cal recognized, as she did, that the differences between them were too fundamental. The hole in her midsection seemed to deepen.

Ridiculous. She'd only known him for weeks. But when she looked at him, she realized that wasn't true. Maybe in chronological terms they hadn't known each other long, but she'd met him at a time when her emotions were stretched to the limit and her normal barriers suspended.

And since then she'd relied on him in a way that startled her when she looked at it rationally. Did she have anyone else, even back in Philadelphia, that she would turn to for help as naturally as she'd turned to him?

No. She didn't. And that was a sad commentary on the quality of her life.

Cal apparently wasn't engaging in any deep thoughts over the prospect of her leaving. He was frowning toward the small window in the side wall.

"Shouldn't we be able to see the reflection of the garden lights from here?"

She followed the direction of his gaze, vague unease stirring. "Yes. I'm sure I could see the glow the last time I looked that way."

Cal rose, walking quickly toward the hallway and the back door. She followed. They stopped at the door, peering out at the garden, which was perfectly dark.

"Something's happened to the lights." She couldn't erase the apprehension in her voice.

"It may not be anything major." Cal opened the door, switching on his flashlight. "I connected the new lights to the fuse box in the toolshed. Could have blown a fuse, I guess. I'll go check." He stepped out onto the patio.

"Be careful."

Already at the edge of the patio, he turned to smile at her. "I always am." He lifted the flashlight in a little salute, and then stepped off the flagstones. In an instant he was swallowed up by the dark.

She clutched the door frame, hands cold. Irrational, to be worried over something so simple, but then, plenty of irrational things had been happening. She yanked open the door and stepped outside, driven by some inner compulsion.

The beam of his flashlight was the only clue to Cal's location, halfway to the toolshed. She should have gone with him. She could have held the light while he checked the fuses.

The stillness was shattered by an engine's roar. Lights blazed, slicing through the darkness. She whirled. Something barreled from behind the garage— something that surged across the grass, sound and light paralyzing her.

Cal. Cal was pinned in the powerful twin headlight beams. Before she could move the massive shape rocketed across the garden, straight toward Cal.

Screaming his name, she darted forward. The vehicle cut between them with a deafening roar. She couldn't see—the light from Cal's torch was gone. Where was he?

THIRTEEN

Cal dived away from the oncoming lights, instinct taking over from thought. The roar of the motor deafened him. Something struck his head, and he slammed into the ground.

He couldn't breathe, couldn't think, facedown in the damp grass. He gasped in a gulp of cool air, shaking his head and wincing at the pain.

Think. Look. Try to identify the car.

No, truck—a four-by-four, by the sound of it. He shoved up onto his knees. The vehicle careened through the garden, ripping up flower beds, smashing the birdbath.

He forced his brain to work. It would be gone in an instant. He had to try and identify it. No license plate to be seen—the rear lights were blacked out. He fought the urge to sink back down on the grass, trying to clear his head. It didn't seem to work. Someone was shouting his name.

Andrea. She flew toward him, barreled into him. He winced and would have toppled over but for the hard grasp of her hands.

"You're all right—I thought you were hit." Her fingers clutched at him, and her voice caught on a sob.

He touched his forehead and felt the stickiness of blood, warm on his palm. He leaned on her, aware of the roar of the truck's engine. If he could get a good look at it before it disappeared around the building...

The dark shape had reached the pond. It turned, wheels spinning in the mud left from yesterday's rain. He could make out the shape, not the color. The driver would cut off down the lane....

He didn't. He spun, straightened, and bucketed straight toward them.

He clutched Andrea. Closest shelter, no time—

"Run! The patio—"

Clutching each other, stumbling a little, they ran toward the patio. He forced his feet to slog as if through quicksand, the truck was coming fast, they weren't going to make it, Andrea—

He shoved her with every bit of strength, flinging her toward the stone patio wall. Threw himself forward, the truck so close he felt the breath of the engine. Landed hard again, pain ricocheting through his body.

Metal shrieked as the truck sideswiped the patio wall, scattering stones. He struggled, trying to get to his feet, dazed, left wrist throbbing. Strength knocked out of him. If the truck came back, he was a sitting duck....

Then Andrea grabbed him, pulling him onto the patio, dragging him to safety. The truck made a last defiant pass through the flower beds, charged past the garage, clipping it, and roared off down the dark country road, disappearing into the trees.

Andrea clutched him, her breath coming in ragged gasps. "Are you hurt?"

He shook his head, wincing at the pain. "You…"

It was more important than anything to know that she was safe, but he couldn't seem to form a question.

He tried to focus on her face, white and strained in the circle of light from the door. Katherine stood in the doorway, saying something he couldn't make out, Rachel behind her in the chair.

He had to reassure them. He staggered a step toward them and collapsed onto the flagstones.

"I'm not going to the hospital. I'm fine." Cal might look pale and shaken, but his voice was as firm as always.

Andrea found she could breathe. He'd be all right. That terrible moment when she thought the truck had hit him—she could stop thinking about it now.

But she couldn't kid herself about her feelings for him any longer. That brief instant when she'd thought he was gone had been a lightning flash that seared heart and soul, showing her exactly how much she cared.

The paramedic leaned on the back of a kitchen chair, looking at him doubtfully. "Might be a good idea to let the docs check out that wrist."

"It's a sprain." He cradled his left wrist in his other hand. "The wrap is all I need."

She'd urge him to let them take him to the hospital, but she knew that was futile. She wrapped her fingers around the mug of coffee someone had thrust into her hands, wondering how long it would take for the shaking to stop.

Grams's kitchen was crowded with paramedics and police, but for the first time in her memory, Grams seemed to have given up the reins of hospitality. She sat at the end of the table, robe knotted tightly around her, her face gray and drawn.

Love and fear clutched at Andrea's heart. Grams had to be protected, and she was doing a lousy job of it.

Please, Father, show me what to do. I have to take care of them, and I'm afraid I can't.

The paramedics, apparently giving up on Cal, began packing up their kits, leaving the field to the police.

There were two of them this time. The young patrolman who'd come before stood awkwardly by the door, and the township chief sat at the table. Obviously the authorities took this seriously. As they should. Cal could have been killed.

The chief cleared his throat, gathering their attention. Zachary Burkhalter, he'd introduced himself— tall, lean, with sandy hair and a stolid, strong-boned face. He must be about Cal's age, but he wore an air that said he'd seen it all and nothing could surprise him.

"Maybe you could just go over the whole thing for me, Mr. Burke. Anything you saw or heard might help."

Cal shoved his good hand through his hair, disturbing a tuft of grass that fluttered to the table. She probably had her own share of debris, and she thought longingly of a hot shower.

"I didn't see much. Seemed like it took forever,

but it probably wasn't more than a couple of minutes at most. We noticed the outside lights had gone off. I thought it was a fuse, started across toward the toolshed where the box is. The four-by-four was behind the garage, out of sight."

She nodded, agreeing, and the chief's gaze turned to her instantly. Gray eyes, cold as flint.

"You agree with that, Ms. Hampton?"

"Yes. I saw the truck come out from behind the garage. To be exact, I heard it, saw the lights. It crossed the back lawn to the pond, turned around and came back, went past the garage again and down Crossings Road. It took less than five minutes, certainly."

And they'd fought for their lives the whole time.

"Can you identify the driver?" His gaze swiveled back to Cal.

"Too dark without the security lights. As Ms. Hampton said, they'd just gone off."

"That ever happen before?"

"No." Cal's voice was level. "It hadn't."

She knew what he was thinking. Someone could have tampered with the fuse box. Would they have had time to do that and get back to the truck before she and Cal went outside? She wasn't sure, but she couldn't say how long the lights had been off.

"And the truck?" Burkhalter obviously wanted a description they couldn't give.

"The rear lights of the vehicle had been blacked out somehow. It was a four-by-four, some dark color—that's about all I could see." Cal was probably berating himself that he didn't get a better look.

Burkhalter nodded. "We've found it, as a matter of fact."

Cal's brows shot up. "That was fast work, Chief."

"Abandoned down Crossings Road, keys missing, scrapes along the fender from hitting the wall. The back lights had been broken."

"Whose is it?" The question burst out of her mouth. If they knew who was responsible…

Burkhalter's gaze gave nothing away. "Belongs to Bob Duckett. Easy enough for someone to take it— he leaves the garage door standing open and the keys hanging on a hook."

Of course he would. Half the township did that, probably, thinking this place was as safe as it had been fifty years ago.

"Bob Duckett wouldn't do anything like this." Grams finally spoke, her voice thin and reedy.

"No, we're sure he didn't." Burkhalter's tone softened for Grams. Then he looked back at her, and the softness disappeared. "You reported an earlier incident, Ms. Hampton?"

"Yes." She glanced toward the patrolman. "We had a prowler."

"This was considerably uglier than prowling."

She glanced toward Rachel, shaken by the bereft look on her face. Rachel had expended hours of work and loving care on the garden, only to have it devastated in a matter of minutes.

"You have any idea who might want to do this?" He glanced around the table, aiming the question at all of them.

Grams straightened, clasping her hands together.

"No one could possibly have anything against us, Chief Burkhalter."

Andrea moved slightly, and Burkhalter was on to it at once. "You don't agree?"

She was conscious of her grandmother's strong will, demanding that she be silent. Well, this once, Grams wouldn't get her way.

"There are people who are opposed to another bed-and-breakfast opening here," she said carefully.

"What people?" Burkhalter wouldn't be content with evasion.

She had to ignore Grams's frown. "Margaret Allen, for one. And I understand Herbert Rush and some of the other old-timers don't like the idea."

"It's ridiculous to think they'd do this."

Grams's tone told her she'd be hearing about this for a while. Grams couldn't imagine anyone she knew stealing a four-by-four to drive it through the grounds, but someone had.

She shivered a little, her gaze meeting Cal's. *Do I say anything about Levi? Surely he couldn't be involved. He doesn't drive, for one thing.*

Cal cradled his left hand, his expression giving nothing away. A bruise was darkening on his forehead. Her heart twisted.

"Could have been teenagers," Burkhalter said. "Hearing their elders talk about the inn, deciding to do something about it. Clever enough, though, for him, or them, to put the vehicle behind the garage while they tampered with the lights. No one would see it there unless they were driving down Crossings Road, and likely enough not even then."

And no one was likely to be going down Crossings Road at this hour. It led to several Amish farms, but they were probably dark and quiet by this time.

"I trust you're not going to just dismiss this as casual vandalism." Rachel spoke for the first time.

"No, ma'am." Burkhalter's gaze lingered on Rachel for a moment, but Andrea found it impossible to read. "We won't do that." His glance shifted, sweeping around the table. "Anyone have anything else to add?"

Someone stood outside the house one night. Someone might have pushed me into a closet. Someone probably followed me back from the Zook farm yesterday. Someone—Margaret, for choice—tampered with our reservations. There were good reasons for saying none of those things.

"We don't know anything else." Grams's voice had regained some of its command. "Thank you for coming."

Burkhalter rose. "We'll be in touch." He jerked his head to the patrolman, who followed him out the door.

Grams waited until the outer door closed behind them. She stood, pulling her dignity around her like a robe. "Cal, you must stay in the house tonight. Come along, I'll show you to a room. Andrea, please help Rachel back to bed."

She was too tired to argue. Besides, if she did have a chance to speak to Cal privately, what could she say? Her feelings were rubbed too raw to have a hope of hiding them. Maybe it was better this way.

Andrea walked into the breakfast room the next morning, wincing as the bright sunlight hit her face.

The French doors stood open, and Rachel sat in her wheelchair on the patio.

She walked outside and put her hand on her sister's shoulder in mute sympathy. Rachel reached up to squeeze it.

"Stupid to cry over a garden." Rachel dashed tears away with the back of her hand. "It's just—"

"It was beautiful, and you and Grams made it." Andrea finished the thought, her stomach twisting as she looked at the damage. Dead or dying flowers lay with their roots exposed, and deep ruts cut through the lawn. The birdbath was nothing but scattered pieces, and the patio wall where she and Cal had sat bore a raw, jagged scar where stones had been knocked out. The only thing that hadn't been hit was the gazebo, probably because it stood off to one side.

"It's hard to believe that much damage could be done in a few minutes." Something quivered inside her. It could have been worse, much worse. It could have been Cal or her lying broken on the lawn.

"I am so furious." Rachel pounded her fists against the arms of the wheelchair. "If I could get my hands on the person who did this, I'd show him how it feels to be torn up by the roots."

The fury was so counter to Rachel's personality that Andrea was almost surprised into a laugh. Rachel was a nurturer, yet when something under her care was hurt, she could turn into a mother lion. "Maybe it's a good thing we don't know, then. I'd hate to see my little sister arrested for assault."

"It might be better," Rachel said darkly. "Then I wouldn't have to see the guests' faces. They'll be here the day after tomorrow, Dree. What are we going to do?" The last words came out almost as a wail.

"We're not going to waste time on anger." She had to give Rachel something to focus on other than the fury that could give way, too easily, to helplessness. "You make a list of what you want, and I'll head out to the nursery first thing. I'll spend the rest of the day putting new plants in. They'll at least last while the guests are here."

Rachel's brows lifted. "You? When was the last time you dug in the dirt?"

"Probably when I left the sandbox stage, but you'll tell me what to do. Look, I know it won't be the same—"

"What about the wall? And the lawn, and the birdbath? It would take an army to get things in shape by Saturday."

Andrea grabbed the chair and turned Rachel to face her. "Look, this is no time to give up. Now stop acting like a baby and go make that list."

"You stop being so bossy." Rachel glared at her for an instant, and then her lips began to quiver. "Um, re-mind me how old we are again?"

Laughter bubbled up, erasing her annoyance. "About ten and twelve, I think." She gave the chair a shove. "Go on, write the list. We'll make this work. I promise."

Smiling, Rachel wheeled herself through the door-way.

"Rach?"

She turned.

"Has anyone checked on Cal this morning?" She forced the question to sound casual.

"Grams said he was dressed and gone an hour ago," Rachel said. "I'll get some coffee started while I make up the list." At least she looked more herself as she wheeled toward the kitchen.

Andrea walked to the patio wall and surveyed the damage. She might be able to plant flowers, given enough instruction, but this she couldn't fix. Disappointment filtered through her at Cal's absence. She'd expected that today, of all times, he'd be here to help.

Well, he had a business to run. Once that would have been a guaranteed excuse, at least from her perspective. She'd changed, if all she could think was that he should be here.

Stepping over the patio wall, she began to gather the stones that were scattered across the grass. Maybe she couldn't fix the wall, but she could make the area look a little neater.

The stones proved far heavier than she expected. She straightened her back, frowning at one particularly stubborn one.

"Take it easy." Cal's voice spun her around. "I'll do that." The bag he carried in one arm thudded against the wall.

"I thought you left." Did she sound accusing?

"I went to get cement mix to repair the wall." He lifted his eyebrows. "Not very complimentary that you thought I'd desert you this morning."

She wasn't sure what to say to that. "Well, you do have a business to take care of."

"Friends come first," he said shortly.

Are we friends, Cal? What would he say if she blurted that out? She wasn't sure she even wanted to hear the answer.

Movement beyond him on the lane distracted her. "What on earth…?"

Cal turned. "Looks like the Zook family think friends come first, too."

Her breath caught, and tears welled in her eyes. Three buggies came down the lane, packed with people, and a large farm wagon bore so many flowers that it looked like a float in the homecoming parade.

She could only stand and stare for a moment. And then she bolted toward the house.

"Rachel! Rachel, come here this minute! You're not going to believe this!"

Andrea sat back on her heels, admiring the snapdragons she'd just succeeded in planting with Nancy's help.

"Looks good already." Nancy, Emma's daughter-in-law, smiled, brushing a strand of dark hair back into the neat coil under her prayer cap. "We brought enough flowers, I think."

She nodded. They'd certainly brought enough help. Eli and Cal fitted the last stone into place on the wall, while Nancy's small son stood by holding the bucket with cement. Nancy's husband and another Amish man, their red shirts a bright contrast to black trousers, used a lawn roller to smooth out the ruts. The grass seemed to spring into place in their wake. And the flowers…

"You must have gotten up at dawn to dig all of these plants to bring. We can't thank you enough for this."

"We always get up at dawn," Nancy said. "This is just being neighborly."

All along the flower border figures knelt, setting out new plants to replace the ruined ones. Children ran back and forth, fetching and carrying, the girls with bonnet strings streaming, the boys small replicas of the men.

Funny. When she'd spread the Sunshine and Shadows quilt over her bed this morning, she'd felt that they were locked into a dark stripe. Now the sun had come out. She glanced at Cal, who seemed to be keeping himself busy well away from her. Or maybe it would be more accurate to say that the dark was interwoven with the bright.

A time to plant and a time to pluck up that which is planted.

A clatter of spoon against pan sounded. Emma stood in the doorway. Her face was still red and painful-looking, but she'd arrived with the others and marched into the kitchen. "Breakfast when you are finished. The flowers must be in before the sun is high." She vanished back inside.

The comment seemed to inspire a fresh burst of industry. Nancy handed her another flat of blooms. "Impatiens," she said. "Along where it's shady."

Andrea nodded. The move brought her next to Levi, who was setting out clumps of coralbells. When he saw her, his round blue eyes became even rounder.

"Hi, Levi. Thanks for helping." In the light of day,

her suspicions of him seemed silly. Levi was, as he'd always been, an innocent child at heart.

He ducked his head, coloring a little. "Help is good." He seemed to struggle with the words, and she realized he'd be far more comfortable with the language of the home. Unfortunately, she'd forgotten whatever German she'd learned as a child.

"Yes. You're good neighbors."

He stared at her, and she saw to her horror that his eyes were filling with tears. "Sorry. Sorry."

He scrambled to his feet, arms flailing awkwardly, and ran toward the barn.

She was still staring after him when Nancy knelt next to her, picking up the trowel he'd dropped and finishing the planting in a few deft movements. "It makes no trouble. Levi will be fine. One of the children will get him when it's time to eat."

"I didn't mean to upset him."

"He's been—" she paused, seeming to search for a word "—funny, just lately. He'll be all right."

"You don't know what's causing it?"

Nancy shrugged. "He doesn't talk so much. Sooner or later he will tell his mother, and she will make it right. Some simple thing, most likely."

Nancy was probably right. She certainly knew Levi better than Andrea did.

Still, she couldn't help but wonder. Why had Levi begun to cry at the sight of her? And why had he said he was sorry?

FOURTEEN

Cal pulled into the driveway and stopped close to the back garden. He'd seen Rachel mourning over the pieces of the birdbath earlier. The one he'd found at the garden store out toward Lancaster should be a decent replacement.

He got the wheelbarrow from the utility shed in the garage, struggling to manage it. Even with his wrist taped, using that hand was awkward. Lucky it wasn't the right, or he'd be out of work until it healed.

Andrea emerged onto the patio, carrying a watering can. She checked at the sight of him, then waved and began sprinkling the potted plants along the edge of the patio.

Maybe Andrea hadn't quite figured out what had changed between them last night, either. He hefted the birdbath onto the wheelbarrow with one hand. They were both trying to look busy, which probably meant they were both confused.

During those moments when they'd fought for their lives, there hadn't been time to think, only to act and feel. Trouble was, he felt too much.

Lord, does it make any sense at all for me to fall for

someone like Andrea? If You've taught me anything in the past year, isn't it that this is the life that's right for me? Andrea could never be content with that. She's itching to race back to the city the minute she's free.

If he told her what he felt—but that could only lead to pain and awkwardness between them.

He was maneuvering the birdbath into place when Andrea caught the opposite side and helped him.

"This is lovely. Where did you find it?"

"Little place over toward Lancaster." If he looked at her, he might weaken, so it was better to concentrate on getting the birdbath into exactly the right spot. "I thought it would please Rachel."

"She'll be delighted." Her tone had cooled in response to his.

He hated that. But wasn't it better for both of them in the long run? Why start something that could only end badly?

Andrea touched a scalloped edge. "About last night..."

He tensed, but before she could say anything else, a buggy came down the drive, the horse driven at a fast trot. "It's Eli." He went to meet the buggy, aware of Andrea hurrying beside him.

Eli pulled up. "Have you seen our Levi since this morning?"

"No, not since we were working on the lawn." He glanced at Andrea, and she shook her head. "Is something wrong?"

"No one has seen him all day." The lines of his face deepened. "That's not like him. He never goes far, and he always tells his mother. We are starting a search."

Cal glanced at his watch. Nearly five. Levi had been missing for something like seven hours.

"What can we do to help?" Andrea said.

"Search all your buildings. And pray."

"We'll do both," he said quickly. "If we spot him, we'll ring the bell." He nodded toward the old-fashioned dinner bell that hung next to the kitchen door.

"I must tell the other neighbors." Eli was already turning the buggy, and he rolled off without another word. The Amish habit of leaving off the niceties of conversation could seem abrupt, but it was certainly understandable now.

Andrea glanced toward the house. "Grams and Rachel are resting, and they wouldn't be much help in any event."

He headed for the garage. "They don't need to know yet. We can start at this end and work our way out toward the barn."

While he checked the cars and the garage loft, Andrea opened the door to the attached utility shed.

By the time he came back down, she was dusting her hands off. "Nothing in there but a lot of spiderwebs." She hesitated a moment, as if something was on her mind. "You know, Levi was a little odd this morning."

"Odd in what way?" He headed for the old brooder coop, which stood next in the line of outbuildings.

"He was upset when he realized I was working next to him." She seemed to be choosing her words carefully. "I tried to talk to him, but all he'd say was that he was sorry. Then he ran off, almost in tears."

"You didn't get a sense of what it was all about?"

She shook her head. "When I mentioned it to Nancy, she said he'd been withdrawn lately, but she didn't take it seriously."

"What could he have been sorry for? For what happened last night?"

"I don't know." She brushed her hair free of the collar of her shirt with an irritated movement. "Does that seem very likely? He doesn't know how to drive, does he?"

He flung open the door of the brooder coop. It was packed solidly with furniture. "A mouse couldn't hide in here." He closed the door again. "I wouldn't think Levi could drive, but a surprising number of Amish people can. Learn when they are teens, most of them. What direction did Levi head when he ran off?"

"Toward the barn—yours, not the old one. But wouldn't you have seen him if he were there?"

"I haven't been in all day. Too much else to do. Maybe we'd better check there next."

She nodded, trotting beside him as he quickened his pace. It wasn't the first time Levi had wandered off, but he didn't generally go farther than the Unger place. Levi could have decided to take refuge in the barn, he supposed, hiding from some imagined misdeed.

They hurried up the earthen ramp, and he pulled the door open.

"Levi! Levi, are you in here?" The words echoed in the barn's lofty spaces.

Andrea grabbed his arm. "The trapdoor to the lower level. It's open."

He swung around, following the direction of her

pointing finger. The hatch, used long ago to throw hay down to the stalls in the lower level, was always kept closed and bolted. Now it yawned open.

He was there in an instant, bending to peer down into the shadowy depths. His heart jolted into overtime.

Levi lay on the floor below, arms outstretched, blood darkening the straw beneath his head. His hands were open, palm up, and next to his right hand, glinting in the shaft of sunlight that pierced the dimness, lay a ring of car keys.

Andrea sat on the plastic chair in the hospital waiting room. She glanced at her watch. How much longer? Surely the doctors knew something by now. At least they'd been given this secluded room in which to wait, rather than sitting out in the open where others could stare at the quaintly dressed Amish.

Grams sat bolt upright on her chair, as if to show any sign of weakness would be a betrayal. She had her arm around Emma, who wept softly into a handkerchief. Nancy sat on Emma's other side, having left the children with Rachel, who'd been quick to say she'd be more trouble than she was worth at the hospital.

Men clustered in a group in the far corner, drinking coffee and talking in low voices. Every now and then the door opened and more Amish appeared, quickly segregating themselves by sexes. A carryover from their separation in church or simply a male desire to be as far away as possible from female tears.

The men's black jackets, the women's black bonnets seemed almost a sign of mourning. She shook off that thought. Levi would be all right. He'd been breathing on his own when they brought him in. That was a good sign, wasn't it?

Each time the door opened, all eyes went to it. Each time, Emma sobbed a bit more.

"I don't understand." Emma's wail was loud enough to startle even the men. "Why did Levi go to the barn? How did he fall?"

Grams took the twisting hands in hers. "We'll know when he's well enough to tell you," she said firmly.

Eli came to his wife and patted her awkwardly on the shoulder. "We must accept," he said. "It is God's will."

Was it? The questions that had hovered at the back of Andrea's mind since she and Cal found Levi forced their way to the front. Her eyes sought out Cal. He was filling his foam cup at the coffee urn, but, as if he felt her gaze on him, he looked up and brought the cup to her.

"Have some. I know it's awful, but at least it's hot."

She took the cup, rising and moving toward the window, where they had the illusion of privacy. "Do you really believe Levi could have driven that truck?" She kept her voice low.

He glanced toward the group around Eli before answering. "It's starting to look that way. Samuel admits that Levi was fascinated by cars. He thinks some of the local teenagers might have thought it was funny to show him." He shook his head. "I just can't figure out how he'd get away from home last night. Emma has been keeping pretty close tabs on him."

"She has, but she was probably exhausted. I don't see how he'd have gotten the keys if he didn't do it. Unless the driver dropped them someplace and he picked them up. And assuming they're the keys to the truck."

"Maybe we're going to find out."

The door had swung open again. This time it was Chief Burkhalter. He glanced around the room, seeming surprised to find it so crowded.

"Any word yet on the boy's condition?" He directed the question to Eli.

Eli shook his head. His normally ruddy face was gray with pain. "The doctor will come when they've finished, he said."

"In that case..." His gaze singled out the two of them. "Maybe you'd step outside so we can have a word, since you found him."

She was grateful for Cal's hand on her back as they followed Burkhalter out into the hallway, knowing everyone watched them go. In the corridor, he gestured them into a room a few doors away.

It was a replica of the other waiting room with its pale green walls and generic landscapes. The chairs looked just as uncomfortable. Burkhalter jerked three of them into a circle. At his commanding look, they sat.

She had nothing to feel guilty about, did she? So why did she feel as if she wanted to look anywhere except into Burkhalter's face?

"Tell me about finding him."

Cal nodded. "Eli came over to tell us he was missing and asked us to search the property. Ms. Hampton and I happened to be out in the garden at the time. We started searching the outbuildings."

"It didn't occur to you to look in the inn first?"

Andrea blinked. "I suppose I knew it was unlikely

Levi would go inside. He's—well, skittish around strangers." She thought of the rabbits that looked askance when she came out onto the lawn and hopped quickly away.

"So you started searching. What took you to the barn?"

"I remembered that he had gone that way when he left the group that was repairing the damage from last night." She closed her mouth, reluctant to say anything that might contribute to his suspicion.

"Did you talk to him at all this morning?" The man seemed to have radar for evasions.

"Yes, a little. He seemed upset." She darted a glance toward Cal, but he couldn't help her. "He said he was sorry."

"Sorry about what?" Burkhalter's response was like the crack of a whip.

"He didn't say. He ran off." She shook her head to forestall any questions. "There's no point in asking me anything else. That's all I know. I remembered he went toward the barn, so we went there. We saw the trapdoor open." Her voice shook a little, and Cal's hand closed hard over hers. "We found him."

Burkhalter transferred his gaze to Cal. "That trapdoor. You always leave it open?"

"No. I always keep it closed and bolted."

"What did you do after you spotted him?"

"Called the paramedics. Went down to see if we could help him." Cal had apparently decided he could be as laconic as Burkhalter.

"I ran back to the house to ring the dinner bell,"

she said. "We'd agreed that's what we'd do if we found him."

Burkhalter nodded, his gaze fixed on her face. "You know, Ms. Hampton, whenever the police get called in, people get choosy about what they say. Mostly it's innocent enough, but they don't want to say more than they have to. Wouldn't you agree, Counselor?"

If Cal was surprised that the chief knew about his past, he didn't betray it. "Maybe so, if they think it's unimportant."

"Cops get so they have a sense when someone's hiding something." He turned on Andrea. "How about it, Ms. Hampton? What aren't you telling me?"

She blinked. He really did have radar. "It's nothing."

"Tell me anyway, and let me decide if it's nothing."

She brushed the hair back from her face. She had no choice, and surely nothing she said could make matters any worse now.

"There was another incident, after the prowler call. I was locked in the downstairs pantry. I thought it was an accident—maybe I bumped the door myself."

"And what else?"

"One night when it was storming, I went to close the windows. I saw someone standing out on the lawn, watching the house." She hesitated. "It appeared to be a man in Amish clothing. I couldn't identify him any further."

"She called me," Cal said. "I came over—didn't catch him, but I found the place where he'd been standing. Judging by the way the grass was trampled, he'd been there for quite a while."

Burkhalter made a show of consulting a small notebook. "I understand your housekeeper had an accident with the stove."

"Yes." Levi wouldn't do anything to hurt his own mother. Surely Burkhalter could see that. "The repairman couldn't say whether someone had tampered with it or not. It could have been an accident."

"Quite a string of bad luck you folks have been having," he observed.

She waited for him to probe more deeply, but to her surprise, he rose.

"You can join the others, if you like."

"Chief." Cal's voice stopped him at the doorway. "Those keys—were they the keys to the stolen truck?"

He didn't move for a moment. Would he answer?

"Yes," he said. "They were."

The stack of green ledgers in the middle of the library desk gave Andrea pause. Rachel, searching in the lower kitchen cabinets for a bundt cake pan, had unearthed yet another batch of Grandfather's records that she'd put away in an unlikely place. Andrea had delivered a lecture on organization, but doubted whether it would do any good.

Andrea pushed the ledgers to one side and switched on the computer, feeling too tired to deal with much of anything this morning. The doctors had come out at last and announced that Levi had a severe concussion and several broken ribs, but would mend. Emma's tears had turned to rejoicing, and the bishop, a local farmer named Christian Lapp, led a lengthy prayer of thanksgiving.

Finally she'd persuaded Grams to come home. It

had been nearly one before the house was quiet, and then she'd lain awake, unable to turn off the questions in her mind.

They'd all come down to one, in the end. Why? Why would Levi do such a thing? Until he told them, no one would know.

Guests were arriving tomorrow. She shoved her hair back and called up the reservations on the computer screen. Were they ready? Aside from a sense that all of them would have difficulty playing the genial host, she thought so.

The front door opened. "Hello?"

"In the library." She shoved her chair back, but the visitor came in even as she rose.

Betty. For a moment it seemed odd, seeing the woman anywhere but behind her desk at Unger and Bendick.

"Betty." She gave what she hoped was a welcoming smile. "What brings you to see us?"

There was no returning smile. Betty marched to the desk and set down a stack of file folders and several computer disks. "Mr. Bendick asked me to bring these to you."

Andrea stared at them blankly. "I'm sorry?"

Betty's lips pressed together in an offended line. "Mrs. Unger informed him that you would be handling all her finances in the future."

With everything else that had been happening, she'd forgotten that vote of confidence from Grams. "I see. I didn't intend for you to bring those over. I'd have come in to talk with Uncle Nick."

"He thought this would be best." Even Betty's hair,

piled in some sort of complicated knot on her head, seemed to quiver with indignation.

It looked as if she'd have to mend some fences. "My grandmother didn't intend any lack of confidence in Uncle Nick. She appreciates everything he's done, but she thought she'd have me do it rather than to take advantage of him, as busy as he is."

Betty leaned over to flip open the top folder. "There are forms here that Mrs. Unger must sign. Please have her do so."

Obviously Betty was offended on Nick's behalf. She found it hard to believe that Nick cared all that much. Surely managing Grams's affairs was an extra burden he didn't need.

"I'll have her sign them when she gets back from the hospital."

Betty paused, and Andrea could see her need to hold on to the grudge battling her curiosity. The curiosity won.

"Is she visiting that Zook boy who caused all the trouble?" Incredulity filled her voice.

"My grandmother is good friends with the Zook family." Andrea stood. "Thank you for dropping these off. I'll take care of them."

Betty glared at her for a moment. Then she turned and stalked out. The front door slammed.

"She isn't too happy with you." Cal walked in from the kitchen as she sat down.

She felt the little jolt to her heart that seemed to come with his presence. "Did you bring my grandmother back from the hospital?"

"She wanted to stay a while longer, so Emma arranged for someone to pick them both up. I told Katherine I'd stop by and update you."

"How is Levi?"

He came and perched on the corner of the desk. "The doctors seem satisfied. He should come home in a few days, if all continues to go well."

That was good news, but where did they go from there? "Has he said anything? Explained?"

He shook his head. "He's conscious, but he doesn't seem to remember much about his injury. Burkhalter tried to question him, but Levi got so upset he gave up." He shrugged, clearly not happy with the situation. "Levi had the vehicle keys, so there doesn't seem to be much doubt that he did it."

"Why?" She shoved the desk chair back. "That's what kept me up half the night. What could Levi possibly have against us?"

"Emma was afraid she had the answer to that. It seems the Zooks got worried that if the inn was successful, your grandmother might decide she wanted to use the property they lease from her. She thinks Levi heard them talking and misunderstood. Got some foolish idea he was helping them. And Emma finally said that he does get out at night sometimes."

Her throat tightened. "Poor Emma. It would be hard for her to admit that."

"Well, your grandmother assured her the land is theirs to use as long as they want it, and when I left they were holding each other and crying, so I think they're going to be all right."

He shifted position, not looking at her. "You know, I have an offer to go out to the Zimmerman farm and work on a cabinetry job. I kept putting it off because of everything that's been going on here, but now that it's resolved, I should go."

"I see." She sensed he was saying more than the words indicated. "When will you leave?"

"This afternoon. It'll take a few days, so I suppose you'll be gone by the time I get back."

For a moment she couldn't speak. This was it, then. Cal was letting her know, in the nicest possible way, that he didn't want a relationship with her.

Well, that was for the best, wasn't it? They were committed to completely different values. This wasn't about the distance between Churchville and Philadelphia. It was a question of what they wanted from life. Since that couldn't be reconciled, it was better to make a clear break before anyone got hurt.

She managed to smile, forced herself to hold out her hand. "Thank you again for everything you've done to help us get under way. I'm sure I'll see you when I come back from time to time."

He nodded, holding her hand for a moment as if there was something else he wanted to say. Then he turned quickly and was gone.

She sank back in the chair. She'd been wrong about one thing. It was already too late to keep from getting hurt.

FIFTEEN

Barney whined, lifting his head from the library carpet to look at Andrea. He probably wondered why she was still at the computer when everyone else in the house was asleep. Over the past week, she'd gotten into the habit of keeping the dog downstairs with her after Grams went to bed, letting him out for one last time and then putting him into Grams's room when she went up.

"It's all right, boy." She leaned back in the desk chair, covering her eyes with her hands for a moment. The figures on the computer screen had begun to blur, particularly when she tried to compare them with the cramped writing in Grandfather's last couple of ledgers.

Maybe it would be better to take all of the financial records back to the city with her on Monday, so that she could go over them at her leisure. She'd begun to find discrepancies. It looked as if Grandfather had been failing more than she'd imagined in his final years.

She studied the portrait above the mantel, her grandfather's painted features staring back at her. Was that what happened? Had he really lost that sharp business sense of his and been too proud to admit it? She was startled to realize it hurt to think of him that way.

Aware of the dog whining again, she closed down the program and stacked the ledgers on the edge of the desk. "All right, Barney. You can go out, and then we'd both better get some sleep."

Barney, understanding the words *go out,* trotted toward the back door. When she opened it, he darted outside with a sharp woof.

She leaned against the door, trying not to look in the direction of the barn. Of Cal's empty apartment.

Working on the financial records had, for a few hours, absorbed her mind completely. She could get lost in the rows of figures as easily as other people got lost in a good book.

Now the pain came rushing back. Cal had shut the door on whatever might have been between them. She understood his reasons, but he could have given her some say in the matter. At least, he could have if he felt what she did.

Maybe she was wrong about that. Maybe those close moments between them, those kisses, had been merely attraction to him, with nothing more solid behind it.

Her mind fumbled with an unaccustomed prayer. *I'm trying to find my way back to You, Lord. For a while, I thought Cal was going to be part of that, but I was wrong. Still, no matter how much it hurts to lose him, knowing him has helped me look at things more clearly. Please, guide me to live the way You want.*

No lightning flashed. She didn't have a burst of insight. But peace seeped into her heart, easing the pain and giving her comfort.

Barney barked, the sound muted. Frowning, she stepped outside and called, "Barney! Here, boy!"

Nothing moved anywhere in the lighted area of the yard. He must have gone farther afield while she stood there lost in thought.

Everything looked perfectly peaceful, but somewhere beyond the fringe of outbuildings, the dog yipped.

She reached back inside to slip the flashlight off its hook. She'd have to get him—if she went up to bed without him, Grams would have a fit. And he'd probably wake the house with his barking.

At least, with Levi in the hospital, she didn't have to worry about encountering any prowlers. Poor Levi. Would charges be brought against him? Surely not, if Grams had anything to say about it.

She crossed to the toolshed, shining the light around. Beyond the range of the security lights it was pitch-black, the sliver of a new moon providing little illumination.

She called again, her voice sharp. This time the answer was a whining cry that sounded distressed, and her fingers tightened on the flashlight. Was Barney hurt? Trapped in some way? She hurried toward the sound, behind the row of outbuildings, into the blackness.

Yards ahead of her, across the overgrown lane, loomed the dark bulk of the old barn. A shiver went down her spine. The sound seemed to be coming from there.

The building had been kept in repair, but it hadn't been used for anything in years. Still, there might be something that Barney's collar could have become hooked on.

That must be it.

She trotted toward the earthen ramp to the upper level, flicking the flashlight around as she went, hoping she wouldn't spot any night creatures larger than a mouse. But the dog's presence had probably frightened away any other animals.

One of the big double doors stood ajar just enough for Barney to get through. She'd have to see that it was secured—something else to add to her to-do list. They couldn't have inn guests wandering around where they might get hurt.

She entered, swinging the light. The space was empty, an oil mark on the floor mute testimony to the farm vehicle that had once been parked there. Grandfather must have had the barn cleared out when it was no longer in use.

Her flashlight beam picked up a small door opposite the entrance. The dog's now-frantic barking came from there.

She hurried across the dusty floorboards and grabbed the door, yanking it open. A foul, metallic aroma rushed out at her. Memory stirred. They'd kept fertilizers and pesticides in here long ago. Her light bounced off floor-to-ceiling shelves, still laden with rusty cans. The place looked like a toxic waste dump. Her grandfather's care of the building hadn't extended to clearing this out, apparently.

Barney's eyes shone in the light, and he wiggled with impatience. "Barney." She was embarrassed at the slight tremor in her voice, even though there was no one but the dog to hear. "What happened, baby? Are you stuck?"

Sure enough, the dog's collar was caught in the prongs of an old harrow that lay on the floor. She hurried to kneel beside him. When she patted him, she had to try to quiet his excited leaps and attempts to lick her face.

"Hold still, you silly thing. I can't release you when you're doing that." She put the flashlight down, fumbling with the collar, the dog's jumps nearly knocking her over. The flashlight rolled, illuminating what lay in the corner.

Nick Bendick. Uncle Nick. He sprawled against the wall, unconscious. Alive? Her heart seemed to stop.

"Uncle Nick?" She hurried to him, dropping to her knees next to the inert form.

She groped for his wrist, breathing again when she felt a pulse—weak, but at least he was alive. She grabbed the flashlight, trying to focus with hands that were shaking. It looked as if he'd stumbled on the harrow, hitting his head against the wall. But what on earth was he doing here?

The circle of light wavered, and she forced herself to steady it. It touched Nick's hand, lying lax on the barn floor. Her breath caught, and the world seemed to spin.

In Nick's hand was a dog leash, next to it a torn paper bag, dog biscuits spilling from it.

She couldn't seem to move. Barney hadn't gotten tangled up on his own. Nick had been waiting, knowing she always let the dog out the last thing at night. Had trapped Barney, apparently intending to use him to lure her here.

Her mind struggled to the obvious conclusion. The financial records. Anger swept through her. This was about her interest in the financial records. Grandfather hadn't been losing his touch. Nick had been cheating him.

She had to get help. Run to the house, call the paramedics and the police, let them sort it out. She hurried back to the dog, struggled with the collar for another moment, and finally got it free.

Uncle Nick. It was impossible to believe. Could he really have intended to hurt her? Surely he'd never hurt anyone in his life.

Except Levi. Her mind seemed to leap from one understanding to another. Levi, lying on the floor with the keys planted next to him. How much of what had been happening had been caused by Nick's frantic efforts to keep her from looking into the financial records? He must have realized she was the one person who would understand what he'd done.

The authorities would figure it out. Barney beside her, she hurried toward the door. Cool night air hit her like a slap in the face. Get help. That was all she could do now.

She darted toward the distant house, the circle of light bouncing ahead of her, and Barney woofed at the unexpected excitement. If Grams heard him, came out—well, she'd have to know the truth about the man she'd trusted soon, in any event.

If Cal were at the barn, she'd call on him for help. But he wasn't. He'd left. Ridiculous, to feel that she needed him.

She rounded the corner of the toolshed and flew straight into someone.

She stumbled back, gasping. The security light showed her Betty, of all people. Another surprise in a night of surprises. She grasped the woman's arm.

"You have to help me. It's Nick—he's hurt. He—"

"I'll help."

Betty patted her reassuringly with one hand. The other lifted something. Light reflected from a long, silvery shaft. It swung down, pain exploded in her head, and the ground came up to meet her.

Andrea struggled to open her eyes, but her head spun and ached. She'd just lie here another minute...

Then consciousness came rolling back. Nick. And Betty. Betty had hit her with a golf club. Impossible, but it had happened. Nick and Betty must be doing this together.

A warm, furry body next to her, a rough wet tongue washing her face. "Barney," she whispered, coughing on the word.

She moved, aware of hard wooden boards beneath her, of the acrid smell that made her want to gag. She was back in the tiny storage room in the old barn. Barney was with her.

Something hard poked into her ribs. She rolled, feeling for it, and pulled out the flashlight. Fumbled for the switch, thinking if she had to stay in the dark another instant she'd start screaming...

The light came on. Maybe this was worse. She could see the tall shelves on either side of her, enclosing her with their load of poison. She sucked in a breath and was instantly sorry when the air burned her throat.

Then she saw what still lay against the wall. Nick. Her mind spun.

Get out. She had to get out. She stumbled to the door, groping for the handle. Locked. Incredibly, Betty had locked her in here. Betty. How could she even have gotten her here? It was impossible.

Then she identified the sound that rumbled from beyond the door. A car's engine. Betty must have driven up the overgrown lane behind the outbuildings and hauled her in here.

She pounded on the door. "Betty! Let me out of here. You can't get away with this."

"Can't I?" Betty's voice was muffled by the thick door, but she must be standing close to it on the other side. "I think I can. You've always underestimated me, all of you. My plans have been made for a long time, my money safely salted away under another name. I knew Nick would break down at some point. He always had such a soft spot for your grandmother."

She sounded like an indulgent mother, admitting a failing in her child.

"You were stealing from the firm." Hard to think it through, with the fumes fogging her brain. "But Nick—was he in it with you? Is that what this was all about?"

"Nick had a little gambling problem, you see. Borrowed some money from the accounts. He wasn't very good at it. Your grandfather would have found him out in a week if it hadn't been for me." There was a trace of pride in her voice.

"Betty, think about what you're doing." She forced herself to be calm. Rational. One of them should be. "Just let me out, and we'll go to the police together. I'll get you a lawyer—"

Betty chuckled. "Dear Andrea, always so sure you know what's best. I have no intention of going to the police. You and Nick are going to have an unfortunate accident, and I'm going to be far away by the time it's sorted out and they start to look for me."

"Accident..." She tried to move, but her muscles didn't obey. She could lie down, just rest for a moment; it would be all right....

Shock sent her upright. Her mental fog wasn't just from the closed room and the cans of chemicals. The car was running because Betty was pumping carbon monoxide into the room.

She dropped to her knees, fingers fumbling along the bottom of the door. Yes, there was the mouth of a hose, thrust under the corner of the door.

Please, Lord, please, Lord, help me know what to do. If I can just block it...

She swung the light around, picking up an old feed sack shoved onto a shelf. Grab it, twist a piece small enough to fit into the hose, stuff it in, coughing and choking, prayng it blocked enough to give them a few more precious moments to live....

A few moments. Not enough. No one would look for her until morning, probably. How long would it take until they searched here?

She slumped back, trying to force her numbed wits to move. The walls were closing in. She couldn't stop them, and she felt the familiar panic, blurred by her fogged mind, but there, creeping in, loosening her control.

Father, help me hold on. If I panic, I'll die. Forgive me for drifting away from You. Hold me in Your hands, living or dying.

Hands. Hands reaching out to her, pulling her free. She shook her head, knowing it was a memory, but a memory of what?

It wouldn't come. Think. What else could she do?

Noises outside the door. A car door opening and closing. The car driving away. Betty was gone.

She was still alive, and so was Nick from what she could tell. But not for long unless she could think of something. She swung the light around. Metal shone for an instant on the shelf—she reached, hand closing on a bar about the size of a tire iron.

Excitement flooded her, clearing her mind. If she could get the door open...

But a moment's effort showed her that was impossible. The door was solid, resisting her feeble efforts to open it.

Think. Think. If you can't get out, maybe you can get air in. The wall behind her was solid stone, the end wall of the barn. Nothing there, but the wall to her right must be an outside wall.

She crawled over to it, dragging the bar. Barney, whimpering a little, struggled to her side. Was it her imagination, or was the air a little better here? The dog seemed to think so. He put his nose at the base of the wall, right where the siding boards came down to meet the floor.

Nick. She crawled back to him, grabbed his arms,

and dragged him toward the wall. No time now to worry that she was injuring him further. If she didn't get them some air, they would die.

Adrenaline pulsing, she ran her hand along the joint, feeling the slightest crack between the boards. Big enough to wedge the bar in? Her fingers seemed to have grown stupid along with her brain. It took three tries before she forced the bar in.

Wiggle it, shove it, find something to hit it with— but there she ran out of luck. There was nothing loose in the room sturdy enough to hit the bar. She'd have to keep wiggling it, trying to force it through to the outside, but her mind was fogging again.

Ironic. She'd filled up the slight crack with the pry bar, cutting off whatever air might come through.

Give me strength, Lord. Help me. I know You're here with me. I know whatever You intend is right. But I can't stop trying, can't stop fighting....

"To everything there is a season, and a time for every purpose under Heaven. A time to live and a time to die..."

Barney slumped to the floor. Poor boy. He'd go first. She and Nick were bigger, so they'd last longer. Push, keep pushing, a little farther...

"A little farther, Drea." Her grandfather's voice. He was the only one who'd ever called her that. "Just a little farther. Don't stop now. Another inch, and you'll reach my hands."

Another inch. A vague dream of Grandfather's strong hands, tight on hers, lifting her out into the cool air, holding her close. Safe. She'd always been safe with him.

Safe in God's hands. Living or dying…

Another inch. She pushed the bar, felt the resistance give way as it slid through. Befuddled. Taking a moment to realize she had to pull the bar back out.

Feel the cool air on her face, rushing in through the hole she'd made. Drinking in long gasps of it. Drag Nick's limp form, then Barney, up to the opening, feeling the dog stir.

But tired. So tired. She slumped down, head on Barney's fur.

SIXTEEN

Cal eased off on the accelerator when he hit the outskirts of Churchville. He was making a fool of himself, rushing back at this hour, but the urge to see Andrea again, to clear the air between them, had been too strong to ignore.

He'd tried hiding from life, and it hadn't worked. He couldn't hide. Life kept finding him.

And beneath that urge to see Andrea had been something he couldn't explain, a sense that all was not right. An urgent feeling that he was needed.

Well, he was here, and how he'd explain arriving at this late hour, he didn't know. They'd all be asleep, probably, and he'd have to wait until morning to see Andrea anyway.

But as he turned into the drive at the inn, he saw the glow of lights in the library. It had to be Andrea, sitting up late at the computer. Relief flooded through him, making him realize just how tense he'd been.

A glimpse of movement drew his attention. From beyond the outbuildings, a dark car spurted out, hit the winding country road and raced away.

Cal jammed on the brakes and slid out, leaving the

motor running, all his instincts crying out. That was wrong, very wrong. He ran toward the back door, and the minute he saw it, he knew his instincts were on target. The door stood open, light pooling out onto the patio, and no one was there.

His feet thudded across the patio. None of them would go off and leave the door standing open at this hour. He bolted inside and ran for the library. Lights on, computer on, desk chair pushed back. It looked as if Andrea had just walked away.

Some rational part of his mind kept insisting that there could be a logical explanation, but he didn't believe it. Rachel—Rachel was sleeping on this floor now, in the little room off the kitchen.

He saw the light go on as he ran to it. He was probably scaring her to death.

"Rachel, it's Cal. Is Andrea with you?"

"No. What's happening?" Fear laced her voice.

He flung open the door. Rachel sat up in bed, pulling a robe around her.

"The back door is standing open, and I can't find Andrea."

"If she took the dog out—"

He felt as if he'd been doused with cold water. "That must be it. Sorry. I'll just check."

Logical explanation, see? But the fear drove him back out to the patio. "Andrea! Andrea, are you out here?"

A light went on overhead, and he heard footsteps on the stairs. Katherine. She hurried toward him.

"Cal, what are you doing back? Why are you calling for Andrea?"

"Is she upstairs?"

"No." She glanced toward the library and paled. "She and Barney were still down here. She must have taken him out. But why didn't she hear you call?"

"I'll look for her. Where's a flashlight?"

She pulled a drawer open and thrust a heavy torch into his hand. "I'm calling the police."

He jerked a nod and hurried out the door. Better a false alarm than a tragedy. He'd never been one to go on instinct, but this sense was stronger than he'd ever experienced.

Is it You, Lord? If it is, help me to listen. Show me where to go. Please, keep her safe.

He ran across the lawn toward the outbuildings. The car that had no possible reason for being there— it had come from behind the outbuildings. He swung the light around.

"Andrea! Where are you?"

Nothing. The buildings were dark and silent, the security lights reflecting from them, mocking him. They hadn't kept Andrea safe.

And the dog—the dog must be with her. "Barney!" he yelled. "Here, boy. Barney!"

Not even an answering woof. He paused by the toolshed, the urgency pounding along his veins like a power in his blood, telling him to hurry, hurry. But where?

Lord, help me. If this is from You, help me.

He took a breath. Think. The car came down the disused lane behind the outbuildings—the lane that led only to the old barn. He ran, heart thudding in his ears. Behind him, from the house, the bell began clanging insistently. Katherine, trying to rouse the Zook family to come and help.

The circle of light bounced. He rounded the corner, saw the barn doors, and knew the instinct that drove him was right. Both doors stood open, and the grass leading to them was bent down from the passage of a car.

He thudded inside. A car had been in here—he could smell the fumes. Strong, too strong. He swung the light around. Empty, nothing...

The light flashed on a door—solid as the barn, the old-fashioned latch dropped down into its pocket, securing it. He ran toward it, stumbling on a length of hose, righting himself, reaching the door.

Flung it open and staggered back from the fumes. Andrea. He took a deep breath and threw himself through the door. Woman and dog lay together against the outer wall. Another figure—a man. Bendick. Still, too still.

He grabbed Andrea, stumbled back out, through the barn, out into the cold night air. Think, remember your CPR training, but even as he thought it she coughed, choked and gasped in a gulp of air.

Tears filled his eyes. *Please, God, please, God.* He knelt in the damp grass, holding her against him. "Andrea, wake up. Say something. Breathe."

She stirred, murmured something, then sank limply against him. But she was breathing. Her eyelids fluttered.

"I've found her!" he shouted at the top of his lungs. "Call the paramedics." Poor Katherine must be terrified, but he couldn't do anything else. He'd have to go back in for Bendick....

Lights bobbing toward him—Eli, his son and the oldest grandson with him, running with trousers pulled on over nightshirts.

"In the barn, the back room. Bendick and the dog. Mind the fumes." Samuel nodded and pelted into the barn with the boy, while Eli knelt beside him.

"Will she be all right, then?"

"She's breathing." He looked at the older man, not ashamed of the tears that spilled over. "She's alive."

"Thank the Lord," Eli said.

The wail of a siren split the night.

Yes, thank You, Father. Thank You.

Andrea toyed with the piece of dry toast that was all she thought she could get down. They sat around the breakfast table in various stages of exhaustion. Emma kept pressing food on people, as if that were the only cure for the night they'd been through.

Since she'd missed most of it, either through being unconscious or at the hospital, she tried to concentrate on what Chief Burkhalter was saying, but her gaze kept straying to Cal.

His face was drawn, the skin pulled tight against the bone, as if he'd been in battle and wasn't sure it was over. She'd had no chance to talk with him alone, and still didn't know what had brought him back. She only knew he'd come in time to save her. That was enough.

Barney padded around the table from Grams to her, sighed, and thudded heavily to the floor next to her, as if he'd decided that she needed his protection.

"…caught up with the woman on the other side of Harrisburg," Burkhalter was saying. "She tried to bluff it out. Might have gotten away if Burke hadn't gotten to you in time." He eyed her soberly. "Just glad you're okay."

She nodded, not sure she trusted herself to speak. The memory was too fresh.

"I don't understand." Grams seemed to have aged overnight. "I'd believe anything of Betty, but Nick— we've known him and trusted him for thirty years."

"Are they talking?" Cal asked.

Burkhalter shrugged. "The woman clammed up tight and asked for a lawyer. Bendick is still in the hospital, but he's babbling like Conestoga Creek." He turned to Grams. "Might make you feel a little better to know that apparently Bendick never intended to steal from the company. He had gambling losses he was ashamed to admit to your husband, took money to pay them off intending to replace it, he says, but the secretary found out and started blackmailing him. I imagine a thorough look into the books will prove she helped herself to quite a bit. Whether you'll ever get it back again is another question. The lawyers will have to sort that out."

"I still don't understand," Rachel said. "What was the point of all of the tricks they pulled? Was that Uncle Nick or Betty?"

"According to Bendick, they figured Andrea was the one person who might make sense of their doctored records, especially if she got hold of her grandfather's ledgers. The secretary was pulling the strings, blackmailing him to try and scare Andrea away. He claims he couldn't take it anymore, was coming here to tell you the truth when she attacked him."

The timing suddenly made sense. "I had the ledgers on my desk in the afternoon, when Betty stopped in. She must have thought I was on to them."

"We found the ledgers in her car," Burkhalter said. "Looks like they had some hope of locating them before you did. And he thought if Mrs. Unger gave up the idea of the inn, you'd go back to the city and leave things alone."

"Levi saw him." Emma spoke unexpectedly, her hands holding tight to the back of Grams's chair. "He finally told us. He saw Mr. Bendick here when he shouldn't of been. He wanted to tell Andrea, but he was too shy. Mr. Bendick said to meet him in Cal's place, so he could explain. Instead he pushed him."

"Levi—he was trying to tell me that night when he stood outside the house. And he followed me when I left the farm."

Emma nodded. "He meant to help. He didn't know how."

It was all starting to fall into place. "What about Rachel, the hit-and-run? Did they do that?"

"Bendick claims not," Burkhalter said. "We'll keep looking, but we may never know the truth about that."

Grams reached up to clasp Emma's hand. "At least Levi and Rachel are going to be all right."

"And Ms. Hampton," Burkhalter added. "The secretary hoped we'd think Bendick was guilty, at least long enough to let her get away." He shifted his gaze to Cal. "What made you come back, Burke? Did you suspect it was something to do with the books?"

Her breath stopped. *Why, Cal? How did you know?*

"No, not at all." He looked as if he were blaming himself. "I just..." He hesitated. "I just had a feeling."

Grams glanced at the clock and got to her feet. "Goodness, we'll be having guests here before you know it. We have to get ready." She bustled around the table, making shooing motions with her hands. "Andrea, you go and rest before you fall over. We'll take care of everything. Go on now."

People began to scatter. If Cal intended to tell her anything, it would have to wait.

The final guests left on Monday afternoon, heaping delighted praise on Three Sisters Inn. Andrea looked at Grams and Rachel. They wore grins just as goofy as hers probably was.

"We actually did it," she said. "I'm not sure I believed it would work."

"I did." Rachel patted her arm. "Thanks to you, and Grams, and Emma, and Nancy, and everyone else who helped out."

"They all said they'd be back." Grams sounded a little surprised. "Two couples have already booked for a second visit."

"You know, Grams, if you're able to recover the money Betty stole, you might not have to run the inn." She was fairly certain she knew the answer to that, but they may as well get it out in the open.

Grams looked astonished. "Not run the inn? Of course we will. This is the most fun I've had in years."

Andrea hugged her. It looked as if she'd been wrong

about a lot of things, but this was one time when she didn't mind that.

Grams patted her. "You should go and rest. You both should."

"Sounds good." Rachel stifled a yawn.

"I think I'll go out back and get some fresh air first." Andrea whistled to Barney, who scurried to her side. She patted his head. "You're my self-appointed watchdog, aren't you?" So maybe he wasn't the brightest dog in the world, but he was loyal.

Afternoon sun slanted across the lawn, filtering through the trees to touch the brilliant colors of the flowers. The sandstone patio wall glowed golden. Cal sat, just where she thought she might find him.

The dog padded quietly at her heels as she stepped off the patio and went to sit beside him.

He gave her a questioning look. "You're not turned off by the view out here after what happened to you?"

That was a nice, safe way to start what they had to say to each other. "It's still beautiful." She managed to look at the dark bulk of the old barn where it lifted above the outbuildings. "I guess there's something about nearly dying that makes you appreciate life."

"I should have been here," he said abruptly, emotion roughening his voice. "I shouldn't have left until I was sure everything was all right."

Sorrow deepened. It would have been better if he'd said he shouldn't have left at all, but he hadn't. She'd have to accept that.

"You came back in time, that's all that counts." It took an effort to keep her voice even. "What made you come back, Cal? I need to know."

He touched her hand lightly, and that touch seemed to reverberate through her. "I kept thinking I'd been unfair, leaving the way I did without talking to you. I tried telling myself I'd done it for the best, but I wasn't very convincing." He looked at her then. "I'm sorry."

She nodded, trying to dispel the lump in her throat. "That's why you came back last night? Because you'd been wrong to leave without talking to me?"

"Not exactly." His brow furrowed. "I don't know if I can explain. I just felt an overwhelming pressure to come, not to wait for morning, not to delay, just to come." His fingers wrapped around hers. "I think God was giving me the push I needed. That's the only explanation I have."

"It's all you need." The feelings she'd had when she was trapped came flooding back—the assurance of God's presence, the half-remembered dream about Grandfather. "Remember when you asked me what brought on my claustrophobia?"

He looked startled by the change of subject, but nodded.

"I found out. Some of it I remembered, some Grams told me. When I was five, I fell into an abandoned well behind the old barn."

"That would certainly do it."

She nodded. "Grandfather was out in the field with Eli and some of the men. They heard me cry. My grandfather had the men hold his legs and lower him down so that I could reach his hands. He pulled me out."

"And you didn't remember it?"

"No. I asked Grams why they didn't tell me, but apparently they thought it was better forgotten. Last night—last night I remembered, some of it at least. When I was digging the airhole, I could feel God's presence with me. Somehow I'd lost that certainty of His presence, but now it's back. And I remembered my grandfather's voice, telling me to reach farther so I could take his hand. It kept me going."

Cal held her hand between his palms, and his touch comforted her. "You feel differently about your grandfather than you did when you came."

She nodded, wanting to articulate it. He needed to understand how she'd changed. "I can see him more clearly now, and look at the situation like an adult instead of a child. He was a strong, stubborn, fallible human being, not a superhero. He loved and he made mistakes, like we all do. But the loving—that was the important part."

"I'm glad," he said simply.

She turned to face him. "Understanding that made me see that I want things to be straight between us. No long silences or things left unsaid."

"That's asking a lot. I'm not sure I'm brave enough for that."

"I think you are." She had to give him the choice. Either they could take the risk of loving each other, or he could go back to hiding from the world in his safe, peaceful sanctuary.

He looked down at their clasped hands. "You know why I left. I'd started to care about you too much. I knew the kind of life you want, and I couldn't ask you to change. It seemed better—safer, I guess—if we parted before it became too difficult." The corner of his lips curled slightly. "I was wrong. It was more than difficult. It was impossible. Andrea, I know that hiding isn't the answer for me. I choose this life because it's right for me, but I don't want it to come between us."

Something lifted inside her, and she wanted to laugh. They'd been so foolish, trying to protect themselves from falling in love. God had known better than they had.

"Funny thing about that." She couldn't help the lilt to her voice. "Being here with family again, seeing how unreasonable my boss is and how cutthroat my colleagues, made me take a serious look at what I want out of life. Maybe that security I was looking for doesn't mean I have to have the biggest office, or make the most money."

He was looking at her with so much love shining in his eyes that she didn't know whether she should laugh or cry.

"I was thinking I might start a little bookkeeping business of my own, where I could be my own boss. You know any small towns that might need a business like that?"

He slid his arm around her and drew her close. "I think we might be able to find the right place. And I know a carpenter who'll give you a good price on office furniture."

She leaned into him, feeling his strength, knowing his character and his faith. She'd been looking for security in the wrong place, just as Cal had been looking for peace in the wrong place. God was calling them to love and to dare, not to hide and be safe.

She lifted her face, meeting his lips, and knew this time she was home to stay.

* * * * *

Dear Reader,

Thank you for picking up this first story in The Three Sisters Inn series. With this series I come back to my beautiful rural Pennsylvania and the good, neighborly people who live here, especially that unique group, the Amish.

I am indebted to Chris and Jim, proprietors of the lovely and welcoming Churchtown Inn Bed & Breakfast, for giving me an inside look at their operation and answering my questions. But please don't think that any of the dangerous doings in my story happened there—they are all the product of my own imagination! I hope you'll let me know how you felt about the story. I've put together a little collection of Pennsylvania Dutch recipes that I'd be happy to share with you—some from my own family, some from friends. You can write to me at Love Inspired Books, 233 Broadway, Suite 1001, New York, NY 10279; email me at marta@martaperry.com; or visit me on the web at www.martaperry.com.

Blessings,

Marta Perry

Questions for Discussion

1. Can you understand the need for security that drives Andrea into being something of a workaholic? Have you ever felt that financial security is the most important thing in life?

2. Cal seeks isolation as a way of dealing with the terrible mistake he made. Do you sympathize with his feelings, even if you may not approve of his reactions?

3. Andrea has a close relationship with her sister, even though they no longer live together closely. Do you have a sister or a woman friend with whom you have the sort of relationship that isn't damaged by distance?

4. The struggle to heal the wounds of the past is central to this story. Have you ever gone through a similar struggle? What helped you the most?

5. Andrea begins to see that being called back home is part of being called back to God. Have you ever felt that God has led you to a particular place or situation?

6. Andrea finds comfort and insight through the Sunlight and Shadow quilt and the Scripture passages she associates with it. Has an object ever provided similar comfort and insight to you?

7. Cal finds healing in the people he meets in his new home and in making furniture. Is there an art or craft in which you can find pleasure and relief from daily tensions?

8. In the scriptural theme, we see reflected the passages of life. What particular incidents in your life are brought to mind by this verse?

9. Most Old Order Amish believe that by living separate from the world, they can serve God more clearly. Do you understand their attitude, even if you don't share it?

10. Have you ever felt that technological advances like cell phones and computers are detracting from your family time or your religious life? If so, how do you deal with that?

BURIED SINS

Draw near to God, and God will draw near to you.
—*James* 4:8

This story is dedicated to my Love Inspired Books
sisters, with thanks for your support.
And, as always, to Brian with much love.

ONE

She was being followed. Caroline Hampton pulled her wool jacket around her, fingers tight on the Navajo embroidery, but even that couldn't dissipate the chill that worked its way down her spine.

Santa Fe could be cold in early March, but the shiver that touched her had nothing to do with the temperature. She detoured around the tour group in front of the central monument of the plaza. Ordinarily, she might stop there to do a little people-watching, her fingers itching for a pad and a charcoal to capture the scene. But not when she felt that inimical gaze upon her.

Evading a vendor determined to sell her a *carnita,* she hurried across the square, only half her attention on the colors, movement and excitement that she loved about the old city. She was letting her active imagination run wild; that was all. This persistent sense that someone watched her was some odd aftereffect of shock and grief.

She stopped at a magazine stand, picking up a newspaper and pretending to study it as she used it for a screen to survey the crowd. There, see? No one was paying any attention to her, or at least, no more attention than her tousled mass of red curls and artistic flair with clothing usually merited. Everything was fine—

Her heart thudded, loud in her ears. Everything was not fine. The man had stopped at a flower stand but his gaze was fixed on her, not on the mixed bouquet the vendor thrust at him. Short, stocky, probably in his forties, dressed in the casual Western style that was so common here—he looked like a hundred other men in the plaza at this moment.

But he wasn't. She'd spotted him before—when she was leaving the gallery after work, when she returned to the apartment she and Tony had shared overlooking the river.

This wasn't grief, or an overactive imagination. This was real.

She shoved the newspaper back on the rack, hurrying toward the Palace of the Governors. It was bustling with tourists, its entrance turned into a maze by the Native American craftspeople who spread their wares there. She'd lose him in the crowd; she'd go back to the gallery....

But he'd been at the gallery. He knew where she worked, where she lived. The chill deepened. Her fingers touched the cell phone that was tucked inside the top pocket of her leather shoulder bag. Call the police?

Her stomach seemed to turn at that, emerging memories of the moment they'd arrived at her apartment door to tell her that her husband was dead. To ask her questions she couldn't answer about Tony Gibson.

She wound her way among the craftspeople, nodding to some of the regulars. Ask them for help? But what could they do? They'd want to call the police.

The knot in her stomach tightened as her mind skirted the older, darker memory that lurked like a snake in the recesses of her mind. She wouldn't think of that, wouldn't let herself remember—

She risked a quick look around. The man was no longer in sight. The tour group, apparently released by their guide, flooded to the crafts vendors on a tide of enthusiasm, swamping everything in their path.

All right. She'd slip around the Museum of Fine Arts and make her way to the city lot where she'd left her car. It would be fine. She rounded the corner.

The man stepped from a doorway to grab her arm.

Caroline took breath to scream, jerking against his grip, trying to remember the proper response from the self-defense class she'd taken last winter.

"You don't want to scream." His voice was pitched low enough to hide under the chatter of the passing crowd. Cold eyes, small and black as two ripe olives, narrowed. "Think of all the questions you'd have to answer about Tony if you did."

"Tony." Her mind seemed to skip a beat, then settle on the name. "What do you have to do with my husband? What do you want?"

"Just the answers to a couple of questions." He smiled, nodded, as if they were two acquaintances who'd happened to meet on the street. "We can stay here in full view of the crowds." The smile had an edge, like the faint scar that crossed his cheek. "Then you'll feel safe."

She summoned courage. Act as if you're in control, even if you're not. "Or you can beat it before I decide to scream."

She yanked at her arm. A swift kick to his shins might do it—too bad she didn't have heels on today. She'd—

"Just answer me one thing." His tone turned to gravel, and his fingers twisted her wrist, the stab of pain shocking her. "Where is Tony Gibson?"

She could only stare at him. "Tony? Tony's dead."

Fresh grief gripped her heart on the words. The fact that Tony hadn't been the man she thought him, had lied from the first moment they'd met—none of that could alter the fact that she grieved for him.

Incredibly, the man smiled. "Nice try. Where is he?" The fingers twisted again on her wrist—her right hand, she'd never be able to finish the project she was working on if he broke it, she—

Think. Focus. She'd pray, but God had deserted her a long time ago.

"I'm telling you the truth. Tony died over two weeks ago. His car went off the road up in the Sangre de Cristo Mountains. Check the papers if you don't believe me. They covered the story."

With a photograph showing the burned-out car that was all that was left of her month-long marriage.

"I saw it. A handy accident is a nice out for a man who'd made Santa Fe too hot to hold him." He sounded almost admiring. "Maybe the others will even buy that. Not me." He leaned closer, and she fought not to show her fear. "Your husband owes me a hundred thousand. I want it. All of it. From him. Or from you."

He released her so suddenly that she nearly fell. She stumbled back a step, rubbing her wrist, trying to find the words that would convince this madman that Tony was dead and that she could no more produce a hundred thousand dollars than she could fly.

"Tell Tony." He moved away, raising his hand in a casual goodbye. "Tell him I'll be in touch."

Before she could speak he was gone, melting away in the crowd of camera-laden tourists who rounded the corner. She stood, letting them flow past her, forcing her mind to work.

Run. That was all it would say. *That's what you do in a situation like this. You run, you find a new place, you start over.*

As she had when she'd come to Santa Fe. As she always did. She shoved the strap of her bag back on her shoulder and walked quickly in the direction of the car park. She could go north, head for Colorado, get lost in Denver. Or west to LA.

An image formed in her mind, startling her—peaceful green fields dotted with white barns, farmhouses, silos. Gray Amish buggies rattling along narrow roads.

She had a choice. For the first time in years she had a choice. She could choose to run home.

Zachary Burkhalter, Chief of Police, pulled the squad car into his favorite place to watch for drivers speeding through his town. The hardware store shielded him from the view of anyone coming east who was inclined to think the residents of tiny Churchville, Pennsylvania, weren't serious about the twenty-five-miles-per-hour speed limit.

They'd be wrong. One of his charges from the township supervisors was to make sure this isolated section of Lancaster County didn't become a speedway for tourists who were eager to catch a sixty-mile-per-hour glimpse of an Amish wagon or a farmer in black pants and straw hat plowing his field behind a team of horses.

No favors, no leeway, just the law. That was what Zach preferred—a nice, clean-cut line to enforce, with none of the gray fuzziness that so often marred human relationships.

Ruthie, with her mop of brown curls and her huge brown eyes, popped into his head as surely as if she were sitting there. She was almost six now, the light God had brought into his life, and he knew that sooner or later she'd start asking questions about how her parents died. He'd rehearsed his answers a thousand times, but he still wasn't sure they were right. He didn't like not being sure.

A blur of red whizzing past brought his attention back to the present. With something like relief at the distraction, he pulled out onto Main Street in a spray of gravel. He didn't even need to touch the radar for that one. Where did the driver think she was going in such a hurry?

He gave a tiny blare on the siren, saw the woman's head turn as she glanced at the rearview mirror. She flipped on the turn signal and slowed to pull off the road.

He drew up behind her, taking his time. New Mexico license plates—now, there was something you didn't see in Pennsylvania every day. For some reason the image stirred a vague response in his mind, but he couldn't quite place it.

Never mind. It would come. He got out, automatically checking the red compact for anything out of place.

The woman's hair matched her car, swinging past her shoulders in a tangle of curls. She had rolled down the driver's-side window by the time he neared it. Her long fingers tapped on the side mirror, as if she had places to go and people to see, and a silver bangle slid along her left wrist with the movement.

Memorable, that's what she was. He sorted through the computer banks in his mind, filled with all the data anyone could want about his township, and came up with the answer. Caroline Hampton, youngest of the Hampton sisters who owned the Three Sisters Inn, just down the road. The one who lived in New Mexico.

"I wasn't speeding, was I?" She looked up at him, green eyes wide.

So apparently they were going to start with innocence. "I'm afraid you were, ma'am. Can I see your license and registration, please?"

She grabbed the oversize leather bag on the seat next to her and began rummaging through it, her movements quick, almost jerky. Irritation, because he'd caught her speeding? Somehow he didn't think that was it.

So Caroline Hampton had come home again. She'd been at the inn at Christmas. They hadn't been introduced, but he remembered her. Any man would—that wild mane of red curls; the slim, lithe figure; the green eyes that at the moment looked rather stormy.

"Here." She snapped the word as she held out the cards.

His hand almost brushed hers when he took them.

And *there* was the thing that set his intuition on alert—her almost infinitesimal recoil from the sleeve of his uniform jacket.

Sometimes perfectly innocent people reacted as if they were serial killers when confronted by the police. It wasn't unusual, but it was something to note.

"How fast was I going? Surely not that much over the speed limit." She tried a smile, but he had the feeling her heart wasn't in it. "I'm afraid I didn't see the sign."

Amusement touched him at the effort. He didn't let it show, of course. He had the official poker face down pat, but even if he hadn't, generations of his Pennsylvania Dutch forebears had ensured that his stolid expression didn't give away much.

"The speed limit drops to twenty-five when you enter Churchville, Ms. Hampton."

Funny. In spite of some superficial resemblance, she wasn't much like her sisters. Andrea, the efficient businesswoman; Rachel, the gentle nurturer. He'd come to know them over the past year, to consider them acquaintances, if not close enough to be friends.

"You know who I am." Those jewel-like green eyes surveyed him warily.

He nodded. "I know your grandmother. And your sisters."

No, Caroline Hampton was a different creature. Jeans, leather boots, chunky turquoise jewelry that spilled out over the cream shirt she wore—she definitely belonged someplace other than this quiet Pennsylvania Dutch backwater.

"I'm on my way to see my grandmother. I guess

I got a little too eager." The smile was a bit more assured, as if now that they'd touched common ground, she had a bit of leverage.

He ripped off the ticket and handed it to her. "I'm sure Mrs. Unger would prefer that you arrived in one piece."

The flash of anger in those green eyes was expected. What wasn't expected was something that moved beneath it—some vulnerability in the generous mouth, some hint of...what?

Fear? Why would the likes of Caroline Hampton be afraid of a hick township cop?

For a moment she held the ticket in her left hand, motionless. Then she turned to stuff it in her handbag. The movement to grasp the bag shoved up her right sleeve.

Bruises, dark and angry, even though they'd begun to turn color, marred the fair skin.

"Can I go now?"

He nodded. "Drive safely."

There was no reason to hold her, no excuse to inquire into the fear she was hiding or the marks of someone's hand on her wrist. He stepped back and watched her pull out onto the road with exaggerated caution.

No reason to interfere, but somehow he had the feeling Caroline Hampton wasn't there on an ordinary visit.

"Thank you, Grams." Caroline took the delicate china cup filled with a straw-colored brew.

Chamomile tea was Grams's solution to every ill.

Declaring Caroline looked tired, she'd decided that was just what she needed.

The entrance of Emma Zook, Grams's Amish housekeeper, with a laden tray looked a little more promising. One of Emma's hearty sandwiches and a slab of her shoofly pie would do more to revive her than tea.

Rachel hurried to clear the low table in front of the sofa, giving Emma a place to deposit the tray. Since Rachel, her two-years-older sister, and Grams had turned the Unger mansion into a bed-and-breakfast inn, the room that had once been Grandfather's library was now converted into a sort of all-purpose office and family room.

The walls were still lined with books, and Grandfather's portrait presided over the mantel, but the desk held a new computer system. Magazines devoted to country living overflowed a handmade basket near the hearth, and Grams's knitting filled one beside her chair.

Caroline took a huge bite of chicken salad on what had to be fresh-baked whole wheat bread. "Thank you, Emma," she murmured around the mouthful. "This is wonderful."

Emma nodded in satisfaction. "You eat. You're too skinny."

That surprised a laugh out of her. "Most women I know would consider that a compliment."

Emma sniffed, leaving no doubt of her opinion of that, and headed back toward the kitchen and the new loaf of bread she no doubt had rising on the back of the stove.

Grams's blue eyes, still sharp despite her seventy-some years, rested on her in a considering way. "Emma's right. You don't look as well as you should. Is something wrong?"

Since there was no way she could tell just part of the story, she couldn't tell any of it. "I'm fine. Just tired from the trip, that's all. It's good to be here."

"If you'd let us know, I'd have had a room ready." Rachel was ever the innkeeper. "Never mind. It's just good to have you home."

Now was not the moment to point out that this hadn't been home to her since she was six. After beginning her prodigal-daughter return with an encounter with the police, she was just relieved things were going so well with her grandmother and sister.

Her mind cringed away from that moment when she'd heard the wail of the siren. It was not the local cop's fault, obviously, that the sound still had a power to evoke frightening memories. Still, he hadn't needed to give her a ticket. He could have just warned her.

Pay the two dollars, as the old joke went. Just pay the fine, which was likely to be considerably more than that, and forget the whole thing.

Barney, Grams's sheltie, pressed at her knee, and she broke off a tiny piece of sandwich for him and then stroked the silky head. Tiredness was settling, bone deep. She hadn't stopped for more than a few hours all the way back, pushed onward by a panic she'd only just managed to control. That was probably why she'd been speeding when she hit the Churchville village limits—that unreasoning need to be here.

She glanced across the table at Rachel, who was

curled up in an armchair, nibbling on a snickerdoodle. Neither she nor Grams had asked the question that must be burning in their minds: Why had she come?

She ought to have created some reasonable explanation during that long trip, but she hadn't. How could she begin? They didn't even know she'd gotten married.

It had seemed like such a sweet idea when Tony proposed it—to wait until they had time to make the trip east and then tell both her family and his in person about their marriage. He'd said his people lived in Philadelphia. Was that true, or was it a mirage, like so much of what he'd told her?

As it had turned out, it was just as well that her family didn't know. If they did, it would be one more reason for them to look at her with the faintly pitying, faintly censoring expression they so often wore.

Poor Caro, the one who's always in trouble. Poor Caro, the one who can't seem to get her life together.

"You look beat," Rachel said, getting up abruptly. "We can catch up on things later. I'll make up a room so you can get settled and take a nap if you want."

Grams stopped her with a slight gesture. "It occurred to me that Caroline might want to have Cal's apartment. Now that he and Andrea are living over in New Holland, it's just standing empty."

Rachel stared at her. "But...won't she want to be in the house? Why would she want to be out in the barn apartment by herself?"

When she'd been here at Christmas, Caro had seen the apartment her older sister's husband had built in one end of the barn where he'd started his carpentry business. It was simple and uncluttered, with a skylight that would give her plenty of natural light for painting. As she so often did, Grams had known exactly what she needed.

"It would be perfect." She interrupted Rachel's argument about her quarters ruthlessly. "Grams, you're a genius. I'd love to have the apartment. If you're sure— I mean, you could rent it to someone else."

"Nonsense." Grams's smile warmed her heart. "It's yours. I thought it would suit you."

Rachel still looked troubled at the idea, but she nodded. "Well, fine, then. It's clean and ready. I'll help you move your things in."

"Great." It seemed to be a done deal. She'd gone from mindless running to having a home. The thought, was oddly disorienting.

Had she really been thinking rationally when she'd packed up what she could fit in the car, arranged to ship the rest, written a note to her boss at the gallery and fled Santa Fe without a backward glance? What would Rachel think if she knew? Or worse, Andrea, the oldest of the three of them, with her sensible, businesslike approach to every problem?

She couldn't explain it, even to herself. She'd just known she couldn't stay there any longer. The urge to run was too strong. The frightening encounter in the plaza had tipped her over the edge, but the need to leave had been building since before Tony's death— probably from the moment she'd realized she'd married a man she didn't really know.

She could only be grateful Grams and Rachel hadn't asked for explanations. She didn't think she could lie to Grams, certainly not under Grandfather's judicious eyes, staring wisely from the portrait. Maybe, somehow, after a little rest, she could figure out what part of the truth she could bear to tell.

The doorbell chimed, startling her. Rachel, already on her feet, headed for the hallway, muttering something about not having any reservations for today.

A low rumble of voices, the sound of footsteps in the hallway. She set down her cup and rose, something in her already steeling. It couldn't be anything to do with her, could it?

The cop—the one who'd stopped her earlier— paused for a moment in the doorway and then came toward them.

"Chief Burkhalter wants to see Caro." Rachel, behind him, looked perplexed. "What…"

She forced a smile. "The chief has already given me a speeding ticket today. Maybe he wants to make sure I'm going to pay up."

Slate-gray eyes in a lean, strong-boned face studied her. "I'm not worried about that, Ms. Hampton." He took a step toward her, and she forced herself not to move back. "Fact is, I've had a call inquiring about you. A call from the Santa Fe Police Department."

TWO

Zach was aware of the sudden silence that greeted his words. The room was so still he could hear the tick of the mantel clock and the thud of the dog's tail against the Oriental carpet.

But there was nothing peaceful about it. Tension flowed from Caroline Hampton. And, to a lesser extent, from her sister and grandmother.

It was a shame they were here, but there wasn't much he could do about that. If he'd come to the door and asked to speak to Caroline privately, it would only have raised more questions.

The plain fact was that something was going on with this woman, and if it had to do with the law, it was his responsibility. And he knew there was something, would have known it even if not for that call from the Santa Fe P.D. He could see it in those brilliant green eyes, read it in the tense lines of her body.

"I can't imagine why you'd hear from the Santa Fe police about me. Did I leave behind an unpaid parking ticket?"

He had to admire, in a detached way, the effort it had taken her to produce that light tone.

"Not that I know of." He was willing to pull out the tension just a little longer in the hope that she'd come out with something that wasn't quite so guarded.

"I don't understand." Katherine Unger sat bolt upright in her chair, chin held high. He'd never met anyone who had the aristocratic manner down any better than she did. "Why on earth would the police be interested in Caroline?"

The words might have sounded demanding. But there was a sense of fragility underneath that made it clear he couldn't prolong this.

"Apparently your granddaughter left Santa Fe without telling her friends where she was going. They're worried about her."

Caroline's eyes narrowed. "Are you saying someone reported me missing?"

"Raised an inquiry is more like it. The police department down there was willing to make a few phone calls to allay the woman's fears." He made a play of taking his notebook out and consulting it, although he remembered perfectly well. "Ms. Francine Carrington. I gathered hers was a name that made the police sit up and take notice."

"Caroline, wasn't that your employer at the gallery?" Mrs. Unger glanced from her granddaughter to him. "My granddaughter had a position at one of the finest galleries dedicated to Southwestern art in the state."

She nodded stiffly. "Francine was my boss. And my friend."

"Well, then, why didn't you tell her where you were

going?" Rachel looked puzzled. Obviously, that was what she'd have done under the circumstances.

"Because—" Caroline snapped the word and then seemed to draw rein on her anger. "I left a letter of resignation for her, planning to call her once I got here. I certainly didn't expect her to be so worried that she'd call the police."

So she'd left what was apparently a good, successful life at a moment's notice. In his experience, people didn't do that without a powerful reason.

"Apparently she told the officer she spoke with that you'd been despondent over the recent death of your husband. She—"

A sharp, indrawn breath from Mrs. Unger, a murmured exclamation from Rachel. And an expression of unadulterated fury from Caroline. Apparently he'd spilled a secret.

"Husband?" Mrs. Unger caught her breath. "Caro, what is he talking about? Does he have you confused with someone else?"

Shooting him a look that would drop a charging bull, Caroline crossed the room and knelt next to her grandmother's chair.

"I'm sorry, Grams. Sorry I didn't tell you. Tony and I planned to make a trip east this spring, and we were going to surprise you. But he—" She stopped, her voice choking, and then cleared her throat and went on. "He was killed in an accident a few weeks ago."

It was his turn to clear his throat. "I apologize. I thought you knew all about it, or I wouldn't have blurted it out that way."

Caroline stood, her hand clasped in her grandmother's. She had herself under control now, and again he found himself admiring the effort it took her. "I intended to tell my family when I got here, but I haven't had the chance."

"I understand." But he didn't, and he suspected Mrs. Unger didn't, either.

"I'm sorry that I worried Mrs. Carrington. I'll give her a call and let her know I'm all right."

There was more to it than that. He sensed it, and he'd learned a long time ago to trust that instinct where people were concerned. Caroline Hampton was hiding something.

She'd left Santa Fe in such a rush that she hadn't even talked to the people closest to her. That wasn't a trip. It was flight.

"I'll be in touch with the department in Santa Fe, then. Let them know you're fine and with your family."

She nodded, eyes wary. "Thank you."

And that was just what worried him, he realized as he headed out the door. Her family.

Mrs. Unger had welcomed her granddaughter with open arms, as was only natural. But from everything he'd heard, she didn't know a lot about the life Caroline had been living in recent years.

It was entirely possible that Caroline Hampton had brought trouble home with her. Someone ought to keep an unbiased eye on her, and it looked as if that someone was him.

Caroline woke up all at once, with none of the usual easy transition from dreams to morning. Maybe because it wasn't morning. She stared at the ceiling in the pitch-black, clutching the edge of the Amish quilt that covered the queen-size bed in the loft of the apartment, and willed her heart to stop pounding.

She'd been doing this for so many weeks that it had almost begun to seem normal—waking suddenly, panic-stricken, with the sense that something threatened her out there, in the dark. Nothing. There was nothing. There was never anything other than her own haunted memories to threaten her.

She rolled over to catch a glimpse of the bedside clock. Four in the morning. Well, it served her right for getting onto such a crazy schedule. As it was, she'd slept twelve hours straight after that encounter with the cop and the endless explanations to Grams after the man had finally left.

Much as she'd like to blame every problem in her life on Zachary Burkhalter, she really couldn't in all honesty do that. And it wasn't his fault that just seeing him sent her mind spinning back crazily through the years, so that she was again a scared sixteen-year-old, alone, under arrest, at the mercy of— *No.* She jerked her thoughts under control. She didn't think about that ugly time any longer. She wasn't a helpless teenager, deserted by her mother, thrust into the relentless clutches of the law. She was a grown woman, capable of managing on her own. And if she couldn't sleep, she could at least think about something positive.

She shoved pillows up against the oak headboard and sat up in bed. Her new brother-in-law was certainly talented. Most of the furniture in the apartment, as well as the barn apartment itself, had been built by him. Since so much of the furniture was built-in, he'd left it here, and she was the beneficiary.

She couldn't blame Burkhalter, she couldn't blame the comfortable bed, and it was pointless even to blame the stress of the trip. She hadn't slept well in months, maybe since the day she'd met Tony Gibson.

She'd been working on a display of Zuni Pueblo Indian jewelry for the gallery, repairing the threading of the delicate pieces of silver and turquoise, set up at a worktable in the rear of the main showroom. That had been Francine's idea, and Francine had a sharp eye for anything that would draw people into the Carrington Gallery.

As usual, there was a cluster of schoolkids, accompanied by a teacher, and a few retirement-age tourists, in pairs for the most part, cameras around their necks. She'd already answered the routine questions—what did the designs mean, how valuable was the turquoise, did the Pueblo people still make it and, from the tourists, where could they buy a piece.

She gave her spiel, her hands steady at the delicate work as a result of long training. Eyes on her—she was always hypersensitive to the feeling of eyes on her—but she wouldn't let it disrupt her concentration.

The group wandered on to look at something else eventually. Except for one person. He stood in front of the table, close enough to cast a long shadow over the jewelry pieces laid out in front of her.

"Did you have another question?" She'd been aware of him the entire time, of course. Any woman would be. Tall, dark, with eyes like brown velvet and black hair with a tendency to curl. An elegant, chiseled face that seemed to put him a cut above the rest of the crowd. Even his clothing—well-cut flannel slacks, a dress shirt open at the neck, a flash of gold at his throat—was a touch sophisticated for Santa Fe.

"I was just enjoying watching you." His voice was light, assured, maybe a little teasing.

"Most people like seeing how the jewelry is put together." She wasn't averse to a little flirting, if that was what he had in mind.

"They were watching the jewelry," he said. "I was watching you."

She looked up into those soulful eyes and felt a definite flutter of interest. "If you want to learn about Zuni Pueblo jewelry," she began.

"I'd rather learn about C. Hampton," he said, reading her name badge. "What does the *C* stand for? Celeste? Christina? Catherine?"

"Caroline. Caro, for short. And you are?"

"Anthony Gibson. Tony, for short." He extended his hand, and she slid hers into it with the pleasurable sense that something good was beginning.

"It's nice to meet you, Tony."

He held her hand between both of his. "Not nearly as nice as the reverse." He glanced at the gold watch on his wrist. "I have a meeting with Ms. Carrington about the Carrington Foundation charity drive. Shouldn't take more than half an hour. Might you be ready for coffee or lunch by then?"

"I might."

"I'll see you then."

He'd walked away toward the stairs, his figure slim, elegant and cool against the crowd of tourists who'd just come in. Well, she'd thought. Something could come of this.

Something had, she thought now, shoving the quilt back and getting out of bed, toes curling into the rag rug that covered the oak planks of the flooring. It just hadn't been something nice.

She would not stay in bed. If there was one thing she'd learned in the weeks of her disillusionment about her marriage, the weeks of grief, it was that at four o'clock in the morning, thoughts were better faced upright.

She pulled her robe around her body, tying it snugly. She wouldn't go back to sleep now in any event, so she may as well finish the unpacking she'd been too tired to do earlier. She slung one of the suitcases on the bed and began taking things out, methodically filling the drawers of the tall oak dresser that stood on one side of the bed. The loft was small, but the design of closets and chests gave plenty of storage.

Storage for more than she'd brought with her, actually. She'd packed in such a rush that it was a wonder she even had matching socks. Anything she hadn't had room for had been picked up by the moving company for shipment here. When it arrived, she would figure out what to keep and what to get rid of.

Especially Tony's things. Maybe having them out of her life would help her adjust.

She paused, hands full of T-shirts. When had it begun, that sense that all was not right with Tony? Was it as early as their impulsive elopement, when his credit card hadn't worked, and they'd had to use hers? It had grown gradually over the weeks, fueled by the phone calls in the middle of the night, the money that vanished from her checking account, to be replaced a day or two later with only a plausible excuse.

The fear had solidified the evening she'd answered his cell phone while he was in the shower. He'd exploded from the bathroom, dripping and furious, to snatch it from her hands. She'd never seen him like that—had hoped never to again.

Yet she'd seen it once again on the night she'd confronted him, the day she'd realized that her savings account had been wiped out. She still cringed, sick inside, at the thought of the quarrel that followed. She'd always thought she was good in an argument, but she'd never fought the way Tony had, with cold, icy, acid-filled comments that left her humiliated and defenseless.

Then he'd gone, and in the morning the police had come to say he was dead.

She dropped a stack of sweaters on the bed and shoved her hands back through her unruly mop. This was no good. The bad memories were pursuing her even when she had her hands occupied.

She'd go downstairs, make some coffee, see what Rachel had tucked into the refrigerator. She'd feel better once she had some food inside her, able to face the day and figure out where her life was going now.

Shoving her feet into slippers, she started down the open stairway that led into the great room that filled the whole ground-level space. Kitchen flowed into dining area and living room, with its massive leather couch in front of a fieldstone hearth.

She'd start a fire in the fireplace one evening. She'd put some of her own books on the shelves and set up a work table under the skylight. She'd make it hers, in a sense.

She went quickly into the galley kitchen, finding everything close at hand, and measured coffee into the maker that sat on the counter. The familiar, homey movements steadied her. She was safe here. She could take as much time as she needed to plan. There was no hurry.

A loaf of Emma's fruit-and-nut bread rested on the cutting board. She sliced off a couple of thick pieces and popped them in the toaster. She had family. Maybe she'd needed this reminder. She had people who cared what happened to her.

She could forget that sense of being watched that had dogged her since Tony's death. She shivered a little, pulling her robe more tightly around her while she waited for the toast and coffee. She'd confided that in only one person, telling Francine about her urge to give up the apartment, get rid of Tony's things, try to go back to the way she'd been before she met him.

Her boss had been comforting and sympathetic, probably the more so because it hadn't been that many months since she'd lost her own husband.

"I know what I was like after Garner's death," she'd said, flicking a strand of ash-blond hair back with a perfectly manicured nail. "I could hardly stand to stay in that big house at night by myself. Jumping at every sound." She'd nodded wisely. "But what you need is stability. All the grief counselors say that. Don't make any big changes in your life, just give yourself time to heal. And remember, I'm always here for you."

Caro smiled faintly as the toast popped up and busied herself buttering it and pouring coffee into a thick, white mug. Dear Francine. She probably didn't think of herself as the nurturing type, but she'd certainly tried her best to help Caro through a difficult time.

The smile wavered. Except that their situations weren't quite the same. Garner had died peacefully in his bed of a heart attack that was not unexpected. Tony had plunged off a mountain road after a furious quarrel with his wife, leaving behind more unanswered questions than she could begin to count.

And it hadn't been grief or an overactive imagination. Someone had been watching her. She shivered at the thought of that encounter in the plaza. Someone who claimed Tony owed him an impossible amount of money. Someone who claimed Tony was alive.

She hadn't told Francine about that incident. She would the next time they talked. Francine had known Tony longer than she had. She might have some insight that eluded her.

Something tapped on the living room window. She jerked around so abruptly that coffee sloshed out of the mug onto the granite countertop. She pressed her hand down on the cool counter, staring.

Nothing but blackness beyond the window. The security lights that illuminated the back of the inn didn't extend around the corner of the barn.

A branch, probably, from the forsythia bush she'd noticed budding near the building. The wind had blown it against the glass.

Except that there was no wind. Her senses, seeming preternaturally alert, strained to identify any unusual sound. Useless. To her, all the sounds here were unfamiliar.

Something tapped again, jolting her heartbeat up a notch. The building could make dozens of noises for all she knew. And everything was locked up. Rachel had shown her, when she'd helped bring her things in, still worried at the idea of her staying alone. But even Rachel hadn't anticipated fear, just loneliness.

How do you know that's not what it is? You're hearing things, imagining things, out of stress, grief, even guilt. Especially guilt. Tony might be alive today if that quarrel hadn't sent him raging out onto the mountain road.

She shoved that thought away with something like panic. She would not think that, could not believe that.

Setting the mug on the countertop, she turned to the window. The only reasonable thing to do was to check and see if something was there. And she was going to be reasonable, remember? No more impulsive actions. Just look where that had gotten her.

She walked steadily across to the window and peered out. Her eyes had grown accustomed to the darkness, or maybe that was the first light of dawn. She could see the outline of the forsythia branches, delicate gray against black, like a Chinese pen-and-ink drawing.

Her fingers longed for a drawing pencil. Or a charcoal, that would be better. She leaned forward, trying to fix the image in her mind.

Something, some sound or brush of movement alerted her. She stumbled back a step. Something man-sized moved beyond the window. For an instant, she saw a hand, fingers widespread, dark and blurry as if it were enclosed in a glove, press against the pane.

Then it was gone, and she was alone, heart pounding in deep, sickening thuds.

She ran back across the room, fingers fumbling in her handbag for her cell phone. Call—

Who would she call? Grams or Rachel? She could hardly ask them to come save her from whatever lurked outside.

The police? Her finger hovered over the numbers. If she dialed 911, would Zachary Burkhalter answer the phone?

The man was already suspicious of her. That wouldn't keep him from doing his job, she supposed. It wasn't his fault that she feared the police nearly as much as she feared the something that had pressed against the window.

She took a breath. Think. The apartment was locked, and already the first light of dawn stained the sky. She had the cell phone in her hand. He...it... couldn't possibly get in, at least not without making so much noise that she'd have time to call for help.

The panic was fading, the image with it. It had been so fast—was she even sure that's what she'd seen? And if she wasn't sure, how did she explain that to a skeptical cop?

Clutching the phone in one hand, she snapped off the light. Safer in the dark. If someone were outside, now he couldn't look in and see her. She crept quickly toward the stairs, listening for any sound.

Upstairs, she pulled the quilt from the bed and huddled in the chair at the window, peering out like a sentinel. She stayed there until sunrise flooded the countryside with light, until she could see black-clad figures moving around the barn of the Zook farm in the distance.

THREE

In the light of day, sitting in the sunny breakfast room at the inn across from her sister, Caroline decided that her fears had been ridiculous. Already the images that had frightened her were blurring in her mind.

The figure—maybe a branch moving, casting shadows. What she'd thought was a gloved hand could well have been a leaf, blown to stick against the window-pane for a moment and then flutter to the ground. There were plenty of last year's maple leaves left in the hedgerow to be the culprit. Her overactive, middle-of-the-night imagination had done the rest.

"Thanks." She lifted the coffee mug her sister had just refilled. "I need an extra tank of coffee this morning, I think."

"Did you sleep straight through?" Rachel looked up from her cheese omelet, face concerned. "You looked as if you could barely stay on your feet. Grams wanted to wake you for supper, but I thought you'd be better for the sleep."

"You were right." If not for what happened when she woke up, but that wasn't Rachel's doing. Besides, she'd just decided it was imagination, hadn't she?

She'd looked in the flower bed when she went outside this morning. Crocuses were blooming, and tulips had poked inquisitive heads above the ground. The forsythia branches, so eerie in the night, were ready to burst into bloom. There had been no footprints in the mulch, nothing to indicate that anyone had stood there, looking in.

She'd clipped some sprigs of the forsythia, brought them inside and put them in a glass on the breakfast bar as a defiant gesture toward the terrors of the night.

She put a forkful of omelet in her mouth, savoring the flavor. "Wonderful. Your guests must demand seconds all the time. Did Grams eat already?" She glanced toward the chair at the head of the table.

"Emma thought she looked tired and insisted she have her breakfast in bed. When Emma makes up her mind, not even Grams can hold out."

She put down her fork. "Was she that upset because of me?" Because of all the things Caro hadn't told her?

"Don't be silly." Rachel looked genuinely surprised. "She's delighted to have you here. So am I. And Andrea. No, it's just Emma's idea of what's right. You'll see. When people are here, Grams is the perfect hostess, and no one could keep her in bed then."

"It's going well, is it?" Rachel and Grams had started the inn in the historic Unger mansion at the beginning of last summer on something of a shoestring, but they seemed to be happy with how things were going.

"Very well." Rachel's eyes sparkled. "I know people thought this was a foolish decision, but I've never been happier. Being a chef in someone else's restaurant can't hold a candle to living here, working with Grams and being my own boss."

"And then there's Tyler to make you even happier." Her sister was lucky. She'd found both the work that was perfect for her and the man of her dreams. "How is it working out, with him in Baltimore during the week?"

"Not bad." Rachel's gentle face glowed when she spoke of her architect fiancé. "Right now he's in Chicago, but usually he works from here a couple of days a week, while his partner handles things at the office."

"I'm glad for you." Caro reached out to clasp her sister's hand. Rachel deserved her happily-ever-after. She just couldn't help feeling a little lonely in the face of all that happiness.

Rachel squeezed her hand. "I shouldn't be babbling about how lucky I am when you've had such a terrible loss."

"It's all right." What else could she say? Rachel didn't know that the real loss was the discovery that Tony had lied to her, cheated her and then abandoned her in the most final way possible.

That was what happened when you trusted someone. She'd learned that lesson a long time ago. Too bad she'd had to have a refresher course.

She *could* tell Rachel all of it. Rachel would try to understand. She'd be loving and sympathetic, because that was her nature. But underneath, she'd be thinking that poor Caro had blown it again.

It was far better to avoid that as long as possible. She didn't need to lean on her sister. It was safer to rely on no one but herself.

She took a last sip of the cooling coffee and rose. "I'm going to drive down to the grocery store to pick up a few things. Do you need anything?"

Rachel seemed to make a mental inventory. "Actually, you could pick up a bottle of vanilla and a tin of cinnamon for me. Otherwise, I think I'm set. Just put everything on the inn account. Your stuff, too."

"You don't need—"

"Don't argue." Rachel was unusually firm. "If you were staying in the house, you wouldn't think twice about that."

She nodded reluctantly. There was independence, and then there was the fact that her bills were coming due with no money in her bank account, thanks to Tony. *What did you do with it all, Tony?*

She felt a flicker of panic. How could she have been so wrong about him?

Main Street was quiet enough on a Tuesday morning in March that he could patrol it in his sleep. Zach automatically eyeballed the businesses that were closed during the week, making sure everything looked all right. They'd open on the weekends, when the tourists arrived.

The tourist flow would be small awhile yet, and his township police force was correspondingly small. Come summer, they'd add a few part-timers, usually earnest young college students who were majoring in criminal justice.

He enjoyed this quiet time. He liked to be able to spend his evenings at home, playing board games or working puzzles with Ruth, listening to the soft voices of his parents in the kitchen as they did the dishes.

Families were a blessing, but worry went along with that. Look at Caroline Hampton, coming home to her grandmother with who-knows-what in her background. No matter how you looked at it, that was an odd story, what with her not telling her family she was married, let alone that her husband died. The sort of odd story that made a curious cop want to know what lay behind it.

He'd poked a bit, when he'd called the Santa Fe P.D. back to let them know that the lost sheep was fine. The officer he'd spoken with had been guarded, which just increased his curiosity.

It might have been the city cop's natural derision for a rural cop, or something more. In any event, the man had said that there was no reason to think the death of Tony Gibson was anything but an accident.

And that way of phrasing it said to him that someone, at least, had wondered.

He slowed, noticing the red compact pulled to the curb, then a quick figure sliding out. Caroline Hampton was headed into Snyder's Grocery. Maybe it was time for his morning cup of coffee. He pulled into the gravel lot next to the store.

When he got inside, Etta Snyder gave him a wave from behind the counter. "Usual coffee, Chief?"

"Sounds good."

Caroline's face had been animated in conversation, but he saw that by-now-familiar jolt of something that might have been fear at the sight of him. It could be dislike, but he had the feeling it went deeper than that.

She cut off something she was saying to the only other customer in the shop—tall guy, midthirties, chinos and windbreaker, slung round with cameras. He'd peg him as a tourist, except that tourists didn't usually travel in the single-male variety, and the cameras looked a little too professional for amateur snapshots.

"Here's the person who can answer your questions," she said, taking a step toward the counter. "Chief Burkhalter knows all about everything when it comes to his township."

He decided to ignore the probable sarcasm in the comment, turning to the stranger. "Something I can help you with?"

The guy looked as if he found him a poor substitute for a gorgeous redhead, but he rallied. "Jason Tenley, Chief. I was just wondering what the etiquette is for getting photos of the Amish. I'm working on a magazine photo story, and—"

"There isn't any," he said bluntly. He'd think any professional photographer would have found that out before coming. "Adult Amish don't want their photographs taken, and it would be an invasion of privacy to do so."

"What about from behind? Or from a distance?"

The guy was certainly enthusiastic enough. "You can ask, but the answer may still be no. Sometimes they'll allow pictures of the children, but again, you'll have to ask."

"And you'd better listen, or the chief might have to give you a ticket." Caroline, turning toward them, seemed to have regained her spunk along with her purchases.

"That's only for speeding," he said gravely. "Although I've been known to ticket for blocking public access, when some outsider tried to take photos of an Amish funeral."

"I'll remember that." The photographer didn't act as if the prospect was going to deter him.

Caroline seemed ready to leave, but they stood in front of the doorway, and he suspected she didn't want to have to ask him to move. Instead she sauntered to the bulletin board and stood staring at it.

"Well, thanks for your help." Tenley glanced at Caroline hopefully. "Goodbye, Ms. Hampton. I hope I'll see you again while I'm here."

She gave him a noncommittal nod, her attention still focused on the bulletin board.

Tenley went out, the bell jingling, and Zach moved over to stand behind Caroline at the bulletin board.

"What are you looking for? The mixed-breed puppies, or that convertible sofa bed? I should warn you that the puppies' parentage is very uncertain, and the sofa bed is one that the Muller kid had at his college apartment."

"You really do know everything about everyone, don't you?" That didn't sound as if she found it admirable. "Neither, but I've found something else I need." She tore off a strip of paper with information about the upcoming craft show at the grange hall.

She turned to go, and he stopped her with a light touch on her arm. She froze.

"I wanted to tell you that I'm sorry for bringing up your husband's death in front of your grandmother. I shouldn't have assumed she already knew about it."

"It doesn't matter." She seemed to force the words out. "I was about to tell her, anyway. If you'll excuse me—" She looked pointedly at his hand on her arm.

He let go, stepping back. *What would you do if I asked you why you're so afraid of me, Caroline? How would you answer that?*

It wasn't a question he could ask, but he wondered. He really did wonder.

Caroline drove straight to the barn by way of the narrow lane that ran along the hedgerow. She pulled up to the gravel parking space near the apartment door and began to unload. She would put her own perishables away before running the vanilla and cinnamon over to Rachel at the house. Maybe by then she'd have controlled her temper at running into Chief Burkhalter once again.

Arms filled with grocery bags, she shoved the car door shut with her hip. And turned at the sound of another vehicle coming up the lane behind her.

It was with a sense almost of resignation that she saw the township police car driving toward her. Resignation was dangerous, though. This persistence of Burkhalter's was unsettling and unwelcome. She'd dealt with enough lately, and she didn't want to have to cope with an overly inquisitive country cop.

She leaned against the car, clutching the grocery bags, and waited while he pulled up behind her, got out and walked toward her with that deceptively easy stride of his. If he were anyone else, she might enjoy watching that lean, long-limbed grace. But he wasn't just anyone. He was a cop who'd been spending far too much time snooping into her business.

Her fingers tightened on the bags. "Why are you following me around? Police harassment—"

His eyebrows, a shade darker than his sandy hair, lifted slightly. "Etta Snyder would be surprised at the accusation, since she sent me after you." He held up the tin of cinnamon. "She thought you might need this."

Her cheeks were probably as red as her hair. "I'm sorry. I thought—" Well, maybe it was better not to go into what she'd thought. "Thank you. That's for my sister, and she'll appreciate it." She hesitated, realizing that probably wasn't enough of an apology. "I am sorry. I shouldn't have jumped to conclusions about you."

Those gray eyes of his didn't give anything away. "No problem. Let me give you a hand with the bags."

Before she could object, he'd taken the grocery bags from her. Snatching them back would only make her look foolish, so instead she fished in her purse for the key.

She was very aware of him following her to the door. Knowing his gaze was on her. The combination of cop and attractive, confident male was disturbing.

"Does Etta often turn you into a grocery delivery-man? I'd think police work would be enough to keep you busy, even in a quiet place like this."

"You haven't been here on a busy Saturday in tourist season if you find it quiet," he said. "Dropping off something you forgot at the store is just being neighborly."

Neighborly. She didn't think she was destined to be neighborly with the local cop. She reached the door, key extended. The door stood ajar. Panic froze her to the spot.

"What is it?" His tone was sharp.

She gestured mutely toward the door. "I locked it when I left." Her voice was breathless. "Someone's in there."

"It doesn't look as if it was broken into. Anyone else have a key?"

She took a breath, trying to shake off the sense of dread that had dogged her in Santa Fe. She was being ridiculous.

"Of course. You're right." Her voice was still too high. "Rachel has a key. She might have brought something over from the house. I'm being stupid."

She stepped forward and ran into an arm that was the approximate strength of a steel bar.

"Probably it's one of the family." His voice was casual, but his expression seemed to have solidified in some way, and his eyes were intent. "But let's play it safe. You stay here." It was a command, not a request.

She opened her mouth to protest and then closed it again. He was right.

He put the bags down and pushed the door open gently with his elbow. She wrapped her arms around herself, chilled in spite of the warmth of the sunshine.

No one would be there who shouldn't be. The things that had troubled her after Tony's death were far away, in a different world, a different life. They couldn't affect her here.

Zach's footsteps sounded on the plank floor, softened when he crossed the braided rugs. She could follow his progress with her ears. First the living room, then the adjoining dining area, then around the breakfast bar into the kitchen. That sound was the door to the laundry room; that, the door to the pantry.

When she heard him mounting the stairs to the loft, she could stand it no longer. She sidled inside. It wouldn't take him long to look around the loft bedroom. Had she made her bed before she left? She hoped so.

Then he was coming back down, frowning at her. "I thought you were going to stay outside."

"This is my home." Brave words, but she wasn't feeling particularly brave.

"There aren't any obvious signs of a break-in. Maybe you'd better check upstairs for any money or valuables you have with you."

She hurried up the steps, brushing against him as she did so, and was a little startled by the wave of awareness that went through her.

She had made the bed, and thank goodness nothing embarrassingly personal was lying out in plain sight. Although Grams would probably find it embarrassing that she'd left things half-unpacked. Grams was a great one for finishing anything you started.

In a moment she was starting back down. "I don't see anything missing upstairs. I was in the middle of unpacking, so it's a bit hard to tell."

And the truth was that neatness had never been her strong suit. Or even a virtue, as far as she was concerned.

Zach stood at the worktable she'd pulled out from the wall, staring at the cartons that held her supplies for jewelry making. She'd wanted those things with her, because it was both a vocation and avocation. Or it would be, if she could ever find a way to make enough money to live on. She patted her pocket, where she'd tucked the information about the local craft show.

He held up a box that contained the supply of turquoise she'd brought. "This must be valuable, isn't it?"

"Fairly. I don't have any really expensive stones. I've been experimenting with variations on some traditional Zuni designs in silver and turquoise." She touched a stone, tracing its striations with the tip of her finger, longing to lose herself in working with it.

"I doubt anybody's been in here with the intent to rob you, or they'd have gone for the obvious."

She nodded, reassured. "Thank you. I—well, I'm glad you were here. I probably overreacted for a moment."

He shrugged, broad shoulders moving under the gray uniform shirt. "A break-in didn't seem likely, but we have our share of sneak thieves, like most places. It's always better to be cautious." His voice had softened, as if he spoke to a friend. "And you've been through a rough time with your husband dying so suddenly."

The sympathy in his voice brought a spurt of tears to her eyes. He was being kind, and she never expected kindness from someone in a uniform.

"We quarreled." The words she hadn't spoken to anyone here just seemed to fall out of her mouth. "We had a fight, and he drove off mad. And in the morning they came to tell me he was dead."

Strong fingers closed over hers, warming her. "It was not your fault. Survivors always think that if they'd done something differently, their loved one wouldn't have died. Don't let yourself fall into that trap."

He had a strength that seemed contagious. She could almost feel it flowing into her. Or maybe she was starting to see him as a man instead of a cop.

"Thank you." She turned away, willing herself to composure. "I appreciate your kindness."

"Plenty of people around here are ready to be neighborly. Just give them a chance."

She nodded, shoving her hair back from her face. Something lay on the breakfast bar—a white sheet of paper that looked as if it had been crumpled and spread flat again. She took a step toward it, recognizing that it was something out of place even before she reached the counter.

She stopped, staring down at the paper, unwilling to touch it. She couldn't seem to take a breath.

"What is it?" Zach covered the space between them in a couple of long strides. "What's wrong?"

She turned, feeling as if she moved all in one piece, like a wooden doll. "That letter." She took a breath, fighting down the rising panic. "Someone has been in here."

Zach grasped her arm, leaning past her to look at the paper without touching it. "Why do you say that?" His tone was neutral, professional again.

"It's a letter my husband wrote to me. I threw it away before I left Santa Fe. Someone came into the house and left it here for me."

FOUR

Zach took a moment before responding. Was this hysteria? Caroline was upset, but she didn't seem irrational, no matter how odd her reaction to that letter.

"Are you sure about that?" Careful, keep your voice neutral, don't jump to conclusions. Getting at the truth was a major part of his job, and he didn't do that by prejudging any situation.

He pulled a pen from his pocket, using the end of it to turn the paper and pull it toward them. "Take a closer look and—"

Before he could finish, she'd snatched up the letter, adding her fingerprints to whatever was already on it. Still, even if what she said was true, returning a letter that belonged to her to begin with probably wasn't a crime.

"I know what I'm talking about." Her voice was tight, and her fingers, when she grasped the letter, showed as white as the paper.

A highly strung person might imagine things after a tragic loss. Her actions in leaving Santa Fe so abruptly weren't what he'd call normal, but she might have reasons no one here knew about. That was what worried him. As well, there were those bruises he'd seen on her arms.

"Isn't it possible this was among the things you brought with you? It could have fallen out when you were unpacking." He glanced toward the stack of boxes that overflowed one of the armchairs. "Maybe Emma or your sister came in, tidying things up, found it and put it there."

That generous mouth set in a firm line, and she shook her head. "They couldn't find something I didn't bring."

Stubborn, and the type to flare up at opposition. Well, she hadn't known stubborn until she'd met a Burkhalter. He could be as persistent as a cat at a mouse hole if necessary. His fingers itched to take the letter and find out what had her so upset about it.

"How can you be so sure it's the same one?"

"Look at it," she commanded. She thrust the paper into his hands, just where he wanted it. "You can see the marks where I crumpled it up before I threw it away."

She was right. The marks were visible, even though the paper had been smoothed out before it was put on the counter. He read quickly, before she could snatch it away again, not that there was much to read—just a single page, written in a sprawling, confident hand. A love note.

Caroline grabbed it. "I wasn't asking you to read it."

"Not many men write love notes anymore, I'd think. Too easy to e-mail or text message instead." And not many women would throw such a message away, especially when the sender had just died. "He must have been thoughtful."

Her expressive face tightened. "Tony could be very charming."

That was the kind of word that could be either praise or censure. "How long were you married?"

She turned away, as if she didn't want him to see her face. "Just over a month."

At that point most couples were still in the honeymoon-glow period. "I'm sorry. That's rough."

She swung back again, temper flaring in her eyes. "You obviously think I'm imagining things. I assure you, grief hasn't made me start to hallucinate. I threw the letter away in Santa Fe. It reappeared here. Now that's real, not imagination, whatever you may think."

"Okay." He leaned back against the granite countertop, taking his time answering. "Question is, do you want to file a complaint about someone entering your apartment?"

"You said the door hadn't been forced." She frowned, the quick anger fading. "I know I locked it when I left."

"The windows are all securely closed now, with the locks snapped." A sensible precaution when no one had been living here, especially since the entrance to the apartment wasn't visible from the main house. "Let's take another look at the door."

He crossed to the entry, and she followed him. He bent to study the lock, moving the door carefully by its edge. The metalwork of the lock was new enough to be still shiny, and no scratches marred its surface.

"I don't see any signs the lock has been picked or forced."

"So only someone with a key could get in."

He shrugged. "Unless it wasn't locked. Easy enough to forget to double check it."

"I suppose." But she didn't sound convinced.

"Look, if you want to file a complaint—"

"No." She backed away from that. "I don't. As you said, there could be some rational explanation."

He studied her face for a moment. "You're not convinced." He wasn't too happy about the situation himself, but he didn't see what else he could do.

Caroline raked her fingers back through that mane of hair, turquoise and silver earrings swinging at the movement. "I'll talk to Emma and my sister. Find out if either of them was in here this afternoon. If not—" She shrugged, eyes clouded. "If not, I guess it's just one of those little mysteries that happen sometimes."

He didn't like mysteries of any size. And he was about to take a step beyond normal police procedure.

"You know, if you were to tell me what made you leave Santa Fe in such a hurry, I might be able to help you."

Her eyes met his for an instant—wide, startled, a little frightened. "How did—"

She stopped, and he could almost see her struggle, wanting to speak. Not trusting him. Or having a good reason why she couldn't trust whatever it was to a cop.

"I don't know what you mean." Her voice was flat and unconvincing.

"Neither of us believes that," he said quietly. "I can understand that you don't want to talk to me about your private life, but talk to one of your sisters. Or move into the house, where there are people around all the time."

"I'd rather stay here."

He let the silence stretch, but she had herself under control now. She didn't speak. And he couldn't help her if she wasn't honest with him.

"If you want me, you know how to reach me." He stepped out onto the flagstone that served as a walk.

She summoned a smile, holding the door to close it as if he'd been any ordinary visitor. "Yes. Thank you."

She might change her mind. Decide to tell him about it. But he suspected he was the last person she'd choose to confide in. He just hoped Caroline's secrets weren't going to land her in a mess of trouble.

They were eating dinner around the long table in the breakfast room, but Rachel had made it both festive and formal with white linens, flowers and Grams's Bavarian china. Caroline discovered that the sense of being welcomed home was a bit disconcerting. Nice to know they considered her arrival a cause for celebration, but at the same time, that welcome seemed to call for a response from her that she wasn't sure she was ready to make.

Depend on yourself. That was what life had taught her. Rachel and Andrea were her sisters, but they hadn't lived under the same roof since she was fifteen—longer than that with Andrea. They'd left their mother's erratic existence as soon as they could, as she had.

Andrea and Rachel had left conventionally for college. She was the only one who'd gotten out by way of a correctional facility.

"Great roast, Rachel." Cal, Andrea's husband of

four months, leaned back in his chair with satisfaction. "You are one inspired cook. You ought to give the guests breakfast, lunch and dinner."

"No, thanks." Rachel flushed with pleasure at the compliment. "We have enough to do as it is. I'll save my favorite dinner recipes for family."

Andrea nudged her husband. "Haven't I mentioned to you that it's not the wisest thing to praise someone else's cooking more than you praise your wife's?"

"You make the best tuna fish sandwiches this side of the Mississippi," he said, leaning over to kiss her cheek.

Andrea tapped his face lightly with her fingers, eyes sparkling in the glow of the candles. "Sweet-talking will only get you more tuna fish," she warned.

Caro's gaze crossed with Grams's, and she saw an amusement there that was reflected in her own. Marriage had taken away some of Andrea's sharp edges. She'd always be the businesslike one of the family, but Cal had softened the crispness that used to put people off a bit. You could even see the difference in the way she looked, with her blond hair soft around her face and wearing slacks and a sweater instead of her usual blazer.

Had she and Tony ever looked at each other with that incandescent glow? If so, it had been an illusion.

Cal tore his smiling gaze away from his wife. "How do you like the apartment, Caroline? If you find anything wrong, all you have to do is give me a shout."

"Everything seems to work fine." *Except for the fact that someone got in while I was out*. She wasn't sure she wanted to tell them that, wanted to have them look at her the way Zach Burkhalter had, with that doubt in their eyes. "You're obviously a good craftsman."

"He is that," Andrea said. "You have to come over to our new house, so you can see how we've fixed it up. Cal built my accounting office on one end, and his workshop and showroom are in a separate building in the back."

"I'd like to." She could hardly say anything else.

How would they react if she asked how many keys to the barn apartment were floating around in possession of who-knew-who? Would they think she was afraid—the baby sister who couldn't manage on her own?

This was ridiculous. She was a grown woman who'd been taking care of herself for years. There was just something about being back at her grandmother's table that made her feel like a child again.

"You fix up the apartment to suit yourself," Cal said. "That's only right. Maybe I ought to put up a few more outside lights." He nodded toward the wall of windows that overlooked the gardens, lit up now by the security lights on the outbuildings.

More lighting sounded like a comforting idea. "Thanks. I'm careful to lock up, but it would be nice to be able to see a bit farther outside at night."

"Why? Is anything wrong?" Andrea, sharp as ever, jumped on that immediately.

"No. Nothing."

They were family, she argued with herself. She could tell them. Except that she couldn't tell them just a piece of her troubles—she'd have to expose the whole sorry story.

"When you asked if I'd been in the apartment earlier—was it because something happened?" Rachel's voice was troubled.

Andrea's gaze whipped round to her. "You thought someone had been in there?"

"It was nothing." She should have remembered that you could never get away with half truths with Andrea. She'd always taken her role as oldest sister seriously. Far more seriously than Mom had taken motherhood, in fact.

"You had better tell us, Caroline." Grams sat very straight in the chair at the head of the table.

She began to feel like a sulky child, being told to behave by her elders. "It wasn't anything serious. I found the door ajar when I came home from the store, and I was sure I'd locked it when I left."

"You probably forgot." Andrea's response had echoes of childhood—of Andrea bringing the lunch she'd forgotten to school or picking up the jacket she'd left at a friend's house. *When are you going to be more responsible, Caro?*

"I didn't forget." She could hear the edge in her voice. "I've been living on my own in the city for years, and it's second nature to lock up."

"Even so—"

It looked as if Cal nudged his wife under the table to shut her up. "To tell the truth, I seldom locked up when I lived there. The latch is probably sticking. I'll stop by in the morning and take care of it."

"You don't need—" she began.

Cal shook his head decisively. "I'll come by."

His tone didn't leave room for argument, so she just

nodded. Apparently Andrea had found herself a man who was as strong-willed as she was.

The entrance of Emma from the kitchen put an end to anything else Andrea might have had to say. Emma placed a platter in front of Caroline. One look, one sniff of the delectable aroma, and she knew what it was.

"Emma, your peaches-and-cream cake. That was always my favorite."

"I remember, *ja.*" Emma's round face beamed with pleasure. "You'd come into the kitchen and tease me to make it when you were no more than three."

For an instant she was back in that warm kitchen, leaning against Emma's full skirt, feeling the comfort of Emma's hand on her shoulder, the soft cadence of her speech, the sense that the kitchen was a refuge from tension she didn't understand elsewhere in the house.

"I did, didn't I?" It took an effort to speak around the lump in her throat.

"You'll have a big piece." Emma cut an enormous slab and put it on a flowered dessert plate. "And there is a bowl of whipping cream that I brought from the farm this morning to top it."

Funny. Cal and Emma, the two outsiders, were the ones who made her feel most at home.

But not even their intervention could change the way the others were looking at her. Wondering. Waiting to say it. Poor Caro, always needing to be bailed out. Poor Caro, in trouble again.

"I'm sure we'll find something up here that you can use for your booth for the craft show." Rachel led the way into the attic the next day. She'd been quick to offer her help when she learned that Caroline planned to sell some of her jewelry at the show. "As far as I can tell, no one has thrown anything away in the history of Unger House. They just put it in the attic."

"I see what you mean." She'd forgotten, if she'd ever known, how huge the connecting attics were, and how stuffed with furniture, boxes, trunks and some objects that defied classification. She picked up an odd-looking metal object with a handle. "What on earth is this?"

Rachel grinned. "A cherry pitter. See what I mean?"

"I see that I wouldn't want to be the one to sort all this out."

"We'll keep that in mind." Rachel worked her way purposefully through a maze of trunks. "I'd vote for Andrea, myself. She's the organized one."

"I doubt she'd appreciate that." She followed Rachel, wondering a little at how easy she was finding it to talk to her sister. The years when their lives had gone in separate directions seemed to have telescoped together.

"Here's the screen I was talking about." Rachel pulled a triple folding screen out from behind a dusty dress form. "This would do for a backdrop, and then you could use one of the folding tables to display your jewelry."

"It's pretty dark. I'd like to find something a little brighter to draw people's attention." She hefted the screen. At least it was easily movable. She'd left most of her craft-show things to be shipped with the apartment's contents, and who knew when the moving company would finally get them here?

"I know just the thing. There are loads of handmade

quilts stored in trunks. Throw one of them over the screen, and you've got instant color."

"That would work." It was nice to have Rachel so willing to support her.

Rachel lifted the lid of the nearest trunk. "By the way, did you ever get in touch with your friend in Santa Fe? The one who was worried about you?"

And that was the flip side of support. You owed someone else an explanation of your actions.

"Yes, we had a long talk. I should have called her sooner."

She hadn't, because she hadn't been especially eager to listen to Francine, who had been appalled that Caro had, as she put it, run away.

Well, what else would you call it? That's what you do. You run away when things turn sour. She'd run from home. She'd packed up and left every time a relationship went bad or a job failed. That was always the default action. Leave.

Rachel, burrowing into the trunk, didn't respond, leaving her free to mull over that conversation with Francine. She'd told Francine what she hadn't told her family—about the man who'd accosted her in the plaza, his demands, his conviction that Tony was still alive.

Surprisingly, Francine hadn't rejected that instantly.

"Honestly, Caro, I can't say I knew Tony all that well." She'd sounded troubled. "We worked on a couple of charity events together, and I knew basically what everyone else did—that he was smart, charming, well connected. As for any problems...well, did you think he might have been gambling?"

"That would be an explanation, wouldn't it?" She'd felt her way, trying that on for size. "I never saw any proof, one way or the other."

It was on the tip of her tongue to tell Francine about the disappearance of her own money, but something held her back. Loyalty, maybe, after the wedding promises she'd made. Or just because it revealed how stupid she'd been.

"One thing I'm sure of," Francine said. "If Tony did fake his death in some bizarre need to get out of a difficult situation, he'd find some way to let you know he's still alive. You can be sure of that."

She hadn't found that as comforting as Francine had obviously intended. How could she?

"Caroline." Rachel's voice suggested that she'd said Caro's name several times. "Where are you? You look a thousand miles away." Her expression changed. "I'm sorry. Were you thinking about your husband?"

"Yes, I guess I was." But her thoughts hadn't been what Rachel probably imagined. She went to help her lift a sheet-wrapped bundle from a trunk. "I'm all right. Really." Her mind flicked back to that conversation over the dinner table. "No matter what Andrea might think."

"Oh, honey, Andrea didn't mean that the way it sounded. Don't be mad at her."

"I'm not." She found herself smiling. "You were always the buffer, weren't you? Sometimes you'd side with me, sometimes with Andrea, but usually you were the peacemaker."

"Well, somebody had to be." Smiling back, Rachel began unwrapping the sheet.

The urge to confide in Rachel swept over her, so strong it startled her. She could tell Rachel, because Rachel had always been the understanding one.

But it wasn't fair to ask Rachel to keep her secrets. And she wasn't ready to risk trusting anyone with her troubles and mistakes.

"There." Rachel unrolled the quilt, exposing the vibrant colors of the design. "It's a Log Cabin quilt, one of the ones Emma's mother made, I think."

"It's beautiful." She touched the edge carefully, aware of the damage skin oils could do to aged fabric. "If you're sure you don't mind—"

"It's as much yours as mine," Rachel said. "There might be something you'd like better, though." She pulled out the next bundle, this one wrapped in a yellowing linen sheet. "Goodness, this is really an old one." She squinted at a faded note pinned to the fabric. "According to this, it was made by Grandfather's grandmother in 1856."

"It should be on display, not stored away." The sheet fell back, exposing the quilt. She frowned. "That's an unusual design, isn't it?"

Rachel pointed to the triangles that soared up the fabric. "Flying geese, combined with a star. I don't know enough about antique quilts to have any idea." She folded the sheet back over it.

Caro felt an almost physical pang as the quilt disappeared from view. To actually hold something that had been made by an ancestress almost 150 years ago—had she been as captivated by color and pattern as Caro was? Had she lost herself in her work, too?

"Well, it certainly needs to be better preserved than

it is. If you don't mind, I'll see if I can find out how it should be kept."

"Be my guest. That's more your domain than mine." Rachel laid the bundle gently back in the trunk.

Taking the Log Cabin quilt, Caroline stood, stretching. "I'll run this down first and then come back and help carry the—"

Her words died as she passed the attic window. She hadn't realized that from this height she could see over the outbuildings to the barn, even to the walk that curved around to the door of her apartment. And to the flash of movement on that walk.

"Someone's out there." She grabbed Rachel's arm, her heart thudding. He was back. The person who'd been in the apartment was back.

"Who? What?" Rachel followed her gaze. "I don't see anyone."

"Someone was there, by the apartment. I'm not imagining things, and I'll prove it." She thrust the quilt into Rachel's arms and rushed toward the stairs.

FIVE

"I told you not to call him." Caroline glanced from the police car that was bumping down the rutted lane to the barn to her sister.

Rachel looked guilty but determined. "If someone's been prowling around your apartment, it's a matter for the police. I know you had a bad experience—"

"That has nothing to do with it." Rachel didn't know just how bad that experience had been, and she had no intention of telling her. "I suppose it won't hurt to talk to the man, but there's nothing he can do."

Zach Burkhalter slid out of the police car, probably in time to hear what she said. Or, if not, he was quick enough to guess at the conversation based on their expressions. He came toward them with that deceptively casual-looking stride.

"You reported a prowler, Rachel?" He glanced from Rachel to her, as if measuring their responses.

"My sister was the one who saw him. She'll tell you all about it." Rachel turned away, as if leaving.

"Wait a minute." Caro grabbed her arm. She was the one who'd called the man. At least she could stick around for moral support. "You're not going."

Rachel pulled free. "I'd better get back to the house and tell Grams everything is okay. Unless you want to have her out here, that is?"

"Of course not." That was hardly something she could argue, but her sister was going to hear about this later.

"Just tell Zach what you saw. You can trust him. He's one of the good guys." Rachel turned and hurried off around the corner of the barn toward the house.

Caro glanced at the police chief, catching a bemused expression on his face. "You look surprised. Didn't you know my sister thought that about you?"

He shrugged. "Plenty of people don't have good opinions of cops. Like you."

The words dismayed her. Was she really that obvious? "I don't know what you mean."

"Ms. Hampton, I suspect you'd be about as happy to see a snake on your doorstep as to see me. But your sister called me to report a prowler, so I'm here."

She would definitely pay Rachel back for this one. "You'd better come in, but I don't know what you can do."

"Why don't you let me figure that one out."

He followed her inside, and the apartment immediately felt smaller than it should. A police chief, even one in a place as small as Churchville, probably found that air of command useful. She just found it unsettling.

She gestured toward the leather couch and sat down opposite him on the bentwood rocker. "There isn't much to tell. Rachel and I were up in the attic of the house, and I glanced out the window. I hadn't realized that you could see the barn clearly from that height. I saw—"

She hesitated. Had she seen enough to be sure?

"Go ahead." He leaned forward. "Just tell it the way you saw it, without second-guessing."

She nodded. That was exactly what she'd been doing. "I could see the end of the walk that leads to the apartment door. I had a quick glimpse of a figure heading toward the door, but he was out of sight almost before it registered."

"Male?"

She closed her eyes, visualizing. "I said 'he' but I'm not sure. It was just an impression of a human figure, probably male, wearing something dark—maybe a jacket."

The face of the man in the plaza came back to her. He'd worn a denim jacket. Would that have looked dark from a distance?

"Did you see anything else? A vehicle, maybe?"

"No. I ran down the stairs, hoping I could get a look at him. But the dog started to bark, and that could have alerted him. By the time Rachel and I got here, there was no one in sight. And before you ask, it doesn't look as if anyone got inside." She shrugged. "I told you it was a wild-goose chase. That was why I didn't want Rachel to call."

He seemed to have a face designed for expressing doubt. "Did you hear a car when you were running out here?"

"I don't think so." She frowned. "There was traffic going by on the road, but I don't think I heard anything any closer. You're thinking that if there really was a prowler, he'd have had to come in a vehicle."

He seemed to suppress a sigh. "Ms. Hampton, maybe you shouldn't be so quick to assume you know what I'm thinking."

There didn't seem to be anything to say to that. "You seem to be on a first-name basis with my sister."

His gray eyes seemed to lighten with his smile. "I've known her a bit longer. And what I was thinking was that it's not a wild-goose chase if you believe you saw someone who shouldn't be here."

She looked down at her hands, clasped in her lap. "All right. Thank you."

"Still, it makes me wonder." His voice was as easy as if they talked about the weather. "What makes you so quick to decide someone's been prowling around?"

Her hands twisted, tight against each other. He thought he'd boxed her in. "Anyone would think that if—"

He was shaking his head. "You're afraid of something. You don't want to talk about it, but you are."

"That's ridiculous." She forced herself to meet his eyes. "I'm not afraid."

"You left Santa Fe in such a hurry that you didn't even tell your friends where you were going. That looks a lot like running. And if someone's been prowling around here, maybe you had a good reason to run."

She couldn't seem to come up with any rational explanation that would satisfy him and send him away.

He leaned toward her, and she stiffened to keep from pulling back. "Caroline, if you're in trouble, the best thing you can do is tell me about it. Because sooner or later I'll find out what's going on, and it would be better coming from you than from someone else."

She wanted to deny it, but she couldn't. She seemed to be poised on the edge of a high dive, ready to plunge into the unknown. "Someone threatened me."

"When? Where?" He didn't raise his voice, but she felt the demand in it.

"In Santa Fe." She pressed her hand to her head. "The day before I left there. He'd been following me, and I kept telling myself it was my imagination, but then he grabbed my arm." Something seemed to quake inside her.

Zach reached out, brushing the sleeve of her shirt back. "He left marks."

She looked down at the bruises, faint and yellow now.

"Did you know him?"

"No. I'd never seen him before I noticed him outside the gallery where I worked. And later outside my apartment building."

"So this man you didn't know accosted you. Why didn't you yell for help? Call the police?"

That was what a normal person would do, she supposed. "Because of what he asked me." She took a breath, feeling as if she hadn't inhaled for several minutes. "He wanted to know where Tony was. My husband. And he'd been dead for over two weeks."

"If he didn't know—"

She shook her head. "He knew about the accident. He said that faking your own death was a good thing to do if Santa Fe was getting too hot for you. And that other people might believe it, but he didn't."

"That took you by surprise?"

She stared at him. "Of course it did. My husband was dead. The police told me—showed me pictures of the burned-out car." She had to force the rest of it out. "The fire—there wasn't much left, but I had a funeral."

His face didn't give anything away. He might believe her. Or he might be thinking she was crazy.

"This man. What did he want?"

"He said Tony owed him a hundred thousand dollars." She closed her eyes for a moment. "He wanted it. From Tony or from me."

"Why did your husband owe him the money?" He was relentless. Of course he would be. He was a cop.

"I don't know that he did. I don't know anything about it. I just knew the man scared me and I wanted to get away." She lifted her hands. "I can't tell you what I don't know, any more than I could have told him."

"Okay." He touched her hand in a brief gesture of…what? Sympathy? Or did he just want to calm her enough to get more answers? "Was your husband a gambler?"

"I don't know." She thought of the missing money. If she told him, it would lend credence to the gambling theory.

But she couldn't. She didn't want him, or anyone, to know just what a sham her marriage had been. "I suppose that makes sense. I can't think of any other way he could owe that much."

Zach leaned back, giving her a little breathing room.

"So this guy scared you. And instead of going to the police or your friends, you left."

At least he hadn't said "ran away." She met his eyes. "I have family here. With my husband dead, I wanted to be with them."

"I can understand that." But his eyes held a reservation. "So, this man. You're an artist. Can you draw his face?"

She blinked at the sudden change of subject when she'd expected more questions about Tony, more about why she'd left. "I did a sketch right after it happened, but then I tore it up. I'll do another. Would that help?"

"It can't hurt. I can fax it to the authorities in Santa Fe, see what they can come up with. If he's in my territory, I want to know it."

"You think he's the one who got into the apartment." She hadn't expected him to agree with her. "How could he have had access to that letter?"

He shrugged. "The letter might somehow have gotten into the things you packed."

"Or he might have searched the apartment in Santa Fe. Found it in the trash." That made sense. "He'd been outside the building. I saw him."

"Possible." His tone didn't give her a clue as to whether he believed her or not. "About that sketch?"

The thought of him watching over her shoulder while she drew that face tightened her nerves. "I'll work on it and drop it off at your office later this afternoon."

"Fine." He rose. "But you don't need to bring it to me. I'll stop by for it."

If she argued, it would sound as if having him here bothered her. It did, but she'd rather he didn't know.

Of course, he'd probably figured it out already.

"All right." She stood, too, walking him to the door as if he were any ordinary visitor. "Thank you."

"Just one other thing." He paused, holding the door. She looked at him, eyebrows lifting.

"What he said about your husband. Do you think your husband is still alive, Caroline?"

"No." The word was out, harsh and emphatic, before she thought. She took a breath. "No, I don't."

Zach nodded. Then he stepped outside and closed the door behind him.

Caroline spread a length of black velvet over the metal folding table Rachel had unearthed for her to use at the craft show. All around her, the cement block fire hall echoed with the clatter and chatter of a hundred-plus crafters getting ready for the event. The doors opened at nine, and everyone wanted to be ready.

The aroma of coffee floated from the food stand at the end of the row. Maybe, once she was set up, she could ask the stall holder next to her to watch the stand while she went for a quart or two of caffeine.

She smoothed out the cloth with her palms and bent to retrieve the first box of jewelry. Silly, maybe, but being here made her feel at home. Veterans of craft shows were a friendly bunch, and Caro had found that no matter what they made, they shared a common bond.

That love of creating something beautiful with your hands was hard to describe but very real. She might not personally understand the drive to make, for instance, the ruffled toilet paper covers that the stand across the walkway offered, but she did know the pleasure of creation.

She began laying out an assortment of turquoise and silver bracelets and necklaces, loving the way they glowed against the black velvet.

"Those are gorgeous." The basket weaver in the next booth leaned over to have a closer look. "I just might end up spending more than I make today. Where did you learn to work with turquoise? Not around here."

Caro shook her head. "Out West. Santa Fe, mostly. The Zunis do some amazing work with silver and turquoise."

"Gorgeous," the woman said again, then grinned and held out her hand. "Karen Burkhalter. Welcome. This is your first time here, isn't it?"

"Yes." She returned a firm grip. Blond hair, hazel eyes, an open, friendly face with a turned-up nose—the woman was probably about her age, she'd guess, with the engaging air of someone who'd never met anyone she didn't turn into a friend.

Burkhalter was a common enough name in Pennsylvania Dutch country. Chances were she didn't even know Zach.

"I'm Caroline Hampton."

"Oh, sure. Your grandmother is Katherine Unger. Everyone knows her youngest granddaughter came home."

"I'm not sure I care for that much celebrity."

Karen grinned. "It's a small township, and most of

us have known each other since birth. You'll get used to how nosy we all are about each other's lives."

That was an uncomfortable thought. "You have a great assortment of baskets." She picked one up, admiring the stripes worked into the weaving with different colored reeds. "Is this an egg basket?"

Karen nodded. "They're popular with the tourists, not that any of them are likely to be gathering eggs."

"As long as they buy." That, after all, was the whole point. If she could make a decent amount on the show, she wouldn't feel as if she dangled on a financial precipice.

"The crafters' slogan," Karen agreed. "It's hard to tell whether people will be in a buying mood or not. Usually around here the shows start pretty small, but as we move on into spring, sales pick up."

"If there's a good turn-out—" She stopped, because a familiar figure was headed toward Karen's booth.

Zach Burkhalter. It wasn't a coincidence, then, about the name.

Karen leaned across the table to hug him. "Hey, it's about time you're showing up. I want my coffee."

In jeans and a flannel shirt instead of a uniform, Zach should have looked less intimidating. He didn't.

His gaze shifted from Karen to her, his hand still resting on the other woman's shoulder. His wife? There was absolutely no reason for that possibility to set up such a negative reaction in her.

"Caroline. I didn't realize you were jumping into the craft-show circuit."

"You two know each other, then," Karen said. "I

should have known. Being the police chief gives my brother an unfair advantage in meeting newcomers."

"You're Zach's sister." And that shouldn't give her spirits a lift, either. The marital status of Zach Burkhalter was nothing to her.

"The woods are full of Burkhalters around here," Zach said easily. "Mom and Dad each had five siblings, and then they had another five kids to add to the mix."

"You're lucky you just have sisters," Karen said. "Brothers can be such a pain." She threw a light punch toward Zach's shoulder.

"Well, I'd better finish setting up." Standing there looking at Zach was not conducive to her peace of mind. It just made her remember those moments when she'd told him far too much. And had had the sense that he understood even more than she'd told.

Things had been quiet since then. With a little luck, they'd stay that way, and she could stop wondering what had become of that sketch Zach had faxed to Santa Fe.

Caro pulled the quilt from its protective covering and slid her metal chair over next to the screen to climb on.

"Let me give you a hand." Before she could say no, Zach had rounded her table. He took the end of the quilt, lifting it over the screen as she unfolded it. "Is this how you want it?"

"Yes. Thanks." *Now please go away, and let me get back to concentrating on the craft show.* It wasn't Zach's fault that he made her tense up, sure that at any moment he'd say something about the prowler. Or the sketch.

He drew the quilt down behind the screen, and she smoothed it out with her hand. It fit perfectly, falling to table height in a cascade of rich, saturated color.

"That's lovely, too." Karen took a step back to admire the quilt. "Handmade. Are you selling Amish quilts, as well as your jewelry?"

Caro shook her head. "I just wanted it to give me a colorful background. My sister found a treasure trove of quilts stored in the attic."

She started to climb down from the chair, and Zach caught her hand, steadying her. Solid, strong, like the man himself. He wouldn't be a featherweight in a crisis, but she guessed he'd expect a lot from anyone he got close to.

"It's a lot better than looking at cement-block walls," Karen said. "Would you mind if I borrowed the idea and did something similar in my booth?"

"Not at all." She took a step away from Zach's supporting hand. She didn't need support. She did quite well on her own.

"As long as you don't try to borrow the quilt, as well," Zach said.

His sister shot him a haughty look. "I happen to have quilts of my own. Although I'm not sure I have anything as fine as that one." She fingered the stitches, so even and neat that it was hard to believe they were done by hand.

Quilts seemed to be a safe topic of conversation. "Do you know anything about restoring antique quilts? I found one that dates back to pre–Civil War, and I'd love to get it into shape to display."

Karen shook her head. "Not me. The person you

should talk to is Agatha Morris. She's a local historian and something of an authority on old quilts and coverlets."

"To say nothing of being the mother of Churchville's mayor, as she'll be sure to point out to you," Zach said.

"You just don't like Keith because he tried to get the county commissioners to cut your budget. And he only did that because you gave him a speeding ticket."

Zach shot his sister a warning glance. "Don't go around saying things like that, Karrie."

She wrinkled her nose at him, in the inevitable manner of little sisters everywhere, and then nodded. "Okay. But how about my coffee? And bring one for Caroline, too. She looks thirsty."

"You don't need—" she began, and then lost track of what she was going to say under the impact of Zach's rare smile.

"Cream? Sugar?" His eyes warmed, almost as if he knew he'd had an effect on her.

"One sugar. No cream." If he kept looking at her that way, she might have to reassess her opinion of him.

Straight-arrow cop, she reminded herself as he sauntered off toward the food stand. Maybe he was one of the good guys, as her sister said, but that didn't mean he could ever understand someone like her.

Zach hadn't intended to spend so much of the day at the craft show. Usually he came by whenever Karrie was exhibiting, just to help her set up or tear down. Somehow today he didn't feel like heading for home.

Ruthie was here, somewhere, with his mother. Mom had been teaching her how to crochet, and that had sparked her interest in Aunt Karrie and the craft show. Thank goodness his daughter had Mom around to handle the girlie stuff. He could teach her how to catch a fish, but he was pretty clueless in some departments.

He rounded the corner of the row of stalls and spotted his sister, leaning across her table to show something to a customer. Beyond her, he could see Caroline, also busy with a customer. Her face was animated as she displayed a bracelet, draping it across her wrist.

His gut tightened at the thought of those bruises on her right wrist. Nobody should treat a woman that way. On the other hand, could he believe her account of how it had happened? He wasn't sure, and until he was, until he knew for sure she wasn't involved in something criminal, he'd tread carefully where Caroline was concerned.

He'd expected to hear something from that Santa Fe P.D. by now about the sketch he'd faxed them, but so far they'd been silent. His request was probably pretty far down on their priority list.

As he neared the stand, he realized that the person she was talking to was that photographer, Tenley. Interesting that the guy was still around. Something about him hadn't quite rung true from the first time Zach saw him.

Zach picked up one of Karen's baskets and turned it over in his hands, trying to separate their conversation from the buzz of talk that surrounded them.

From what he could make out, Tenley was intent on asking her out, and Caroline was equally intent on selling him something. It seemed to be a bit of a stand-off.

"Are you planning to buy a basket today?" Karen

turned to him as her customer moved off, dangling a bag containing one of her smaller items.

"Why would I do that, when you keep giving them to me? If you want your family to buy, you'll have to stop being so generous."

"Small chance of that," Karen said. "You have a birthday coming up, don't you? What kind of basket would you like?"

Caroline, seeming to overhear, turned to smile at his sister. "That's what it is to be related to a crafter. As far as I can tell, my sisters like my jewelry, but they could hardly tell me anything else, could they?"

"Of course they like it," Tenley put in quickly. "Your adaptation of Zuni designs is inspired. As a matter of fact, I'll take the bracelet for *my* sister's birthday."

"Excellent." Caroline beamed. "I'll gift wrap it for you."

"You seem to know a lot about Southwestern design." Zach leaned against the table. "You spend some time out there?"

Tenley looked startled at the direct question, but then he tapped his camera. "My work takes me all over the place. I know enough about Zuni art to appreciate it." He turned quickly back to Caroline, pulling out his wallet. "Don't bother to gift wrap it. I'll take it as it is."

In a moment he'd paid, claimed his package and moved off. Frowning, Caroline turned to Zach.

"You just scared off a customer. I might have been able to sell him something else."

He shrugged. "If someone's scared of the police, it's usually because they have something to hide."

Her reaction to that might have been invisible to

anyone else, but not to him. He was looking for it, and he saw it—that faint withdrawal as muscles tightened, the slightest darkening of those clear green eyes. Caroline took that personally. That meant she had reason to do so.

And that meant he should do the thing he'd been putting off for days—run a check on her and find out just what it was about her past she wanted to hide.

"Caroline, here's just the person you should talk with about your quilt." Karen's voice had both of them jerking toward her. His reaction was mild annoyance, but he suspected Caroline's was relief.

The annoyance deepened when he found Agatha Morris and her son Keith standing behind him. He jerked a nod. "Mrs. Morris. Mayor. Enjoying the show?"

Agatha gave him an icy nod before turning to Caroline. With her iron-gray hair worn in a style reminiscent of Queen Elizabeth, her sensible shoes and the flowered dresses she wore whatever the season, Agatha was a formidable figure. "I understand you're Katherine Unger's granddaughter." The words sounded faintly accusing.

Caroline smiled, extending her hand. "I'm Caroline Hampton."

Agatha glanced toward the jewelry, seeming not to notice the gesture, but Keith slid past her to take Caroline's hand. "Welcome to Churchville, Caroline. I'm Keith Morris."

You couldn't fault Keith's manners, even if you did think him too much of a featherweight to be mayor of any town, no matter how small. Maybe the voters had been bemused by the freckles and aw-shucks smile.

"My son is the mayor of Churchville, you know." Agatha never missed an opportunity to mention that. She cast a critical eye at the quilt. "Karen says you had some question about an antique quilt. If it's that one, it's not nearly old enough or unique enough to be of interest."

Caroline seemed to stiffen at the slur. "No, I'm familiar with the history of this one. I found an older quilt in the attic at Unger House, one made by my grandfather's grandmother during the 1850s. It has an interesting design—a combination of flying geese with a star. I'd like to know more about it."

He expected Agatha to welcome the opportunity to show off her expertise. She could be counted on to launch into a lecture at a moment's notice.

But she didn't. She stood perfectly still for a moment, staring at Caroline as if she'd said something off-color. Then she shook her head. "I'm afraid that would hardly be worth pursuing. Such quilts are rather common—of no historic interest at all." She turned away. "Come, Keith."

With an apologetic glance at Caroline, Keith followed his mother down the crowded aisle between the tables.

"Well." Karen sounded as surprised as he was. "I've never known Agatha to miss an opportunity to tell someone exactly how to do almost anything."

Caroline shrugged. "Obviously she didn't think my quilt was worth her time."

Could be. But it was still odd. Odd things seemed to collect around Caroline Hampton, for some reason, and he'd like to know why. Until he did—

"Daddy!" A small hurricane swept toward him, and Ruthie launched herself as if she hadn't seen him for months, instead of hours. "Grammy said you'd be here."

He lifted her in a hug and then set her back on her feet, overwhelmed as he so often was at the way God had brought her into his life. He ruffled her dark-brown curls as his mother came up behind her.

"Ruthie, you shouldn't run off that way." Mom divided a smile among them, sounding a little out of breath.

"Mom, Ruthie, this is Caroline Hampton."

Ruthie caught the edge of the table with two probably grimy hands and propped her chin on it, eyes wide as she looked at the jewelry. "Wow. Did you make those?" Before Caroline could answer she'd ducked down and crawled underneath the table cover, to pop up on the other side next to Caroline, beaming at her. "I love your jewelry. Someday I want to have earrings just like yours."

Smiling, Caroline bent down to let Ruthie touch the dangling spirals of silver that danced from her earlobes. His daughter touched the earring, making it shimmer.

"Ruthie, come out of there now." Instead of waiting for her to crawl under, he reached across the table and lifted her in his arms. "You know better than to go into someone's booth without permission."

But that wasn't what put the edge in his voice. It was the sight of his daughter leaning against Caroline.

Caroline took a step back, her face paling as if he'd struck her. He was sorry. He didn't want to hurt her.

But like it or not, Caroline was a question mark in his mind. He'd give the woman the benefit of the doubt in any other instance, but not where his daughter was concerned.

SIX

"You really don't need to stay and help me." Caro opened the trunk of her car, peering around the lid at Rachel, who'd walked over from the house to help unload.

"It's no problem." Rachel seized a cardboard box. "Andrea wanted to stop by the show to help out, but she's swamped, with tax time approaching."

Rachel seemed to take it for granted that the family would pitch in to help. A wave of guilt moved through Caro. She hadn't done much in the way of helping Rachel or Grams since she'd been back, had she?

"You have the inn guests to worry about. I'm sure you should be prepping for tomorrow's breakfast or something." She tried to take the box from Rachel's hands, but her sister clung to it, laughing a little.

"Don't be so stubborn, Caro. How many times did I say that to you when we were kids?"

"Pretty often. But not as often as Andrea did." She had to return the smile. "That used to be her theme song when it came to me, as I recall."

"And how you resented it."

Yes, she had. She'd wanted to do things for herself,

but Andrea, always trying so hard to be the big sister, had been just as determined to help her.

Until Andrea had left, headed for college, and she hadn't come back. And then Rachel had taken off in her turn. She could hardly blame them for that, could she? Except that it had left her alone with Mom.

"I'm a big girl now. I've been doing my own loading and unloading from craft shows for a long time—" She looked up, startled, at the sound of another vehicle pulling up behind hers.

Rachel lifted a hand in greeting to Zach as he slid out of the car. "Okay," she said. "I'll let Zach do the heavy lifting, then."

"Glad to," he said, approaching. "Believe me, my sister has me well trained in the whole craft-show routine." He reached past her to begin sliding the folding screen out of the trunk.

Rachel gave her a quick hug. "Come over and we'll raid the refrigerator for supper whenever you're hungry. Grams won't want much after her tea party today." She scurried off, leaving Caro alone with Zach.

He hefted the screen. "You want to get the door?"

"Actually I want to know why you're here. Again." She unlocked the door as she spoke. After all, there was no point in refusing a hand in with the heavy things.

"There's something I need to talk to you about." He stepped inside and set the screen against the wall.

She paused on the doorstep, stiffening. Whatever it was, she didn't want to hear it.

Zach leveled that steady gaze at her. "You look like you're tensed up for bad news."

"I can't imagine that you're here to bring me good news." She shoved the door shut behind her, aware of the alien scent almost before she registered it mentally. Her head lifted, face swiveling toward the kitchen.

"Coffee smells good." Zach's tone was casual, but his eyes were watchful.

"Yes." She had to force the word out. "But I didn't make any coffee this morning."

He frowned, and then crossed the dining area and rounded the breakfast bar into the kitchen. "Somebody did. The pot's still on—the mug rinsed and left in the drainer. You sure you didn't start it and then forget about it?"

"I didn't make any." She walked to the counter. "I didn't have time."

Her mind flickered to those moments when Zach had brought her coffee at the show. When she'd actually felt as if they were becoming friends. It had been an illusion, like so much else.

"I don't see how you can be sure," he began.

"Because I know what I did and what I didn't do." She snapped the words. "Because even if I had planned to make coffee, I wouldn't have made that kind. Hazelnut. I don't care for hazelnut. I don't have any in the house." Her voice was starting to veer out of control, and she caught herself, breathing hard.

"Who does like hazelnut?" he asked quietly. As if he knew the answer already.

"Tony." It took an effort to swallow. "Tony liked hazelnut. It was all he drank."

He stood for a moment, watching, and then came to

plant his hands on top of the counter. "Tony's dead. So how could he be here, making coffee in your kitchen?"

She sank onto the stool, her legs trembling. "He couldn't. He couldn't."

"You said the man who threatened you claimed he was alive." His gaze was so intent on her face that she could feel its heat.

"He was wrong. Or lying. Tony died in that accident. If he hadn't, he'd have come back."

Or would he? He'd already taken everything she had. What else was there to bring him back?

"There's more to it than that." Zach's frown deepened. "That man, the one you drew the sketch of—"

"You've identified him." Her gaze flew to his face. "You know who he is."

"I had a call from the police in Santa Fe. They're familiar with him. His name is Leonard Decker. Mean anything to you?"

She shook her head slowly. "Leonard Decker. I don't remember hearing the name. What was he to my husband?"

"Good question." Zach ran his hand absently along the edge of the granite counter. "According to the officer I talked to, Decker has a finger in a lot of pies, some of them probably illegal. They've never managed to convict him, but he's been under suspicion several times—fencing stolen goods, gambling, that sort of thing."

"Gambling." She repeated the word, her heart sinking, mind flashing back to Francine's speculations about Tony.

"You have any reason to think your husband was involved in anything like that?"

She started to shake her head, but something about that steady gaze seemed to stop her. She didn't trust Zach. But what was the point of denying something he already seemed to guess?

"There was money missing from my account." She pushed her hair back from her face, aware of the throbbing in her temples. "That was what we fought about, that last night. He'd cleaned out my savings and checking accounts."

"Did he say why he needed the money? Give any explanation?"

"No." His only defense had been in cruel, cutting remarks. "He seemed to think I'd cheated him in some way, letting him believe I had family money when he married me." That accusation had left her numb and speechless. How did you defend against that?

Zach was silent for a moment. Maybe he knew there was nothing safe to say in response to that.

Finally he spoke. "Sounds as if Decker is nobody to fool around with, but I can't see what he'd hope to gain by following you here. Unless he thinks you're going to lead him to Tony."

"Tony is dead." But not even she was convinced by her tone.

"If he isn't, would he contact you?"

"I don't know." Everything she'd thought she knew about Tony had turned out to be a lie. How could she be sure of anything? "Francine—my friend at the gallery—thinks so, but she doesn't know everything."

"You haven't told anyone else about the money."

"No."

She thought he was going to ask why she'd told him, but he didn't. He just shook his head.

"Why not move into the house? Nobody would risk paying you any surreptitious visits there, to make coffee or anything else."

"That's why." She pressed her palms down on the counter. "Don't you see? If Tony is alive, I have to know. If he's trying to get in touch with me, I have to be where he can reach me."

"Why wouldn't he just walk in, then? Why fool around leaving you hints that he's been here?"

"I don't know. We didn't exactly part on the best of terms. Maybe he's afraid I'm being watched. I don't understand any of it." She squeezed the back of her neck, trying to press the tension out. It didn't help. "But I can certainly understand why you didn't want your daughter anywhere near me."

"Ruthie." His gaze was startled, but she could read the truth there. To do him credit, he didn't try to deny it. "She's my child. I can't expose her to—"

"A criminal like me?"

"I was going to say to someone who might be surrounded by trouble."

"You're a wise parent." If her own parent had been a little wiser, how different might her life have been? She wouldn't have ended up spending those terrifying months in the juvenile detention facility. She wouldn't have carried that around with her for years. Or would she have ended up the same even with good parents?

"I try. Picking it up along the way, I guess. I'd like to help you, Caroline. I'm not sure what I can do."

"There's nothing anyone can do." Anyone except Tony. If he was alive, sooner or later he'd show himself. And then what? Did they try and put the pieces back together again, when there'd been nothing real to begin with?

"Get in touch with me if anything happens that worries you." He put his hand over hers where it lay on the granite, and his grip was warm and strong. Reassuring. "If there's any way I can help you find the truth, I will."

Tears stung her eyes, and she blinked them back. "Thank you. But I don't think—"

His grip tightened. "Promise me. If there's a way I can help, you'll tell me."

There wasn't a way anyone could help, so the promise was a small price to pay to be left alone.

"All right. I promise."

What would anyone have to gain by making Caroline believe that her husband was still alive? Zach drove slowly down the bumpy lane to the main road, his mind still revolving around that odd incident with Caroline.

And the coffee. Was that remotely believable? He came back to the same question. If someone had gone into the apartment while she was out today and deliberately made a pot of her husband's favorite coffee—

It was stretching his imagination to believe that much, but Caroline's reactions had seemed genuine.

So get back to the question. If someone had done that, what would his or her purpose have been? To taunt Caroline about her husband's death? To accuse her, in some veiled way, of contributing to that death? Or to make her think that her husband was still alive?

To think that. Or fear that. He didn't believe for a moment that Caroline had told him everything about that relationship. Had there been reasons why she might have feared Tony Gibson? He hadn't forgotten the bruises on her wrist, and his natural skepticism had made him question her explanation.

Still, the Santa Fe police had identified Leonard Decker, and there was a certain logic that would fit Tony Gibson into the picture with him.

On the other hand, and he had the feeling he was now on his third or fourth hand, Caroline could have engineered the entire story herself. He didn't pretend to be a psychologist, but he'd seen enough human behavior in his years as a cop to know it was seldom entirely rational, especially when driven by strong emotion. If Caroline felt guilty in regard to her husband's death, she might find a way to punish herself through these hints that he was still alive.

He knew a bit about survivor's guilt himself— enough to accept that such a thing could happen, at least. He couldn't forget—would never forget—that Ruthie might not be an orphan if he hadn't failed to do his duty. He ripped his thoughts away from that. This was about Caroline, not him.

There was the least-palatable explanation—that Caroline had set up the situation deliberately, for reasons that had nothing to do with her feelings for Tony. Think about it. What would have happened if Zach hadn't come along just when he did?

Rachel would have helped her carry the craft show

things into the apartment, and Rachel would have been the one to hear the odd story about the coffee. She wouldn't have his skepticism. She'd rush to her little sister's defense.

He couldn't dismiss the niggling fear that this could all be part of some elaborate scheme to get money out of Katherine Unger. She'd do anything if she believed her granddaughter needed her help.

Caroline could be telling the exact truth as she understood it, in which case she deserved sympathy and help, not suspicion. But he was a cop, and he couldn't stop thinking like one. In any event, the only way to help anyone, innocent or guilty, was to find the plain, unvarnished truth.

He pulled up to the curb at the police station, glancing at his watch. It was past time he went home for supper, but he had something to do first.

He unlocked the door and went inside. It was just as well that everyone was gone. He didn't want anyone listening to the conversation he was about to have, always assuming he could reach the detective in Santa Fe he'd talked with earlier.

A few minutes later he was leaning back in his chair, listening to Detective Charles Rojas of the Santa Fe P.D., who had still been in his office thanks to the time difference.

Rojas seemed to have decided to be a bit more forthcoming. "The thing is, and this is strictly in confidence, Gibson had been under investigation in the weeks before his death."

"Investigation of what?"

Silence on the line.

"Look, someone has been dropping hints to his widow that Tony Gibson is still alive. If through some bizarre chance that's true, it's in both our interests to work together on this." He waited.

A rustling of papers sounded through the phone. "You've got a point there." There was a thud, as if Rojas had propped his feet up on his desk. "Okay, here's the story. Gibson was thought to have been involved in a fairly sophisticated series of scams."

"Thought to be? If he tried to con someone, they ought to be able to identify him."

"You don't know these people." Rojas's voice betrayed his frustration. "Upper-crust society, whatever you want to call them. They don't relish letting the world know they've been made fools of. Seemed like most of them would rather write off the con and forget about it. No one would identify Gibson directly. Maybe, eventually, we'd have pinned it to him, but he drove his car off a cliff first."

"You're sure about the identification of the body?" That was the crux of the matter, as far as he was concerned.

Silence again for a moment. "The car burned badly. Very badly. So far we haven't received complete confirmation as to the driver's identity. But Tony Gibson was seen driving the car about fifteen minutes before it went over the cliff. I think it's a pretty safe assumption that he was the one in the bottom of that ravine."

"If he's dead, who would want his widow to think he was still alive? And why?"

"Good question. And a good reason for you to keep an eye on the Hampton woman. Thing is, she had access to the kind of people Gibson liked to con, through that gallery job of hers. There's no reason to believe she was involved, but there it is. She could have been."

A few more exchanges, and he was off the phone, but he sat staring at it. Rojas had talked because he wanted to keep a line on Caroline Hampton, however tenuous.

If Tony Gibson had been involved in the kind of scam Rojas suspected, he had been a dangerous man to know. Caroline might be an innocent victim.

Or she might be involved.

He knew more now than he had fifteen minutes ago, but he couldn't say that it made him any happier.

Caroline had never intended to go to church that Sunday. However, she hadn't been prepared to combat Grams's calm assumption that of course she'd go to the worship service at the small church across the road from the inn.

If she'd thought about it, she might have come up with some reason, or rather some excuse, that wouldn't hurt Grams's feelings. As it was, she'd nodded, smiled and tried to close her eyes and ears to the service.

She had a deal with God. He left her alone, and she left Him alone. She didn't want to change that, but she also didn't want to try to explain it to Grams.

The churchyard gate creaked shut as they exited, and she took a breath of relief. It was over, with no harm done. Next Sunday she'd be ready with an excuse.

Grams linked arms with her as they started across the street, Rachel behind them, chatting with Andrea and Cal. "What did you think of the service, Caro?"

Caroline glanced back at the stone church that had stood within its encircling stone wall for the past two hundred and fifty years. The green lawn was splashed with color from spring dresses—in Churchville, people obviously still believed that worship called for their best. In their own way, they were as traditional as the Amish, meeting in someone's house or barn today.

Realizing Grams was looking at her for an answer, she managed a smile. "Nice." That didn't seem to quite cover it. "I noticed Zach Burkhalter with his little girl." She was sorry the moment the words were out. She didn't want to sound as if she were asking about him.

"Not just Zach," Rachel commented as they reached the sidewalk in front of the inn. "I think the Burkhalters have expanded to two pews, haven't they? That was his mother, sitting on the far side of Ruthie."

"I met her at the craft show. And Karen was very helpful." Did that sound stilted? Probably. She hadn't been able to forget the way Zach had snatched his little girl away from her, as if her troubles were contagious.

"They're all helping him raise that child," Grams said. "It's a lovely thing to see."

"He's not married?"

Grams shook her head. "Oh, no. Ruthie is the daughter of some friends he made when he was stationed in the Middle East with the military. The parents were killed very tragically, and Zach adopted her."

She blinked. "I didn't realize." She'd been making assumptions that were amazingly far from the truth.

"She's a dear little thing." Grams smiled. "And so appropriately named. Ruth, finding a home in an alien place."

She nodded, the story from long-ago Sunday school days coming back to her. Apparently this little Ruth had found the place where she belonged, thanks to Zach.

She'd figured him for a straight arrow, but he obviously wasn't the cold fish she'd assumed. She'd seen that when she'd seen him with his little girl.

"I have a casserole in the oven." Rachel headed back toward the kitchen the moment they got inside. "We'll be ready for brunch in a few minutes."

"I'll help you." Caroline followed her to the kitchen, catching the look of surprise that was quickly hidden by Rachel's smile.

Fair enough. She hadn't been much help to anyone since she'd come back, obsessed as she was with her own problems. It was time she changed that.

"What can I do?" She washed her hands quickly and turned back to Rachel, who was pulling a casserole from the oven, her cheeks rosy.

"There's a fruit salad in the fridge that goes on the table. I'll just stick the rolls in to heat up for a minute."

She nodded, lifting the glass bowl from the fridge and removing the plastic wrap that covered the assortment of melon, blueberries, pears and bananas. "Lovely."

Rachel shrugged. "Everything's left over from the guest breakfast. Makes Sunday easier—otherwise I'd never make it to church."

That would suit her. Maybe she could offer to stay behind and make dinner next week, but somehow she didn't think Grams would agree to that.

"Your schedule is pretty tight. I didn't realize what went into running a B & B."

"It's worth it." Rachel's expression softened. "I feel as if I came home when I came back here. Mom certainly never gave us anything that was remotely like a home."

She carried the fruit in and set it on the table. Rachel, following her, took silverware from the massive corner cupboard.

"You and Andrea had more memories from this place than I did. I was too young to have built up much." Was that jealousy she felt? Surely not.

"Doesn't mean you can't start now." Rachel set the table swiftly. "I saw Keith Morris talking with you after service. What do you think of our mayor?"

"Not bad, but his mother tried to freeze me dead with a look. Guess she doesn't fancy me for her baby boy."

Rachel grinned. "She's more likely to snub you for insulting her knowledge of local history."

"On the contrary, I asked very humbly for her advice. About the 1850s quilt we found, remember?"

"You mean she didn't take the opportunity to lecture you on the history of the township?"

"Just said it was 'of no historic interest' and walked off."

"She probably hates that someone else owned it. You ought to talk to Emma's mother-in-law about it. She knows everything there is to know about quilts."

"Who knows everything about quilts?" Grams came into the room, followed by Andrea and Cal.

"Levi Zook's mother. Caro wants to find out more

about the flying geese quilt that grandfather's grandmother made."

Grams nodded. "I think there might be something about it in some family letters your grandfather collected. I'll see what I can find."

"Thanks, Grams. I'd like that. I'm not sure why it fascinates me so. I actually had a dream the other night about the geese." She'd been flying with them, soaring away from everything that held her back.

"You must have the quilt, since it seems to have touched you," Grams said gently.

Tears stung her eyes, sudden and unexpected. "You shouldn't—I mean, it might be valuable, whatever Mrs. Morris thinks."

"It's yours." Grams pressed her hands. "We'll say no more about it."

She looked from face to face, seeing…what? Love? Acceptance?

Panic swept through her for a moment. She'd told herself that what they thought of her didn't matter—told herself that she was better off relying on no one but herself.

It wasn't true. The longer she was here, the more she became enmeshed in something she'd given up a long time ago.

And the more she risked, when they would eventually let her down.

SEVEN

So that was what Caroline was hiding in her past. Zach had known instinctively there was something.

He leaned back in his desk chair, hearing its familiar squeak, and stared at the computer screen in front of him. It hadn't even been that hard to find—the record of the arrest of the then-sixteen-year-old Caroline Hampton, charged in the robbery of a convenience store in Chicago.

Sixteen. The criminal record of a sixteen-year-old shouldn't be so readily available, but sometimes the legal system didn't work the way it should.

He frowned, leaning forward to read through the report again, filling in the blanks from experience. Two older boys had actually done the crime, roughing up the elderly store owner in the process. Caroline had apparently been the driver, waiting outside.

His frown deepened. She was only sixteen, and she hadn't been inside the store when the crime was committed. A good attorney should have been able to get her off with probation, with her record wiped clean at the end of it. That hadn't happened. Why?

There were only two possibilities that he could see.

Either she was far more involved than the bare facts would indicate, or she hadn't had decent representation. Hard to believe that the Unger family wouldn't have hired a lawyer for their granddaughter, but it was always possible they hadn't known. It was the mother who had custody, not Fredrick and Katherine Unger.

He flipped through the text, looking for the resolution of the case. And found it. Caroline Hampton had been confined in a teen correctional facility until her eighteenth birthday.

Pity stirred in him. That was pretty harsh, given her age and the fact that she didn't seem to have been in trouble before. Still, everyone's life wasn't an open book on the Internet. There might have been—must have been—other factors involved.

He drummed his fingers on the scarred edge of the desk. No one had mentioned this serious blip in Caroline's past, at least not to him. Well, they wouldn't, would they?

Still, he'd give a lot to know what the family knew about it. And what they thought about it. Was that a piece of whatever had kept the sisters apart for so long?

More to the point, could it be related to what was happening now? On the surface that seemed unlikely, but he'd learned not to discount anything.

There was a tap on his office door, followed by the creak as it opened. The face of young Eric Snyder appeared. He looked worried, but that meant nothing. Snyder always looked worried, as if he were completely convinced that whatever he decided to do, it was wrong.

As it usually was. He'd never seen anyone with less

natural aptitude for police work, but the boy's uncle was a county commissioner, which meant the police force was stuck with him for the moment.

"What is it, Snyder?"

"Ms. Hampton is here to see you, Chief."

Rachel? Or Caroline? Well, he didn't want either of them to see the report in from of him. He saved the file and clicked off.

"Ask her to come in."

A moment later Caroline sidled through the door, looking around as if expecting trouble. "I wanted to see you," she said abruptly.

He stood, noting the by-now-familiar flinch away from him. Well, now he knew why. That aversion of hers to anyone in a uniform could be a sign of guilt. Or it could be the reaction of injured innocence.

"I promised I'd let you know if anything else happened."

"I'm glad you remembered." He reached out to pull his lightweight jacket from the coatrack. "No reason why we have to stay inside on such a nice day. Let's take a walk and talk about it."

Her sigh of relief was audible. "Good." She turned, moving back through the door so quickly that it was almost flight.

He followed, glancing at Snyder. "I'll be back in a few minutes. Take any calls that come in."

The boy gulped, nodding. He didn't like being left in charge of the office. Again, not a desirable quality in a cop.

Caroline was already out on the sidewalk, waiting in the sunshine, hugging her dark denim jacket around

at seemed to be made
d her silver and tur-
r.

p as she strode away
warmer than yester-
it? Did you enjoy the

comment to relax her, but
opposite effect. She jammed her
ckets of the denim jacket, her shoul-
g. "Yes. It made my grandmother happy
all of us in church with her."

That sounds as if you wouldn't go on your own."

She shot him a look that bordered on dislike. "That doesn't have anything to do with why I came to see you."

He shrugged. "Just making conversation." But he really did wonder where she was spiritually. It seemed as if Caroline could use a solid underpinning of faith right now. "Sorry. Something else has happened?"

They'd walked past the bakery before she nodded. Reluctant. Caroline was always reluctant when it came to him. He understood that a little better than he had before he'd unearthed the story of her past.

"I got something in the mail." Her hands were shoved tightly into her pockets. "I can't explain it."

He came to a halt at the bench in front of Dora's Yarn Shop, planting his hands on its back and looking at her. The pot of pansies next to the bench gave a bright spot of color to the street. "You plan to let me see it?"

She didn't want to—that much was evident in the

apprehension that darkened those gr[...] had she come? She was perfectly capa[...] that promise he'd screwed out of her.

Maybe she'd run out of excuses. Prob[...] the least of a number of bad choices.

She yanked an envelope from her pocket an[...] it toward him. "This came in today's mail. [...] know what to do about it."

He took it, handling it by the edges automaticall[...] business-size envelope, Caroline's name and addre[...] printed in computer-generated letters. No return ad-dress. The postmark read Philadelphia.

She shifted her weight from one foot to the other impatiently. "Open it."

She obviously already had, no doubt further ob-scuring any fingerprints that might have survived the handling of the postal service, unlikely as that was. He teased out the enclosure—a folded fragment of copy paper with something hard inside it.

He flipped it open. The briefest of notes in block printing. A small key held fast to the paper with a strip of cellophane tape.

"It's a safe-deposit key," she said impatiently. "I'm sure of it."

He studied the key more closely. "I think you're right. It may be possible to find out what bank it's from, especially if it's in Philadelphia."

"It will be." She stared at the note as if it were a snake. "Tony had family there. Anyway, he said he did. I never met them. Never even talked to them. Tony was going to tell them about our marriage when we came east. That's what he said, anyway."

He nodded slowly, frowning at the words on the page. "Is this your husband's handwriting?"

She took a breath, the sound ragged, as if she had to yank the air in. "I think so."

Black letters. Three short words. She couldn't be positive from that small a sample, but she probably had a fairly good idea who wrote those words.

"For my wife."

What had possessed her to tell Zach, of all people? He stood there on the sidewalk looking at her, gray eyes intent and watchful, as if weighing every word and gesture. Judging her.

Still, what choice did she have? Who else would she tell?

A brisk breeze ruffled the faces of the pansies, making them shiver, and she shivered with them. The truth was that she couldn't keep this to herself any longer. She didn't know what to do or how to find out what it meant.

She certainly couldn't take this to Grams. And while Andrea's cool common sense might have been welcome, she'd have to tell her everything for the story to make any sense.

At least Zach already knew. She might not be happy about that, but it was a fact.

He nodded, murmuring a greeting to someone passing by. The woman sent a bright, curious gaze Caro's way, and she turned, pulling the collar of her jacket up, as if that might shield her from prying eyes.

Zach folded the envelope and pushed it into his jacket pocket. He took her arm.

"Let's go to the café and have some coffee. You look as if you could stand to warm up. And it won't be crowded this time in the afternoon."

He steered her down the street, turning in to the Distelfink Café. The door closed behind them, and they were enveloped in the mingled aromas of coffee, chicken soup and something baking that smelled like cinnamon.

"See? Empty." Zach led her past several round tables to a booth against the far wall. The tables were covered with brightly painted stencils of the Distelfink, the stylized, mythical bird that appeared on so much Pennsylvania Dutch folk art.

She slid into the booth. The wooden tabletop bore place mats in the same pattern, and the salt and pepper shakers were in the shape of the fanciful birds.

Zach folded himself into the booth and nodded toward the elderly woman who'd emerged from the kitchen. She was as plump and round and rosy as one of the stenciled figures herself. "Two coffees, Annie."

"Sure thing, Zach. How about some peach cobbler to go with it?"

"Sounds good."

She disappeared, and Caroline shook her head. "I don't want any cobbler. I just want to talk about this—"

"If we take Annie up on the peach cobbler, she won't be popping out of the kitchen every two seconds to offer us something else." He turned a laminated menu toward her. "Unless there's something else you want."

She shook her head. The menu, like everything else,

was decorated with stenciled figures—birds, stars, Amish buggies. She flipped it over.

"I see they still offer a free ice cream to any child who memorizes the Distelfink poem."

He smiled, his big hands clasped loosely on the table in front of him. "Sure thing. It's a rite of passage in Churchville. You must have done it."

"Oh, yes." Memory teased her. "As I recall, I insisted on standing up on my chair and declaiming it to the entire café. I'm sure I embarrassed my family to no end."

"I imagine they thought it was cute. Ruthie's been working on it every time we come in. She'll probably get the whole thing mastered by the next time we're here."

His doting smile told her that he wouldn't be embarrassed by anything his little daughter chose to do.

Annie bustled out of the kitchen with a tray, sliding thick white coffee mugs and huge bowls of peach cobbler, thick with cream and cinnamon, in front of them.

"Anything else I can get for you folks?"

"We're fine, Annie. Thanks." Something in his voice must have indicated this wasn't the time for chit-chat. The woman vanished back into the kitchen, leaving them alone.

Caro took a gulp of the coffee, welcoming the warmth that flooded through her. But it wouldn't— couldn't—touch the cold at her very center; the cold that she'd felt when she saw the letter.

Zach didn't pull the envelope out again, and at some level she was grateful. "Have you showed it to your family?"

"No." She thought of all the reasons why not. "I haven't told them much about Tony. Showing them this would mean I'd have to tell them everything. They'd be upset, and I don't want that."

That wasn't all the reason. She knew it. Maybe he did, too. He watched her, the steady gaze making her nervous.

"Your choice," he said finally. "Question is, do you really think it's genuine?"

She stared down into her mug, as if she could read an answer there. "It looks like Tony's handwriting. I'm not an expert."

"If someone had a sample, it wouldn't be that hard to fake three words."

"I guess not." She pressed her fingertips against her temples, as if that might make her thoughts clearer. "What would be the point of faking it?"

He shrugged. "What would be the point of sending it, even if it's genuine?"

"Exactly." At least they agreed on that. "It's not as if the sender is asking me to do anything. It's just a key."

"Seems like if someone sends you a key, they intend you to use it to open something," he said mildly.

"I get that." She found she was gritting her teeth together and forced herself to stop. "It's postmarked Philadelphia. As I told you, Tony said he had family in Philadelphia."

"That's a link. Still, it's odd, assuming this is from your husband—"

"I don't think we—I can assume that. It could be a fake, or it could be something Tony wrote that someone else sent me."

"Why?"

"I wish I knew." She rubbed her temples again. "Just when I get a line of logic going, it falls apart on me. Why would anyone do any of the things that have happened?"

"Good question." He was silent for a moment, but she felt his gaze on her face. "Should I assume you want to get to the bottom of this?"

"What I want is to be left alone, but it doesn't look as if that's going to happen." *You could run,* the voice whispered at the back of her mind. *You could run away again.*

But she couldn't. At some point, for a reason she didn't quite understand, she'd stopped running. She was here. She was staying. So—

"Yes," she said, surprised by how firm her voice was. "I want to get to the bottom of this whole thing. But how?"

She looked up at him when she asked the question, finding his gaze fixed on her face. For a moment she couldn't seem to catch her breath. He was too close.

Don't be ridiculous, she scolded herself. *He's clear across the table.* But he seemed much nearer.

"I might be able to identify the bank where the safe-deposit box is." He frowned a little. "And with some more information, I might also be able to trace any family he had. What did he tell you about them?"

"Not much." Almost nothing, in fact. Now that seemed suspicious, but at the time, it hadn't surprised her. After all, she didn't see much of her family, so why would she expect something else from him?

"What exactly?" He sounded remarkably patient,

and he pulled a small notebook and pen from his pocket, setting it on the place mat in front of him.

She took a breath, trying to remember anything Tony had mentioned. Trying not to look at those strong, capable hands that seemed to hold her future.

"He was named for his father, I know he said that. Anthony Patrick Gibson. He mentioned a married sister once. I helped him pick out a piece of jewelry for her birthday."

Zach scribbled some unreadable notes in a minuscule hand. "Any idea where in Philadelphia? City or suburbs?"

She shook her head slowly. Incredible, that she knew so little about the man she'd married. "I suppose it would all have been in his PDA, but that was in the car with him. I had the impression they lived in the suburbs, maybe on the Main Line."

Nothing definite, she realized now. Tony had managed to convey, just by how he looked and acted, that he'd come from money. Society, the kind of people who learned which fork to use before they learned their ABCs.

Zach raised his eyebrows. "Money?"

"I guess that's what I thought." That was what Tony had thought about her, wasn't it? That Unger House, the grandfather who'd been a judge, the great-grandfather who'd served in the state senate, had automatically conveyed an aura of wealth and privilege.

"Look, we just didn't talk about our families all that much. I suppose, if I'd thought about it, that it was odd I didn't know more, but we were going to see them when we came east. I'd have found out all about them then." She blinked, realization dawning. "But there was an address—there must have been, because the police said they'd notified his family. I don't know how I could have forgotten that."

She'd been numb—that was the only explanation. She'd gotten through those days in a fog of misery, not thinking much beyond the next step she had to take.

"Well, that gives us a place to start, anyway. I'll make some calls and see what I can come up with."

She looked at him, wondering what was really going on behind that spare, taciturn expression. "I...I don't know. Maybe I should just let it drop. I mean, without anything else to go on, how much can I expect to learn?"

He put his hand over hers where it lay on the table, startling her. "Let me tell you what just happened. You've been stewing about that letter since the mail came this morning, working yourself up until you had to tell someone about it. And then you told me, and saying it out loud relieved some of the pressure. So now you're thinking that it's not so bad after all."

"Are you setting up as a psychiatrist on the side?" She couldn't help the edge to her voice, because he'd nailed it. That was exactly how she'd felt—that pressure to tell someone, that feeling that she couldn't carry it another minute by herself. And then the release, as if by saying the words, she'd convinced herself it wasn't so bad.

"Normal human nature," he said. His fingers tightened around hers. "Don't kid yourself, Caroline. There's something going on here. Something—" he paused, as if wanting to be sure he had the right word

"—something malicious about all this. I think we need to find out what's behind it. We, not you."

His gaze was steady on hers. Questioning: Will you let me help you? Will you trust me that much?

She bit her lip. She didn't trust, not easily, and certainly not a cop. But she was running out of options, and Zach Burkhalter was the best choice she had.

Something winced inside her, but she managed to nod. "All right. Will you help me find out what's going on?"

His grip eased fractionally. "Okay. Assuming I can get any answers by then, let's go to Philadelphia tomorrow."

For better or worse, they were committed.

Caroline's hand clenched on the car's armrest, but her nerves had nothing to do with the traffic Zach encountered as he took the off-ramp from the interstate toward the Philadelphia suburb where he'd determined the bank was located.

He shot a sideways glance at her. "Don't you trust my driving?"

"It's not that." She released the armrest and slid her palms down the creases of her lightweight wool slacks. Well, not hers, exactly. The art of dressing to impress a banker was Andrea's style, so she'd borrowed the tan pantsuit from her sister. Even brightened with her favorite turquoise necklace, it didn't look like her.

"There shouldn't be any difficulty accessing the safe-deposit box." Zach glanced in the rearview mirror before swinging around a double-parked car. "You brought all the paperwork, didn't you?"

"Yes." Not only had Zach found the bank, he'd determined what she'd need in order to prove her right to claim the contents of the box. "I'm not worried about that. I was just thinking about how fast you were able to get the information. And how much more of my life must be spread out there for anyone to see who has the skill and the authority."

He glanced at her, his gaze shielded behind the amber sunglasses he wore. "You don't care much for authority, do you?"

That tightened her nerves, but she managed a cool smile and what she hoped was an equally cool tone. "My sisters would tell you that I've always been the rebel."

Whether he wanted to or not, Zach exuded authority. Even today, wearing khakis and a dress shirt instead of his uniform, there was no mistaking that. It was present in the calm gray eyes, the strong planes of his face, the whipcord strength of his long muscles. He was a man who would always take control, whatever the situation.

"You were the one to test all the rules, I guess." He frowned at the GPS system on the dashboard, as if assessing its accuracy.

With their mother the rules had been whatever capricious notion had taken her fancy at the moment, but Caroline had no desire to get into that. "Pretty much. Andrea was the perfect one, of course, and Rachel was the peacemaker. The role of rebel was open, so I took it."

His hand flexed on the gearshift. "I was the oldest in my family. Does that make me perfect?"

"It probably makes you think you are."

"Touché." His glance flickered to her. "Does that rebellion of yours extend to God?"

Her stomach clenched. How had she given so much away to this man that he could even guess that?

"Let's just say I never want to get too close." She hoped he'd let it go at that, but suspected he wouldn't.

"I've felt that way at times, I guess when things were going fine and I thought I could handle everything on my own. Unfortunately in my line of work I get plenty of reminders that I can't, and I have to come running back, looking for help."

She stared out the window, not wanting him to see her face. "And do you get it?"

"Always. But not always in the shape I think it should come."

What about not at all? But she didn't want to hear his answer to that, did she?

The GPS beeped, its metallic voice announcing a right turn at the next intersection. Zach jerked a nod toward the unit.

"Be nice if God was like that, always alerting you when you were about to make a wrong turn. I guess sometimes you just have to make the mistake first before you're ready to admit it."

"So God stands back and lets you sink." She snapped the words out before she could censor them.

"Was that what you felt happened when you landed in trouble as a teenager?"

She winced as if he'd hit her. So he knew. Well, was that so surprising?

"I take it my so-called criminal record is out there for anyone to see."

"Not anyone." His voice softened, as if he knew he'd hurt her. "The records should have been sealed, given your age, but mistakes happen."

"Don't they, though." And always, it seemed, in someone else's favor. "Well, now that you know, I'm surprised you're helping me. Or maybe you're not. Maybe you're just trying to prove I've done something wrong."

He wouldn't find anything else, no matter how much he searched her past. She'd been scrupulous since the day the gates of Lakecrest closed behind her. No matter how hard he looked, he wouldn't find so much as a parking ticket—nothing to involve her with the police, ever.

Until now. Maybe Zach wasn't dressed like a cop today, but that was who he was, bone deep.

"Look, I didn't want to try and hide the fact that I'd checked into your past. That doesn't mean I'll let it influence my attitude toward you."

Her chin lifted. "As far as I can tell, your opinion of me was set from the first moment you saw me. This was just confirmation, wasn't it?"

He didn't answer for a moment, occupied with turning into a parking lot. The bank parking lot, she realized, and her stomach churned.

Zach pulled into a parking space and switched off the ignition. Then he turned to her. He pulled off the glasses, and his eyes were intent on her face, so intent that it seemed her skin warmed.

"I'm probably not going to convince you of this, but

I came into the situation thinking you're innocent, not thinking you're guilty. Of anything. The fact that you got into trouble as a teenager doesn't have any bearing on anything." He paused, and a muscle twitched at the corner of his mouth. "Except, maybe, that it's made you prejudiced against anyone who wears a uniform, including me."

He didn't give her time to come up with an answer. He just turned and slid out of the car.

EIGHT

"Now, Mrs. Gibson, if you've brought all the proper documentation, I'll just need to have a look at it."

Caroline swallowed hard as she pulled papers from her shoulder bag and handed them to the bank officer. She couldn't stop being aware of Zach, sitting in the chair next to her. Anyone looking at the scene might think them a married couple, applying for a home loan or something else equally routine.

But there was nothing ordinary about this situation. She glanced at the man behind the desk—Dawson, that was it. His name had gone into her brain and fallen back out again as quickly, a tribute to the nerves that seemed to be doing a tango at the moment.

Thin and balding, with a fussy, precise manner, he peered so intently at each document that it seemed the bank itself, with its arched ceilings and echoing tile floors, might tumble down around them if he didn't get this right.

"Mrs. Gibson—"

Her fingers clenched. "Ms. Hampton, please. I kept my birth name."

"Yes, of course." He frowned as if that were, in itself, a suspicious action. "If you don't mind waiting a few minutes, I'll just need to make copies of these."

She nodded, leaning back in the chair with an assumption of ease. Mrs. Gibson. No one had ever called her that, other than a desk clerk at the hotel where they'd checked in for their three-day honeymoon. She'd never had a chance to get used to the name. Maybe that was just as well.

Zach seemed perfectly ready to wait as long as it took. He had a gift of stillness, and for an instant her fingers itched for a pad and pencil to capture that.

But if she did, what would it say about the man? The ease of his long body in the chair, the carefully neutral expression on his face—everything about Zach seemed designed to camouflage his emotions, assuming he had any.

Well, of course he did. She was being ridiculous. She'd seen him with his daughter, and there was certainly no lack of feeling there. The fact that he wore that shuttered look with her just confirmed that he saw her as part of his job, nothing else.

He knew about her past. She still had difficulty swallowing that. To do him justice, he hadn't let that prejudice him against her, but she suspected it had to weigh in the balance he kept in his mind, with each new fact he learned about her being dropped on the scale.

He didn't know everything. Her stomach twisted. He couldn't. The ugliest thing about that time would never appear in any official report, even though it had left an indelible stain on her life.

She straightened her back, clasping her hands

loosely in her lap and trying to behave as she imagined Andrea would in such a situation—cool, confident, perfectly at ease.

"He's been gone a long time." The words came out before she could tell herself that saying them made her sound anything but cool and confident. "Maybe he found something wrong."

The faintest of frowns made a crease between Zach's level eyebrows. "What could he find wrong?"

"Nothing. Nothing at all." She'd say she was just nervous, but that was probably pretty obvious to him. "I…I don't like this."

"Why?" He leaned forward, his gaze probing.

"I just feel that way. Does there have to be a reason?"

He considered that calmly. "There usually is."

She clamped her mouth shut to keep from snapping at him. She counted to ten. "All right." Maybe she should have made it twenty. "I guess it bothers me to feel that I'm being manipulated. That I'm doing exactly what someone wants me to."

To her surprise, he nodded. "I understand. And you're probably right, but what other choice did you have?"

"None." Unfortunately, he was right, too. "That doesn't mean I have to like it."

"I'd say the best thing would be to move cautiously. No matter what is in that box, you don't have to act on it today."

"Right." She took a deep breath and tried a smile. "You're right. Whatever it is, I don't have to rush into dealing with it."

Dawson came toward them, sliding papers into a file. "Here are your originals back, Mrs.—Ms. Hampton." He handed them to her. "Naturally, I'd like to express our sympathy in your loss."

"Thank you."

"As you probably know, Pennsylvania law requires that a safe-deposit box be sealed upon the death of the owner until it can be inventoried by a representative of the Department of Revenue."

"No, I didn't know that." If she had, she wouldn't be here. What was the point of this exercise, if she couldn't access the box?

"However, since you and your husband rented the box jointly, that's not an issue. If you'll just come along, I'll get the box out for you."

Jointly. She felt as if she'd stepped onstage in a play where she didn't know the lines. She hadn't rented the box—at least not knowingly. But the bank officer clearly thought she had.

And Zach—what did he think? Did he assume she'd been lying all along about this?

Moving automatically, she followed the man, aware of Zach, close on her heels. Down one long hall, footsteps echoing on the tile, and then a flight of stairs. Dawson led them into a small room lined with storage compartments, its only furniture a table in the center of the room. Obviously the bank didn't encourage its patrons to hang around here.

Murmuring the number under his breath, Dawson retrieved the box, placing it on the table. Once it was unlocked, he stepped back with a suggestion of duty fulfilled.

"There you are. I'll wait until you're finished."

She was barely aware of the man moving to the doorway, turning his back as if to give them some semblance of privacy. All her attention was focused on the box. On the feeling it aroused.

Dread. There was no other word for it. Whatever Tony had put in that safe-deposit box, she didn't want to know. And however he'd gotten her name on the box, she didn't want to know that, either.

"Would you like me to wait outside?" Zach said.

She shook her head slowly. "No. Stay. Whatever it is, I think I'd like a witness." Besides, if she didn't let him stay, that would simply make him more suspicious.

"If that's what you want."

He was probably pleased. He saw this as one more step toward solving a puzzle, nothing more.

She couldn't be that detached. Tony's secrets hadn't died with him, and she was about to see one of them. Somehow she didn't think it could be anything good.

She reached out, her hands a little unsteady, and lifted the lid from the box. It clattered when she dropped it back onto the table. She heard a swift intake of breath from Zach.

She didn't seem to be breathing at all. She took an involuntary step back, not wanting to admit what she was seeing.

Money. The safe-deposit box was stuffed to the brim with cash.

Zach leaned against the back of the park bench, trying to look anything but as tense as he felt. Caroline was upset enough already. The last thing she needed was for him to add to that.

She sat on the other end of the concrete-and-redwood bench, staring out over the wide, placid river, as if intent on the rowing sculls that zipped along its surface like water bugs. But her hands clasped each other so tightly that the knuckles were white, and even the warmth of the spring sunshine didn't keep the occasional shiver from going through her.

"Have a little more of your coffee," he urged.

She lifted the foam cup to her lips and drank without looking at it. When they'd finally gotten out of the bank he'd wanted to find a restaurant where they could sit and talk, but she'd just kept shaking her head.

Well, he could understand why she didn't want to feel hemmed in. He'd finally gone through a fast-food drive-through and ordered her a large coffee with sugar. Something hot and sweet seemed the right remedy for shock.

Was the shock genuine? The analytical part of his cop's brain weighed her reactions. She'd certainly acted surprised when Dawson had pulled out the rental lease with her name on it. To suppose that she'd already known about the box was to imagine she'd been taking him for a ride all along, and he didn't think he was that gullible.

And she couldn't have mimicked that shock when she'd flipped the box lid back and seen the money. Whatever she'd expected to find in that safe-deposit box, it wasn't that.

"You feel like talking about it now?" He edged a little closer, even though there was no one within earshot.

The ground sloped gently from where they sat down to the river, and the few people who were in the park at this hour were on the paved path that led along the water—a couple of joggers, a couple of women pushing strollers.

Caroline lifted her hand, palm up. "I don't know what to say. I don't understand any of it."

"You didn't have any idea Tony had rented that safe-deposit box in your names?"

She shook her head, the movement setting her dangling silver earrings dancing. "No. I didn't even know he'd been in Philadelphia. Why wouldn't he tell me that? I wouldn't have found it suspicious if he'd said he had to go there on business."

Some people lied even when it would be easier to tell the truth, but it seemed pointless to say so. "The rental form had what looked like your signature on it."

She rubbed her forehead. "I guess it's faintly possible that he slipped the form in with some other papers to sign, and I didn't notice what it was."

She didn't sound convinced. Well, he wasn't, either. Caroline might be something of a free spirit, maybe a tad irresponsible, but he doubted she'd sign something without even looking at it.

"And the money? You didn't know he had that much salted away?"

Nearly two hundred thousand dollars. Caroline had refused to so much as touch the contents of the box, but finally she'd agreed to let him count it.

Afterward, he'd put the cash back into the box, and Caroline had returned it to the bank's care. What else was there to do? If it hadn't been for Caroline's name on that lease, the bank officer would have sealed the box himself, not letting them do anything but look for a will until someone was present from the Department of Revenue.

Caroline transferred her gaze from the sculls to him. "It's not my money."

She'd been saying that, in one variation or another, since they'd left the bank.

"If it belonged to your husband, then it belongs to you, unless he made a will leaving it elsewhere."

"As far as I know, Tony didn't make a will. But then, there's a lot that I don't know, obviously." Her voice held an edge.

"Barring a will, it would go to you as next of kin."

"I don't want it." The suppressed emotion in her voice startled him. "Even if it did belong to Tony, I can't imagine that he came by it honestly."

"You said he took money out of your account. You could probably legitimately claim that, even if—"

He stopped, because she was shaking her head. "I don't want it, I tell you. I just want to forget I ever saw it."

Her voice had the ring of truth. She had to be hard up for money, if Gibson really had cleaned her out, but she seemed adamant about that.

"I can understand, I guess," he said slowly, "but I don't think you're going to be able to do that. Seems to me you ought to notify the Santa Fe police."

Fear flared in those green eyes. "No! I mean, I don't want to have anything to do with it."

Anything to do with the police—that was what she meant. He hated to push her. What he wanted to do was put his arm around her shoulder, pull her close and tell her everything was going to be all right.

But he couldn't. It wouldn't be professional, for one thing. And he couldn't promise things were going to be fine. His instincts told him a law had been violated somewhere in all of this, even if he couldn't put his finger on it yet.

"Where do you think the money came from?" Maybe if he could get her thinking, the fear would leave her eyes and they could talk about notifying the police in a rational manner.

"I don't know." She rubbed the sleeves of her suit jacket. "Based on when he rented the safe-deposit box, it was several months ago. I just can't imagine, but obviously I didn't have a clue about his finances."

"What about gambling winnings?"

She winced a little, but she kept her back ramrod straight, reminding him of her grandmother. "I guess that's one possibility."

She clearly didn't want to admit that, but it seemed the obvious answer to a lot of the problems she'd been having. A compulsive gambler, losing money he couldn't repay, might resort to stealing from his wife or even driving his car off the side of a mountain.

The trouble with that scenario was that it didn't fit the facts. Tony, with a safe-deposit box stuffed with cash, didn't look like any loser he'd ever seen.

He studied Caroline's face. Those normally clear green eyes were clouded, the shadows under them looking like bruises on the fair skin. There were lines of strain around her generous mouth, and he had the sense that she was hanging on to her composure by a thread.

Sooner or later, information about the money would have to be passed on to the Santa Fe police. Since Tony's death wasn't being investigated, he didn't feel an urgency to do it today.

He could give Caroline another day, maybe. But if she hadn't decided by then to talk to the New Mexico cops, he'd have to do it.

"Do you want to head home now?" He planted his hand on the top slat of the bench, ready to get up.

She looked up, startled. "We're going to try and find Tony's family, aren't we? You said that you had a possible address."

"I do. But I thought maybe you'd had enough for one day."

She managed a smile. "Think how offended my grandmother would be at the idea that an Unger wouldn't do her duty, no matter what."

"You don't have to prove anything, Caroline." But maybe, in her mind, she did.

She rose, slinging the strap of her leather bag on her shoulder. "I'd rather get it over with. If Tony has family here in Philadelphia, I think it's time I met them."

"Are you sure this is the right address?" Caroline stared through the windshield. The row house, its brick faded and stained, sat behind its wire mesh fence with an air of cringing away from the street. Small wonder. This wasn't the worst neighborhood in Philadelphia, but it had an air of having come down in the world considerably in recent years.

Zach consulted the address in his notebook, checked the GPS monitor and nodded. "This is it, all right. Not what you expected?"

"No. I can't imagine Tony growing up here." She thought of the safe-deposit box stuffed with money, and her stomach tightened. "But I seem to have been wrong about plenty of things where Tony was concerned."

Tony, who were you? Was there anything real about our marriage?

The look Zach sent her seemed to assess her stability. "Are you sure you want to do this now?"

She took a deep breath. In a situation like this, her grandmother would rely on her faith. For a moment she felt a twinge of something that might be envy. To feel that Someone was always there—

But she couldn't. She grabbed the door handle. "Let's go."

"Wait a second." He reached across her to clasp her hand before she could open the door. For a moment she couldn't seem to breathe. He was too close, much too close. She could smell the clean scent of his soap, feel the hard muscles in the arm that pressed against her.

"Why?" She forced out the word, her voice breathless.

He drew back, as if he'd just realized how close he was. "Maybe it would be better if I took the lead in talking to them. If they don't already know that Tony was married—"

"Yes, of course you're right." That was yet another nightmare to think about. Tony's family would have no reason to welcome, or believe in, a previously unknown wife. "Just—"

"What?"

She hesitated a moment and then shook her head. "I was going to say be tactful, but maybe there's nothing left to be tactful about."

He squeezed her hand, so lightly that she might have imagined it. "I'll do my best."

She slid out of the car and waited until he joined her on the sidewalk. The gate shrieked in protest when he pushed it open, and she followed him up the walk, stepping over the cracks where weeds flourished unchecked.

Three steps up to a concrete stoop, and then Zach rapped sharply on the door, ignoring the doorbell. Moments passed. The lace curtain on the window beside the door twitched. Someone was checking them out.

They must have looked presentable, because the woman swung the door open. "Something I can do for you?"

She was probably not more than thirty, Caro guessed. Blond hair, dark roots showing, was pulled back into a ponytail. She wore a faded navy cardigan over a waitress uniform, and the bag slung over her shoulder seemed to say that she had either just come in or was just going out.

"We're looking for Anthony Gibson. Does he live here?"

She jerked a nod and turned to look over her shoulder. "Somebody for you, Tony. Listen, I have to go. I'll see you later."

She held the door so that they could enter and then slid past them as if eager to make her departure.

"What do you folks want?" The tone held a trace of suspicion. The man thumped his way toward them with a walker. Tall, like Tony, with dark eyes.

But the world was full of tall men with dark eyes. Surely this couldn't be Tony's father. The setting was wrong, and he must be too old—he looked nearly as old as Grams, rather than being a contemporary of her mother.

"You're Tony Gibson?" Zach nudged her forward as he spoke.

"That's right." The man came to a stop at a mustard-colored recliner and sat, shoving the walker to one side.

"I'm Zachary Burkhalter, Chief of Police over in Churchville in Lancaster County. This is Caroline Hampton. We wanted to talk to you about your son."

She opened her mouth to say that this couldn't be her Tony's father, and then she closed it again, because Tony's picture sat on top of the upright piano in the corner. A much younger Tony, but that smile was unmistakable.

The lines in the man's face seemed to grow deeper. "My son died a month ago. If he owed you money, you're wasting your time coming here for it."

"No, nothing like that," Zach said easily. "We're just trying to clear up some questions that came up after Tony's death. We weren't sure we had the right family."

The old man—Tony's father, she reminded herself—leaned back in the recliner, grabbing the handle so that the footrest flipped up. "My son, all right." He pointed to the picture on the piano. "If that's the Tony Gibson you're looking for."

"Yes." She forced herself to speak. "Yes, it is."

"Died out west. New Mexico, it was." He didn't look grieved, just resigned. "I always figured it would happen that way. Somebody'd call and tell us he was gone."

"What made you think that?" Zach's voice had gentled, as if he recognized pain behind the resignation.

He shrugged. "Always skating too near the edge of the law, Tony was. You can't keep doing that and not get into trouble at some point."

"Had you heard from him lately?" *Did he tell you about me?* That was what she wanted to ask, but something held her back.

"Not for months. He sent Mary Alice a hundred bucks back in January, I think it was. Said she should get Christmas presents with it."

Mary Alice was apparently the woman who'd opened the door to them. Tony's sister, she supposed, left here to look after their ailing father.

"Were you expecting a visit from him this spring?" She put the question abruptly, hearing Tony's voice in her mind. *We'll go back east in the spring, sweetheart. We'll surprise both our families.* He'd spun her around in a hug. *My folks will be crazy about you.*

"No. And I wouldn't have believed him if he had said so." He planted his hands on the arms of the recliner and leaned toward her. "What is all this, anyway? Why do you want to know about my son? What are you to him?"

"We just—" Zach began, but she shook her head.

"Don't, Zach." She took a breath. For good or ill, the

man had a right to know she was his son's widow. "I'm sorry to blurt it out this way, Mr. Gibson. I'm actually Caroline Hampton Gibson. I was married to Tony."

He didn't speak, but a wave of red flushed alarmingly into his face. He jerked the recliner back into the upright position with a thump.

She took a step backward. "I don't want anything from you. I just thought you ought to know—"

"You're crazy, that's what you are." He grabbed the walker and took a step toward her. "Or you're trying to pull something. Some of his friends, most likely, just as crooked as he was."

"Nothing like that." Zach's tone was soothing.

The old man ignored him, glaring at Caroline. "I don't know who you are. But I know who you're not. You're not my son's wife. Mary Alice is Tony's wife, and she's the mother of his little girl."

NINE

Caroline spread the old quilt over the table in the barn, handling it as carefully as if it were a living creature. Maybe working on the quilt would distract her from the memory of yesterday's shocking revelations.

Maybe, but she doubted it.

She forced herself to concentrate on the pattern. The research she'd done had told her that the particular way the flying geese and star were combined on this quilt was unusual. She wanted to see it more clearly, but the colors were muted by an inevitable coating of dust. Going over it with the brush attachment of the vacuum cleaner on low power was the recommended process.

The soft hum of the vacuum blocked out other sounds. Unfortunately, it couldn't block out her thoughts. They kept leaping rebelliously back to that disastrous trip to Philadelphia.

Maybe *disastrous* wasn't the right word. The revelations, one after the other, had been painful, but would she be better off if she didn't know? The truth would be the truth, whether she wanted to hear it or not.

She still wasn't sure how she'd gotten out of that house after Tony's father had dropped his bombshell.

Zach had taken over, of course. That would always be his automatic response. He'd soothed the man as best he could and piloted her back to the car.

She hadn't been able to talk about it during the drive back. Maybe it would have been better to get it out, but she couldn't. She'd been numb, maybe in shock.

Zach hadn't pressed her, other than to urge her to tell her grandmother or her sisters what happened. He'd left her with the promise that he'd check the records and find out the facts.

She hadn't taken Zach's advice, good as it probably was. She'd been in limbo, unable to decide anything. She'd spent the evening with Grams and Rachel, taking comfort in their chatter, listening to Grams's stories, reviving a sense of belonging she hadn't had in a very long time.

She switched off the vacuum and stood back to look at the results. The experts appeared to be right—the area she'd gone over was discernibly brighter, the deep, saturated colors coming to life.

The sound of a step had her turning, seeing the shadow he cast in the patch of sunlight on the barn boards before she saw him. Zach stood in the doorway, his figure a dark shape against the brightness outside.

His uniform didn't induce that instinctive revulsion any longer, but her stomach still tightened at the sight of him. He might have found out. He might know the truth about her marriage.

"Hi. Your sister told me I'd find you here." He came toward her, heels sounding on the wide planks. A shaft of sunlight turned his sandy hair to gold for a moment, and then it darkened when he moved out of the light. He studied the quilt. "Are you taking up quilting now?"

"This is the quilt your sister and I were talking about. It apparently dates from the 1850s. I'm trying, very cautiously, to clean it up." She was a coward, but she'd rather talk about the quilt than what had brought him here.

"I'm surprised Agatha Morris wasn't interested. I'd expect her to be here leaning over your shoulder, telling you you're doing it all wrong."

"I may be, but eight out of ten experts on the Internet agreed that vacuuming with a soft brush was a good first step."

"What would we do without the Internet?"

He said the words casually, but she heard something beneath them that alerted her.

"You've found out, haven't you?" She let go of the vacuum hose, and it clattered to the floor.

He nodded toward a bench against the low wall that separated the hay mow from the rest of the barn floor. "Let's have a seat. I see Cal left behind some of the improvements he made when this was his workshop."

She followed him, not interested in whether her brother-in-law had made the bench or not, just intent on sitting down before her knees did something stupid.

"The Internet does make searching records easier. Tony married Mary Alice seven years ago in Philadelphia."

She ought to be shaken, shocked and appalled. Maybe she was, but at the moment she mostly seemed numb. "You're sure—" She shook her head. "Of course you're sure, or you wouldn't be telling me. What about the child?"

"Their daughter, Allison Mary, was born seven months later. A shotgun wedding, maybe."

It would be tempting to try and rationalize what Tony had done in that light, but she found she couldn't. He'd had a wife. A child. He had a duty to them, not to her.

"Did he get a divorce?" A voice she barely recognized as hers asked the question.

He hesitated for a moment, as if knowing how much this would hurt her. His very silence told her the answer before he said the word.

"No." His stretched his arm along the back of the bench and touched her shoulder. "I'm sorry, Caroline."

She nodded, trying to think this through. "So the marriage he went through with me wasn't legal. Am I—did I do anything against the law in marrying him?"

"No. He was the bigamist, not you."

She took a deep breath. "I guess mostly I don't understand. He must have known I'd find out the truth eventually. Why would he do such a thing?"

"That's a good question. Can you think of any reason—anything that might explain what was going through his mind?"

"If I could, don't you think I'd have mentioned that by now? There's nothing." She planted her hands on her knees. "Maybe if I threw something I'd feel better—preferably something at Tony's head."

"I don't think that would help." His voice was mild, as it always was. That didn't tell her whether he believed her or not. "It's natural enough to be angry at him."

"He's well beyond the reach of my anger now." That in itself was cause for wrath. Tony had escaped, and left her to deal with everything. "I'm relieved about one thing, though. Since I wasn't really his wife, I don't have to do anything about that money."

He didn't answer. Didn't move. How, then, did she know that he wanted something—something in relation to the money?

"What?" Impatience threaded her voice.

"You should talk to the Santa Fe police about it. They're the ones investigating his death, and it could have an impact upon that case."

"I don't want to." Her fingers twisted together in her lap. He put his hand over hers, stilling the restless movement.

"That's pretty obvious. Would you mind telling me why?"

Zach studied the expression on Caroline's face. What was going on with her? For that matter, what was going on with him? He ought to be looking at this situation, at her, with his usual professional detachment.

He wasn't managing to do that, not where Caroline was concerned. She got under his skin in a way he'd never experienced before.

She wasn't his type. Take that as a starting point. Sure, he was attracted to her. Any man would be. But this was about more than creamy skin and eyes so deep a green that a man could drown in them.

He was drawn by what he sensed beneath that—the

creativity that sparked and sizzled in her, the gentle smile that didn't come often enough, the hint of vulnerability mixed with strength and independence.

His arguments seemed to be heading him in the wrong direction. Against that, he stacked who he was. A cop. A family man. A father who wouldn't bring a woman into his daughter's life unless he was sure she was the right woman. A Christian woman.

He must have been silent too long, because Caroline turned her head to look at him.

"Aren't you going to argue with me?"

"I guess I should." He didn't want to. He sympathized with her, maybe too much. She'd been through a tragedy that would be tough for anyone to handle, especially someone who didn't have a relationship with Christ to see her through.

He looked up at the lofty barn roof, where dust motes danced in the stripes of sunlight. Something about the quiet, open space made him feel as if he was in church.

Lord, show me how to deal with this. Caroline is hurting. I want to help her, but I have to do my duty.

"I don't see why I should do the police's work for them." Caroline's tone was defensive, and she sent him a sidelong glance that was reminiscent of Ruthie when she was in a stubborn mood. "I haven't done anything wrong, and even if Tony did, surely his liability died with him."

He studied her averted face. "Is Tony dead?"

Her gaze flashed to him. "Yes. The police said he was. I buried him."

"So the things that have happened since you came

here—the letter, the coffee, the safe-deposit box—were they coincidences? Someone trying to make you think Tony is still alive?"

Her lips trembled for a moment, and she pressed them firmly together. She shook her head. "I don't know. Nothing else has happened. Maybe nothing will. Maybe—"

"Do you really think that?" He was sorry for her, but he couldn't let her convince herself that she could just walk away from this.

She shoved her hair back from her face in that characteristic gesture. "I'd like to, but I guess I can't. Still, according to you I'm not Tony's wife. So why should I be involved?"

He couldn't tell her that Tony had been under investigation by the Santa Fe police—that was their business, and he couldn't interfere unless they asked for his help. But she already suspected gambling, didn't she?

"If Tony was involved in something that skirted the law, as his father said, that money could be important. The police should know."

"Why should I be the one to tell them? It properly belongs to Mary Alice, doesn't it? Let her tell them."

"She doesn't know about it. Come on, Caroline, stop evading the issue. Why won't you go to the police?"

She swung to face him, anger flaring in her eyes. "You know the answer to that, don't you? I don't know what happens to other people who've been where I was, but I know what effect it had on me. I've spent the past eight years being so law abiding it's painful—obeying every last little rule and regulation, never jay-walking, never so much as getting a parking ticket."

"Because you learned respect for the law." He was feeling his way, not sure what lay behind that vehemence.

"No! Because I can never put myself in that helpless position again. Because I learned I couldn't trust anyone—not my family and not the police."

She swung away from him, breathing hard, as if sorry she'd revealed that much of herself to him. He couldn't let her stop, not when she was so close to letting him see what was going on inside her.

"What happened? Tell me. You got into trouble, but there's more to it than that."

She shook her head, mouth set, eyes shimmering with tears that she no doubt didn't want him to see.

"You were riding around with two guys," he said deliberately. "You stayed outside in the car as a lookout while they went into a convenience store and beat up the elderly proprietor."

"No." The word seemed torn from her. "I didn't. I didn't know what they were doing. I had no idea they were robbing that man." Her voice trembled, the pain in it almost convincing him.

"Did your lawyer bring that up at the trial?"

"My lawyer didn't believe anything I told him." A touch of bitterness. "Or maybe he didn't care."

"Your family could have gotten different representation for you." They hadn't; he knew that. Why not?

For a moment she stared, eyes wide and clouded, as if she looked into the past. "The authorities couldn't find my mother. Turned out she'd run off to Palm Springs with her latest boyfriend. You couldn't expect her to pass up a trip like that just because her kid was in trouble, could you?"

The insight into what her life had been like with her mother shook him. He'd heard bits and pieces from time to time about Lily Hampton, none of it good.

"Your grandparents, your sisters—"

She shook her head. "I guess they tried to help, when they finally heard, but by then I was in the system. There wasn't much they could do. Besides, my mother was my legal guardian." Her voice shook a little. She might deny it, but that youthful betrayal had affected the rest of her life.

He understood, only too well. Once a juvenile was in the system, everything affecting them had to grind through the legal process. "Your grandmother must have been frantic."

"I suppose." Doubt touched her eyes. "At the time, all I could see was that they'd let me down."

"You got through it." He couldn't imagine how much strength it must have taken for her to deal with that situation alone at her age.

"Not without scars."

Lord, help me to understand. "That's not all, is it?" He knew, without questioning how, that there had been more. That something worse had happened to her when she was alone and vulnerable. "Locked up in a place like that—the other kids must have—"

"Not the other kids." Her body tensed, as if she drew into herself. "I dealt with them."

"Who?" He had to force the word out, because he thought he knew the answer, and he didn't want to hear it.

She hugged herself, as if cold in spite of the warmth of the day. "I don't want—"

"Who was it?" His voice was sharp to his ears. "A cop?"

She pressed her lips together. Nodded. "When I was arrested." It came out in a whisper. "He took me into a room by myself at the police station. Left me there. I thought my mother would come, but she didn't. He came back. He—" Her breath caught, as if she choked on the word.

"He attacked you." He managed, somehow, through the red haze of fury that nearly choked him, to keep the words gentle.

The muscles in her neck worked. She nodded. "Someone came in, finally. He said I was faking, trying to get him in trouble. I didn't care what he said, as long as I didn't have to see him again."

She should have filed a complaint, but he could understand why she hadn't. She'd been alone, and she'd just had a harsh lesson in how helpless she was. Small wonder she didn't trust the system or anyone involved in it.

If he'd been the one to walk into that room, he'd have been tempted to dispense some harsh justice of his own to the man who'd abused his position and shamed his badge. Even now he wanted to put his fist through the barn wall.

But that wouldn't help Caroline. He was probably the last person who could help her, but he was the one she'd confided in, and he had to try.

"He was a criminal wearing a badge, and I'd like to see him get the justice that's due him. But he was only one person. You had the misfortune to have run up against him."

To say nothing of the poor excuse for a mother she'd had. Seemed as if Caroline had been given the raw end of the deal too many times.

"I know." She straightened, quickly blotting a tear that had escaped as if ashamed of it. "Intellectually, I know that. But that doesn't keep me from wanting to stay as far away from the police as I possibly can."

"Understandable." It was a good thing she'd pulled herself together, because he longed to put his arm around her, pull her close, tell her—

No. There was nothing he could tell her. He might understand her better now, but that understanding had only served to emphasize the barrier between them.

She pushed herself off the bench, taking a few quick steps away from him. Maybe she sensed the feelings he was trying so hard to suppress.

"Look—about the money. You could tell the Santa Fe police about it, couldn't you? Tell them it isn't mine. That I don't want anything to do with it."

"I can tell them." That wouldn't end her involvement, but he didn't have the heart to tell her that now. Push her too hard, and Caroline might just run again.

He could understand why she always seemed to perch on the edge of flight. Nothing in her life had given her the assurance that she could trust people, and running away had been her only defense.

"It'll be okay." He stood, went to her. Wanted to touch her, but he didn't quite dare, knowing what he did. "You're not a helpless kid any longer, and you have family to love and protect you."

She had him to protect her, too, even though she probably didn't believe that and wouldn't welcome it. Still, he was the one she'd told. That had to mean something.

"Since you haven't called me again, I realized the only way I'd find out how you're doing is to call you." Francine's voice was clear and crisp over the cell phone. Possibly a little annoyed, as well.

"I'm sorry." Caroline curled into the corner of the leather sofa. She'd closed the curtains against the darkness outside and told herself she was perfectly safe. Still, it was good to hear another person's voice. "It's been so hectic here, getting settled and trying to get into the craft-show circuit. That's no excuse. I should have called."

"Craft shows?" The words were dismissive. "Really, Caroline. You have a position waiting for you here. I've told you that. Why don't you come back to Santa Fe where you belong?"

"I'm not sure I do belong there." Odd, how far away that life seemed now. "Maybe what happened with Tony changed everything."

"Nonsense. You had a good life here before you ever met Tony, didn't you? There's no reason why you can't have that again."

"I'll think about it." That was an evasion, but how could she know what she wanted? She'd been battered by one shock after another until it was impossible to do anything except tense up, waiting for the next one. "What's going on with the gallery? Are you all right?"

"Never mind me. How are you?" Francine's voice

softened on the words. Caro could picture her, leaning back in her custom-made desk chair, her sleek blond hair shining under the indirect lighting she insisted upon. "I didn't mean to snap, but I've been worried about you. So many people have asked how you are, and I don't know what to tell them."

"I'm fine. Really." It was good to feel she had friends who cared about her. "It's just—things have been a little crazy." She could trust Francine, but it didn't seem fair to unload all her worries on her.

"You're not. I can hear it in your voice. What is it? Have you heard from Tony?"

The question had her sitting bolt upright. "Why would you ask that? Tony's dead."

Francine didn't speak for a moment, but her very silence communicated her doubt. "I know that's what the police said. What we all believed. But after you told me about the man who accosted you that day—"

"You've found out something." She was shaken, but at some level she wasn't surprised. Francine knew everyone who was anyone in Santa Fe, and she heard every rumor first.

"Nothing that I'd want to take to the police." Francine sounded unsure of herself, and that was unusual. "People have been talking. People liked Tony. He was good at selling upscale real estate, probably because he was so likeable. But now there are rumors of gambling debts—enough rumors that there must be some basis in fact, I'd think. You had no idea?"

"No." It was hard to look back and see how naive she'd been. "But now—" She didn't want to tell Francine about the safe-deposit box stuffed with money, but if that didn't indicate gambling, what else could it have been?

"Now it seems likely to you. Don't bother to deny it. I can hear it in your voice." Francine had become her usual brisk self. "Well, that increases the possibility that Tony is still alive. And if so, he'll get in touch with you. You're his wife, and he—"

"I'm not." She couldn't let Francine go on any longer making assumptions that weren't true about her relationship with Tony. "I found out yesterday Tony had a wife in Philadelphia. He didn't bother to divorce her before he married me."

"I can't believe it. Caroline, are you sure? He must have been divorced. He couldn't hope to get away with anything else."

"But he did, didn't he? I had no idea the woman existed, any more than she knew about me." Her throat tightened, and she had to force the words out. "He had a child with her."

"Oh, my dear. I'm so sorry."

Somehow the sympathy in Francine's voice broke through the control Caroline had imposed on her emotions. A sob burst out before she could stop it, then another. She could only hold the phone like a lifeline and let the tears spill out, vaguely registering the soothing words Francine uttered.

Finally she managed to take a deep breath, mopping her face with her palm. "Sorry." Her voice was still choked. "I didn't mean to let go that way."

"Well, it's not surprising. But look, are you positive about this? How did you find out? Did your family help you, hire a private investigator?"

"No, nothing like that. I haven't told them about it yet. The local police chief got involved. He's the one who found the record of Tony's marriage, and no record of any divorce."

"A country cop?" That was Francine at her most superior. "My dear, if you're depending on someone like that, you're really in trouble. It sounds as if what you need right now is a friend you can count on."

She pressed her palm over her burning eyes. "I know how lucky I am to have you."

"Well, I'm not much use to you when I'm way out here. Let's see—" she could hear the tapping of computer keys "—there are a few things on my calendar I can't rearrange, but I ought to be free in a couple of days. I'll let you know when my flight gets in."

Her mind grappled to keep up. "You're coming here?"

"Why not? I suppose that inn of yours can rent me a room, can't it?"

"But I can't let you do that. You have so much to do. The gallery—"

"I own the gallery, remember? I can give myself a vacation whenever I want to."

"Francine, I appreciate it." Her voice choked again. "I can't tell you how much. But I can't let you change your plans for me."

"There's no point in arguing about it. I'm sure you think you can handle things by yourself, but right now it sounds as if you can use a friend."

She'd make another attempt to dissuade her, but Francine was right. She did need a friend, and it was far better to rely on someone she'd known for over two years than someone she'd known for less than two weeks.

An image of Zach's frowning face formed in her mind. What did she know about him, really? And what had made her trust him with secrets she hadn't told another soul?

TEN

Caroline folded the tortilla over the chicken-and-pepper-jack-cheese filling. She'd come over to the house to show Grams how the quilt looked after its initial cleaning, and ended up offering to cook supper. She just hoped they'd like her chicken enchiladas. There weren't too many recipes in her repertoire. She'd had to make some substitutions, since Snyder's Grocery apparently considered that one kind of pepper was sufficient for anyone's needs.

Grams came into the kitchen, carrying a large document box—that sort that was used to store fragile paper and photographs. "Here it is. I'm sure you'll find something in this batch of papers and letters about the quilt."

Caro gestured with the tortilla she'd just warmed in the microwave. "Great. I don't dare touch them now, but I'll look through them after supper."

Grams found nothing unusual about her interest in the quilt, attributing it to a natural desire to learn about her family history. Caro didn't think it was that, exactly, but she couldn't explain, even to herself, the fascination the old quilt held for her.

"There's no hurry. You can take the box back to the apartment with you."

Grams turned to set it on the end of the counter, her earrings swinging. Caro couldn't help a smile. Grams wore the earrings she'd made for her almost every day.

"I'll be careful with it," she promised.

"I know you will, dear. And after all, family documents belong to you as much as anyone."

That calm assumption that she had a place here still took her aback, even though she'd already encountered it several times. To Grams, it was as if Caroline's time away was just a visit to another world, and now she was back where she belonged.

"Your grandfather started collecting family papers and letters after he retired, with some idea of writing a family history." Grams's smile was reminiscent. "He should have known he wouldn't be content with something that sedentary. He loved to be out and about, meeting with his friends and taking an interest in civic affairs."

"I wish I had more memories of him." She'd been too young when Mom took them away, and time had blurred whatever memories had been left.

Grams came to hug her, her cheek soft against Caro's. "He loved you, you know. You'd sit on his lap and listen to his stories until you fell asleep in his arms."

Her throat tightened. "Thank you, Grams." For the memory, and for the sense of belonging. She wiped away a tear. "And thanks again for being so welcoming about Francine coming."

"Well, of course it's fine for your friend to come. She can have the blue bedroom. We don't have any guests booked until the weekend." Grams pulled the wooden stool over so that she could watch the enchilada-making. "Goodness, Caro, wouldn't you know we'd welcome your friend?"

"I know nothing hampers your hospitality. I just thought it might be an imposition if you have other guests booked. Although I'm sure Francine will insist on paying."

"She'll do no such thing." Grams's response was prompt. "She's your friend."

Grams and Francine could battle that one out, she decided. They were both so strong-willed that she didn't have a clue which one would win.

She transferred the enchiladas to one of Rachel's ceramic baking pans, trying to concentrate on that instead of on the vague worry that had possessed her since hearing of Francine's plans.

The thing that bothered her about the proposed visit didn't have anything to do with Grams's hospitality. It was more of a reluctance to see two such different parts of her life meeting. The truth was that she felt like a different person since she'd come back to Pennsylvania. With Francine here, who would she be?

She didn't think she wanted to go back to who she'd been in Santa Fe—the woman who'd fallen in love with Tony and who'd also fallen for his lies. But she wasn't sure she was ready to move forward, either.

"Are you all right, dear?" Grams touched her arm, her fingertips light as the wings of a butterfly. "You know I've been worrying about you. And praying for you, of course."

Her throat tightened. "I know. I'm going to be all right."

"Grieving takes time," Grams said, her voice gentle. "You can't rush it."

Shame flooded her. She couldn't keep doing this—couldn't go on letting Grams imagine she was grieving for a beloved husband. She set the casserole dish in the oven, closed the door and turned to face her grandmother.

"It's not what you think. The situation with Tony—" She stopped, because Rachel walked into the kitchen, the dog at her heels.

Rachel glanced from one to the other of them, obviously knowing she'd interrupted something. "Should I make some excuse none of us will believe and go away?"

"No. Don't go. I want both of you to hear this." They deserved to hear the truth. Caro took a breath, trying to frame the words she needed to speak. "I fell in love with Tony at first sight, I guess, enough in love to agree when he wanted to elope. But I didn't know him very well." That was a massive understatement.

Rachel came to lean on the table, as if wanting to be closer to her. "You found out you made a mistake."

"That's a nice way of putting it." She tried to smile, but she couldn't manage it. "It didn't take long to find out that Tony lied constantly—about where he'd been, about his business dealings. He wiped out my savings and checking accounts. When I confronted him—" They didn't need to know about all the hurtful words Tony had thrown at her. "He was furious. He left, and that was the night he died."

"Oh, honey—"

She held out her hand, stopping Rachel's instinctive

embrace. There was more to be said before she could let herself accept comfort. "I never did find out what he was doing, but I think he might have been involved in gambling. The other day, when I went to Philadelphia…" She couldn't watch their reactions. "I learned he was married before. Apparently he never got a divorce. So it looks as if our wedding wasn't even legal."

Silence for a moment. And then she felt Rachel's arms go around her, strong and comforting, the way she had been when Caroline was eight and had broken her arm falling out of a tree. "Caro, I'm so sorry."

She nodded, those weak tears spilling over again. Grams's arms went around both of them, holding them tight.

"You cry all you want, Caro. You don't have to be brave for us."

Maybe that was what she needed to hear to give her strength. "I'm all right." She pressed her cheek against Grams's, and then hugged her sister. "I've cried enough over it. I just wanted you to understand that—" She stopped, not sure what she wanted to say.

"That some odd things have been happening since you got back," Rachel finished for her.

Caroline drew back, shock running through her. "How did you know that? Did Zach tell you?"

"No, he didn't say a word, but I'm not an idiot. I can see what's right in front of me. If he's helping you… well, he's a good man."

"We want to help you," Grams said. "But we don't want you to think we're interfering." Grams brushed her hair back from her face with a gentle touch. "We're on your side, that's all. We love you. Just remember that."

She nodded, wiping tears away, and gave a watery laugh. "I'll remember. I love you, too."

She'd told them the worst of it. No one had blamed her or looked at her with that pitying expression that she dreaded. Only with love.

Caroline came down the stairs from the loft, still yawning, and squinted at the bright sunlight flooding through the living room windows. She crossed to the sofa, mindful of the papers she'd left spread across it and the coffee table.

She'd sat up far later than she'd intended, absorbed in the contents of the box Grams had given her. Those fragile papers, with their faded ink, shouldn't be left where sunlight might touch them. She didn't know much about preserving old documents, but common sense told her that.

Still, her fingers lingered as she started sorting them back into the box. Grandfather hadn't, as far as she could tell, done anything more than put together whatever he'd found relating to the 1850s and '60s. The papers weren't grouped in any way, and she'd found the Civil War enlistment papers of one Christian Unger shoved in among a sheaf of household bills and letters.

The letters were what fascinated her. Most of the ones she'd found so far dated from the 1850s. Elizabeth Chapman Unger, Grandfather's grandmother and the maker of her quilt, had come from Boston, Massachusetts. She seemed to have kept up a lively correspondence with her sister, Abigail, after she married and moved to Churchville. Judging by Abigail's replies, Elizabeth had found plenty to say about her new surroundings and her husband's family, apparently not all of it complimentary.

Caro smiled at one passage, where Abigail urged her sister to be tactful with her new mother-in-law. Human nature hadn't changed very much in the past 150 years.

She laid the papers gently back into the box and put the lid on. There'd been no mention of the quilt in what she'd found so far. Maybe the best thing would be to sort out everything she could find that related to Elizabeth and then go through it chronologically. Grams had promised to continue looking for anything else that related to her. The old house held the accumulated belongings of at least ten generations of the Unger family, and finding any one thing could be a challenge.

Grams had also suggested that Emma Zook would be a good person to give advice about repairing the quilt. She had a long tradition of quilting, as most Amish women did, and she'd know how to handle it.

But that could come later. Right now she was starving, and Rachel had insisted she come to the house for breakfast this morning to taste a new frittata recipe. Over supper last night, as if by unspoken consent, they'd kept the conversation on quilts and food, not on Caro's painful revelations.

She slid the box into the closet and headed out the door, careful to lock it behind her. Nothing had happened recently, but still, she didn't intend to take any chances.

She paused, hand still on the knob, wondering at the turn of phrase. Chances of what? Was she afraid that someone was trying to convince her that Tony was still alive? Or afraid that he was?

Tony wasn't her husband. At some point over the past two days she'd accepted that. She didn't have any obligation to him.

But she'd made the promises before God. She'd meant them, even if Tony had been lying the whole time. Her mind winced away from the memory of that ceremony. Tony, so tall and handsome in the dark suit he'd worn, seeming so solemn when he took his vows.

Had he been laughing inside, even then? She didn't know, and the more she thought about it, the less sure she became that she could rely on anything she thought she knew about him.

Well, standing here obsessing about it wasn't going to help. She started down the path that led around the corner of the barn. She was far better off to get on with things. She'd have breakfast, see if there was anything helpful she could do at the inn this morning.

This afternoon she'd work on the quilt and try to get a few more things ready for the next craft show. Once the moving company got around to bringing the rest of her belongings, she'd have a better choice of things to sell. There was an entire box of jewelry and some weaving that she'd left for the movers.

She ought to be working on jewelry instead of the quilt. Some simple pendants that she could price at under twenty dollars would be a good balance to the more expensive pieces. Plenty of people went looking for bargains, or what they thought were bargains, anyway, at craft shows.

The path led around the pond, past the gazebo toward the house. She glanced back at the barn and stopped. One of the double doors into the barn stood ajar a couple of inches.

Had she left it that way after that disturbing talk with Zach yesterday? Surely not. She was careful to lock things up, although there wasn't much in the barn to attract a thief—just the quilt frame she'd set up and the table on which she'd laid the quilt to vacuum it. She'd packed the quilt up afterward to take to the Zook farm.

Coffee and frittata were waiting at the house. She sighed. It would worry her all through breakfast if she didn't check now, just to be sure.

She cut across the lawn toward the barn doors, the damp grass soaking her sneakers in only a few steps. Well, that was foolish. She should have backtracked along the walk instead of trying to save time.

She went up the gravel ramp to the upper level of the barn, slowing as she reached the door. Silly, to be worried about it. She'd probably left it that way herself. Certainly she'd been cut up enough emotionally after betraying herself to Zach. Hardly surprising if she'd forgotten a little something like shutting the barn door.

But at some level she knew it wasn't true. She'd closed the door and made sure it was latched, just as she always did.

She reached out, grasping the handle. Everything was perfectly still, except for the family of barn swallows who chirped under the eaves. If someone had been there, he or she wouldn't hang around to be found. She shoved the door open and took a step inside.

Sunlight poured through the opening, casting a

spotlight on the interior. Nearly empty, just as she'd left it.

Except that the table she'd been working on had been tipped over, and the quilting frame she'd brought down from the loft had been smashed to pieces.

Zach sat at the kitchen table at the inn, steam rising from the coffee mug Rachel had just set in front of him. By the looks of her, Caroline was the one who needed the coffee, but instead she was holding a cup of chamomile tea that her grandmother had forced on her.

Mrs. Unger and Rachel were hovering over Caroline, so he waited, letting them do all the fussing they needed to before he started in with more questions.

Come to think of it, their concern seemed a bit out of proportion to the cause. If so, that probably meant Caroline had finally told them about her husband. High time, too. They were capable of dealing with that trouble.

He'd sat in this kitchen before. The Hampton women seemed to be—well, not trouble in themselves, exactly. It was more as if they found trouble.

Or in Caroline's case, brought it with her. He took a sip of the coffee, nearly scalding his tongue. Everything that had happened since she arrived had its roots in her life in Santa Fe—that seemed certain.

"You ought to have some breakfast." Rachel gestured toward a casserole that sat on top of the stove, still bubbling from its time in the oven. "I'm sure we called you out before you had time to eat."

"No, thanks. I had breakfast with Ruthie before she left for school. Now, about the damage—"

"It's just a good thing Caro left the quilt in the house last night," Mrs. Unger said. "I'd hate to think what they might have done to it."

So she was assuming the unknown intruders were vandals. Most likely that was true, but he didn't want to take anything for granted.

"This quilt—was it the one I saw you working on yesterday?"

Caroline nodded. Her face was a little pale. Natural enough, having vandalism strike so close to her.

She'd been getting the dust off it with a vacuum brush when he'd come in, he remembered. "Is it valuable?"

She looked up, seeming startled. "I don't know. We hadn't really looked into the value of it."

"I gave the quilt to Caro because she loved it," Mrs. Unger said. "No one is thinking about selling it, so its value is immaterial."

"Not to someone who planned on stealing it," he pointed out.

"Surely this wasn't intended to be a theft." Rachel poured a little more coffee in his cup, even though he hadn't taken much more than a sip. "If someone wanted to steal an antique quilt, they'd hit a quilt shop. There are several between here and Lancaster."

"I suppose, but I can't ignore the possibility. The more valuable the quilt, the more likely, it seems to me."

"I suppose we could find out." Caroline threaded her fingers back through her hair, letting it ruffle down to the shoulder of the white shirt she wore with jeans. That was probably the most conservative outfit he'd seen her wear yet. "I described the quilt to Agatha Morris, though, and she seemed to disregard it."

"Agatha doesn't know everything." Mrs. Unger's voice was tart. "We could call an expert for a valuation, if you think it's important."

"That wouldn't be a bad idea." It also wouldn't be a bad idea if he could speak to Caroline alone, but that didn't seem likely, the way her grandmother and sister were protecting her.

"I'm not worried about what it's worth. There's just something about the quilt that speaks to me." Caroline gave him an assessing look. Can you understand that? That was what it seemed to say.

"Right." He pulled a notebook from his pocket and put it on the table next to his mug. He didn't need to write any of this down, but somehow people seemed to find the action reassuring. "Now, who might know about the quilt?"

She frowned down at the straw-colored brew. "I talked about it at the quilt show, I know. To your sister. She was the one who suggested I speak to Mrs. Morris." She shrugged. "There were a lot of people milling around. I suppose anyone might have heard us. But if someone did want to steal the quilt, why smash up the quilting frame?"

"Good point. It's most likely vandals. Something about spring seems to bring them out of the woodwork. I don't suppose any of you have seen anyone hanging around the place?"

Blank looks, heads shaken. People didn't notice, unless they were the type who saw lurkers in every innocent bystander.

"Maybe you should move into the house." Mrs. Unger's brow wrinkled as she looked at her youngest granddaughter. "If you had run into them, whoever they were—"

Caroline patted her grandmother's hand. "I didn't, and I hope I'm smart enough not to go wandering around investigating strange noises by myself."

"Did you hear any noises?" He slid the question in. She should have—that was the first thing that struck him. The damage had to have made considerable noise, and her apartment was on the other side of the barn wall.

She was already shaking her head. "No. I've been thinking about that, and I should have if they were in there at night. But I spent the evening in the house, and we wouldn't have heard anything from here."

"That explains it, then." He supposed. It got dark fairly early, so the damage could have been done any time after, say, seven in the evening. Still, whoever had done it was taking a chance on being seen.

He wasn't accusing her of lying to him, not even in his mind. But no matter how sympathetic he felt toward Caroline, he couldn't let that affect his judgment.

He put the notebook in his pocket as he stood. "Well, I think that's it for now." He looked at Caroline. "If you'd like to walk out with me, maybe we could have a word about the locks."

She nodded, getting up quickly. "I'll be back in a minute," she said, and followed him to the door.

The patio was sun drenched and bright with spring flowers. Caroline stopped at the low wall that surrounded it and looked at him.

"This isn't about locks, is it?"

"No, I guess not, although it wouldn't hurt to put dead bolts on all the doors. More to the point, why don't you want to move into the house? Seems like that would be the sensible thing to do."

She shrugged, evading his eyes. "No one has ever described me as sensible."

"Your grandmother would probably feel better."

"You mean she'd be able to fuss over me more." She folded her arms across her chest.

"That's not a bad thing, you know." He could understand why she was prickly, given her history, but her grandmother obviously loved her.

"I like my independence." Her mouth set in a stubborn line.

He looked at her for a long moment, weighing how much to say. "I hope that's it," he said slowly. "I hope you're not just staying there because you want to make it easier for Tony to reach you."

He thought she'd flare up at hearing her words parroted back at her. She didn't. She just looked at him, her gaze defiant, and he knew that was exactly why she was so determined to stay.

ELEVEN

"That is just right." Emma Zook smiled at Caro over the quilt that was spread out between them. "You already know how to take the tiny stitches so they will not show."

"I've never done anything like this before." She traced the line of stitches she'd used to repair the fraying edge of a triangle. As Emma said, it was nearly invisible.

Nancy, Emma's daughter-in-law, came to look over her shoulder at the quilt. "That will fix up nice, it will. It is good to keep such a quilt in the family."

"Yes, it is."

Funny. For years she'd told herself she got by very nicely without family. Her priorities seemed to have gotten turned around in recent months.

Nancy smoothed a strand of hair back under the white prayer cap that sat on the back of her head. "Sticky buns are almost ready to come out of the oven. We'll have some with coffee when you finish work."

She'd decline on the basis that a sticky bun contained probably her entire daily allotment of calories, but that would no doubt be an offense against hospitality. Nancy fed her family in the way that Amish women had done for generations, and they seemed to thrive on it. Of course, they had no need for organized activities or gym memberships to keep fit. Dealing with the daily needs of the house and farm without electricity or other modern conveniences did the job.

Emma fingered the binding on the edges of the quilt, frowning a little. "The binding shows wear first. Could be you should just put on a new one."

"I'd hate to replace it with modern fabric. From everything I've heard, that takes away from the value. Maybe I can repair it."

Emma nodded. "It is worth a try. You have the patience to do it right. Like with the jewelry you make."

Emma didn't wear jewelry, of course, but that didn't seem to keep her from appreciating the workmanship that went into it. The difference was, she supposed, that the Amish made useful things beautiful, while she attempted to make beautiful things that were also, in their own way, useful.

"You were the one who started me on the way to being a crafter," she said, putting in a final stitch and knotting it. "You taught me to crochet before I even started school. Remember?"

Funny how that memory had come back to her— of herself and Rachel sitting at the kitchen table with Emma, the woman's work-worn hands guiding their small ones as they made an endless chain of crochet loops to be formed into pot holders.

"Ach, you remember that." Emma beamed. "You were so tiny, but you caught on fast. Like my own girls."

It went without saying that Amish girls knew such useful things, learning them from their mothers almost before they could talk. Had she and Andrea and Rachel learned anything useful from their mother? Offhand, she couldn't think of anything, unless it was how to evade bill collectors.

"I remember you always welcomed us into the kitchen, no matter how busy you were. You'd find something for us to do." Now, looking back, she knew they'd escaped to the kitchen when her mother was in one of her moods or when their parents were quarreling.

"It made no trouble." Emma had probably known why they were there, but she'd never said. "I liked having you with me for company."

Probably Emma had been lonely, working by herself in the kitchen at the mansion instead of in her own kitchen, surrounded by children, visiting with her mother-in-law while they did the routine chores of taking care of a large family.

"You told us Bible stories." Caro smiled. "Sometimes they came out half in German, I think."

"My English was not so *gut* as the children's. But the stories were the same, whatever the tongue."

"Yes." She supposed they were. "I have a feeling I was a pest, always asking questions. I wanted to know why you wore a cap, I remember."

The prayer cap now covered gray hair, instead of blond, but it was identical to the one Emma had worn then.

"The Bible says that a woman should pray with

her head covered, and also that we should pray at all times."

"Do you pray at all times?" The words were out before she could think that Emma might not want to answer so private a question.

But Emma just smiled. "Often enough that I would not want to be taking a cap on and off, for sure. I know the English don't hold with that rule. The praying is the important part, *ja*. And I pray for you, little Caro."

Her throat tightened. "Thank you. I haven't... haven't prayed so much. Not in a long time. God always seems pretty far away to me."

Emma took a final stitch and bit off the thread. "If God seems far off, it is because we have moved. Not God." She stood, apparently feeling that was all she needed to say about it. "Come. We will have coffee with Nancy."

Heart still struggling with the concept, Caro followed her to the farmhouse kitchen. Nancy sat at the long wooden table, her workbasket in front of her, but she greeted them with a smile and set it aside to get the coffeepot from the stove. The room was filled with afternoon sunlight and the mouthwatering aroma of the sticky buns that sat cooling on top of the gas range.

A faceless rag doll lay atop the basket, hair in braids, awaiting its replica of Amish children's clothing. She picked it up, wanting to think about anything but her relationship with God. "This is lovely, Nancy. Is it for one of your daughters?"

"Ja." Nancy's smile was the thank-you she wouldn't say in response to a compliment. "I had a bit of time after finishing the baking to work on it."

She made sewing the doll sound as relaxing as if she'd taken a nap.

"Do you ever sell them at the local craft shows? I'd think they'd be very popular." They were unique in their lack of features, reflecting the Amish adherence to not making any images.

Nancy shook her head. "We put some out when we have our produce stand in the summer, that's all."

"Would you like to have me take some to the shows on consignment?" She had second thoughts almost immediately. Was she breaking any Amish taboos with the suggestion?

Nancy glanced at her mother-in-law, and Emma nodded. "That would be a fine thing, I think. We would like that, Caroline."

Actually, once they committed to it, both Emma and Nancy showed a lot of enthusiasm for the idea. By the time Caroline was ready to go home, she carried not only her quilt and several Amish cloth dolls but also some carved wooden toys created by the Zook men. And the promise of the loan of a quilt frame so that she could finish her work on the quilt more easily.

She pulled the car into her parking space behind the barn and began unloading. Something else was sticking with her from that visit. Emma had played a huge role in her young life, and she hadn't even realized it until this afternoon.

The memories of that time, which came back more strongly with each day she spent here, proved that. Emma, in her quiet way, had made her feel safe. Secure. Loved. Loved by the Heavenly Father who was such a strong presence in Emma's life.

Emma's words came back to her. If she no longer felt God's presence, was it God's fault? Or hers?

Arms filled with a box containing the dolls and toys, the quilt folded on top, she followed the walk that led around the corner of the barn. It was too much. She wasn't ready to face any tough spiritual questions right now. All she could do was try to get through things as best she could. She —

She rounded the corner and nearly walked into the man who stood at her door.

The bag Caroline was clutching slipped from her grasp, but he caught it before it could hit the ground.

"I'm so sorry. I didn't mean to startle you."

Easy smile; open, boyish face; a disarming twinkle in his eyes. Churchville's mayor—she'd met him at the last craft fair. For an instant she couldn't think of his name, and then it came to her. Keith Morris.

"No problem. I just didn't expect anyone to be here. I don't get many visitors, but that doesn't mean I should overreact when someone comes to my door." She fished her key from her bag, hoping she didn't look as embarrassed as she felt.

"I'm sure it's only natural for you to be edgy under the circumstances." Keith's mobile face expressed concern.

Circumstances? For a moment she imagined he knew about Tony, but that was impossible.

"What circumstances?" She pushed the key in the lock, juggling the packages in her arms.

"Here, let me help you with those." He relieved her of her load so quickly she didn't have time to refuse.

"I heard about the vandalism. That's a terrible thing. That's really why I'm here."

"You know something about it?" She could hardly object when he followed her inside since he was carrying her things. She nodded toward the dining room table, and he set everything down.

"No." He looked startled at the suggestion. "No, I don't. I just wanted to apologize on behalf of the town. As mayor, I'm afraid I feel responsible when a newcomer to our little community gets such an unpleasant welcome."

"I could hardly blame the town, could I? But thank you for your concern. I'm sure you have plenty of more important things to do in your position."

"Important?" His right eyebrow quirked. "You do realize that the most significant part of the mayor's role in Churchville is to sign proclamations, declaring that it's Pennsylvania Apple Week, or American History Month. And did you know that this coming week is Community Festival Week?"

She had to smile at the self-deprecation in his voice when he talked about his job. "I'm sure it's more complicated than that."

"A little. I oversee town departments, of course, such as the police department. So I feel a little responsible when our police chief lets vandals run around loose."

"I hardly think it's fair to blame Chief Burkhalter for that." She snapped the words before she could think that it was odd for her to be defending Zach.

"I'm sure you're right." He backed down without, it seemed, a parting glance at what he'd just said. Was telling people what they wanted to hear part of a politician's job?

"Yes, well—" She turned away, appalled at herself for springing to Zach's defense. She didn't owe him that. "I was lucky I didn't have anything very significant in the barn. And believe me, it has a nice, sturdy lock on the doors now."

"Good, good." He rested his hand on the back of a chair. "I have to confess that wasn't the only reason I came to see you."

"No?" She raised an eyebrow, wondering if this was the prelude to a pass.

"I'm interested in the quilt you talked about with my mother. The 1850s one."

She blinked. Did he realize it was one of the things he'd carried in? "I'm pretty fond of it myself."

"I collect quilts—in a minor way, that is. I wondered if you were interested in selling it."

She could only stare at him for a moment. Was this some sort of game he and his mother played to get the price down?

"According to your mother, my quilt doesn't have much historical value." The woman's quick dismissal of her quilt was still annoying.

"I'm sorry about that." Again that boyish smile disarmed. "Mother can be a bit difficult at times. So many people see her as an expert and ask for advice that she just doesn't want to be bothered with it."

"Odd." In her experience, crafters were the nicest people on earth, always willing to help each other. She must be the exception.

"In any event, I think that quilt would be a great addition to my collection. What are you asking for it?"

The usual rule at shows was that everything was for sale if the price was right, but she didn't feel that way about the quilt. "I'm afraid it's not for sale."

"Oh, come on," he said. "Name a price."

She shook her head. "It's a piece of family history."

"One thousand dollars?"

She had to keep herself from gaping. "I'm afraid it's not for sale," she said again, infusing her words with a note of command.

He glanced toward the quilt, lying folded on the table. "Is that it?"

She nodded. Since he'd shown so much interest, she could hardly refuse to show it to him. "Would you like to see?"

"Of course."

He helped her unfold the quilt onto the table. She had to force herself not to say irritably that she'd do it herself. Really, she didn't understand why she was so possessive about the thing.

"There you are."

He took a step back to survey the quilt. "Very interesting. It's an unusual combination of patterns for that time period, from what I know."

"That's what I understand, too." She touched the edging. "Maybe that's why it interests me. I'm trying to research its history, and my grandmother has begun finding some letters and papers that relate to the time period. Hopefully I'll find some mention of the quilt."

He nodded toward one of the torn triangles. "You

know, there are people who specialize in repairing and restoring old quilts. If you'd like, I could give you some names."

"No, thanks. I'd prefer to do it myself." She was sure of that, even if she didn't quite understand why.

"But it's a big job—"

"I can manage." Really, what business of his was it if she wanted to do it herself? She'd already told him it wasn't for sale.

"Now I've annoyed you." He gave her a rueful smile. "I'm sorry. I was just trying to be helpful."

"Well, thank you." She hoped she didn't sound too ungracious. "Everyone has been very helpful—I guess I'm not used to that after living in the city for so long. The Zooks are even bringing over a quilting frame to replace the one destroyed by the vandals."

"That's good. And you said you'd put a new lock on the barn door?"

"My brother-in-law took care of that, but I doubt the vandals would strike twice in the same place."

"Still, better safe than sorry." Keith's smile was a little warmer than friendly. "I'm glad the incident hasn't given you a distaste for our little town."

"Not at all. I'm happy to be here." To her surprise, she realized that was true. In spite of the problems that seemed to have followed her, she felt more at home than she had in years.

"That's good." His smile broadened. "I'm glad."

She couldn't help smiling back. Some simple, uncomplicated flirting was a welcome change from dealing with the betrayal hidden behind Tony's smooth facade.

Or with Zach's intensity. A pair of frowning gray eyes appeared in her mind, and she tried, without success, to dismiss them.

"That is such a clever idea." Karen Burkhalter leaned across from her booth at the Spring Festival to take a closer look at the children's activity Caro had set up.

"Since it's a community event, I thought it'd be good. I've done it at this kind of show before, and most kids like to string beads." She'd made a trip to the nearest craft store for supplies for the simple craft, and it had been a pleasant distraction from everything else that was going on in her life.

"You're really getting into the swing of things here." Karen's pert, freckled face lit with a smile. "I'm glad. That means you want to stay."

Karen's insight startled her. Was her attitude that obvious? "I guess I am enjoying it here." But for how long?

"They're opening the doors," Karen said. "Get ready to be swamped."

She didn't really expect that, but over the next hour it looked as if Karen's prediction would come true. People flooded through the aisles between the booths, locals and visitors alike. She should have realized that it would be difficult to supervise the children's activity and deal with adult customers at the same time.

She was trying to untangle the mess one overeager ten-year-old had made of her necklace when someone slid around the table and into the booth with her. She looked up to see Andrea.

"You can use an extra pair of hands." Andrea shoved a strand of blond hair behind her ear and took the string of beads from her. "I'll do this. You take care of the customers."

"I...thank you. I didn't expect this."

Andrea, who managed to look crisp and business-like even in jeans and a button-down shirt, deftly untangled the beads. "Rachel would have come, but she was too busy at the inn. Hey, it'll be fun."

It would? She enjoyed it, but it hadn't occurred to her that Andrea might. There was a lot she didn't know about her sisters, it seemed. She turned to a woman who wanted to argue her down on the price of the Amish dolls.

"Well, I don't know if my grandkids would like them. Don't you have any with faces?" She picked at the fine hand stitching on the doll's dress, and Caro had to restrain herself from snatching it away from her.

"It's handmade by an Amish woman," she said firmly. "Amish dolls don't have faces because the Amish don't believe in making images of people. If you want a cheap machine-made doll with features, I'm sure you can find that somewhere else."

She held her breath. She didn't usually turn away customers, but she wouldn't insult Nancy by selling her handmade dolls for less than they were worth.

"I guess you have a point at that." The woman looked over the display. "I'll take four of them."

She managed to keep a straight face until the woman had paid and walked away, and then she turned to Andrea, a laugh escaping. "I can't believe I just did that."

"You sounded like my husband. Cal feels the same

about his handmade furniture. If you want cheap machine-made, go elsewhere." Andrea, having a moment's respite from the demands of the children, leaned against the table. "You know, you really have a feeling for Pennsylvania folk art. Maybe that's what you're meant to be doing."

The idea startled her. First Karen, now Andrea pointing out something she hadn't seen in herself.

Andrea glanced over her shoulder. "Looks as if you have another customer."

Caro turned, and her breath caught. The woman who stood on the other side of the table wasn't a customer. She was Tony's wife.

"Mrs. Gibson." Caro said the words with a sense of fatality. Of course the woman would seek her out. What else could she do? She should have seen this coming.

"I thought you were claiming that name." The woman's tone was combative, but Caroline saw past that to what lay beneath. Grief. Despite what he'd done to her, Mary Alice had loved Tony.

"What do you want?"

"To talk, that's all. You can spare me a few minutes, can't you?"

Caro glanced around. They couldn't talk here, not in the midst of the crowd. "Andrea, can you take over for a few minutes?"

Andrea nodded, controlling the questions that no doubt seethed in her mind.

Caro slid out of the booth, struggling to find composure. She had to do this. She didn't want to.

Please. She wasn't sure whether it was a prayer or

not, it had been so long. *Please show me what to say to her.*

"Let's go out back. Maybe we can find someplace quiet to talk." She touched the woman's arm. Mary Alice winced away from her, but she followed when Caro started down the aisle toward the rear of the fire hall.

They got there too fast. She hadn't come up with anything to say by the time she pushed through the metal door and went out to the gravel lot.

The area around the door was piled with boxes left there by the exhibitors, and a couple of pickups were parked nearby, but there was no one around. It was as private a place as they were likely to find in the midst of the festival.

She turned to the woman. "I guess this will have to do. I'm sure you don't want to come back later."

"No. Let's get this over with." Mary Alice's thin face tightened. She'd probably been a beauty once, with those soft curls and huge brown eyes, but years of tending a child and an ailing father-in-law had taken their toll.

For an instant Caro felt an irrational fury at Tony. What right had he to betray this woman—to betray both of them? Hadn't he had any sense of morality at all?

"How did you find me?"

The woman shrugged. "Your friend told Tony he was police chief here. I stopped at the station, asked for you. The guy on duty said you'd probably be here."

Simple, wasn't it? "All right, what can I tell you?"

"You told my father-in-law that you were Tony's

wife." Mary Alice folded her arms across her chest, as if holding back pain. "What did you mean by that?"

"I wasn't trying to hurt you or him. I wanted to find out—"

"Are you after what Tony left?" Mary Alice blurted out the question. "Because if you are, you're going to be disappointed. He didn't leave a thing, and if he had, it would belong to me and his child."

The thought of that child was a fresh source of the pain she'd thought she was finished with. "No. I don't want anything. Just the truth."

"The truth is that Tony was my husband. Maybe not a very good one, but mine." Her thin cheeks flushed. "You have no right to say anything else."

"I'm sorry. I thought I was married to Tony." She tried to harden her heart. She had her own pain to deal with. "We got married in Las Vegas. But if you two were never divorced, then it was all a sham."

"I don't believe you." The woman's face was taut with pain. "Tony wouldn't do that. We were married in the church. He might do a lot of things, but not that."

Caro fumbled in her shoulder bag and pulled out the photo she still carried around. She should have gotten rid of it. Having it was like biting down on a sore lip, but she hadn't been able to bring herself to throw it away.

"Here." She held the image out to the woman. "Is that your Tony?"

Mary Alice took the photo, hand trembling. Looked at it. Shoved it back toward Caro, turning away. Her shoulders shook with sobs.

"I'm sorry." Her voice was thick, too. She grabbed

the picture, taking a brief glance at the smiling bride and groom, and shoved it back in her bag. "I didn't want to hurt you. But I was victimized by Tony, too."

Mary Alice took a deep, rasping breath. She turned back to face her, clearly still fighting for control. "Sorry. I thought—"

"I'd have thought that, too, in your place. But honestly, I don't want anything that was Tony's."

Mary Alice wiped tears away with her fingers, managing a weak smile. "Good thing. As far as I know, he didn't even leave enough to bury him. I guess you did that."

"Yes." A fresh twinge of pain hit at the thought of the tears she'd shed at the graveside. Not only wasn't she Tony's widow, but she couldn't even be sure Tony was dead.

She pushed that thought away. Someone had sent that safe-deposit key, but that didn't mean it was Tony. A thought hit her. If that money had been come by honestly, it would belong to Mary Alice and her child.

"I'm not sure if this is going to help you, but when I came to Philadelphia, it was to check out a safe-deposit box that Tony had rented. It was filled with money."

Something that might have been hope dawned in the woman's eyes. She hated to squelch that, but she couldn't let her believe that her money troubles were over.

"The police out in Santa Fe think Tony might have been involved in something illegal, so don't get your hopes up."

"Hope?" Anger flared in Mary Alice's voice. "What

do you know about it? Hope doesn't feed a kid or put shoes on her feet."

"I know how you must feel, but—"

"You don't know anything about what I feel. Don't you dare feel sorry for me. At least Tony actually married me. What does that make you?"

Before Caro could say a word, she'd whirled and raced away.

Caro stood there for a few minutes, dealing with the emotions that boiled up and threatened to explode. She didn't have the luxury of collapsing in tears or even kicking a few of the stacked boxes. She had to pin a smile on her face, go back inside and take over her stand. So that's what she'd do.

The crowds seemed to have thinned out as she moved through them to the stand. Maybe most people had gone outside to the food stands and the rides. Andrea sent her a questioning look.

"Everything okay?"

She summoned a smile. "Fine. Do you want to take a break? I can manage."

"Maybe a little later." Andrea gestured toward the children's table. "I still have a few customers."

Caro glanced at the four children grouped around the table. Three flaxen heads—common in this area with its German heritage. And one little girl with curly dark hair and an engaging smile. Ruthie, Zach's daughter.

He wouldn't like the fact that Caro was anywhere near his little girl. He'd made that clear at the last show. But what could she do about it? She could hardly chase the child away.

Even as she had the thought, the little girl lifted the necklace she was working on. "It's pretty, isn't it?"

Since Ruthie was looking right at her, she could hardly avoid answering. "It sure is. Are pink and purple your favorite colors?"

She nodded gravely. "My daddy says they're princess colors. My princess doll has a dress that color."

"Your daddy will really like your necklace, I'm sure."

"Someday I want to make pretty necklaces like yours." Ruthie leaned across the table and reached up to touch the aqua and silver cross Caro wore. "It's be-yoo-tiful."

Karen, overhearing, grinned at her niece. "I'll bet you could ask Daddy to get one just like that for your birthday. Maybe Ms. Caro would even make it, wouldn't you?"

"Well, yes, of course, if he wanted me to." It wasn't Karen's fault that she was in such a sticky situation. Karen didn't know that her brother's only interest in Caroline was that of a police officer.

She turned away, relieved, at the sight of a potential customer, and went to the other end of the booth, switching places with Andrea, determined to stay as far away from Zach's daughter as possible.

Once she'd persuaded the woman that she shouldn't pass up the earrings that went with the necklace she wanted, the other three children had wandered off to look at something else. To her surprise, Ruthie still bent over her necklace, totally absorbed in stringing beads on the cord.

Her sketching pad, never far away, lay on the corner

of the table. A pencil in her hand was usually a sure remedy for thinking about things she'd prefer to ignore.

Her gaze was drawn back to the little girl, and the pencil started to move. She didn't have quite the angle she wanted, so she edged closer quietly, not wanting to distract the child. She didn't want to talk to Ruthie— she just wanted to capture the intent look an artist, no matter how young, had when absorbed by the work.

She didn't know how much time passed before she realized someone was watching her—had probably been watching her for some time. She looked up to find Zach leaning against his sister's booth, his gaze fixed relentlessly on her face.

Her heart seemed to skip a beat and then proceed to thud too loudly. Foolish, but she couldn't seem to ignore the effect the man had on her.

"Your daughter decided to make a necklace." He could hardly blame her. The activity was open to any child who wanted to do it.

Ruthie looked up at her words. "Daddy, Daddy!" She launched herself into his arms.

"Hi, sweetheart." He caught her, his face lighting with a love that made Caro's breath hitch. "What are you doing?"

"Making a necklace, see?" She scurried to hold it up for his inspection. "It's all finished. Isn't it pretty?"

"It's beautiful." The pink-and-purple creation dangled from his strong hand. "I'm proud of you."

"Ms. Caro showed me how." Ruthie turned to her, and her gaze touched the sketch pad. Her eyes widened. "Is that me?"

Caro nodded. And what exactly would Zach think of that?

He took the pad, his fingers brushing hers, and turned it so that he could see. It seemed to Caro that his face gentled. "Look, Ruthie. It is you."

While Ruthie exclaimed over the image and called her aunt Karen over to see, Zach's gaze met hers. For once there was nothing guarded in it.

"You've really captured her. That expression of total concentration—I've seen that so often, always when she's making something."

"You have an artist on your hands," she said lightly. She tore the sketch carefully from the pad and handed it to him. "For you."

"Thank you." His voice was low, and she couldn't seem to look away from his gaze.

After a long moment, Zach turned away. He took Ruthie's hand. "Say thank you to Ms. Caro, honey. We'll find Grammy and show her what you made."

"Thank you, Ms. Caro." Velvet brown eyes sparkled, and a pair of dimples flashed in her cheeks. "I love your necklaces."

"You're welcome, Ruthie. I'm glad you came." She would not let her confused feelings for Zach affect the way she treated the child. "I hope I'll see you again."

Zach wouldn't like that, she supposed. Well, too bad.

He gave her a slight smile, raised one hand in a sketchy salute and walked off with his daughter.

TWELVE

All Ruthie could talk about for the next several hours was her new friend, Ms. Caro. Zach eventually turned her over to his mother at home, still chattering, and headed back to the festival.

They'd be closing down now, and he'd take a quick look around the grounds to be sure everything was all right. And if he saw Caroline, well, that was inevitable, wasn't it?

The bond that had started to form between his daughter and her Ms. Caro would be a nice thing to see, if only Caro were not involved in who-knew-what.

She could be perfectly innocent of any wrongdoing. But even so, he didn't want his daughter around someone who seemed such a magnet for trouble.

Caroline knew that. He'd seen it in her eyes when she looked at him.

He didn't like the thought that his attitude hurt her. She'd been hurt and betrayed enough. But that was all the more reason to be cautious of any relationship with her. Duty came first for him, and that duty could very well cause him to do something that would hurt her still more.

All very good reasons for staying away from her. So why was he headed straight for the spot where her booth had been?

His sister was already gone. One of his brothers must have stopped by to help her pack up.

Caroline seemed to be down to several boxes that looked ready to take out. He stopped behind her as she picked up one.

"Can I give you a hand with those?"

The box she balanced wobbled in her arms at the sound of his voice, and he grabbed it. "Sorry. I didn't mean to startle you."

"That's fine." She tightened her grip on the box. "I didn't hear you coming. Thanks, but I can manage these."

"No point in making two trips when one will do," he said. He picked up the rest of the boxes. "Lead the way."

Her brow furrowed, as if she were about to argue, but then she shrugged. "My car's out back."

They made their way to the back door, sidestepping folks tearing down their booths. "The festival had a good turnout." He addressed her straight back, since that was all that was visible to him. "The craft shows have become quite a draw for tourists. How did you make out with the things you brought on consignment for the Zooks?"

She looked at him over her shoulder. "How did you know about that?"

He shoved the door open, holding it with his shoulder until she maneuvered her box through. "I hear just about everything, it seems."

"I guess that's a valuable trait for a police officer. Everything sold pretty well—the dolls in particular. I think Emma and Nancy will be pleased." She crossed the gravel lot to her car and opened the hatchback. "Everything should fit in here. If I keep on with the craft shows, at some point I'll need to borrow a bigger vehicle."

He wedged the last box in on top of the things she'd already loaded and closed the hatchback. "There you go. What happened to your sister? She didn't hang around to help you tear down."

"She had a Saturday-night date with her husband, so I chased her off home. I can manage the unloading myself."

"No need. I'll follow you home and help you unload."

Her mouth tightened infinitesimally. "You don't have to do that."

"I want to." He turned toward the side lot where he'd left his car. "I'll be right along." He walked off before she could launch into an argument.

The few minutes it took to drive from the fire hall to Caro's barn were enough time to wonder what he was doing. Not, unfortunately, enough to come up with an answer.

Caroline was already unloading by the time he pulled in behind her car. He thought she was going to reiterate her insistence that she could handle this herself, but instead she gave him a thoughtful look.

"Maybe it's just as well I have a chance to talk to you. I had a visitor today. Tony's wife."

Her expression didn't tell him how she'd taken that. "I suppose that was inevitable. How did it go?"

She shrugged as she headed for the door. He picked up a stack of boxes and followed her.

"Not very happily, as you might imagine. She… well, I guess she needed to vent her anger at somebody."

"What happened wasn't your fault." He held the door while she carried her load inside and then followed her. "If she's going to be angry, Tony ought to be her target."

"Unfortunately, he's not around to hear what we think of him." She crossed to the worktable and set her stack of boxes down, so he did the same.

"What did you tell her?"

"She didn't really want to hear anything from me. I did tell her about the money, though." She swiveled to face him. "Of course, I don't know if it's still there. Did the police take it?"

"Not that I know of." At her skeptical look, he held out his hands. "I'm not in the confidence of the Santa Fe police. I told them about it, as you asked me to. They haven't kept me posted on their plans."

He could guess, but they hadn't told him. If it were his case, he'd probably leave the money where it was to see if anyone showed an interest in it.

"And if they did tell you, you couldn't pass anything along to me in any event."

"No, I guess I couldn't. So where does that leave us?"

"Destined to talk about something else, I suppose. Your daughter is adorable."

As a change of subject, it was a good one. "I think so, but I might be prejudiced."

"The proud father." Her smile seemed to relax. "I can understand that."

"You had a nice activity for the kids today. Not many of the vendors bothered to do that."

She moved into the kitchen and began putting coffee on, seeming to assume he'd stay. "Maybe they didn't think of it. I've been at other shows where vendors have had kids' activities. Or had displays of work in progress. That always seems to draw an audience."

"You enjoyed participating in the show." He didn't really need to ask. She'd been completely wrapped up in what she was doing.

"I did, yes." She leaned against the counter, waiting for the coffee to brew. "I'd gotten away from the craft-show circuit when I was working at the gallery. Francine always seemed to have so much going on that there wasn't time for anything else."

"What kind of things?" He put his elbows on the breakfast bar countertop, curious about what her life had been like in Santa Fe.

"Charity events, for the most part. Francine's late husband, Garner, was very active in the social scene in Santa Fe, and running charity auctions was something he'd started. She got involved and then carried it on after his death." The coffeepot clicked, and she lifted a couple of mugs from the shelf. "I was busy so many Saturdays that I got out of the craft-show circuit. Besides—"

"What?" He liked that she was talking to him so easily, as if they were friends.

She shrugged. "Much as I love the Southwestern art, there's just something about Pennsylvania folk art that speaks to me. It feels so familiar."

"It's part of your childhood, even if you got away from it for a while." He wrapped his hand around the mug she shoved toward him. "Sometimes I think I should be trying harder to keep Ruthie's Afghan culture alive for her, but I'm not sure how to do it. And her parents were Christian, so they were already isolated from their culture to some extent."

"I didn't realize." She leaned on the counter opposite him, so that they were close but with a barrier between them. "How old was she when you brought her back here?"

"Four. She still has some memories, mostly of her parents. I hope she doesn't remember the fighting."

"Were her parents killed?" Her voice was very gentle.

He nodded. It wasn't easy, even after all this time, to think about that. "They were both doctors, doing good work in an isolated area of Afghanistan, but there was a lot of prejudice against them because of their faith. When our team was sent there, we got to know them pretty well."

"How did they—" She stopped. "I'm sorry. I shouldn't bring up something so painful."

His fingers tightened on the mug. "It's okay. The good Lord knows my memory of that is never very far away. What happened to them was my fault."

"Zach—" Her voice was troubled.

He shook his head. "Sorry. I didn't mean to sound melodramatic, but that's how I see it. I left my post because a car overturned in front of me and I ran to help. The terrorists were waiting for that—they got into the village and attacked the clinic. David and Miriam were both killed. Thank goodness Ruthie survived."

Her hand closed over his. "I'm so sorry you lost your friends. But anyone would have done the same."

"Maybe. But if I'd stayed at my post, they'd be alive today."

"You don't know that."

He shook his head.

"Zach—" Her fingers moved comfortingly on his hand. "If something I did made you think about it, I'm sorry."

"Not your fault." He turned his hand, so that he clasped hers. "I guess it was seeing her so absorbed in making that necklace. Her mother loved to make things, too. She'd do these little crafts with Ruthie whenever she had the time. Seeing her like that reminded me of Miriam."

"They'd be proud of the way you're raising their daughter."

"I hope so."

"I know so." Her mouth curved in a smile. "Anyone can see how she adores you."

"The feeling is mutual." He smiled back at her, and somehow those smiles seemed to touch a deep well of understanding. Her green eyes darkened with awareness. But she didn't look away.

The moment drew into an eternity. And then he leaned across the counter and kissed her.

Her lips were soft under his, and she made a small sound that might have expressed surprise. Then she leaned into the kiss, reaching up to touch his cheek with her fingers.

The counter was a barrier between them. Maybe that was just as well. It forced him, eventually, to pull back.

Caro's eyes were soft, almost dazed. He touched her hair, and one of those wild curls tangled around his fingers, seeming to cling with a mind of its own.

He couldn't do this. He drew back, shocked at himself. "I'm sorry. I shouldn't have."

She turned away. "No. I mean…we shouldn't. It's not a good idea."

It wasn't. But that didn't keep him from wanting to kiss her again.

So probably he'd better go before he got himself into any more trouble.

Caroline folded the quilt carefully, wrapping a sheet around it. She'd come to the house for a family dinner and couldn't resist showing off the repair work she was doing on the antique quilt. "I've actually found references to a quilt Elizabeth was making. I'd like to believe it was this one, although there's no proof, of course."

"It's like a treasure hunt," Andrea said. She folded napkins, setting the table with the same efficiency she used to prepare a spreadsheet. Rachel's Tyler had come up from Baltimore for the weekend, and she was busy in the kitchen, having chased the others out to the breakfast room to set the table. "I wonder if there are any other primary sources. Journals, other letters, family histories—that sort of thing."

"I hadn't thought of that." Caro carried a stack of Grams's favorite Lenox plates to the table. It was far better to keep herself occupied with the mystery of the quilt rather than let her mind stray to Zach and that kiss.

He'd known immediately that it was a mistake. They both had. Why did she find it upsetting that he'd been so quick to admit that? She knew as well as he did that there couldn't be anything between them.

"Caro?"

She blinked, jerking her mind back to the present to find Andrea looking at her questioningly.

"Sorry. My mind was wandering. What did you say?"

"I asked if you wanted me to do an Internet search to see if I could locate any other information."

"That would be great. As it is, it's like listening to only one side of the conversation. If only I had Elizabeth's letters to her sister, instead of just her sister's to her."

"That would be pure gold if I could find that," Andrea said. "And about as rare. But let me take a look and see what I find."

"Are you talking about the quilt?" Grams carried a pitcher of daffodils to the table.

"If it is the same quilt, and that's a big *if,* Elizabeth's sister mentions getting the pattern for her from a Reverend Albright. You wouldn't expect a minister to be passing on quilt patterns."

"Maybe it was from his wife." Grams tweaked the blossoms. "I think everything is ready in here. Do we dare interrupt Rachel to see if she's ready?"

"Not I," Caro said quickly. Rachel was the mildest of creatures, but she could turn violent if interrupted in the midst of culinary creation.

"Nor I," Andrea said quickly.

Caro grinned. "Up to you, Grams."

Grams gave a ladylike snort. "I'll get her."

But the kitchen door popped open, and Rachel burst through carrying a laden tray. "Where are the men? The food is ready now."

"We're here." Cal's voice sounded from the hallway. He never strayed far away from Andrea, she noticed. Tyler loomed behind him, and Rachel's gaze caught his.

Something clutched Caro's heart. Surely she wasn't jealous, was she? Her sisters deserved to find happiness with good men who loved them.

It was just that she felt…bereft, she supposed. Not at the loss of Tony, but at the realization that what she'd imagined they'd meant to each other was an illusion.

There was no one for her, and she was left standing on the outside, watching her sisters' happiness but unable to share it.

Rachel carried platters to the table, and for a few moments all was confusion as she and Andrea brought the rest of the food, filled water glasses and finally took their places around the long table.

Grams reached out, and they all linked hands around the table. She'd forgotten, in all those years away, that family custom. Rachel held her hand on one side and Andrea on the other. She could almost imagine she felt love flowing through the link as Grams asked the blessing on the meal and on the family.

They loosed hands at the Amen, and platters began to fly around the table—fried chicken, baked corn, fluffy mashed potatoes, the relishes that were characteristic of a Pennsylvania Dutch dinner.

"Rachel, you've outdone yourself." Cal took a biscuit and passed the basket to Grams. "This is wonderful."

"Well, she had an incentive," Andrea teased, with a sidelong glance at Tyler. "Tyler was coming."

Tyler grinned. "Then you should thank me, right?"

"I guess so." Andrea took a forkful of mashed potatoes and looked at Grams. "Can we tell Caro yet?"

"Tell me what?" She couldn't help a spasm of apprehension. Most of the surprises in her life had not been happy ones.

"I suppose we'd better, since you've given it away," Grams said.

"What?" Surely they wouldn't all be smiling at her if it were bad news.

"We've seen how much you love dealing with the local arts and crafts," Grams said. "So we thought a good addition to the bed-and-breakfast would be a crafts shop in the barn. Which you would run, of course."

She could only stare. "But...that would be very expensive, renovating the barn, getting the stock. I don't have any cash to put into a project like that."

Thanks to Tony. If he hadn't wiped her out, this might be a possibility. But if he hadn't, she might never have come home and realized that what she wanted was right here.

"Your contribution would be your expertise," Andrea said. "Grams will front the start-up costs with the settlement she received from the embezzlement of Grandfather's business. And I'm sure I can get you a small-business loan for whatever else we need."

Her mind whirled with possibilities, and for a moment she let herself hope. "But the renovations—"

"You have a carpenter and an architect right in the family," Tyler said. "I've already drawn up some preliminary plans, but Cal and I need your input. We thought you might want some space for craft classes and groups to meet."

She tried to combat the tears that welled in her eyes. "I can't let you do all this for me. It's too risky. There are other craft and gift shops...."

"You have access to Amish-made crafts that many others don't." Grams smiled, her eyes soft with tears. "Emma loves you as if you were one of her own children."

"She mentioned the idea to begin with," Andrea said. "Rachel and I just took it and ran with it."

"So, Caroline." Grams smiled through her tears. "What do you say? Will you do it?"

She couldn't speak. Couldn't say anything in the face of this overwhelming love. She could only nod and put up her hands to try and stem the tears that overflowed, washing away the barriers that remained between them.

Zach had stayed away from Caro for several days, trying to forget that kiss. It hadn't worked. Still, he'd managed to rationalize it to a certain extent.

They were attracted to each other, and they'd had a

moment of closeness that took them both a little too far. More serious for him than for her. There was no actual investigation going on, so he hadn't violated any regulations, but he knew in his heart that was a cop-out.

Attraction or not, he had a responsibility to check on her. The Santa Fe P.D. might not want to involve him in their investigation of Tony Gibson, but he wouldn't ignore the odd things that kept happening in Caroline's vicinity.

At least, that was what he told himself when he pulled up to the side door of the inn. He wanted to touch base with Rachel. If she could talk her stubborn sister into moving into the house, he'd feel a lot better about Caroline's safety.

But when he tapped at the door nearest the kitchen, it was Emma who answered. "Morning, Emma. Is Rachel around?"

"She has gone to New Holland for groceries. Is there some way I can help you, Zachary?"

Emma had moved to a first-name basis with him when her son had been injured last year.

"It's nothing important. I'll catch her later. What about Caroline?"

"Ach, she is not here, either. She has gone to the airport to pick up her friend who comes for a visit."

That was the first he'd heard of a friend coming. Someone from her life in New Mexico? Maybe someone who knew Tony? "Was that her friend from Santa Fe?"

"*Ja,* the lady she worked for out there. I have the blue bedroom all ready for her."

"Guess it wasn't my day to find anyone home. Stay well, Emma."

She nodded, shutting the door.

That was a pointless trip. Still, it was interesting to learn that her employer was coming. Francine Carrington—the woman who'd reported her missing.

He went down the steps, glancing toward Caroline's apartment, and came to a stop. Caroline might not be there, but someone was. He caught sight of a flicker of blue, maybe a shirt, disappearing around the corner of the barn.

Could be nothing. Could be the person who'd been in the apartment a couple of times, back for another try.

He glanced toward the patrol car, but it would be faster on foot. He jumped lightly off the patio and ran across the grass.

Better this way, in any event. The prowler, if that's what he was, would hear a car coming. This way, he'd catch him unawares.

It worked out just about that way. He rounded the end of the barn, moving quietly on the grass instead of the path, and there the man was, looking in the window.

"Police. Stop right there and turn around."

Somehow he wasn't entirely surprised when the man turned around. Jason Tenley, supposed photojournalist. He hadn't bought that from the moment he'd met the man.

"Just looking for Ms. Hampton, Chief. That's all." Tenley held his hands up, palms toward him, as if to show he wasn't holding a weapon.

Not that he expected a weapon. If the prowler had

intended harm to Caro, he wouldn't do it by making coffee.

"Looking in her window?" He shook his head. "You'll have to do better than that, Mr. Tenley. Suppose we go back to my office and talk about it."

Tenley looked chagrined. "You're not really going to arrest me, are you? I suppose technically I'm trespassing, but…"

"*Prowling* was the word I had in mind," Zach said. Something was off-key here. The man wasn't reacting the way he should be, having been caught by the police.

"Guess maybe it's time to come clean." Tenley tried a disarming smile.

"It wouldn't hurt." He wasn't disarmed.

"I'm not a peeping Tom. I'm an insurance investigator. Let me reach into my pocket, and I'll show you my ID."

Zach gave a curt nod. Insurance investigator. The words sounded more reasonable than the photojournalist bit.

Tenley handed over an ID folder. Zach studied it and then slid it into his pocket.

"You won't mind my hanging on to this until I check it out."

"Wouldn't do any good arguing, would it? Especially since I'd like your cooperation."

"It's a bit late for that."

"I guess it looks that way from your viewpoint."

"From any cop's viewpoint." The guy might be legit, but that didn't mean he was letting him off easily. "If you come into my jurisdiction on an investigation, you ought to know enough to check in with me. Now, why are you here?"

And what did it have to do with Caroline?

"You're right. I shouldn't have tried to take a short cut. The truth is, my company is on the hook for a substantial sum over a charity auction in Santa Fe, and they're not eager to advertise the fact that they've been had. A very expensive piece of Native American jewelry that was donated for the auction has turned out to be a skillful fake."

He didn't need the man to connect the dots for him. "Caroline Hampton was, I assume, the jewelry expert on the gallery's staff."

Tenley nodded. "She's the only one, so far as we've been able to determine, who had the skill to make such a convincing switch."

"I take it you don't have any actual evidence, or this would be coming from the police."

"That's about the size of it." Tenley ran a hand over his graying hair, then massaged the back of his neck. "It's been a real headache. Both the owner and the insurance company want to keep this a private matter as long as there's a chance of regaining the object."

"And what progress have you made?" He wouldn't let himself focus on the Caroline he'd grown to know. He couldn't.

"Precious little." Tenley spread his hands. "Ms. Hampton hasn't made a suspicious move since she's been here. Only thing that might have caught my attention was that trip to Philadelphia, but since she went with you, I assume she wasn't contacting any fences."

"No." He was tempted to hold the man until he'd

checked out his story, but that would be more a product of his own irritation than good police work. "Where are you staying, Mr. Tenley?"

"White Rose Inn, out on the highway."

"All right." He gave a curt nod. "Stop by my office tomorrow afternoon. I'll have checked this out by then. In the meantime, stay off this property. We clear?"

"Right." If Tenley was relieved, he didn't show it. "I'll be on my way."

He went quickly, rounding the end of the barn at a lope. A moment later his car bounced out the lane toward the road. Zach watched, automatically noting make and model, license number.

Now what? Go back to the office, check out the story Tenley told.

It would check out. Tenley wouldn't make up something so easy to disprove. And then—well, then he was going to have to tread very carefully.

He'd begun to have feelings for Caro. But those feelings could explode and hurt both of them if she wasn't the woman he thought her to be.

On the other hand, if she was innocent in all this, she'd feel betrayed when she learned he'd been investigating her. And she'd been betrayed too many times in her life to forgive that again. There was no possible happy ending in all of this that he could see.

THIRTEEN

"Now we're getting into typical Pennsylvania Dutch country." Caroline nodded toward the dairy farms spread across the rolling landscape. Once she'd picked up Francine at the airport in Philadelphia, she'd been eager to get off the interstate and out into the country again.

"Very pretty." Francine barely turned her expensively coiffed ash-blond head to glance out the window.

"You didn't look," Caro accused, half laughing.

It was good to see Francine again, but rather odd, too. They'd had a good relationship, a friendship even, but she'd always been aware of their employer/employee relationship.

Francine gave an elaborate sigh. "Really, Caroline. You should be aware that I'm not a scenery person."

"True. I've never known anyone who was more urban than you." Even in Santa Fe, where most people gloried in the magnificent outdoors, Francine had looked slightly too sophisticated to fit in.

She'd been surprised that Francine hadn't gone back to her native San Francisco after her husband's death, but she'd been devoted to running the gallery and continuing Garner's charities. There had been rumors of a suit launched by Garner's children from his first marriage, contesting his will, but Francine had never mentioned it.

Francine touched her hand. "Now you know how much I care about you, to be willing to spend time in this rural wilderness. I suppose there's not even a decent coffee bar in this small town of yours."

"Well, no." She tried to imagine one of the stolid Pennsylvania Dutch farmers picking up the latest mocha cappuccino before heading out to do the milking. "But my sister makes a fine cup of coffee."

How long would Francine last here? Probably not for more than a few days, but she was touched that Francine would make the effort at all.

"I'll defer judgment on your sister's coffee until I've tasted it, if you don't mind. Now tell me. Has anything more happened with regard to Tony?"

She'd been keeping Francine up to date at her insistence, so there wasn't much new to tell. "Not since I talked with you after we found out about that safe-deposit box and Tony's wife. Believe me, that was enough of a shock to last quite a while."

Francine frowned for an instant and then smoothed the frown away, always careful to preserve her flawless complexion. "I'm not sure it was a good idea to take the local cop along on that expedition. Why tell the police something they don't already know?"

"He's all right." She pushed the memory of that kiss away. "Anyway, I could hardly hide the existence of all that money. If Tony was involved in something illegal, I don't want it in my possession."

"I suppose not. But as for that first wife—well, darling, he should have told you about her, but I refuse to believe there wasn't a divorce. Tony was hardly the type of man to commit bigamy."

She had to smile, even though the situation wasn't humorous. "Is there a type of man likely to do that?"

"You know what I mean." Francine dismissed that with a wave of her hand. "I'm relieved nothing else has happened. Perhaps whoever was playing games has tired of it."

"Maybe." She wasn't convinced she was at the end of this trouble, but maybe she was just being pessimistic.

"So, are you about ready to give up your rural solitude and come back to Santa Fe where you belong?"

"I don't think so." She couldn't imagine how Francine was going to take her news. "As a matter of fact, my family wants me to create and run a crafts center and shop in conjunction with the inn."

Francine's head swiveled to give Caro the full effect of a disbelieving stare. "You're not going to tell me you're settling in here for good."

"Well, maybe not forever. But for the foreseeable future, anyway."

To her surprise, Francine didn't jump into telling her what she should do, as was her usual practice. Instead she turned back, to stare absently at the winding road ahead for a long moment.

"Much as I hate to say this, maybe that's the best thing for now."

An odd note in her voice set Caro's nerves on alert. "What do you mean?"

"That's really the reason I came." Francine didn't seem to want to look at her. "I hate to be the bearer of bad tidings, but I feel as if I have to warn you."

"Warn me about what?" Her hands tightened on the steering wheel.

"Something happened at that last charity auction we ran." Francine's voice was slow. Reluctant. "There was an elaborate turquoise and silver pin—an original design by a noted Zuni artist. Do you remember it?"

"Yes, of course I remember it. I set up the display and did the photographs." She'd held the beautiful thing in her hands, marveling at the artistry and craftsmanship, knowing that however good she was, she'd never make anything that perfect.

"The new owner had it valued. It's a fake."

Her head spun. "How could that be? I worked on it. I know it was genuine. It was checked out by the insurance expert before it went on display. Surely they don't think that the gallery had anything to do with the fraud."

"Not the gallery," Francine said. "You."

Caroline narrowed her eyes, trying to make out the sign that was nearly hidden by a rampant growth of wild roses. It would be hard enough to see in the daylight; in the dusk it was nearly impossible. She had to come to a stop to read the sign, and even then it wasn't reassuring. She wasn't supposed to be on Twin Forks Road, was she?

She'd followed Emma's directions to reach the Stoltzfus farm and arrived there without incident. Even now, several carefully wrapped quilts rested on the backseat, ready to be shown in the craft center once it opened. Now getting back home was the problem.

Maybe she was jumping the gun, collecting materials for the shop while it was still in the planning stages, but she wanted to be sure she had enough inventory to give her new project a chance of success.

Besides, it had been a distraction from the bad news Francine had brought with her when she arrived three days earlier. Since then they'd gone over the counterfeit backward and forward, exploring every possibility, without coming to any conclusion.

Francine had reiterated her support a number of times, but Francine was also concerned for her gallery's good name. She wouldn't sacrifice that for the sake of friendship, and Caro didn't want her to. But where did that leave her?

She hadn't been able to bring herself to tell her grandmother and sisters about this new complication. How long could she expect even their support to last?

Grams would say that there was Someone who was always there to support her. Emma had said that if God seemed distant, it was because she had moved away, not God. Maybe that was true, but if it was, how did she bridge that gap?

Lights flashed in her rearview mirror and she looked up, startled. Apparently she wasn't the only one on this lonely road. Good. It felt a little less isolated. It must lead somewhere, hopefully to a road whose name she'd recognize before it was completely dark.

The driver behind her came up fast—too fast on this narrow road. His lights reflected in her eyes, and she flipped the rearview mirror to diminish the glare.

Irritation edged her nerves. If he was in that much of a hurry, why didn't he just pass her?

She eased ever so carefully closer to the side. There could be a ditch or a drop-off, hidden by the lush undergrowth. She raised her hand to motion him around—

The car rammed her, snapping her neck back and taking her breath away. Shock ricocheted through her, and she stepped on the gas in an automatic reflex.

The car surged forward, but he was right on her tail, bumping her again and sending the car fishtailing before she regained control. Crazy—he had to be crazy.

She clutched the wheel, hunched forward as if to ward off a blow, pressing down on the gas. *Please, please. Help me.*

No hills to deal with, thank goodness, but she went shrieking around the bends blindly, terrified that she'd meet someone coming, but at least then she wouldn't be alone out here with a maniac on her tail—

He came up fast, lights glaring, and rammed her again. She fought the wheel, but it did no good, she couldn't regain control, she was losing it—

The car spun dizzyingly and plunged off the road. Her body was thrown backward, then forward as the car lurched to a stop in a mass of rhododendron bushes. The airbag deployed, muffling her. For a moment she couldn't move, couldn't even assess whether she was hurt.

But she had to move. She could hear the other car, coming back toward her, engine roaring. She had to get out, now, before he reached her.

She fumbled with the seat belt, freeing herself,

shoving at the folds of the airbag, and slid across to the passenger door, shoving it open, clambering out.

Taking a quick glance toward the road, she saw the car stop, a dark figure get out. No time to see more; she just ran. Into the dark, anywhere away from him.

She stumbled through the undergrowth, brambles tearing at her clothes, and then burst into the woods where dry leaves rustled with every step.

She couldn't worry about being quiet—he was too close behind her. She rushed through the woods blindly, panic harsh in her throat, breath dragging painfully.

She'd gained a little on him, hadn't she? She could hear him crashing through the underbrush. Stop. Think. Once he got in the clear he'd overtake her easily.

She looked around, eyes adjusting to the dimness. There—that clump of trees surrounded by bushes. If she could get in there before he came any closer, she could hide.

Please, please. She ran to the bushes, threw herself on her stomach and squirmed her way beneath, reaching back to ruffle the dry leaves so that she'd leave no telltale traces.

Just in time. She could hear him now, closer, so close she could hear the ragged gasps of his breath.

She curled into a ball, hiding her face against her knees. *Please, Lord. Please. If You're there. If You hear me, protect me.*

The footsteps came closer, crunching the leaves. A low chuckle chilled her bones. Did he see her?

A whisper, so soft it might have been a flutter of birds' wings. It came again, a little louder.

"Caro." A whisper, just on the edge of hearing. "Caro, come out. Come out."

She pressed her face tight against her knees, clenching her teeth. He knew where she was, she would feel a hand grabbing her, dragging her out—

He turned. His feet rustled through the leaves, going back toward the road.

She let out the breath she'd been holding. *Wait, wait, don't move yet, not until he's farther away.*

Finally she couldn't hear him any longer. She crawled out. Don't go toward the road, he could be waiting. The other way—that was the only safe thing. She moved slowly, cautiously, one step at a time.

Nothing. If he heard her, if he was coming, she'd know it. She hurried blindly through the woods, away from the road, falling, getting up, running, falling again, until finally she was in a field, the stubble of grass under her feet, and ahead of her the lights of a farmhouse.

The brightness of electric light, not Amish, then. They'd have a phone. She started toward the house at a staggering run. She was safe.

Thank You. Thank You.

Zach sent a cautious glance toward Caroline as he drove down the lane from the Miller farm to the main road. "Are you sure you don't want to stop by the E.R., just to be on the safe side?"

Caro shook her head, reaching up to lift a strand of hair away from the bandage that adorned her forehead.

"You heard Mrs. Miller. Nothing but bumps, bruises and abrasions."

"Margo Miller is used to patching up three accident-prone sons, but that doesn't make her a doctor."

She turned her head slightly to smile at him. "I'm all right, really. I just want to go home."

"If you're sure." His stomach had been tied up in knots since he got the call from John Miller that Caro had turned up at his door. It began to ease, just a little, at the smile. "Have you thought of anything else about the car?"

She moved restlessly. "We've already gone over all that."

They had, but he suspected she needed to talk it out before she reached the inn. "Sometimes something else comes back once the initial shock has passed."

"I didn't really get a good look—just lights in my rearview mirror." Her voice tightened on the words, as if she didn't want to relive those moments.

"What about when you got out of your car? Did you try to see where the other vehicle was?"

She glanced toward him, her breath catching. "You're right. I did. It was just a dark shape, but I'm sure it was a sedan. I guess that doesn't help much."

"It eliminates all the pickups in the county," he said lightly. "We might find something when we go over your car. When he rammed you, he might have left a paint chip that would tell us the color."

"I didn't think of that." She shook her head. "I haven't been thinking of much of anything, to tell the truth. Just...scared."

"That's not surprising." It took an effort to keep his

voice level when he thought of her in danger out on that lonely road. "You're entitled after what you went through. Any chance you got a look at the driver?"

"It was dark. I couldn't see anything about him." Her voice tightened, alerting him. There was more, he was sure of it.

"Notice how he walked? Did he give the impression of a young man?"

"I didn't see him, I told you."

"Hear him, then. Did he speak?"

Her hands twisted together in her lap. This was it. She'd heard him.

"Not to say 'speak.' He…whispered."

He wanted to reach out, to cover those agitated fingers with his, but he couldn't. "What did he whisper?"

"My name." Her voice was the whisper now.

"You're sure?"

At her nod, his jaw clenched. It wasn't a random thing, then. He hadn't really thought it was, but there was always a chance. He glanced at her.

"There's something else, isn't there?"

She held out against the question for a moment, and then she nodded. "He didn't say Caroline. He said Caro." Her fingers twisted again. "Tony called me that. He… I didn't believe he could be alive. But who else would know?"

She sounded at the end of her rope, and for a moment he couldn't think of her as a suspect, only as someone he cared about, someone who was hurting.

"I don't think you can assume that." He tried to keep his feelings from sounding in his voice. It wouldn't do either of them any good to let her know he cared. "Your sisters call you Caro. I've heard them. Probably a lot of people around here have."

"I suppose." She didn't sound convinced.

He could hardly blame her. The bottom line was that the attack on her wasn't a random thing, so whether the attacker was Tony or someone else, this situation had taken a turn to the dangerous.

They were almost at the inn, and once her grandmother and sisters saw her, to say nothing of her friend, he wouldn't have a chance to say anything in private.

"Look, I want you to promise me something."

She looked at him. "What?"

"Promise me that you'll stay at the inn tonight, okay?"

She nodded. Her eyes were wide and frightened in the intermittent illumination of the streetlamps. "That's not a permanent solution. Why is this happening, Zach?" Her voice choked on a sob. "I have to know."

He did reach out then, clasping her hand briefly in his. "I wish I could answer that. But I won't stop looking until we know the truth. I promise."

FOURTEEN

Caroline turned away from the stove and nearly tripped over Barney. When she'd made it clear she was returning to the apartment the next night, Grams had insisted that if she wouldn't listen to reason, she'd at least take the dog along for protection.

"You'll take care of me, won't you, sweetie?" She ruffled Barney's silky fur, and he gave her a foolish grin and a soft woof.

She was afraid Grams didn't understand her insistence on coming back to her own place. It wasn't about asserting her independence, not anymore. She loved and trusted them.

Just as important, she'd taken her first step toward trusting God again last night. Funny. She'd wrestled with how that would happen, and then when it came, it had been as natural as breathing.

She walked into the living room, carrying her mug of coffee, and Barney padded at her heels. Much as she'd learned to love this place, it did seem lonely with darkness pressing against the windows. But she hadn't really had a choice. Danger was coming closer, and she wasn't going to let it get anywhere near her family. She'd face it here.

Barney put his head on her knee, as if he sensed that her thoughts were getting too grim. She petted his head. "Sorry. I guess I'm not very good company, am I? Maybe if I talk to you, I can keep from thinking about what happened last night."

But she couldn't. She kept hearing that voice whispering her name. She'd heard it last night, too, but at least she'd had the comfort of Rachel's soft breathing in the other twin bed to help block it out.

Caro. No one in Santa Fe had called her that but Tony. Still, Zach was right. Plenty of people here had heard the nickname. Even Zach had used it once or twice. Wasn't it more rational to assume that the dark figure was someone, anyone, other than Tony?

She was thinking too much again. She took a sip of the coffee and made a face. Why on earth had she made coffee? It would keep her up all night. Not that she expected to do much sleeping, in any event.

Barney's ears pricked, and he raised his head, giving a soft woof. A knock at the door followed a moment later.

The dog didn't act as if it were a stranger. She went to the window nearest the door and drew the curtain back. Her sisters stood on the doorstep.

She'd thought this was settled. She opened the door, trying to look perfectly calm and confident.

Before she could say a word, Andrea had elbowed her way in, arms laden, with Rachel right behind her.

"Since you won't come to us, we've come to you," Andrea announced. She tossed a couple of sleeping bags on the rug in front of the fireplace. "We're going to have a pajama party."

"Andrea, Rachel—" She choked up before she could say anything else.

"Don't argue." Rachel carried her bundles to the kitchen. "We have the makings of a first-class pajama party—brie, crackers, fruit, my special panini sandwiches, hot chocolate and marshmallows, the works."

Andrea grinned. "Doesn't sound remotely like any pajama party food I can remember."

"Well, I trust our palates are a little more sophisticated now." Rachel moved from stove to countertop to refrigerator as if she were perfectly at home. Maybe, for Rachel, any kitchen was home.

"I hope Tyler knows what a treasure he's getting." She crossed to the breakfast bar.

Andrea followed her. "She reminds him with every meal. I'm sure when Cal faces one of my meals, fresh from the deli, he thinks he's married the wrong sister."

"I had first shot at Cal, you'll remember, and he never got past looking at me as a little sister." Rachel turned the heat on under the hot chocolate pot and slapped a fry pan onto the front burner. "He took one look at Andrea and he was a goner."

Andrea's smile was tender and reminiscent. "He didn't act that way. Spent most of his time yelling at me for one thing or another, as I recall."

"He adores you, and you know it." Caro looked from Andrea to Rachel. "You're lucky, you know. Both of you, to find such good men."

Andrea gave her a quick hug. "Baby, it's going to happen for you, too. Just because Tony turned out to be a jerk—"

Rachel made a soft murmur of dissent, but Andrea shrugged that off.

"Don't give me that look, Rach. We all know the man was a con artist if not something worse, and Caroline deserves way better than that." She glanced at Caro's face. "Okay? Or would you like to slug me?"

That surprised a laugh out of her. "Tact isn't your strong suit, is it? But you're right. It's just taken me a while to accept."

Rachel turned a sandwich. "I can understand that. It's one thing to accept something intellectually, but another to really get it in the heart."

Caro could almost feel the tension drain out of her. "How did I get two such wise older sisters?"

"It took us a while." Andrea's expression grew serious. "We let you down. We know that now. We were both so eager to get away from Mom that we didn't think about what it was going to be like for you, left alone with her."

Tears welled in Caro's eyes. It was far more than she'd ever expected to hear from Andrea, who was always so sure of herself. "It's okay." She forced the words past the lump in her throat. "Really."

"Okay, enough serious stuff." Rachel slid plates in front of them, then turned back to get the platter of brie, grapes and crackers. "Wrap yourself around that, and I guarantee you'll feel better. Prosciutto, goat cheese, roasted red peppers, sautéed mushrooms—"

"And your secret sauce?" Andrea teased.

Caro took a bite, the flavors exploding in her mouth. "Wow, Rachel. This is prize-winning food. You're right. This would bring a dying man back from the brink for one more bite."

"Oops, almost forgot." Andrea turned to scrabble through her bag. "I brought something that's going to cheer you up almost as much as Rachel's food." She put a sheaf of fax papers onto the countertop. "My Internet research paid off faster than even I expected. I found a family historian in Boston who is writing a history of Elizabeth's family. And—wait for it—he actually had some of Elizabeth's letters written to her sister from Pennsylvania."

Caro put down her sandwich. "You're kidding! How on earth did you find him that fast?"

"Genealogy sites." Andrea smiled, a little smugly. "You'd be amazed at what's out there, and most of the serious researchers are eager to share. He faxed these when I promised to send him photos of the quilt and any additional information we find."

"Hurry, look at them," Rachel urged. "Andrea wouldn't let me get even a peek. She said you had to be first."

Caro bent over the faxed sheets, deciphering the faint, faded script. It had become easier since she'd been reading the letters from Elizabeth's sister, and she was able to go through them fairly quickly, reading out pertinent bits to her sisters.

"Listen to this." She frowned at the page. "She says, 'I have completed the quilt according to the pastor's instructions, and I eagerly await the first opportunity to put it out.' That's a little odd, isn't it?"

"Maybe she just means to use it," Rachel said, scooping up melted brie with a cracker.

"Could be." But something was niggling at the back of Caro's mind—something she'd read or heard, that had to do with quilts.

"Listen to this one." Andrea had picked up another of the sheets. "This really is odd. She says, 'Thank you, my dear sister, for your concern. I am upheld by your prayers. As you say, this venture can be dangerous, but when I think of the perils of those we help, our dangers are nothing. If only I could be sure who to trust. A Friend was taken into custody two nights ago, and all are praying for him and questioning who could have betrayed him.'"

"Wow," Rachel said again. "I always pictured women of those days living a pretty quiet life. Sounds like Elizabeth had something more serious on her plate. I wonder what it was."

"Well, my new genealogy friend promised me more letters in a few days, so maybe the answer will be there." Andrea looked toward the stove. "Are you going to give us some of that hot chocolate, or just let it steam away over there?"

"Goodness, I forgot." Rachel scrambled to get the hot chocolate served up, along with a shoofly pie that she said was Emma's contribution to the party.

Between the food and the lively chatter her sisters put up, Caroline realized to her surprise that she actually wasn't worrying any longer. She had a new life, and plenty of new things to occupy her mind. With so much support, she'd get through this dark time.

They cleaned up together, chattering in a way she couldn't remember since they'd been children. Her sisters had grown into women to be proud of. Andrea, so smart and efficient, but with a new softness about her since she'd come back home and met Cal. And gentle Rachel—there was strength behind that gentleness that surprised her.

What did they think of how she'd turned out? She wasn't sure she wanted to know. She'd certainly made more than her share of mistakes.

They finally settled in front of the fireplace with refills of hot chocolate. "I guess we should have asked your friend to join us," Rachel said. "But she went out to dinner, and I didn't like to interfere with her plans."

"You mean you thought she'd put a damper on the party," Andrea said, smiling.

"It's just as well," Caro interceded. "I don't think Francine is the pajama-party type." And Francine certainly didn't have to tell Caroline where she was going for the evening, although she was a little surprised that she hadn't.

"It was nice of her to come here to support you," Rachel said.

"It was. She's bravely doing without her gourmet coffee for the sake of being here for me."

"I did manage to fix some hazelnut this morning that she said wasn't half-bad." Rachel's grin said that she wasn't offended.

Andrea stretched. "Look at the time. I'd better get some sleep. I'm supposed to meet with a new client in the morning."

Caro was about to say that they could go and sleep in their own beds when the noise came. Rachel froze, half into her sleeping bag, and stared at the back wall—the one the connected to the barn. "Did you hear that?"

"How could you help but hear it?" Andrea demanded. "Somebody knocked something over. Sounds like your vandals are back, Caro." She was already dialing her cell phone. "Cal, there's someone in the barn. Yes, all right. We will, just hurry."

She snapped the phone shut. "Cal says to stay inside and keep the door locked. He's on his way, and he's calling Zach."

When Caro would have moved, Rachel grabbed her. "It's all right. They'll be right here. Cal was staying in the house tonight. It'll only take a couple of minutes."

"I don't have a couple of minutes." Caroline pulled free and headed for the door, seized by a compulsion she didn't really understand. "I can't wait. Don't you see? The quilt is in there. Vandals—" Words failed her, but the pictures filled her mind—some ignorant kids slashing at the quilt, stretched on its frame, throwing paint at it—

She reached the door and grabbed the flashlight that hung next to it. Barney, excited, jumped at her heels, barking. "I'll be all right. I'll take Barney—"

"We'll all go." Andrea coolly pulled a poker from the fireplace rack. "It's our history, too."

"Right." Rachel rushed to the kitchen and returned brandishing the fry pan. "Let me at them."

Caro's fear was swept away by the desire to laugh. "All right. Let's go."

She opened the door. Barney ran ahead of them, barking wildly. How they must look, running after the dog in the dark. The fear she'd felt the night before in the woods was a distant memory. She could take on anything with her sisters behind her.

They rounded the corner of the barn. Barney gave a fierce bark, followed by snarling and snapping, and a man's frightened cry. She swung the torch's beam wildly, trying to focus on the melee.

The dark figure—was it the man from last night?—tore free of the dog and started to run.

But there was no place to run. The police car surged down the lane, siren wailing, just as Cal, breathing hard, burst out of the path from the house.

The man froze, caught in the converging beams of the headlights and the torch. Zach got out of the police car and came toward him.

"Out kind of late, aren't you, Mayor?"

The man turned, full into Caro's light. Keith Morris stood there, and in his arms was the antique quilt.

Zach led Keith to a straight-backed chair in the barn apartment and planted him in it, none too gently. In his opinion, Keith should be sitting in the police station right now, but he'd given in, partly because of Keith's frantic appeals to be allowed to explain, but mostly because Caroline said she wanted to hear him. After what she'd been through, she deserved to hear.

At the moment Caroline and Rachel had spread the quilt on the table and were going over it, stitch by stitch, to be sure it hadn't come to any harm. Andrea had given up her poker, a little reluctantly, and now sat in the corner on the sofa, her husband's arm around her.

"Okay, Keith." He frowned down at Churchville's mayor. "Let's have an explanation. Breaking and entering, theft—those are plenty serious charges."

"No, no, you can't arrest me." Sweat broke out on

Keith's forehead, and his gaze swiveled from side to side and settled on Caroline. "You have to believe me. I just wanted a look at the quilt, that's all. I wanted to know what you had before I made an offer. But then I heard the dog barking, and I ran without thinking."

"You expect us to buy that? You could have come to Caroline anytime and asked to see the quilt if you were interested in buying."

"He already saw it," Caroline said. "He offered to buy it."

"I...I hardly got more than a glimpse then." Keith looked at him and quickly away. "I mean, I thought the price would go up if I showed too much interest— she'd already turned me down once."

"If all you wanted was to look at it, why did you take it out of the frame?" Andrea leaned forward, apparently unable to stay out of it any longer. "You were trying to steal it."

Keith shied away from the words. "I couldn't help it. I mean, it was my mother." He looked up at Zach again. "You know what she's like. She's so proud of being the final authority on things historical in the area, proud of her ancestors being First Proprietors, going back to William Penn and all that. She couldn't take the idea that someone might have something of more historical significance than she does." He sat up straighter, apparently gaining confidence from this line of argument, which just might be closer to the truth.

"So you decided to steal the quilt for her?" He let skepticism weigh his voice.

"Not steal, no. I thought if I showed it to her, maybe she'd decide it wasn't that great and lose interest. Or if not, I'd return it, come to Caroline, make her a fair offer. I thought I'd have it back before anyone even knew it was missing. You don't want to arrest me for that. Think of the ugly publicity."

That was the wrong argument to use on him. In his book, no one was above the law. Maybe it would be tough to go up against the Morris family, but—

"That's not why your mother wants the quilt." Caroline walked toward Keith, her gaze fixed on him.

Zach took a sidestep that put his body between them, shocked by the wave of protectiveness that surged through him. "What do you mean?"

She didn't veer from her focus on Keith, and she spoke to him as if there were no one else there. "You don't know what we found out. We already had Elizabeth's letter from her sister. Now we have copies of the ones she wrote."

Zach shot a glance toward Andrea, who seemed like the one most likely to give him a sensible explanation.

"The Elizabeth Unger who made the quilt," she said. She turned her attention back on her sister. "Go on, Caro. What did you figure out?"

"Elizabeth talked about making the quilt according to the directions she'd been sent. About putting it out for its first use. About a Friend being betrayed and arrested, and how their courage was nothing to that of the people they were trying to help." She turned toward the others then, her eyes alight with excitement. "Don't you see? I remember reading about it—some scholars believe that quilts were used as signals on the Underground Railroad, guiding escaping slaves to safe houses."

"This area was one of the major routes." Everyone knew that. There was even a historical tour of Underground Railroad sites.

"Elizabeth was a perfect person to get involved— deeply religious, coming from Boston, which was a center for the abolitionist movement." Caroline went on as if he hadn't spoken. "The Friend she talked about... the word was capitalized because she literally meant Friend, one of the local Quakers who were part of the network. She said someone in the area betrayed him to the slavecatchers." She swung back on Keith. "That's what your mother didn't want me to find out."

He'd become so involved in her story that he'd almost forgotten about Keith. Now he saw that the man's face had blanched.

"What about it, Keith? Time to stop dancing around the truth."

"One of your mother's prized ancestors was the traitor. That's it, isn't it?" Andrea was on her feet now, shaking off her husband's restraining arm. "You're trying to save your family reputation."

Keith shook his head helplessly, sagging in the chair. "Mother knew the family stories about it. When she heard about the quilt, heard that Caroline was going to display it, was looking into the history—she thought it was all going to come out. She wouldn't let me alone about it. She said I had to destroy the quilt, make it look like vandals had broken in, anything. I didn't want to, but I couldn't help it."

Zach planted his hands on his hips. "And what about the rest of it? Breaking into this apartment, forcing Caroline's car off the road last night."

Cal cleared his throat, the sound breaking through Zach's fury. "Much as I hate to sound like the attorney I used to be, Chief, don't you think you ought to caution him before he answers that question?"

The words restored his common sense. He was appalled at himself. He was letting his feelings for Caro get in the way of his duty.

He reached for Keith's arm. "Come on. Let's continue this down at headquarters."

"No, no, don't." Keith shrank away from him. "I don't need an attorney. I didn't do anything else, I swear it. I heard about her troubles, but it wasn't me. And I couldn't have done anything last night—you should know that. I was at the town council meeting. It went on until nearly eleven. The council members will tell you. I was there the whole time."

"I won't press charges."

The quiet statement had him swiveling toward Caro. "What are you talking about? He's admitted it."

"But he didn't do the other things. I never thought he did."

No, she wouldn't have believed it could be that easy. Besides, she believed Tony was still alive. "We caught him red-handed running away with that quilt in his arms."

"We got it back. There's no harm done." For a moment she looked ready to burst into tears. "I don't want the trouble it would cause."

"That's not an excuse for not doing your duty." Now it was as if they were the only two people in the room. She knew how he felt about duty. And why.

"Your duty. Not mine." She looked immeasurably

tired. "If I don't press charges, you can't arrest him, can you?"

"No. He can't." Keith straightened. "I'm very grateful, Caroline. I hope you won't—"

"That's not all." Now it was Rachel. He'd always thought her the gentle one of the sisters, but at the moment she had fire in her eyes. "There's a condition to not pressing charges."

Zach's gaze crossed with Cal's. Cal gave a rueful shrug. "I suggest both of us contract temporary deafness. Whatever she's going to propose, we shouldn't hear."

That was probably good advice, but he couldn't pretend none of this ever happened.

"You resign." Rachel said, the tone of her voice allowing no wiggle room. "It's in the paper tomorrow, or we press charges. And you and your mother walk on eggshells around us from now on. No more tricks, no gossip, nothing."

"I agree. Anything. Everything." Keith was practically babbling in his efforts to get this over with. "I'll do it."

Rachel glanced at her sisters. She must have seen agreement in their faces. "That's it, then."

He watched, fuming, as Keith gave them all a vague, meaningless smile and bolted from the apartment. He couldn't arrest him if they wouldn't press charges. He resented having the decision taken out of his control. His duty—

"Relax, Chief." Cal nudged him. The sisters were hugging, half laughing, half crying. "It wasn't done according to the book, but at least my wife isn't going to jail for braining the mayor with a poker, Caroline knows the story of her quilt, Rachel got her licks in and Keith is losing the thing that's most important to him. Besides, you're getting rid of the worst thorn under your skin who ever took office in the township. It might not be according to Hoyle, but seems to me it worked out pretty well."

"Not according to the law."

Cal shrugged. "The law has its limitations. I'd rather see justice."

It wasn't his interpretation of doing his duty, but clearly he could do nothing about it. He went to Caro. "I'll be leaving, then."

This wasn't over, not by a long shot. Keith might be removed from the running, but Caro was still in trouble, whether she knew it or not.

"Thank you." Her green eyes glistened with tears when she looked at him.

"You're welcome. I hope the three of you know what you're doing."

He thought about the possible charges hanging over her in regard to the museum theft. She'd been generous to Keith. He suspected the insurance investigator wouldn't be generous toward her.

Zach sat in his office the next afternoon, scowling at the day's issue of the *Churchville Gazette*. True to his word, the announcement of Keith's resignation appeared prominently on the front page. Keith must have run straight home and called the paper to make the deadline.

He tossed the paper aside. Maybe Cal had a point,

but he still wasn't satisfied. He had a duty that Cal didn't, and he didn't like being finagled out of doing it for the sake of convenience.

He ignored the phone ringing in the outer office, shoving his chair back. He knew what was really sticking in his craw. He'd let himself start to care about Caro Hampton against his common sense, against his professional duty, against everything he knew was right and sensible. He'd told her more about himself than he'd told anyone other than family, and look where it had gotten him—compromising his duty for a woman who obviously didn't return his feelings.

Eric Snyder opened the door without knocking and poked his head in. "You'd better take this call, Chief. It's the Santa Fe police."

Zach glared at him. "I've got it. Shut the door. And hang up."

He picked up the phone, waiting until he heard the click that told him the line was private. "Chief Burkhalter here."

"Chief. This is Charles Rojas. We spoke a while back about Tony Gibson and his widow."

"I remember, Detective." The neutral tone of his voice must have alerted the man that he wasn't feeling particularly cooperative. They'd pretty much told him to buzz off, hadn't they?

"Yes, right," Rojas said quickly. "And you were real helpful, sending along that sketch of Leonard Decker the way you did."

He grunted. That hadn't seemed to lead anywhere, as far as he could see.

"Ms. Hampton still there, is she?"

"Yes." He sat up straight. Something was going on. The Santa Fe P.D. hadn't called him just to chat. "What about it?"

"We just found his body."

He clutched the receiver, mind working feverishly. If Leonard Decker was dead in Santa Fe, it was highly unlikely he'd been running around this part of Pennsylvania trying to make Caro believe her husband was still alive. "When?"

"That's the thing." The tone of the detective's voice told him there was bad news coming. "He's been in the river, but the ME pegs the time of death as somewhere around the same time Ms. Hampton left Santa Fe. We consider that an interesting coincidence."

"If you're suggesting that Ms. Hampton killed him—" He stopped. He wouldn't do Caroline any favors by alienating the investigator. Not that he could do her favors in any event. His duty was all he could do. "Do you know anything about the forgery of some jewelry at the gallery where she worked?"

He could almost sense the interest on the other end. "How do you know about that, I wonder? Have you been holding out on us, Chief?"

"I might ask you the same thing, Detective." This was his jurisdiction, after all.

Rojas paused. "Okay," he said finally. "We've been hearing rumors, but no one is talking—not the gallery people, not the victim, certainly not the insurance investigators."

"One of the insurance investigators is here. Keeping an eye on Ms. Hampton. He claims she had the expertise to make the switch, but no proof."

Rojas whistled softly. "Told you more than they have us, then."

"He had to. I was about to arrest him for trespassing."

"That'll do it, all right." Rojas chuckled. "Look, Chief, seems to me it's time for us to put our cards on the table. Maybe we can help each other."

And who will help Caroline? The voice at the back of his mind was insistent, but he managed to silence it. If she was innocent, Caroline would only be helped by finding out the truth. And if she was guilty—

If she was guilty, his feelings had nothing to do with it. He'd do his duty.

"I'm listening," he said.

FIFTEEN

Caroline stood by the barn doors, watching as the movers carried the remnants of her life in Santa Fe into the barn. With a new lock once again installed by Cal and with Keith frightened off for good, her things should be safe until she had the heart to go through them.

She fidgeted restlessly as box after box was carried inside. Who would have thought she had so much stuff? If she'd packed it herself, she'd have gotten rid of things, including most of Tony's belongings. As it was, she'd simply taken what would fit in her car and left the rest to the movers. They'd have packed everything down to the Sunday paper and the cans of tuna fish in the cabinet.

Tony's things rightfully belonged to Mary Alice now. Would she want them? That was yet another hurdle, one she didn't want to face.

Speaking of facing things, maybe she ought to admit what was really bothering her. Not the task of sorting through her old life. It was the fact that she hadn't seen Zach since the night before last, when they'd exposed Keith's activities.

She should have realized she was treading on his devotion to duty when she took matters in her own hands and settled with Keith. But didn't he see that she and her sisters had done him a favor? If it had come down to the chief of police arresting the mayor, it would have been a three-ring circus. No one could predict how something like that would turn out. Zach might have been the one to suffer most, not that he'd let that stop him.

She sensed movement behind her and turned to see Francine picking her way along the path gingerly as if it were lined with snakes. She wore capri pants and a snug top with a pair of high-heeled sandals that were inappropriate anywhere outdoors.

She teetered to a stop next to Caro. "I see your belongings have finally arrived. It might have been faster to have sent them by mule train."

Caro shrugged. "I suppose. I wasn't in any hurry to get them. It just means I have to sort everything out."

"No need to rush into doing it." Francine touched her lightly, sympathetically, on the arm, surprising her. Francine wasn't a touching person, generally. Caro had never seen her hug anyone other than her late husband or a potential big donor to one of her charities.

Hearing Francine voice what she'd just been thinking made her reconsider. "Thanks, but I'd better face it. After all, Tony's things don't really belong to me."

"If you believe that hick sheriff knows what he's doing." Francine's tone made it clear that she doubted it.

"Police chief, not sheriff," she corrected, a little

pang reminding her that she was unlikely to be talking with Zach on that subject, or any other, anytime soon.

"At least that business with the quilt has been cleared up." Francine seemed to be looking for something to distract her from that rather sad parade of belongings. "The things these small-town folks don't get up to. Imagine committing robbery to cover up something that happened 150 years ago."

"If someone threatened to expose something harmful about Garner's family, you'd jump into action quickly enough."

Francine stiffened a little at the mention of her late husband, but then she smiled and shrugged. "Believe me, I'd find a better way of dealing with it. A little blackmail goes a long way in some circles."

"Maybe so. Keith isn't as sophisticated as you."

"You're convinced he wasn't the man who forced you off the road? Maybe your police chief was too quick to accept that alibi."

"Not my police chief. And no, it couldn't have been Keith, unless he has an identical twin no one knows about. He was in full view at a town council meeting all evening."

"Well, I suppose it'll sort itself out." Faint lines appeared between Francine's brows. "If there is any chance it was Tony, that's another reason not to do anything about his belongings, you know."

"I suppose so. But I hate having this unfinished business hanging over me. And, frankly, I'm not sure I owe Tony any kind of loyalty at this point."

"But, Caroline—" She stopped, because a familiar police car was pulling up behind the moving van.

Zach got out, very stiff and correct, dark glasses hiding his eyes. Something in her tensed as he approached. If only he'd let her explain why she'd intervened with Keith, maybe she could clear that air between them.

"Zach." She forced a cheerful note into her voice. "You remember my friend Francine Carrington."

He gave Francine a curt nod and turned back to her.

"I'm afraid I'll have to ask you to come down to the police station with me."

She blinked. "Look, if this is about Keith again—"

"It has nothing to with that."

"What, then?" She couldn't keep her voice from rising. "What's going on? You're scaring me."

A tiny muscle twitched at his jaw, the only acknowledgment of her words. "You need to come with me now. Two detectives from Santa Fe will be arriving shortly to question you."

She heard Francine's sharp, indrawn breath. She didn't seem to be breathing at all. "Question me about what? Tony?"

"About Leonard Decker. The man you said threatened and harassed you."

"I've already told you everything about that." Why are you doing this? That was what she wanted to say. Why are you looking at me as if I'm a criminal?

"He's been found. Dead. He was murdered about the time you ran away from Santa Fe."

She was vaguely aware of Francine murmuring that she'd get her sisters and hurrying off toward the house, teetering a little on her heels. Silly, to notice that at a time like this.

And then all she could feel was the iron grip of Zach's hand on her arm as he led her to the police car.

They filled up Zach's tiny office at the police station—she, Zach and the two officers from Santa Fe—one short and burly, the other tall, young, almost elegant in his Western dress. She felt as if they were using up all the air in the room, leaving none for her.

"Now, Mrs. Gibson, you must see that it's in your best interest to be honest with us." The younger one was smooth and persuasive.

"Hampton." That was all she could think of to say. "We—I found out that Tony had a wife in Philadelphia he hadn't bothered to divorce before he married me."

That probably only increased their suspicion of her, but she was too tired to think what was the best thing to say. If Zach, who knew her, could believe her capable of murder, what chance did she have of convincing anyone else?

Zach. The pain cut deeper than any she'd ever known, even deeper than the knowledge of Tony's betrayal. Maybe that was because she'd always suspected, at some level, that Tony wasn't honest. Zach was a man of integrity. If he believed this, maybe she really wasn't worth being loved.

Zach moved slightly in his chair. "Ms. Hampton has not been apprised of her right to have an attorney present."

The detective shot him a look of dislike. "I'm sure Ms. Hampton would rather have a friendly talk with us than a formal interrogation with an attorney present."

What Zach would have said to that she didn't know,

because the door opened and Cal burst in. Zach shot to his feet. "Burke, you're not licensed to practice law in Pennsylvania. Get out."

"I'm not, but I've brought someone who is." He ushered in a graying, distinguished-looking man who reminded her in some way of Grandfather. "Caro, this is Robert Hanson. He's an old friend of your grandparents' and he's your attorney. Don't answer any questions unless he tells you to." Cal bent to press his cheek against hers before anyone could object. "It's going to be all right," he whispered. "We're all waiting outside and praying for you."

"Out." The older of the detectives grabbed Cal and shoved him out of the office. He grinned and gave her a thumbs-up as he went.

The ice that encased her began to thaw. They were here. They were taking care of her. Even Zach, in his way, hadn't let them bully her into talking without an attorney. Maybe somehow she was going to get through this.

There were moments when she doubted that, over the next two hours, when the wrangling between Hanson and the detectives turned into a blur of noise that made her dizzy. When that happened, she clung to the thought of them—her family, waiting for her.

Someone else was here with her. *Draw near to God, and He will draw near to you.* She'd looked for a reference to what Emma had said in the Bible she'd found on her bedside table. Those were the words that expressed Emma's thoughts perfectly. *Draw near to God, and He will draw near to you.*

She listened to the attorney and answered only the

questions he allowed, convinced that those questions made no sense. She'd never spoken to Decker before that day in the plaza, never heard Tony mention his name. She didn't know what Tony had been involved in. He'd lied to her from the first time she met him.

Maybe her voice had trembled on that, because the attorney's hand had closed warmly over hers, as if it were Grandfather there next to her.

"I think that'll be all Ms. Hampton will answer today," he said.

The detective lost his urbane charm, leaning toward her with a quick, threatening movement. She didn't think she reacted, but Zach was between them in an instant.

"You heard the attorney. Now either you're going to charge Ms. Hampton or let her go."

"Stay out of this, Burkhalter. This is our case."

"This is my jurisdiction." Zach's voice carried no expression at all, but it was like a door clanging shut. "Charge her or let her go."

"Of course Chief Burkhalter knew perfectly well they didn't have enough evidence to charge her." Robert Hanson leaned back in the leather chair that had once been her grandfather's, accepting a mug of coffee from the tray Emma held. They'd all come back to the library at the inn for a council of war once she'd finally been released. "He's a good man to have on your side, my dear."

She could only stare at the man from her place on the couch between her sisters. "I don't think he is."

"Listen to Mr. Hanson," Cal advised. He took a tray

of sandwiches Emma had put on the table and began forcing them on people. "That could have been a lot worse if Zach hadn't been looking out for your rights."

Her rights. Yes, she supposed Zach would do that for anyone. It was part of doing his duty. She suddenly felt an overwhelming urge to cry.

She got to her feet, drawing startled glances. "I…I know we have to talk this over, but I can't seem to think. I need to take a hot shower, change my clothes, and then maybe I'll be able to eat something."

Cal glanced toward the attorney. "Maybe we'd better get this over now, Caro. Mr. Hanson has a busy schedule."

But Hanson waved with a thickly piled ham sandwich. "Not at all. I'll just sit here and catch up with Katherine. Take your time, my dear. I know the atmosphere of suspicion can seem to contaminate you when you're not used to it."

Andrea and Rachel stood up, one on either side of her. "We'll go with you," Andrea said firmly, and took her arm.

All she wanted was to be left alone to let the tears out, but she knew she'd never get rid of them that easily. She let them walk with her back to the apartment, trying to nod and smile at their attempts to distract her.

Once Rachel had run a hot tub, more relaxing than a shower, she insisted, and Andrea had laid out a change of clothes, she shooed them toward the door.

"I can handle the rest of it," she said firmly. "I know how to take a bath by myself. I'll come back as soon as I feel a little more together. You go now and keep those two lawyers from scaring Grams with their stories, all right?"

Her sisters exchanged glances. "She has a point," Andrea admitted.

"Maybe we are hovering a little," Rachel said. "All right. But if you're not back in an hour, we're coming for you."

"I will be. Go." She shoved them out the door and locked it behind them.

The confident manner only lasted until the door closed. She had to drag herself back up to the loft. She peeled off her clothes, tossing them to the back of the closet. Maybe she'd throw them away.

Only when she lay back in the tub did the tears come. Whatever they might say about Zach defending her, she knew things were over between them. She'd known all along it couldn't possibly work, but she hadn't been able to quash that tiny flicker of hope. Well, now it was gone for good.

She sat up, sloshing water over the tub. How ridiculous was this, hiding away to cry while people who loved her made plans for her defense. She wasn't a child who needed protection, much as she appreciated what they were trying to do.

The familiar urge to run had disappeared completely, she realized with surprise. She'd grieve, and go on grieving for the loss of whatever she might have had with Zach, but she wouldn't run. She'd stay and face this.

She got out, dried herself, made up her face and brushed her hair free of tangles. Then she put on the clothes her sister had laid out and went down the stairs.

They'd be surprised to see her back so soon. Well, she was surprised, too. But it was time she started acting like one of the grown-ups.

She opened the door, stepped outside and turned to shut it. She sensed movement behind her, felt a fierce pain in her head and then slid into blackness.

SIXTEEN

Zach leaned back in his chair, leveling a gaze at Rojas, the senior of the detectives. The past hour had been an exercise in futility since Caroline left, surrounded and supported by friends and family.

Not by him. He'd done what he could for her, but it hadn't been enough.

Doubt had been growing in him throughout the endless afternoon. If you followed the rules, you got the right result. That was what he'd always believed, but it didn't seem to be working out that way this time.

Where is the truth in this, Lord? Help me to find it, whatever the cost.

"Let's stop the posturing, Rojas. It's pretty obvious you don't have anywhere near enough evidence to charge Ms. Hampton in Decker's death. What's this really about?"

Williams, the younger man, opened his mouth for what would probably be another jab at hick cops, but Rojas waved him to silence.

"Go out there and get the dispatcher to give you a cup of coffee."

Williams gave him a mutinous look, but he went.

When the office door closed behind him, Rojas spread his hands wide.

"Okay. Here's the truth, or as much of it as I can tell you. Tony Gibson was involved in a scam worked through a series of charity auctions at the gallery where Ms. Hampton was employed. Someone at the gallery had to be involved, and she seemed the obvious suspect."

"*Obvious* isn't always good enough."

A slow anger simmered inside him. If Rojas was content with the obvious, the truth would never come out.

"True," the man admitted. "We don't know how long this was going on. The people involved aren't ones to run to the cops if they think they've been defrauded. More likely to write it off or hit up their insurance company." He shrugged. "You figure they're smart enough to handle fortunes, but seems like they check their business sense at the door when it comes to these fancy society affairs. The Carrington name means something in those circles."

"That'd be Francine Carrington's late husband?"

Rojas nodded. "Carrington had a heart condition. That seems to be common knowledge. He died, and the widow kept up the charities he'd started. Everybody found that admirable. Just lately, though, Carrington's kids from his first marriage have been making noises about the merry widow."

"You knew she came to see Ms. Hampton," he said slowly. "That's why you're here." If the detective was suspicious of a woman in Mrs. Carrington's position, he wouldn't want to raise the wrath of his superiors by leaning on her. "You figured it was safer to lean on Ms. Hampton than on her."

Rojas looked affronted. "Hey, don't tell me it doesn't work the same in your little corner of the world. Some people you just can't jump in and accuse, not if you want to come out with your job intact."

He thought of Keith Morris. "It's better to risk that than to harass an innocent person."

"Well, now, we don't know that Ms. Hampton is innocent, do we? She could be involved, could be the one who faked the pieces. Or maybe she knows something. There has to be a reason why those two women are here together."

The anger was coming to a boil now. It wasn't his case, the sensible side of his mind insisted. It was his jurisdiction, though. His obligation to find the truth.

"You decided Ms. Hampton was the weak link. You figured if you leaned hard enough, she might break."

"It works, more often than not," Rojas said.

"Not when you're leaning on an innocent woman." A woman who deserved better than she'd ever gotten from the law he and Rojas both claimed to represent.

Rojas's brows lifted. "Sounds to me as if you've gotten involved with the woman."

Zach shoved his chair back. "I'm going to get some air. Feel free to use my office." He slammed out before he could say something he'd regret.

The day had slid away while they were arguing. Dusk was drawing in. Unease trickled down his spine.

Caro was safe. Of course she was. Her family would protect her. So why did he have the urge to drive over there, just to be sure?

He shouldn't approach her now, not when she was part of an ongoing investigation conducted by another department. Doing so could cost him. He had to follow the rules on this one.

But maybe following the rules wasn't good enough. His job was a small sacrifice in exchange for the truth. Or for Caroline's safety.

Driven by a need stronger than anything he could explain, he slid into the cruiser and pulled out.

Voices penetrated the darkness, forcing Caroline's eyelids to flutter. She didn't want to wake up. She couldn't. Her head hurt. She wanted to lie here quietly....

But she wasn't in her bed. Hard wooden boards beneath her, not a soft mattress. And the voices—

"You shouldn't have hit her that hard." Francine, but a Francine who sounded different. "We'll never find it without her help."

There was the sound of something heavy sliding along the floor. Her mind began to function. The apartment. She'd been leaving, going back to the house. Now...she opened her eyes a cautious slit.

Now she lay on the barn floor, amid the boxes the movers had brought in this morning. Francine had one of the boxes open, hauling things out and holding them up to examine in the dim light.

"...don't see why I had to hit her at all." It was a voice she struggled to recognize. "You should have offered to help her unpack and sort things out, like any good friend would."

He stepped into the light. Jason Tenley. The photographer. Except that he obviously wasn't. Why was he here with Francine?

"And what if she found it first?" Francine's tone was waspish. "You should have made sure you had it before you killed Tony."

The words penetrated, and Caro gasped. A tiny sound, but they heard. They were on her in an instant, the man hauling her to a sitting position. The movement sent pain shooting through her head. She struggled and realized her hands were tied behind her back.

"Now we're getting somewhere." Francine leaned over her. "Think, Caroline. Where would Tony have hidden something of value? Something quite small. It has to be here. We've looked everywhere else."

"I don't know what you mean." Which was the truth, and better than any lie she could imagine. "What are you doing, Francine? Who is he?"

Francine didn't bother to answer the questions. She surveyed Caroline for a moment. Then, before Caro could guess her intent, she slapped her.

"Think," she demanded. "Where did he hide it? Help us, or my brother might have to do to you what he did to Tony."

She could only gape at the woman. Her friend. The person she thought she knew. She hadn't known Francine, any more than she'd known Tony.

"Shut up, Francine." The man, Tenley, if that was really his name, smiled pleasantly. "You talk too much."

"It doesn't matter what she hears now." Francine turned on her. "Help us, if you want to go on living. We're not leaving here without it."

They didn't intend to let her live in any event. She knew that as surely as she'd ever known anything. That was what Tenley meant. Francine wouldn't talk so freely in front of her if she was going to let her live.

Tenley intercepted her gaze. "Yes, she really is my sister. Half sister, at least."

"You're not a photographer." Think, keep them talking. Don't sit here and wait for them to kill her.

"Just an honest insurance investigator. Until I ran into my dear sister, and she suggested that there was far more money to be made by skirting the law a little."

Francine gave a low sound that might have been a laugh. "You were never honest, whatever else you were. Stop chatting. We have to find it. If she won't help us—"

The menace in her voice sent a surge of energy through Caro. She wouldn't be a helpless victim. "I'll help you. I know what should be in the boxes. But you have to tell me what I'm looking for."

Francine frowned at her for a moment. Then she came to Caro, bent over and fumbled with the bonds at her wrists. "All right. You're looking for a pill vial. Find it, and you might get to go on living."

"And do be careful, my dear." Jason Tenley waggled the thing that was in his hand. A gun, small and deadly. "I'd hate to have to use this."

No, he wouldn't want to use a gun. They'd want it to look like an accident, like Tony's death. Or even suicide. Widow, depressed over her husband's death, under suspicion herself, decides to end it all. That made sense.

She stumbled to her feet, rubbing her hands together and then grabbing the nearest box. She had to think. *Please, Lord, help me think. Show me what to do. Someone could come looking for me at any moment. Walk in the door and face a man with a gun. Please, help me.*

She felt her control slipping as she pulled things from the box and took a deep breath. *Draw near to God, and He will draw near to you.* The words seemed to steady her.

Please, Lord. Let me feel Your presence. Show me what to do.

If Zach came—she didn't doubt Zach's ability to handle Tenley. But Zach wouldn't come. Zach thought she was guilty.

Be with me, she prayed again. She opened another box, this one containing clothing, and began feeling carefully in the linings and pockets. Her hands felt stiff and cold.

"Something so small could be anywhere," she said, needing to hear the sound of a voice. "Why do you need it?"

"You don't want to know the answer," Tenley said, leaning against a stack of boxes, the gun drooping.

"What does it matter?" Francine tossed aside a file folder that was probably from Tony's desk. "She's the reason all of this fell apart." She turned on Caro, face twisting with anger. "You never even realized, stupid little idiot. You didn't know what you were saying when you told Garner the one thing that showed I was playing his wealthy friends for suckers."

"I did?" She could only stare at Francine. "I hardly

knew Garner. He died the night of that first charity event, right after I came to work…" Her voice trailed off.

Her first event. She hadn't been working at the gallery for more than a few weeks, and she'd been so eager to do well. Garner Carrington, tall, courtly, distinguished, coming into the gallery unexpectedly looking for his wife. He talked to her, probably seeing how nervous she was, and she'd babbled about whatever it was Francine had her working on. He'd already been suspicious, or something she'd said had tipped him off. Francine must already have been substituting fakes for the real donated objects.

"Yes, you." Francine stalked toward her, fury filling her face. "I never planned to harm Garner. I just wanted to make sure I came out of that farce of a marriage set up for life. You're the one who forced the issue."

Horrified, Caro could only stare at her. Garner's heart attack, that very night. Francine, the grieving widow, mourning that if only she'd gone to his bedroom sooner, she'd have found him in time to help.

But she could only be this frantic to find a pill vial if it were somehow evidence that she'd killed him. And the only way it could have come into Tony's possession—

"Tony knew." The words came out before she could suppress them. Tony had known and done nothing.

"Tony knew." Francine shrugged. "We were having a little fling, Tony and I. Nothing serious, but he was coming to the house that night. He was out on the balcony, and he saw me with the pill bottle. He took it. Blackmailed me. If he hadn't gotten so greedy—"

"This is futile." Tenley walked between them. Before Caro could guess his intent, he knocked her to the floor. Pain shot through her. Half-conscious, she felt him pull a rope tight around her wrists and ankles.

"What are you doing?" Francine clawed at his arm. "We have to find it."

"We can't." He shook her off. "We've played around with this stupid plan of yours for too long. The only solution is to burn the place down. The vial will be destroyed, and your little friend with it."

"The police—" Francine began.

"The police don't know a thing," he said shortly. "I'm going to get the gas cans. Here." He handed her the gun. "Make sure she behaves." He stalked toward the door, switching on a penlight as he did. His figure was a dark silhouette in the doorway for an instant, and then he disappeared.

Nearly dark. How long had she been here? They'd come looking for her—Andrea and Rachel would come—

No, Lord. Don't let my sisters walk into this. Keep them safe. Protect them. Protect me. She reached out in longing, in certainty, and felt His presence.

She couldn't be sure how much time passed. She didn't attempt to talk to Francine. She just waited, wrapped in God's love.

Footsteps finally, coming back. A dark figure appeared in the doorway, carrying a flashlight. Awareness shot through her. A bigger, heavier torch than the tiny penlight Tenley had carried, surely.

"About time," Francine said, apparently not noticing anything wrong.

But she would, she'd see— Shoving with her elbows, she pushed herself toward Francine as the fierce beam of the flashlight shot into the woman's eyes. Francine lifted the gun, arm flying up to shield her eyes. Caro raised her bound feet and aimed a frantic kick at Francine's legs.

Deafening shots, flashes of light, loud voices. She didn't know where Francine was. Zach—was that Zach's voice?

The overhead lights went on, blinding her for an instant. Then her vision cleared and she saw Zach, holding Francine in a hard grip. Other men rushing in—the detectives, local patrolmen. And a moment later Zach was holding her, releasing her bonds, drawing her gently into the safety of his arms.

"Now, you sit quietly here on the bench, and you can watch them work on your new business for a while." Rachel, at her most maternal, guided Caro to a seat on a garden bench that had a view of the barn. "You know what the doctor said."

"He said I should take it easy for a couple of days," Caro pointed out. "Not that you and Grams and Andrea should coddle me for the rest of my life."

Still, she had to admit that it had been healing to spend the past two days doing nothing, floating in a soft cocoon of family concern. She hadn't seen Zach. No detectives had come with questions.

All of the belongings she'd had stored in the barn

had been taken away for a police search. Maybe that was just as well. She was ready to concentrate on the future, not the past.

Right now that future was taking shape before her eyes. Rachel had stopped to talk to Tyler, looking very professional with his hard hat and blueprints. Inside the open doors of the barn, she spotted Cal with a crew of Amish carpenters, beginning the work that would transform the barn into the Three Sisters Arts and Crafts Center. It was an ambitious title they'd decided upon. She just hoped she could live up to it.

The quilt would have a place of honor, hung in a glass case inside the entrance, with as much as they knew of its history posted beside it.

That history wouldn't include any mention of treachery, she'd decided. That could be left for others to argue. She simply wanted to celebrate how the work of a woman's hands had helped lead courageous souls to freedom.

She leaned against the bench, half dreaming in the warm sunshine, and watched as a familiar police cruiser pulled up. Zach. She'd known he'd come at some point. What she didn't know was what they would say to each other.

He came toward her slowly and stood looking down at her. "Any chance you feel up to talking? If so, I'll risk your sister's wrath and sit down."

She gestured to the bench beside her. "Please. I think it's time I stopped floating and found out what's happening."

He sat down next to her, studying her face with that

intent gaze. "Is that what you've been doing? Floating?"

"Pretty much," she admitted. "You can tell me. You don't need to hedge around the subject. Did you find the vial?"

He nodded. "Stuffed inside a ski boot, as a matter of fact."

"They were right to be worried. That's one of the first things I'd probably have gotten rid of, since I don't ski."

"That was what motivated all of this, apparently." Zach linked his hands on his knee. "Francine had to find the vial before you did and got curious about why Garner Carrington's medicine was with your husband's things."

"She thought if I believed Tony was still alive, I wouldn't get rid of them." Her brain was starting to work again. Apparently she'd figured some things out while she'd been drifting. Everything Francine had engineered—the love letter, Tony's favorite coffee, the sense someone had been watching her, even sending the safe-deposit key, had one aim—to keep her thinking Tony was alive, so she wouldn't do anything with his belongings until they'd found the evidence.

"That's what her brother claims." Zach wore an expression of distaste. "They're tripping over themselves to blame each other for everything that happened. I guess that'll be for the Santa Fe courts to sort out. They're out of my jurisdiction, anyway."

"They're gone? Don't the detectives want to talk to me?"

"Not at the moment. Rojas seems satisfied that your role was that of an innocent bystander."

"A stupid bystander, you mean." She shook her head. "I can't believe I didn't see anything. I worked on those charity events with Francine and never suspected a thing."

"Francine was one careful lady. Sorting out the truth from the accusations, I'd say she started the scam with help from her brother. Carrington must have already been suspicious the day he spoke with you, though."

She nodded slowly. "I've been thinking about that. At the time, I thought he was just being nice to a new employee, but in light of what happened, he must have been trying to see what I knew. Whatever I told him confirmed his suspicions."

"He let her see that he was on to her. A deadly thing to do with a woman like that. She acted immediately."

"And Tony saw her." The words tasted bitter, but she got them out. "She told me that. She and Tony were having an affair, and he saw what she did. He took the pill bottle and blackmailed her."

Some of the tension in Zach's face eased, as if he was relieved he didn't have to convince her of what Tony had been. "According to the brother, Tony got greedy, and Francine decided he had to go. They thought they'd have plenty of time to search for the vial."

She nodded. "I had a feeling that someone had been in my apartment several times during the couple of weeks after Tony died. I thought it was Decker, the man who threatened me, but it must have been Francine."

"Decker messed up their plans. He scared you into running, and suddenly your belongings were out of reach. Tenley followed you here to keep tabs on you while Francine, playing the devoted friend, found out that most of your things were in a moving truck, making their way slowly east."

"So they had to wait until everything got here to find it," she said. "But I don't understand what happened to Decker. Was he one of the people they scammed?"

"Rojas thinks so. He figures when Decker couldn't get the money out of you, he went to Francine, and she killed him. But neither of them are talking about that, and we may never know."

Maybe it didn't matter whether she knew. Let the law take care of Francine and her brother. But there was one thing she had to come to terms with before she could move forward.

"About Tony." She looked down, realizing she didn't want to see Zach's face when she asked this. "Why? Why did he get involved with me? Why marry me?"

His hands clenched. "Tenley claims Francine told Tony to make sure you weren't suspicious about her husband's death. As to the marriage—well, we know it wasn't the real thing. He may have thought it gave him more leverage over Francine, having you and anything you might remember about Carrington in his pocket, so to speak. Or maybe he just couldn't resist." His voice softened. "People have been known to fall in love. Even the bad guys."

She took a breath, feeling the last of whatever shackled her to Tony falling away. "You're trying to spare my feelings, but you don't need to. I know now it wasn't love with Tony."

"I..." He hesitated, as if not sure what to say. "Is that a good thing?"

She nodded, managing a smile. "I think so. I'd rather know what love isn't, so I can recognize what it is."

Zach touched her hand, very gently, and her breath hitched. Her heart seemed to be fluttering somewhere up in her throat.

"I'm sorry," he said softly. "For the times when I doubted you—"

"Don't." She closed her hand over his. "There were times when I doubted my own sanity. Anyway, you wouldn't be you if you hadn't questioned. You're a man of integrity, and you did what you thought was right."

His fingers moved caressingly on hers. "If there's anything I've learned, it's that when there's a choice between duty and right, God expects me to do what's right." His voice roughened, as if with emotion he was trying hard to control. "Look, I know you're going to need time to come to terms with everything that happened to you. I just hope you'll do it here. I'll be waiting."

She turned to look at him and saw the love shining in his eyes. Her heart melted, and she reached up to touch his cheek, feeling the strong line of bone and the warmth and aliveness of his skin.

"Not so much time," she said softly. "I've stopped running now."

God had brought her back to the place where she

belonged—the place He'd been preparing for her all along. And the man He'd intended for her from the beginning.

Zach's arms went around her, and she was home.

* * * * *

Dear Reader,

Thank you for picking up this third story in the Three Sisters Inn series. With this series I come back to my own beautiful rural Pennsylvania and the good, neighborly people who live here, especially that unique group, the Amish.

I really enjoyed writing Caroline's story, maybe because, as well as being the artist of the family, she was the youngest of three, as I am. I've tried to convey some of the deep bonds I believe can exist between siblings, which I've certainly experienced in my own life.

I hope you'll let me know how you felt about this story. I've put together a little collection of Pennsylvania Dutch recipes that I'd be happy to share with you—some from my own family, some from friends. You can write to me at Love Inspired Books, 233 Broadway, Suite 1001, New York, NY 10279, email me at marta@martaperry.com, or visit me on the web at www.martaperry.com.

Blessings,

Marta Perry

Questions for Discussion

1. Can you understand the conflict between the need to be independent and the longing for family support that drives Caroline? Have you ever struggled to balance two seemingly conflicting needs?

2. Zach is a man of integrity who is driven by his sense of duty. Do you sympathize with his need to do what he feels is the right thing even when it brings him into conflict with people he cares about?

3. Caroline feels that her sisters let her down, even though she tries to look at her experience through adult eyes. Do you have experience of the complicated relationships that can exist between sisters?

4. Caroline's answer to trouble is to leave, but when she comes home she realizes that she's not willing to run away again. Do you think a place or a person can give someone the courage to fight instead of run?

5. Caroline withdrew from God because she felt that He let her down, just as she felt her family did. Emma tells her that if we feel distant from God, it is because we have moved, not God. Do you agree with that? Why?

6. The handcrafts of the Amish and the quilt made by her ancestor move Caroline emotionally in a

way she finds difficult to explain. Do you ever have that feeling about objects?

7. Zach has a close relationship with God, but he still has not entirely forgiven himself for his actions. Is there anything that you tend to hold back from God?

8. The scripture verse for this story is a very short one, but it packs some powerful meaning in a few words. Have you found this verse to be true in your life?

9. Caroline finds a community in the other crafters because of their devotion to something she loves. Do you have a hobby or skill that brings you into relationships with people you might otherwise never meet? How can God work in a situation like that?

10. Caroline eventually finds her way back to a relationship with God through the life-threatening events of the story. Do you think we turn to God more readily when times are difficult? Why or why not?

CLASSICS

Enjoy these four heartwarming stories from
your favorite Love Inspired authors!

NO PLACE LIKE HOME and DREAM A LITTLE DREAM

by Debra Clopton

NO PLACE LIKE HOME

Dottie Hart made a promise and has to get to California. But when the
candy maker gets stranded in Mule Hollow, Texas, handsome sheriff
Brady Cannon—her polar opposite—has her dreaming of staying
forever. With the help of town matchmakers, she may find a way to call
Mule Hollow home for good.

DREAM A LITTLE DREAM

After writing about the lonely ranchers in Mule Hollow, reporter
Molly Popp is responsible for all the would-be wives who travel to the
Texas town. One confirmed bachelor cowboy isn't too pleased—especially
when he can't seem to get the pretty city slicker off his mind.

A TREASURE WORTH KEEPING and HIDDEN TREASURES

by Kathryn Springer

A TREASURE WORTH KEEPING

Teacher Evie McBride plans to spend a quiet summer on Cooper's
Landing. Yet when handsome Sam Cutter asks her to tutor his troubled
teenage niece, she can't turn them away. Soon enough, it's Evie and Sam
who are learning more about love and faith than they ever expected.

HIDDEN TREASURES

All Cade Halloway wants is to sell the family vacation home that
reminds him of bad memories. But now his sister insists on marrying
there. Wedding photographer Meghan McBride and her camera just
may help him discover the treasures of family and love.

Available in October 2013
wherever Love Inspired Books are sold.

www.LoveInspiredBooks.com

LIC1013

REQUEST YOUR FREE BOOKS!
2 FREE RIVETING INSPIRATIONAL NOVELS
PLUS 2 FREE MYSTERY GIFTS

YES! Please send me 2 FREE Love Inspired® Suspense novels and my 2 FREE mystery gifts (gifts are worth about $10). After receiving them, if I don't wish to receive any more books, I can return the shipping statement marked "cancel." If I don't cancel, I will receive 4 brand-new novels every month and be billed just $4.74 per book in the U.S. or $5.24 per book in Canada. That's a savings of at least 21% off the cover price. It's quite a bargain! Shipping and handling is just 50¢ per book in the U.S. and 75¢ per book in Canada.* I understand that accepting the 2 free books and gifts places me under no obligation to buy anything. I can always return a shipment and cancel at any time. Even if I never buy another book, the two free books and gifts are mine to keep forever.

123/323 IDN F5AC

Name	(PLEASE PRINT)	
Address		Apt. #
City	State/Prov.	Zip/Postal Code

Signature (if under 18, a parent or guardian must sign)

Mail to the **Harlequin® Reader Service:**
IN U.S.A.: P.O. Box 1867, Buffalo, NY 14240-1867
IN CANADA: P.O. Box 609, Fort Erie, Ontario L2A 5X3

**Are you a current subscriber to Love Inspired Suspense books
and want to receive the larger-print edition?
Call 1-800-873-8635 or visit www.ReaderService.com.**

* Terms and prices subject to change without notice. Prices do not include applicable taxes. Sales tax applicable in N.Y. Canadian residents will be charged applicable taxes. Offer not valid in Quebec. This offer is limited to one order per household. Not valid for current subscribers to Love Inspired Suspense books. All orders subject to credit approval. Credit or debit balances in a customer's account(s) may be offset by any other outstanding balance owed by or to the customer. Please allow 4 to 6 weeks for delivery. Offer available while quantities last.

Your Privacy—The Harlequin® Reader Service is committed to protecting your privacy. Our Privacy Policy is available online at www.ReaderService.com or upon request from the Harlequin Reader Service.
We make a portion of our mailing list available to reputable third parties that offer products we believe may interest you. If you prefer that we not exchange your name with third parties, or if you wish to clarify or modify your communication preferences, please visit us at www.ReaderService.com/consumerschoice or write to us at Harlequin Reader Service Preference Service, P.O. Box 9062, Buffalo, NY 14269. Include your complete name and address.

LIS13R

SPECIAL EXCERPT FROM

Love Inspired

*Brian Montclair is about to go from
factory worker to baker.*

Read on for a sneak preview of
THE BACHELOR BAKER
by Carolyne Aarsen, the second book in
THE HEART OF MAIN STREET *series from*
Love Inspired. Available August 2013!

He took up her whole office.

At least that's how it felt to Melissa Sweeney.

Brian Montclair sat in the chair across from her, his arms folded over his chest, his entire demeanor screaming "get me out of here."

Tall with broad shoulders and arms filling out his button-down shirt rolled up at the sleeves, he looked more like a linebacker than a potential baker's assistant.

Which is what he might become if he took the job Melissa had to offer him.

Melissa held up the worn and dog-eared paper she had been given. It held a short list of potential candidates for the job at her bakery.

The rest of the names had been crossed off with comments written beside them. Unsuitable. Too old. Unable to be on their feet all day. Just had a baby. Nut allergy. Moved away.

This last comment appeared beside two of the eight names on her list, a sad commentary on the state of the town of Bygones.

When Melissa had received word of a mysterious

benefactor offering potential business owners incentive money to start up a business in the small town of Bygones, Kansas, she had immediately applied. All her life she had dreamed of starting up her own bakery. She had taken courses in baking, decorating, business management, all with an eye to someday living out the faint dream of owning her own business.

When she had been approved, she'd quit her job in St. Louis, packed up her few belongings and had come here. She felt as if her life had finally taken a good turn. However, in the past couple of weeks it had become apparent that she needed extra help.

She had received the list of potential hires from the Bygones Save Our Street Committee and was told to try each of them. Brian Montclair was on the list. At the bottom, but still on the list.

"The reason I called you here was to offer you a job," she said, trying to inject a note of enthusiasm into her voice. This had better work.

To find out if Melissa and Brian can help save the town of Bygones one cupcake at a time, pick up
THE BACHELOR BAKER
wherever Love Inspired books are sold.

Copyright © 2013 by Harlequin Books S.A.

LIEXP0713

Love Inspired®

CARING Canines

Both Abbey Harris and Dominic Winters long for a second chance at love, and it'll take two adorable dogs and a sweet little girl to bring them together.

Healing Hearts
by Margaret Daley

Available August 2013
wherever Love Inspired books are sold.

www.LoveInspiredBooks.com

LI87830

The Master Matchmakers

Emma Pyrmont hopes to convince single father
Sir Nicholas Rotherford that there's more to life than calculations
and chemistry. As she draws him closer to his young daughter,
Nicholas sees his daughter—and her nanny—with new eyes.

The Courting Campaign

by

REGINA SCOTT

Available August 2013 wherever
Love Inspired Historical books are sold.